PARTNERS FOR THE JOKER-NAT WAR

"Stalin? A wimp. Hitler? A weenie. The Khmer Rouge rubbed out a third of Cambodia's population."

Mark gaped at him. It felt as if all his blood was draining into a seething pool in the pit of his belly. "These people were *involved* in that?"

Belew shrugged. "Lots of them are early to mid thirties now, which would've made them early to mid teens back in 1975. Golden Age of the Khmer Rouge, those middle teens."

"But—mass murderers—they're your *friends*?"

"They're combat vets. And we have *history* together. Blood is thicker than water; I can rely on them."

Don't miss any of the WILD CARDS series from Bantam Spectra!
Ask your bookseller for the titles you have missed:

TURN
OF
THE CARDS

A Wild Cards Novel

by Victor Milán

SPECTRA ™

®

BANTAM BOOKS
NEW YORK · TORONTO · LONDON · SYDNEY · AUCKLAND

TURN OF THE CARDS

A Bantam Spectra Book / February 1993

ISBN 0-553-56152-9

Published simultaneously in the United States and Canada

PRINTED IN THE UNITED STATES OF AMERICA

RAD   0 9 8 7 6 5 4 3 2 1

For Mike Weaver. Thanks for it all.

Part One

FRIEND OF THE DEVIL

Chapter One

If the tall man had not been to an alien world, he would never have seen the danger.

Spring on the *Damplein*, with the North Sea sky above, blue and astringent as the taste of peppermint, as if to cut the smell of the IJ docks beyond the rail yards. Mark Meadows said, "Huh?" and came back to himself with a sensation like a bubble bursting.

A newspaper had wrapped itself around his shins like an affectionate amoeba. He reached down, picked it up. It was a two-day-old copy of the *International Herald Tribune* in English. He glanced at the headlines. Governor Martínez was announcing victory in the War on Drugs. The UN was still debating whether the American suppression of the jokers on the Rox had been genocide—a twinge went through his soul at that. He'd had friends on the Rox, and it hadn't been the fault of the poor jokers who had gathered there to defy an increasingly hostile nat world that he'd had to flee for his life.

Bloat, man, I'm sorry. K.C. was right. The Combine couldn't let you go, and they were just too damned much for you. Requiescat in Pace.

In other news, the European Council was convening a summit on wild cards affairs. Nur al-Allah terrorists had bombed a free joker clinic in Vienna. The government of Vietnam declared it would keep the revolutionary socialist faith until the end of time, no matter that everyone else from South Yemen to the USSR was dropping it like a rabid rat.

It was as if he'd never left.

3

Mark would rather have his nails pulled out than litter; he wadded the paper into a back pocket of his secondhand khaki trousers. Now that he had been pulled back out of that remote place inside his head where he'd been spending so much time of late, he blinked in the thin noonday light. A lunchtime mob was squeezed in between the Palladian-style Royal Palace—with its green statues of mythological figures and its seven symbolic archways that led, symboli-cally, nowhere—and a lot of boxy old brown buildings with gabled roofs. The scene felt comfortable but just a bit drab, which struck Mark as a perfect microcosm of what he'd ex-perienced of Dutch life in the few weeks since he'd re-turned to Earth.

People were looking up and pointing. He raised his head too. He had to squint against the sky's brightness, but right away he saw what they were looking at: a slim figure, high above the Earth, flying without aid of an aircraft.

Where he came from, that was no big deal; flying aces were as regular a feature of New York's sky as smog and traffic helicopters. The Europeans had less experience with such phenomena. They still got excited.

Mark shaded his eyes, tried to make out who it was. The suit seemed to be blue, hard to pick out against the sky, and it trailed a voluminous white cape. The getup belonged to no one he'd met personally, but it was familiar from countless TV broadcasts.

"Hmm," he said. "Mistral. Wonder what she's, like, doing over here?"

Nobody stepped forward to enlighten him. He noticed that something was going down on the Vischmarkt side of the square. He had some free time—very little but, in fact—and had been vaguely acting on an urge to wander down and check out the Central Station again. It was the product of the same daffy late-nineteenth-century romanticism that led Bavaria's Mad King Ludwig to build the original of what Walt Disney would make into Sleeping Beauty's Castle, all gingerbread and silly towers that its builder fondly believed was Renaissance. Just to Mark's taste, in other words.

Curious, Mark dared the stream of lorries and buses and bicycles pedaled by puffing businessmen and Indone-sians whose limbs and faces seemed carved of polished ma-hogany to cross the broad street called Damrak or Rokin, depending on where you were, that split the square in two. Speakers had been placed among the concentric rings that circled the white cement dildo of the war memorial. A young man with baggy paratrooper pants and his hair cropped to a silvery-blond plush was striding back and forth between them, hollering into a cordless mike. He was attracting a crowd, mostly young.

"What's going on?" Mark asked the air in general. Amsterdammers tend to be reserved, but they're also cordial, and have a seven-hundred-year tradition of taking strangers in stride. As Mark anticipated, one caught hold of the conversational line he'd thrown.

"The young man is a Green," came a reply in an old man's voice that made the Dutch-accented English sound gruff. "He is speaking about the wild cards."

"Wild cards?" Mark frowned. He rubbed at his beard—it was growing in nicely, full this time instead of the goatee which had been his trademark for so long, and he wasn't entirely used to feeling hair on his cheeks. *Have things changed since I left?* he wondered. "I thought the Greens were, like, an environmental party."

The young orator was pointing after Mistral, about to vanish to the southwest. His exhortation had cranked up a notch in pitch and vehemence.

"They are." The old man nodded precisely, once. He had a dark suit and dark Homburg and leaned on a dark cane. Time seemed to have reduced him to the bare essentials except for round red cheeks. With his snow-white Imperial he looked like a shrunken Colonel Sanders. "But they are a political party, and so they must have an agenda for everything."

"What's he saying?" Mark didn't know much about the Greens except for what he read in *Time* and the *Village Voice* or saw on the *CBS Evening News*, but he'd always had the impression they were pretty right-on. Still, whenever he heard people talk about wild cards and politics in one breath, he got that old familiar ice-water trickle down the small of his back.

"He says that the new Europe must make all those touched by the wild card wards of the state."

"What?" His daughter had been a ward of the state for a while. Getting her out of kid jail—where she'd been thrown because the government disapproved of both her parents, not because she had done anything wrong—was the reason he was living undercover in a foreign land. One of them, anyway. "That—that's discrimination. It's like racism."

"Indeed. It does seem that way. The young man assures us it is for everyone's good. The jokers must be cared for in the interests of compassion, the aces must be constrained in the interests of public safety. In this way only can an environmentally pure Europe emerge."

He shook his head. "I do not like this myself. The earnest young man has the right to say his piece, no true Amsterdammer would deny him. But I remember another group that wanted to single a particular group out for special treatment. They were very concerned with the purity of the environment; they were quite Green, in fact. This very monument commemorates their victims."

"The Greens aren't the only ones who, uh, have it in for the wild cards," Mark said. He'd seen English-language telecasts of debates in the European Parliament in the Hague on RTL.

"No, indeed. It is a very popular point of view these days. Very progressive. The Eastern Europeans can turn on wild cards instead of Jews, now that the Soviet boot is off their necks, and no one will criticize them." He looked at Mark closely. "Once again, you Americans lead the way."

"It's not something I'm proud of, man."

"Good. Good for you."

He held up a hand. "Wait. Listen: 'There is nothing natural about the wild cards. That is not their fault; they are innocent victims of an alien technology more monstrous than even American technology. But like Styrofoam or the products of gene-engineering, their access to our threatened biosphere must be supervised and carefully restricted.' "

"At least we're easily recyclable, man," Mark said.

His stomach dropped away toward the center of the Earth when the old man's eyes caught his and held them and he realized what he'd said.

"I hope you have not correctly grasped the thrust of what that very sincere young man is saying," the old man said, "but I very much fear you have."

Feeling strange, feeling as if the Beast's mark the fundamentalists said listening to rock 'n' roll would give you was finally glowing to red life on his forehead, 6-6-6, Mark mumbled thanks and started away. The old man called him back.

"I hope you will forgive my saying so, young man, but you look just like the Jesus of the Calvinists, with your long blond hair and your beard," the old man said. "Fortunately I am Catholic."

Mark blinked and smiled sheepishly, as startled at being called "young" as by the rest of what the old man said. He was in his early forties, and he didn't *feel* young.

Then purposeful movement caught the corners of his peripheral vision, and alarms rang in his skull.

On Takis the assassin's knife is just part of the decor. You reflexively learn to pick it out of the background, the way an antique freak could spot a Louis Quinze chiffonier in the clutter of an Amsterdam spring market. Or you die.

"Get down," Mark said to the old man. He turned to run.

"Hey!" A voice shouted behind him—American English, bright and brassy as a trumpet. "Hey, you son of a bitch, stop!"

That was it. The dogs were on him. He thought it would take them longer to sniff him out. He stretched his long legs and ran like hell.

"Mother*fucker*," the slender dark-haired man snarled. His hand dove inside the summer-weight off-white jacket he wore without a tie.

His beefier, blonder comrade grabbed at his arm. "Lynn, *no*—"

The Czech *Skorpion* is a true machine pistol, which is to say it's pistol-sized and it shoots full-automatic like a machine gun. Not appreciably accurate but nice and concealable, just the thing for chopping up people at handshake range. It was a popular number with the Euroterrorist set, like the West German Red Army Fraction before the Wall came tumbling down.

The Colt Scorpion is entirely different. It's manufactured in America for use by various government agencies, which is to say the DEA. It looks like the Czech *Skorpion*, it works like the Czech *Skorpion*, and it fires the same round as the Czech *Skorpion*. But the Czech *Skorpion* is used by terrorists, and the American Scorpion is used by the good guys. No similarity at all.

The man called Lynn used his Scorpion the way they teach at all the better law-enforcement academies: you fire short bursts and sort of slash the thing around as if it's a scimitar. People screamed and fell. A loudspeaker popped and died. The plush-headed young man in the para pants goggled and ran for cover behind the white pillar of the monument.

The Netherlands was a peaceful place, and proud of it. Though first socialism and then Greenthink had made them self-conscious about it, the Dutch still regarded trade as a more elevated calling than murder made legal, made sport. They lacked gunfire reflexes.

Most of the crowd was just standing and staring, not realizing where the sudden loud sounds were coming from or even what they were. The tall man took instinctive advantage of this, darting this way and that through the crush like a frightened earthbound crane, his shoulder-length gray-blond hair flying a head above the crowd but not offering any kind of shot, even for someone calm enough to draw bead.

The man with the Scorpion wasn't. His dark eyes burned like drops of molten metal, and beans of knotted muscle stood out inside the hinge of either jaw. The veins and bones of his hands seemed about to burst through the skin as his partner wrestled them and the machine pistol into the air.

"Lynn, Jesus, take it easy," the big blond kid gasped. "There's gonna be hell to pay if you cap too many natives."

Lynn tore away from him with a wordless curse, raised the weapon again. Their quarry had darted behind the white cement demilune that backed the monument pillar and vanished.

The good burghers were belatedly getting the message that something was *very wrong*, and diving to the pavement to join those who were rolling around clutching themselves and screaming. "You son of a *bitch*, Gary," Lynn raged, swinging the Scorpion both-armed in front of him like José Canseco in the on-deck circle. "You let him get away!"

"Yeah," Gary said, hauling on the sleeve of his Don

Johnson pastel sport jacket. "Now we'd better think about getting away before the cavalry comes."

He dragged Lynn, still screaming, through a now-panicked crowd. The Amsterdammers didn't seem to be paying them any attention, as if they didn't associate the two Americans with the abrupt irruption of noise and pain. They dodged across Damrak/Rokin and down the street that ran along the north side of the square, to a silver and blue cicada of a Citroën parked in front of the Nieuwe Kerk.

A figure dropped down from the sky to meet them. Her slim form was encased in a uniform of blue and silver. A parachutelike cape deflated around her shoulders as she touched down. Her hair was brown.

"You missed him," she said in a flat voice.

Lynn slammed his Scorpion back into its shoulder holster. "If you'd been down low covering us instead of showboating way the hell up there in the wild blue yonder, he never would've gotten away."

She gave him a haughty look. She was well equipped for it, with the kind of narrow nose and fine features that wouldn't look out of place on the cover of a glamour magazine, and hadn't. There were dark circles beneath the green-hazel eyes, though, and a haunted look within them.

"I had no idea you were going to move so quickly. I thought we were going to set this up carefully and then move. Forgive me if I don't quite have the hang of your methods."

"Lynn saw the sucker," the blond agent said. "It just kind of set him off. There's *history* between them, y'know?"

"I suppose I shouldn't be surprised," the ace said. "I'd figure that going off prematurely would be one of your friend's difficulties."

Lynn gave her a look black and hot as the flank of a potbellied stove. Then he turned and kicked the Citro's door. "He's just a hippie. A fucking burned-out *hippie*. How the hell could he make us?"

"Somebody must have told him," his partner said. "Somebody turned us over."

'These damned Dutch uncles. They don't have the stomach for the War on Drugs. They've been jacking with us since day one." He shook his head. "If I hadn't cut loose on him the second I spotted him, we'd never—"

The sirens had tuned up, their little voices rising and falling like a computer-simulated doo-wop group. The woman's face went white. "You trigger-happy half-wits!" she snarled. "You just sprayed a crowd with *bullets*?"

"He's an ace," the bigger man said defensively. "What do you want Lynn to do, Ms. Carlysle, let Meadows have first crack at *him*? A good man's already died on the trail of this puke."

"Shot accidentally by NYPD," the woman said, "as a result of his own carelessness."

"You fucking *bitch*." Lynn started forward as if to strike her.

A whistling rose around the agent. A cloud of dust swirled upward to surround him. His dark hair began to whip in his face, and his clothing to flap as if he were caught in the midst of a whirlwind. He opened his mouth, but suddenly seemed to have no air to speak with.

His partner laid a hand on his arm. "Lynn, take it easy. She didn't mean anything."

The whistling stopped. Lynn fell back against the car, briefly and resentfully touched the base of his throat with his fingertips.

"I'm quite capable of taking care of myself, Agent Hamilton," the woman said. "Your being so quick on the draw is going to cause us serious problems with our hosts."

Lynn had recovered enough to show her a smirk. "So what? They can't touch us. We're DEA."

"If innocent people died—"

"Hey, baby, we're in a war," Lynn said. "In war, people die. The sooner these fatass Dutchmen wake up and smell that cup of coffee, the sooner they're gonna fit into this new Unified Europe thing."

Mistral Helene Carlysle gave him a final angry look and got into the driver's seat. The two agents piled hastily in after her. They squealed away from the ancient church as emergency vehicles flooded the square behind them.

Chapter Two

On Eglantier Straat the narrow ancient houses leaned gently toward one another across the canal, the tulips in the boxes at every sill like overemphatic splashes of makeup on the faces of aging tarts. Mark Meadows collapsed in the doorway of the house where he rented a flat, and just breathed. It was a questionable move, however necessary. The streets in this district were all named for flowers—its name, *Jordaan*, was the nearest the Dutch could come to phonetically spelling its old name, which was the French word for garden—but the Eglantine Canal that ran right past the house front smelled more like a sewer.

After a while old Mrs. Haring's big black tom Tyl appeared and jumped on Mark. He made sure to brace his hind feet in Mark's crotch and knead Mark's solar plexus with his powerful forepaws, making it difficult to breathe. Mark thought he loved all animals, but Tyl was an evil bastard.

In the first flush of panic Mark's instinct had been to return here, home, like a fox to its earth. Now that he had a chance to think about it, he wondered if it had been such a good idea.

They've found me. How do I know they're not upstairs waiting? How do I know they aren't up under the gables across the canal, watching, calling to each other on their walkie-talkies, getting ready to yank the snare?

He felt scattered, strange, irresolute. He felt as if maybe he should just lie here in the doorway until they came for him. It was better than having to choose. To act.

He squeezed his eyes shut. *No.* He'd been suffering

11

these bouts of indecision, of the sensation that he was a lot
of dissociated motes flying around without a common center,
since Takis. Dr. Tachyon said they ought to pass, in time, but
that was mostly just to make Mark feel better, not to mention himself. The truth was, Mark's condition was something
entirely new to the psychological sciences of Takis as well as
of Earth.

A part of Mark had died on Takis. Literally.

He reached to his chest, felt the reassuring lumps of
the vials in his shirt pocket, beneath the sweater. Only four
now. He hadn't even thought of them when the shooting
started.

*Would I have had the presence of mind to take one be-
fore . . . before Takis?*

He told himself to hang on. Things had worked out
fine. He hadn't needed a friend; if he'd summoned one,
there might have been a confrontation with his pursuers.
More innocents might have been hurt. As it was, he desperately hoped no one had been killed by the gunfire meant for
him.

And he could not stop from wondering, *What have I really lost?*

He made himself breathe slowly, from his diaphragm—
not easy with that damned fifteen-pound cat digging him
there and grinning—and pull his wits together. He wasn't
too hip to modern police procedure, but he understood that
cops were basically lazy. If they *knew* where he was living,
they'd just have waited for him there, rather than roam all
over the city in hopes of stumbling across him. They could
take him easily and unobtrusively here, in this still-slummy
backwater of the generally gentrified district just west of
where the medieval town walls once stood.

. . . If unobtrusiveness was a priority. They had been
willing to spray a crowd of innocents with gunfire in broad
daylight. Not exactly *discreet*.

He shivered. *And they were* Americans. Not since Vietnam and his belated rise to consciousness of the antiwar
movement had he felt such shame in the country of his
birth. *What have we come to?*

He was a criminal, of course. A federal fugitive, and
one whom the authorities believed was fantastically dangerous. They were right, too, if you considered raw power. But

he believed, in the core of him, that he had done nothing wrong.

In fact they were primarily hunting him for doing something *right*. The rightest thing he had ever done: rescuing his daughter Sprout from the living hell of the kid jail the kinder, gentler New York authorities had committed her to.

A vague alarm, trilling in the pit of his stomach: *what if they followed me here?* But frightened as he was, he hadn't gone completely stupid. The path he'd taken had been anything but direct. Like a lot of ancient European cities, Amsterdam was compact—tiny, actually, at the core—but it was also as convoluted as Hieronymus Bosch's brain. Ideal for losing pursuers.

He pushed the cat off his chest. Tyl got a good dig into him with foreclaws through sweater and T-shirt, then rubbed purring against Mark's shins as he stood. Hoping to overbalance him so that he'd crack his head on the stoop, no doubt.

He pushed into the house. The stairwell was filled with gloom and the smell of vinegar-intensive Dutch cooking. Mark put his head down and started up the steep steps.

Because the *grachtenhuizen*, canal houses, were painfully narrow—the palaces of the old syndics over on the Bend of the Herengracht no less than the tenements—there was little room for switchbacks in the stairwells. This house had been built with the stairs a straight shot up to the fifth-floor attic flat Mark rented. Mark told himself it was aerobic exercise and kept climbing, though the tendons of his shins were already so tight, it felt as if they'd snap his tibias like Popsicle sticks.

The door opened at what he still thought of as the second floor, though everyone in Europe insisted it was the first. The face of his landlord glared out like a big lumpy fist clutching a wad of wiry black hair, with two round turquoise rings for eyes.

"Ahh," the landlord breathed in a juniper-scented gust of *genever*, the local gin. "Mr. Marcus."

"Afternoon, Henk." As unobtrusively as he could manage, Mark craned to look past him into his apartment, just in case it was packed to the rafters with American narcs and automatic weapons. There was nothing but the usual clutter of bottles, tracts, and porcelain figurines. Henk Boortjes liked to keep a supply of cutesy bric-a-brac, symbols of hypertrophied bourgeois *gezelligheid*, on hand so he could bust them up when the iconoclastic fit was on him.

Henk was an old *kabouter*. The *kabouters*—gnomes—were a posthippie movement of the early Dutch seventies, self-proclaimed anarchists and environmentalists. Some of them still hung on, but their niche in the food chain had been mostly co-opted by the Greens.

The landlord squeezed onto the stairs. Mark managed to sidle past before his belly, which overflowed from the bottom of a well-holed black T-shirt with a red-circled *A* on it, blocked the passage. There was no room for a landing in this narrow scheme of things.

"Have you heard the news?" Henk demanded.

"No, man. I've been out."

"There was shooting, down in the *Damplein*. Someone fired a machine gun at the crowd. Half a dozen were injured, though nobody has died yet."

"That's, uh—that's terrible, man."

Henk fixed him with a red-rimmed glare. "Whenever such things happen, one can be certain there are Americans at the bottom of it."

Mark swallowed. "It wasn't me, man," he joked feebly.

The landlord kept him pinned with his stare. Mark realized the man was half convinced he—Mark—was a CIA spy sent to make sure he didn't singlehandedly upset the applecart of American imperialism. He was guiltily familiar with that kind of self-glorifying paranoia. During his years as a counterculture fringie he'd indulged in a lot of it himself.

Then came the last couple of years, when Mark learned what it was like when they really *were* after you.

Henk nodded suddenly, with a grunt that made it sound as if his neck were a rusty hinge, releasing Mark from the bonds of his eyes.

"I've caught him," he said, with a brown-toothed grimace Mark suspected was a smile.

"Who, man?"

"That old bastard de Groot, down the block."

De Groot was Henk's archenemy. He was an artist, at least to the extent that every few weeks he'd splash some paint on a canvas and then get the Arts Ministry to pay him a totally optimistic price to stick it in one of these enormous warehouses they maintained for the purpose. He was in fact more or less a contemporary of Mark's landlord, and belonged to some rival anarcho-faction that the *kabouters* had splintered into. Mark had a suspicion Henk's real grievance was that he himself couldn't get registered to sell his modeling-clay sculpture to the Ministry, and he suspected his rival of blackballing him.

"What's he done, man?" Mark asked.

"He has violated our fair-housing laws. He's renting to an Indonesian family, and he has too many of them crammed in that tiny flat." He spat on the stairs. Mark yanked his foot up in alarm and almost toppled over. "Exploiter. He won't get away with it; I've notified the authorities."

"So, like, what happens to the Indonesians?"

"Certainly, they shall move out."

"You mean they're gonna get thrown out on the *street*?"

The glare returned. "Their rights must be protected. Obviously you don't understand."

"I guess I don't, man."

Mark's flat was stuffy with the rising heat of midafternoon, up in the attic beneath the bell-gabled roof. He opened the front window and walked back through the apartment.

It was narrow but not really small. The canal-front houses were surprisingly deep, and the flat ran all the way to the rear of the building, a succession of rooms strung together in what Mark thought of as shotgun style. In the bathroom all the way back Mark opened the other window to let the rank Amsterdam breeze in.

As he returned to his living room, Mark took out his wire-rim glasses and put them on. It wasn't vanity that made him leave them off when he was out; he was a skinny six-four American, which did not make him the least conspicuous person in the world. Not wearing the glasses was at least a gesture in the direction of not being spotted by hostile eyes. For a man whose Secret Ace Identity once consisted of dressing up in a purple Uncle Sam suit and matching stovepipe hat, it was a pretty comprehensive gesture.

It didn't seem to have worked, though.

He made himself a cup of coffee and sat on the sill of the open window. Right over his head a massive wooden hoist beam jutted from the face of the house. All the old-time *grachtenhuizen* had them. People rigged blocks-and-tackles to them when they had to move things in and out of the upper floors. You didn't want to try wrestling a piano up those stairs, or anything less wieldy than a loaf of bread.

He was careful not to knock over the window box. It was crowded with red and yellow tulips he'd brought on a day trip to the country, just like the boxes on all the sills on the block and, as far as he could tell, in the whole damn country.

He wasn't, in retrospect, sure what he'd expected to find in Amsterdam—a sort of Hippie Heaven on Earth, perhaps, with naked people chasing each other happily through the streets and screwing in the fountains to the tune of the Dead and the Lovin' Spoonful, all seen through a blue-green scrim of pot smoke. The actuality was staid: a lot of neat reserved plump people who left their front curtains open so you could admire the crowded coziness of their living rooms—Bourgeois Paradise in all truth, though with the occasional startling tangent.

On the other hand, after the never-ending adrenal nerve-whine of palace life and open warfare on Takis, a little *petit bourgeois* calm was not at all unwelcome. Or maybe Mark was getting old.

When it came to flowers, though, the good people of Amsterdam made the Flower Children of the Summer of Love look like developers. Mark had the vague impression that a couple of centuries back they'd actually had a boom-and-bust depression over tulip bulbs. April was tulip season, and the city looked as if it had been invaded by a race of tiny aliens with bulbous brightly colored heads who liked to hang out on windowsills. It made Mark wonder what the tulip *mania* had been like.

Still, a country that could go hock-the-baby crazy over flowers had to have a place for Mark. After everything he'd been through, he was still the Last Hippie.

Gazing at the gaudy flowers and sipping his coffee—an exotic blend with a taste like licorice to it that the little Indonesian guy who ran the coffee store down the street had pressed on him—he thought about his daughter, Sprout. His lips smiled, but his blue nearsighted eyes grew sad behind his glasses.

She would be fifteen now, his daughter. With her mom's features and his eyes and blonde cornsilk hair. He hadn't seen her for almost two years.

She was perpetually four, was Sprout. Though she was physically perfect, quite beautiful, in fact, she was severely developmentally disadvantaged—or whatever euphemism they were hanging on it this year. No matter what name they gave it, the doctors could do nothing to cure it.

Mark loved her desperately. For her he had made the Great Leap Forward from common or garden federal fugitive to perennial guest star on *America's Most Wanted*.

Now there were more tough decisions to be faced. About Sprout.

He rose, set the cracked Delftware cup from the service he'd picked up at one of Amsterdam's innumerable flea markets on the sill beside the planter. He walked between posters he'd bought here in the Jordaan, Tom Douglas's bearded glare answering Janis Joplin's sad, doomed smile, to kneel by the fireplace. He rummaged around up inside the flue. His fingers found a still-strange texture, resilient to the touch. He lifted the pouch off the smoke shelf. It took all his never-great strength to get it over the blade of the damper.

He laid the pouch along the hearth. It was half the length of his arm and gleamed a rich, blue-veined maroon. He ran a thumb along the top. A hidden seam parted. The pouch was Takisian, artifact of a culture that preferred growing things to fabricating them. He wasn't entirely sure the pouch was not in some sense *alive*. He tried not to think about it.

He pushed the pouch open. Inside, faces ignored him with fine Takisian hauteur. Too-sharp features turned profile, captured in crisp relief on soft yellow metal, showed an unmistakable resemblance to Tachyon. Tach's grandfather; by custom, Tach's father had had the gold coins struck on his accession, as a memorial. Mark guessed the Doctor would be having some coins of his own minted now, in honor of his own loved/feared father, Shaklan.

Oh, Tach—Tis. He shut his eyes and squeezed tears out. His closest friend, sometimes it seemed his only friend, now light-years away. Tach had returned home from his forty-year exile to find his father a vegetable, beyond reclamation even by Takisian science, kept alive only to preserve the claim of his branch of the family to rulership of House Ilkazam. One of the first acts by Tachyon—still trapped in the body of Blaise's ex-girlfriend, Kelly—had been to shut down his father's last vital processes by a touch of his mind. The ostensible reason was to ensure Tach's own accession and head off a coup attempt by a hostile line, and Jay Ackroyd still thought he was a monster for it.

Mark thought that, whatever the motive, it had been an act of transcendent mercy. He hoped he would have the moral courage to do the same. He feared he wouldn't.

There were about five pounds of the coins, each a little shy of twenty-three grams, around eighty percent of an ounce. For reasons Mark could not begin to fathom— economic processes were pure alchemy to him—gold prices had really launched of late. He did get the drift, which was that the coins were worth a pretty piece of change.

But they were nothing compared to the jewelry. Rubies, sapphires, emeralds, diamonds, cut in strange geometric shapes. The stones were set in silver, a metal the Takisians—or Tach's House Ilkazam, at any rate—favored over gold. The silverwork was truly breathtaking. Fine filigree, fantasies spun in wire that intertwined like dreams, like the destiny of a race. Mark had never seen work remotely like it. It possessed a hypnotic quality, as if the twining lines could draw the eye of the observer in, draw his soul. Even without the rarity value of being genuine artifacts from an alien world—hard to substantiate, though surely no one could ever really believe human hands had made them—the pieces of jewelry were priceless.

He had no idea what to do with them. He had passed a few of the coins; the canny Dutch were a bit bemused by the unearthly patterns they were struck in, but accepted them readily enough once they satisfied themselves they were real gold.

The loot made him feel strange. He had helped Tach because the Doctor was his friend and needed his help. He had done things for Tachyon that he'd never done for any-body else, that he never imagined he'd be called on to do. But he hadn't done them for treasure.

He had accepted the reward because Tach insisted. Tachyon had his own pride, he knew that. But what Mark wanted was to find a way to make it without becoming re-liant on the alien's beneficence.

He wanted to send the treasure to Sprout. That posed problems too. Under the RICO and Continuing Crime Acts—America's answer to the *Nacht und Nebel* decrees—any property identified as his was liable to confiscation by the federal government.

Even if he could find a way to smuggle it to his daughter, his dad might not accept it. Sprout was in the care of General Marcus Antonius Meadows, recently retired as commander-in-chief of America's Space Command. The aging Vietnam War hero had a pride prickly as any Takisian's.

Mark picked up a bracelet—armlet, maybe, openwork, light as a breath. Set in it was a spherical stone, tawny and pearlescent. It glowed with its own light. The glow grew brighter when he held it in his hand. He traced the patterns of the silverwork in his mind. They seemed to lead him into the heart of the stone. It was warm in there, warm and safe and far from worry and fear and strange, harsh-voiced young men with guns. . . .

When he came back to himself, it was dusk outside. He shook himself, hastily scooped the treasure back into its alien pouch and stuffed it back up the flue. He was spacing out a lot these days. He was doing a little dope—this was Holland, after all, and despite growing pressure from the rest of the European community, they practically gave the stuff away like the Green Stamps of Mark's childhood. His appetite for grass was nowhere near what it had been before his ex-wife Sunflower had come back into his life, bringing with her the child-custody suit that would wind up with Mark on the lam, Sprout in the juvie home, and Sunflower herself committed to a mental institution.

He doubted the dope had anything to do with the fugues anyway. There was a void inside him since Takis. Sometimes when he wasn't careful he wandered into it.

So far he'd always come back.

He closed the window, drew the chintz curtains. At this

altitude nobody could see into his living room anyway, so it didn't look out of place. It would be dark soon, and even though this was the North Sea, the night sky sometimes cleared.

He couldn't handle stars yet.

Chapter Three

Coughing and grumbling, Henk emerged from his doorway as Mark trudged up the stairs next afternoon, a loaf of French bread and an English-language book on silversmithing tucked under his arm. Mark had found the book in a Jordaan shop. He was so entranced with his Takisian silverwork, he had decided that that might be what he should try to do for a living: learn to capture that airy beauty, seduction in pale metal.

Today the landlord wore an apron. As far as Mark knew, he didn't cook. He seemed to subsist entirely on meat pies from a little shop around the corner.

"There has been more about the shooting," Henk announced. "Yesterday. In the *Damplein.*"

"Really, man?" Mark asked, trying to sidle by, waiting to be denounced as a fugitive, as responsible.

"It was an attempt on the life of a noted Green activist. He was speaking on the need for the new European Community to take an active role in wild cards affairs." He waited with his chest puffed out portentously.

"Really?" Mark managed to say.

Henk nodded. "Is it not obvious? They are a conspiracy, these aces. They think they are better than the rest of us. Mark my words, they must soon be controlled, or they will take over."

Mark fled up the stairs.

Night arrived. Mark was heating soup on the cracked-enamel gas stove when someone knocked on the door.

His heart jumped into the base of his throat. His long fingers sought the little leather pouch he wore to carry his vials when he wore a T-shirt without pockets beneath his sweater. After the excitement in the Dam Square yesterday he had stuffed an extra set into it.

Take it easy, man, he told himself. *Don't get paranoid. It's probably only Henk.* Wiping his hands on a linen towel with blue windmills printed on it, he walked to the well and down the short flight of stairs that led to the flat's door.

It wasn't Henk. It was a short man dressed like a tourist, in a navy windbreaker and khaki pants, a New York Yankees baseball cap worn over short hair that had clearly once been brown but was now mostly the color of ash. He had a luxuriant mustache with obviously waxed tips. It was mostly seal-colored. Maybe he dyed it.

"Can I, uh. Can I help you?" Mark managed to ask.

"Mr. Marcus?" Mark nodded. "I'm Randall Bullock. Might I impose on you for a couple minutes of your time?"

The man spoke English in a way that would have been brusque if it hadn't been softened by a hint of southern drawl and an easy down-home smile. He smelled of the rain that had begun to fall lightly in Eglantier Straat. It stained the bill of his cap and stood in beads on his jacket.

"Come on in," Mark said. He turned and walked back up the stairs. It felt as if his feet were lead and his knees were about to disconnect completely. As he reached the top, he fished the pouch out from inside his sweater, making sure to keep his body between it and his visitor.

Pausing at the stove, he asked, "Can I offer you some coffee, man?"

"Any made?" Mark shook his head. "No, thank you. Don't mean to impose."

Wordlessly Mark led his way to the living room.

The sofa was overstuffed, floral-patterned, and threadbare, and Henk the landlord had restrained its tendency to burst at the seams and spew stuffing everywhere with duct tape. Mark waved a spidery hand at it and went and propped his skinny butt on the windowsill as Bullock took his seat.

The man sat on the edge of the sofa with his cap politely in his hands and his elbows on his knees. It was a pose from which he could stand up again very quickly—or launch himself at need. *Funny, how I've started noticing things like that.*

He had also noticed something else about his mysterious visitor, right off the bat. Mark was a military brat. Randall Bullock had *military* scrawled all over him the way Dennis Wilson Key said *sex* was written on Ritz crackers. It was in the short hair and the mustache and his bearing, erect without being stiff. It was in the taut way he filled his skin in spite of carrying virtually no excess weight—in the lack of a spare tire in a man of his obvious age.

He might have been former military, one of those eternal boys who can't let go of the sense of belonging the Green Machine had given him. Mark's gut sense was he was still serving. In one capacity or another.

"Are you with the government, Mr. Bullock?" Mark asked, trying hard to sound casual.

Blue-gray eyes held his for a beat. "Let's just say I'm here in a private capacity, shall we?"

Right. With his thumb Mark popped the plastic cap of the vial he held loosely in his left fist and tossed the contents down his throat with a fluid motion. Blue powder, with sparkles of silver and black.

"Great Caesar's ghost!" Randall Bullock exclaimed, jumping to his feet. He took a step forward.

It wasn't Mark he took a step toward. It was a man not much taller than Bullock was, with pale blue skin and a cowled black cloak.

"Really, can't you let a man have *any* peace?" the blue man asked in a stranger's peevish voice. He hopped lightly to the sill, then stepped through the window, which was still closed.

Randall Bullock's reactions were good. He only stood rooted for a second and a half. Then he strode forward and threw open the window.

"*Doctor Meadows!*" he yelled into the rain. "Doctor Meadows, come back! You're making a terrible mistake!"

At the end of the block he caught a swirl of black, in which stars seemed to glitter, disappearing around the corner. The only reply was a defiant laugh.

Actually, it was more of a nasty snicker.

*   *   *

"Let me suggest the Northern Lights," the waiter said in excellent English. "It is the *spécialité de la maison*. It provides a most mellow experience, and one that you can fully enjoy here in our establishment. The Red Lebanon is also excellent, but I must warn you, it is best sampled in the privacy of your hotel or living quarters. And, of course, you will please remember not to operate a motor vehicle while under the influence of any of our fine smokables."

Lynn Saxon sat back with his arms folded and a cool little smile under his military mustache. Helen Carlysle had her neck at full extension, holding her head over the box the waiter proffered on a silver tray but as far away as she could and still examine its contents, as if they were live but exotic bugs. Gary Hamilton peered carefully inside.

"I think I'll try the Northern Lights," he said.

"Very good choice, sir. I will bring a selection of pipes."

The waiter went away. Hamilton sat back, flushing on his prominent Slav cheekbones. He had on a cream-colored sport jacket over a blue polo shirt with the collar loose around his thick neck. In the smoke-filtered light from the discreet cut-crystal light fixtures, his blond hair appeared to be thinning in front, just a shade. In general he looked like a failed college jock who was just waiting to develop enough of a beer gut to be credible as a football coach. Helen Carlysle stared at him in disbelief.

Saxon leaned his elbows on the table and peered into the candle in its amber-glass vessel in the center of the table. With his dark eyes and hair he looked like an apprentice Gypsy fortuneteller practicing to look mystical for the *gadjo*. He wore a black-and-red soccer jersey and one of those long duster coats, black with white flecks, that had been popular with the hip-hop crowd a couple of seasons ago.

"So when does Meadows show up?" he asked the flame. Then he spoiled the effect by glancing quickly at Helen in her blue-and-silver yuppie skirt-suit to see if she was buying it.

"Mind if I sit down, Ms. Mistral?" a voice asked.

She started, as if the name had stung her, turned in her

chair. "Major Belew," she said. "Ah . . . please. Do sit down. And it's, ah, it's Helen Carlysle. Or Ms. Carlysle."

The newcomer nodded and sat. In his dark-blue three-piece with the conservative pinstripe, he looked far more one with the scene than the other three Americans. The Café Northern Lights of an evening was a dignified, hardwood-paneled sort of place, where a man might sit and sip his coffee and peruse his *Neudeutsscher Zeitung* and choke some hemp in congenial surroundings.

"Certainly, Ms. Carlysle. I wasn't sure whether your ace name might be what the Japanese call *bashō-gara,* 'appropriate to the circumstances.' You can dispense with my title, too, by the way. Plain Mr. Belew is fine. Or Bob—J. Robert to my friends, whom I'd be honored if you'd count yourself among."

"*Mister* Belew," she said.

"The elusive fourth man arrives," Lynn said, sitting back in his chair.

Belew nodded. "We can play bridge now, if that's what you were waiting for."

"What've you been up to?"

"Going to and fro in the Earth, and walking up and down 'in it.' " He looked from one agent to the other. "The Dutch are mightily ticked about that little shooting spree in the *Damplein* yesterday. You wouldn't happen to know anything about it?"

Helen bit her lip. Hamilton glanced quickly at Saxon. His buddy just kept steady eyes on Belew.

"They can't prove anything," Hamilton said sullenly.

Saxon laughed suddenly. "These fuckin' Dutch. They're in a war, and they don't even know it."

"They're operating under the quaint illusion that it *is* their country. And their cops aren't as fat and sleepy and complacent as they look."

Saxon looked at him with apparent shock. "Then what about all *this*?" he demanded, taking in the hash café with a sweep of his hand. Heads raised at the American shrillness. "Look at this shit. They're selling smoke in *public*. The cops do nothing."

"They have a tradition of tolerance hereabouts."

"Well, *excuse me*. But we're the American DEA. And we have a new tradition of tolerance: *zero* tolerance."

"It's the New World Order," Hamilton said.

"It's still hard time for assault with a deadly weapon if they make you for it."

Saxon leaned forward. Small points of light glittered in his black eyes. "Hey, I thought you were Captain Combat. Real hard-core Nam vet. Cowboy for the Company. All that jazz."

"Nobody calls it the Company except in the movies. They say the weapon used in yesterday's attack was a Czech *Skorpion*, or something very much like it. Tell me, Agent Saxon, just where is your sidearm? You have it on you? Of course you do; you sleep with your piece. I've seen your jacket."

He turned to the other agent and plucked at his lapel. "And I've seen *your* jacket, too, Agent Hamilton. That *Miami Mice* coat isn't quite enough to hide your bulge, big boy. Well," he said, leaning back, "all God's children got guns— best-armed pot party in Amsterdam. Except, of course, for Ms. Carlysle?"

She was staring at the dark-stained hardwood tabletop and blushing angrily. "I don't like guns."

"Ah, yes. 'Guns don't die—people do.' Guns are evil, wicked, mean and nasty. Not benevolent, like ace powers." He put his head to the side. "I remember your dad from, oh, my third tour in the Nam. Cyclone. Real kick-in-the-pants, that guy. Used to take your captured Charles up with him to, oh, about a thousand feet. If Charles didn't want to talk to him then, your old man let him come back by himself."

She gave a strangled tiny scream, like a snared rabbit. "No! That's a lie. My father—my father would never do anything like that."

"You know him best, I guess."

"She should," Saxon said, and sniggered. "She killed him."

She went white and started to rise. Then she controlled herself with visible effort, settled back into the chair. For a moment she stared down at her hands, knotting and unknotting in her lap.

"It wasn't me," she said in a tight, tiny voice. "I'd been Jumped. It . . . wasn't me."

"He's a tactful young bloke," Belew said cheerfully. "Would you like me to kill him?"

Saxon was glaring at him when the waiter arrived with a selection of pipes for sale—health regulations forbade lending or renting them out to customers. Somewhat self-consciously, Hamilton selected one. The waiter laid out his hash, along with steaming cups for Lynn and Helen. Belew waved him off.

Helen Carlysle watched Hamilton prepare his pipe with wide hazel eyes that glittered with moisture. "I can't believe you use that poison."

"We've been exposed to it before, ma'am," said Lynn. He gave Belew a *yeah, you were just joking, weren't you?* look and pried his eyes off him. "It's called knowing your enemy."

"I thought your Mr. Bennett said drug use was intrinsically wrong."

Gary Hamilton paused with his pipe to his lips and his disposable lighter poised over the bowl. "It's different for us."

"She's as likely to be talking about your coffee as his hash, Saxon. She doesn't approve of caffeine either. She's a very natural kind of lady, our Ms. Carlysle."

"You seem to know a great deal about me, Mr. Belew."

"I read *Aces* magazine, like anybody."

"We were just wondering why Meadows hasn't turned up in the smoking cafés when you decided to grace us with your presence," Saxon said.

"It was sheer luck that he's been spotted twice," Helen said.

Lynn Saxon frowned. "Don't use that word, babe. It's not luck. It's professionalism. An Interpol stringer made him here initially—*that* was luck. We picked him up yesterday, just out cruising the streets. *That* was skill. The first team is very definitely on the job."

"Our sources say he hasn't been *anywhere*," Hamilton said, letting out a mouthful of smoke and coughing. "Nobody knows him at the clubs. Not Paradiso or the Melkweg or even the Hard Rock Café."

"He's had some pretty rough times," Belew said, "or at least he did before he dropped out of sight for a year or two. Maybe he's just into being a homebody these days."

Saxon laughed. "No way. These old hippies were definitely herd beasts. We got it all down to a science, Belew. We got profiles of every major kind of dealer and user in existence in our computers, plus we got a whole database on Meadows all by his lonesome. Printout looks like the Manhattan phone book. No. I tell you, Amsterdam is the last great preserve of old hippie burnouts on Earth, and Mark Meadows has got to be out rubbing elbows with them. We just haven't worked out *where*."

"I'm glad you set me straight on that, Agent Saxon." Belew grinned boyishly and smoothed back the waxed wings of his own impressive mustache. "Well, it's a good thing our Dr. Meadows is on the distinctive side in appearance. Maybe third time really is the charm."

He signaled for the waiter to come over. "I'll take some of your best Lebanese—the real stuff, not what you palm off on the tourists. And please, spare me the lecture about operating a motor vehicle."

When he came back to himself, Mark drew a deep breath and shuddered. His heart still thudded with terror, and it was more than just a carryover from having been the manic-depressive Cosmic Traveler. They *had* tracked him to his flat. It had just taken them a little extra time.

For some reason his memories of what the Traveler did during his hour of drug-induced life weren't as clear as those he brought back from some of his other personas. It was just as well; he didn't especially like the Traveler, and didn't trust him at all. Traveler was selfish and totally unscrupulous and wouldn't hesitate to abuse his ace powers if the opportunity arose. The fact that he possessed no offensive abilities whatsoever restricted his scope somewhat, but he was resourceful.

Bully and lecher though he was, however, Cosmic Traveler was a coward. A *complete* coward; it was the one reliable thing about him. He was endlessly ugly when he perceived himself as holding the whip hand, but a whiff of threat and he was gone with the wind.

By the smell of the air—grease and dust overlying open water—and the way the sound of his breathing resounded in the darkness, Mark decided Traveler had picked an IJ-front warehouse to go to ground in. Absence of lights or voices or subtler sensory clues indicated there was no one here. A certain stagnant quality to the air, a sense of *intruding*, gave Mark the sensation no one had come here for a while.

It didn't surprise him. You could trust the Traveler to find a secure hiding place, even if that was all you could trust him for.

He felt with his hands. Cement floor, brick cool to the touch at his back. Slowly he stood up.

Squat masses surrounded him. By thin greenish light drooling in a nearby window he made out dormant machinery, angles rounded by tarps. Keeping his palms pressed to the brick, sliding his feet along the floor to lessen the risk of tripping over something and breaking his neck, he sidled toward the window.

Small rustlings receded from him. He smiled despite the adrenaline that still rang in his veins like a gong. The Traveler had been so obsessed with avoiding human contact that he'd forgotten to fear rats.

The window was so grimy that all he could see were big dim, gauzy balloons of light, as if he'd forgotten his glasses. He rubbed at the cool glass with the heel of his hand. For a moment all he did was redistribute grease. Then a patch cleared enough so that he could see a blue light blinking mournfully at the top of a giant crane out across the IJ, and a gibbous moon hanging like an autumn apple in the west.

He jerked back. *Hey, now, it's nothing to be afraid of,* he told himself. *It's only the nighttime sky.*

It was like when he was a kid and he sometimes got scared to look outside at night for fear he'd see a UFO. What with his dad a big-time test pilot and all and the Air Force insisting that UFOs didn't exist (except for the one Dr. Tachyon arrived in), it just *wouldn't do* for him to see a UFO. Also, he was afraid of UFOs.

Except he had no fear of UFOs anymore. His best friend *owned* a UFO—a whole fleet of UFOs, now. He'd arrived back on *Earth* on a UFO. Besides, if he did have something to fear, this wasn't the right sky.

But something inside him whispered, *death. Death waits among the stars.* It came from far deeper than the voices of his friends.

Just to be sure, he turned away from the window and

slid down to the cold, hard cement floor. With his knees beneath his chin and his hands wrapped in the hem of his sweater, he settled in to wait out the stars.

Wherever the space between his eyes was, that's where he went.

Chapter Four

"I'm sorry," the shopkeeper said, shaking his head slowly as if to emphasize the gravity of his regret. All around him clocks looked on with idiot faces, ticking and electronic hum combining into cicada sussuration. "I cannot give you job. No papers."

"Well, thanks anyway, man."

"You want a job?" The stallkeeper was a whole foot shorter than Mark, and his head looked disconcertingly like one of the cantaloupes he had piled in mathematical ranks in the bins, fringed with longish gray hair. "Very difficult these days. Perhaps I can find you something. You can pay?"

Reflexively Mark felt the pockets of his stained and slept-in khaki pants. There was the reassuring weight of a Takisian gold piece, the crinkle and tinkle of some guilders' change.

I thought the point of getting a job was to make *money*, he thought. Besides, the man's manner sang of illegality like fingernails down a blackboard. Mark thought the last thing he needed now was more trouble.

Nodding politely, he turned and walked out of the open-air stand.

"Out! Go away! You police, you provocator!"

The tiny Moluccan restaurant's tiny Moluccan owner waved stick arms at Mark while aproned kids, probably his, scurried for cover with practiced familiarity.

Recoiling, Mark held up his hands in front of his face. "Wait, man, I'm not from the police. All I want is a job."

31

"Ha! Job. Job! I spit." He spat. *"Job!"*

He got up in Mark's face, or at least his sternum. "You American, huh? You no European?" He wound his hands furiously in the towel at his waist as if trying to choke it.

"That's right. I'm American."

"Ha!" The proprietor darted behind a counter that offered candies in bright wrappers covered with pictures of elephants and monkeys and unfamiliar script. He rummaged out of sight, produced a stack of papers that threatened to overflow his small fist.

"See? You see? All papers must be fill out. European Community make man write whole life story, write book to get job. But you American. You no got paper, no got permit. I fill out form on you, I still go to jail!"

It got him going again. He came rushing out flapping the sheaf of Euroforms in Mark's face like a live chicken. "Out! Out now! *Orang besar yang tipis* get Molucca man big trouble!"

Outside, the sun was getting low, and the light was taking on that odd, soft quality of afternoon light in an ancient town in these latitudes, like a sepia-tone print from long ago.

Night coming soon. He shivered, though the afternoon was warm and a trifle muggy and he was sweating in his sweater. He put his head down and began to walk. Quite purposefully, though he had no idea where he was going.

"Marx," the woman said as she wrote the name on a form pinned to a clipboard. "First name?"

"Julius," Mark said.

She wrote that down too. She stood. She was a diminutive woman in a black blouse splashed with purple and a hint of yellow. Black skirt and stockings accented rather heavy legs. Black hair cut in a modified pageboy came down in pointed wings to either side of her triangular chin. She had lavender-and-black eye shadow and a general air of shopworn prettiness.

"Please come with me, Mr. Marx," she said.

She turned and led off from the reception desk in a foyer lit yellow by electric bulbs in sconces in the wall, down a corridor of stone that must have been horribly expensive when it was laid near Spui Square during the troubled sixteenth century. Sint Antoninus Hof had begun life as a Catholic convent. It was now a homeless hostel.

Mark fondled the coin in his pocket and felt guilty as hell. He had money, and here he was trying to jump lodging that might have gone to some homeless person. He didn't dare go back to his flat; the tiny tag-end of Takisian loot he'd had in his pocket when he went out the window was going to have to last him a good long time. That still didn't make it feel right.

But we were talking life-and-death here. More than the money, a hotel would require Mark to surrender his passport. That would be it for him; the police checked hotel registrations on a daily basis. Holland looked with tolerance on its own drug users, but in the face of mounting pressure from the rest of the EuroCommunity as well as Big Brother across the Atlantic they were beginning to cooperate with American drug enforcers. And it wasn't as if Mark was *merely* wanted for the few grams of forbidden chemicals—mainly psychedelics, as far out of fashion in the nineties as elephant bells—he could be proven to have had possession of.

Light spilled out an open door. It had the slightly irreal offcast of fluorescent light, a blue-tinged jitter that imparted a real night-of-the-living-dead look. She led him into its full glare.

Inside was an examining room. It had an old-timey look to Mark, wood where an American room would have been gleaming metal. A young doctor in a white coat sat reading a newspaper with his legs folded. As the woman led Mark in he jumped up, looking outraged.

He sputtered something in Dutch. Dutch always sounded like gargling to Mark; the country was pretty, the people friendly, and he loved the funky old streets of Amsterdam, but the language was just plain ugly. The doctor had long blond hair. It was thin on top.

"Mr. Marx needs shelter," the woman said pointedly in English.

"Very well, Mrs. Wiersma," the doctor said without enthusiasm. "I'll see to him. Here, take off your shirt."

Mrs. Wiersma smiled and nodded encouragement. She showed no sign of going away. As Mark pulled his sweater off, he couldn't help but wonder whether it was because the Dutch had less body modesty or because the hostel staff were used to processing the homeless on the assembly line. There wasn't much of a crowd tonight—Mrs. Wiersma and the doctor were the only people he'd seen. But it was early evening, sun barely down and warm yet. The real crush wouldn't happen until the nighttime North Sea wind really began to bite.

The doctor examined Mark with distracted briskness—poked here, tapped here, placed the cold ring of the stethoscope to his skin and bade him breathe. Mark did.

"Any chronic conditions or communicable diseases?"

"No."

The doctor tapped Mark a last time on the chest. "You sound good for one of ours," he said, frowning slightly. "You smell better than most, also."

"Thanks, man."

The doctor nodded and turned away. Mark sat dangling his long legs off the end of the examining table and tried not to look at Mrs. Wiersma. She was staring at him with the earnest intensity of an indulgent grown-up watching an unusually untalented neighbor child perform in a school pageant: knowing the child will screw up, but trying to beat the odds by sheer positive energy.

"Hold out your arm."

"What?"

The doctor's bored professionalism turned chill. Mark saw he held a hypodermic. "Your arm. I must draw blood. Come along, now, it won't take a minute."

He reached for Mark's arm. Mark snatched it away and held his other hand protectively over the elbow. "What're you testing for?"

Scowling openly now, the doctor turned and said something to Mrs. Wiersma in Dutch. "Certainly he has a right to know," she answered in English. "We are not crowded now. Come, be gentle."

The doctor sighed. "We must test for hepatitis, HIV, and xenovirus Takis-A."

Mark felt as if the flesh of his hairless chest and arms had turned to the marble it resembled in the otherworldly light. "Wild card virus? W-why?"

"It is the law."

"New government regulations," Mrs. Wiersma said hurriedly. "There was much resistance here to the idea of mandatory testing. The European Commission proposed it last fall, and the Council of Ministers passed the directive. Because it concerned health and safety, there was nothing the Netherlands could do. The European Community holds sway."

"Your arm," the doctor said.

"No," Mark said. "Wait. I—can't."

The doctor turned away. "No test, no stay."

"Oh, please," Mrs. Wiersma said. "We wish to help you. We can't if you won't let us."

Mark moistened his lips. He made himself breathe quickly and shallowly, as if a panic attack was coming on. It didn't take much acting skill. "I—I'm afraid of needles. Got it real bad."

"Perhaps if you had a few minutes to think it over, to calm yourself," Mrs. Wiersma said. "Really, it's for your own good."

"I haven't got all night," the doctor complained. "I have other duties."

"Just let me think about it a little," Mark said.

The doctor had lost interest in him, returning to his chair and paper. Mark hurriedly pulled on his shirt and sweater and walked back out to the front. Mrs. Wiersma hovered beside him, cooing at him and touching him dartingly on the elbow.

"I need to go outside a minute," Mark said. He had a catch to his voice, as if he was in danger of throwing up at any moment. He had gotten so frothed up by phony fear of needles and genuine fear of discovery that he really was about to puke.

"Certainly, certainly," Mrs. Wiersma said, alighting behind her little wooden desk. "You poor man."

Mark smiled wanly at her, nodded, walked out the arched front door into the evening, and away.

The naked pink neon woman bent over. The naked blue neon man leaped forward in an arc and thrust his prominently erect member into her from behind. Mark decided they were doing some pretty radical things with neon these days.

A ripening of the breeze drove the rain into him where he huddled in the doorway. The rain pitted the surface of the canal with dark saucers and made the big purple, pink, and magenta oblongs of light tossed onto the water from the houses' big front windows waver and bobble like ectoplasm. Mark shuddered, hugged himself with hands that felt inside and out like the cold wet hands of a statue.

Dutch households liked to leave their front curtains open so that passersby could admire the bourgeois splendor of their decor. The houses that lined the block away from the porn shop with the interesting and educational neon sign were no exception. It was the interior design that was unusual.

In each window sat a woman. Each was scantily clad, in costumes weighted heavily to garter belts and housecoats, though some outfits were tuned to the fetishist eye: a nurse, two nuns, and a probably Indonesian woman in chiffon and fake feathers that Mark had an awful suspicion was supposed to suggest a Native American princess.

The babes looked bored. Several did needlepoint, a couple read, and the Indian maid had a laptop computer propped on her thin bare thighs. Mark wasn't sure how they managed to read in the gloom. The rows of garishly if inadequately lit windows reminded him irresistibly of the aquariums they used to have in cheap lounges back in the early sixties.

It was a poor night for business. No tourists were braving the rain to gawk at the cellulite on display, not even your usually indefatigably horny Japanese businessmen. Even as Mark watched, one of the nuns took off her headgear, tossed it in a corner, and drew the frilly drapes with a flourish of disgust.

He had heard somewhere that whorehouses sometimes offered the cheapest accommodations. Maybe that was true. The problem was, these weren't whorehouses, and the occupants depended on rapid turnover, even if they weren't getting much tonight. He somehow doubted any of them would be in a mood to cut a deal on crash space alone.

He craned his head out of the doorway that provided him largely symbolic shelter. No break in the weather. Maybe he'd drift back to the warehouse and see if any watchmen had yet spotted the window he'd jimmied to get out of his last night's lie-up.

Sprout was a million miles away. Tomorrow morning didn't seem much closer.

At least there weren't any stars.

"Cocaine? Hashish? Heroin?"

Mark put his head down to avoid eye contact and practiced his broken-field running, trying to dodge the West African blacks doing the *Leidseplein* caracole on those funky bikes with the handlebars turned upside-down, like steer horns.

He was on his way to Vondel Park, just south of Leyden Square. You couldn't crash in the huge park anymore, thanks to abuse of the privilege by the trend-followers and wannabes who appropriated the name "hippies" during the mid-seventies. It was still a major nexus for the European counterculture.

Mark, of course, had never actually *been* a member of the counterculture. That was his curse; that was the dramatic irony of his life. From the time he first discovered the glories of the counterculture, as a flat-topped biochemistry major in highwater pants in the fall of 1969, through his days as Cap'n Trips, the ace with the purple Uncle Sam suit and no visible powers whose not-so-secret secret identity was the mild-mannered owner of the last head shop on Manhattan Island, Mark's journey had been a personal one. He had never actually participated to any extent in the Movement.

Of course, maybe that was why he was still keeping the faith in the early 1990s, when all others were become stockbrokers and informers. Mark didn't think that way. He was more inclined to wonder if he'd ever been more than a spectator to his *own* life.

Now Mark, in desperation, was seeking the communal shelter of what remained of the counterculture. These days the kids were lean and mean, with spiked hair in exotic colors or the *Wacht am Rhein* butch cuts of the Greens—long hair and beards went with potbellies and Coke-bottle glasses. Not too congenial, but he was running out of options.

He had lived for a time as a federal fugitive on the streets of New York. But that was his own country, where you didn't need identification papers to find lodging for the night, or a job—at least if you were as blond and tall as Mark. Amsterdam was a tolerant place, and the people friendly in their own reserved way. But for a foreigner on the run, all the colors were wrong and the corners were sharp and unwelcoming, and the rising wind of Euro-unification blew cold through streets that once sheltered the dissident and different.

He noticed the real-world wind coming up, sharp and cold and crisp as a knifeblade across the sunny, complacent heat of afternoon. He pulled his sweater tighter around him, hunched his shoulders. His clothes were still wet from the soaking they'd received last night.

Wind began to whistle in his ears. Scraps of trash brushed his legs like small frightened animals. He found himself leaning forward as he walked; he never realized a gale could come up quite this quickly, even off the turbulent North Sea.

Debris began to swirl around him.

A black pedal-pusher fell off his bike and went tumbling down the street, scattering pedestrians. Mark couldn't hear anything. He was having trouble breathing.

The wind was too much for him. He stopped, and clutched himself, and shivered. He wondered what the hell was going on.

The wind stopped. Something small and hard and metallic rammed into his right kidney hard enough to keep him from recovering his breath.

"Walk this way, motherfucker," an American voice hissed in his ear.

Chapter Five

The brown-haired young woman turned around in the driver's seat of the Citroën and said, "Dr. Meadows. So good to see you again."

She gave him a smile as chill and brittle as late frost and turned back forward to close her own door. Memory belatedly kicked in.

"Hey! I know you. You're Mistral. I saw you—"

He meant to say, *I saw you in* Aces High. But to do so would be to admit that he was Cap'n Trips, which he had some vague idea might prejudice his cause, even though he guessed just about everybody within reach of American satellite broadcasting knew it now anyway. Besides, she had said, "Good to see you *again*" . . . mostly he tripped on his tongue.

As he was doing so, the larger, blond member of the pair that had hustled him into the slope-backed French sedan slid in after him. "She calls herself Helen," he said. "That's Ms. Carlysle to assholes like you."

The smaller, darker one got in the front passenger seat. There was something vaguely familiar about him. Maybe it was the nasty little pistol he'd stuck in Mark's side and now stuck under Mark's nose. Mark knew nothing about firearms, but he thought it was probably some kind of automatic weapon. He also had a suspicion that the little striations on its bullets that ballistics experts looked for under microscopes would bear a marked resemblance to those on the ones dugs from victims of the notorious *Damplein* shooting two days ago.

He closed his door. Mistral—Helen Carlysle?—let the clutch in and drove off.

"You don't know how long I've waited for this," the dark man said. He had the crazy intensity that was so popular in movie cops these days. "You're going to burn, asswipe."

That didn't sound right. "What for?" he asked, a microsecond before realizing it made him sound like a dweeb.

The thin, feral face flushed. "You killed my partner! You killed Dooley, and you're going down for it big time."

Mark blinked. "What are you talking about? I didn't kill anybody." Not on Earth, anyway. He had a hard time dealing with some of what he'd done on Takis, but it was no time to bring that up.

"What about all those people you sold your poison to on the streets?" Carlysle asked in a strained voice.

Mark stared at her. About the only crime he *wasn't* accused of was trafficking. The two male agents turned a momentary look of disbelief her way, then turned back to Mark, obviously choosing to edit her question out of their personal realities.

"Tim Dooley, DEA," the beefy blond said. "His partner. He was killed in a shoot-out in your lab in New York."

"In my *lab*?" Mark was completely disoriented now.

"Over your fucking head shop," the dark-haired one said. "Oh, excuse me. Your New Age deli."

"A couple of years ago," Carlysle said over her shoulder. "About the time you pulled your disappearing act from Judge Conower's courtroom."

Mark had no idea what they were talking about. After Judge Conower's surprise decision—adjudging *both* Mark and his ex-wife unsuitable parents and remanding Sprout to the custody of the New York juvenile justice system—Mark had sort of phased out of the world for a while.

"He was actually shot by a Narcotics Division officer from NYPD," Carlysle said. "It was what you might call a slight misunderstanding."

"That doesn't matter," the dark-haired agent snarled. "You're just as guilty as if you'd pulled the fucking trigger. That's what the law says, dude."

"That's the craziest thing I ever heard in my life!" Mark blurted.

The agent shoved the muzzle of his machine pistol up Mark's right nostril. *"Don't call me crazy!"*

"Hey, Lynn," the big blond agent said, reaching up as if to touch his partner's arm, not quite daring to do so. "Take it easy. Don't want to get blood on the upholstery, you know."

The other man turned him a look of hatred so pure it rocked him back against the rear of the seat. Then he relaxed.

"Yeah, you're right, Gary," he said, actually taking the gun out of Mark's face. "We're supposed to take good care of the little lady, after all. Not subject her to the sight of spilled brains."

"You can knock off the condescending sexist crap," Carlysle said.

Lynn laughed and tucked his piece out of sight beneath the windbreaker he was wearing today. They were driving southeast away from Leyden Square, along the Lijnbaansgracht. Trees and colorful moored houseboats ticked past.

"I think I'm going to throw up," Mark said.

"Jesus," Lynn said, and turned away.

"Go ahead," his partner said. "You'll have to clean it up."

"Wait. My arm. My left arm hurts. Like, what'd you guys do—"

He slammed his right hand against his sternum and doubled over.

Lynn came around in his seat. "What? What the fuck?"

"Hey!" Gary said, holding up a hand to try to keep his partner under control. "Hey, knock that shit off."

Mark uncurled a little. "My—my chest. *Aaah!*"

"Wait!" Carlysle cried, veering a little. "You don't understand. Nausea, pains in the arm—he's having a heart attack, dammit!"

"Oh, bullshit," Agent Gary said. He pulled Mark upright.

"Hey," the blond agent exclaimed. "He put something in his mouth!" His hand went under his sport coat.

Mark grabbed the coat by the collar and yanked it desperately down Agent Gary's back to his elbows, effectively pinning his arms.

He changed.

The blond agent cried out in surprised fear as Mark's skinny body *expanded*, filling the slope-roofed rear of the Citroën. Helen Carlysle looked up to her rearview, saw an immense gray-skinned man crushing Gary against the side of the car, and crashed into a Daihatsu parked facing the canal.

The gray man reared up, crashing up through the tinted-glass fastback. He climbed out of the now-stationary car with a squeal of tearing metal, dragging the terrified Gary with him.

Lynn had his Scorpion out and leveled across the back of the passenger seat. Carlysle knocked its barrel up in the air. "Don't shoot! You'll hit Hamilton!"

The gray man was backing away, dragging the agent with him as a bullet shield. He was big and muscular in a furniture-mover way. His skin was shiny. He wore what looked like gray Speedo racing trunks. His nose and ears were small, and there was no hair visible anywhere on his face or body.

Spitting curses like a cat in a sack, Lynn pulled the lever on his door, kicked it open when it balked. He jumped out on the sidewalk with his Scorpion up in a two-handed Weaver stance.

His partner recovered his senses enough to scream, "Don't shoot!"

Realizing that the dark-haired agent was going to shoot anyway, the gray-skinned man turned and lunged for the canal, still holding onto Gary's coat. The seams gave way, leaving the agent standing there in just the sleeves as his erstwhile captor, still clutching the jacket's torso, turned and launched himself in a racing dive.

As he did, he shifted again. What hit the greasy green surface of the Lijnbaan canal was the sleek, gray form of a *Tursiops truncatus*.

The passengers of a red-and-white canal tour boat crowded against its glass wall to point and mouth at the spectacle of the dolphin streaking past with a vest of some sort draped over its rostrum. Then they tumbled over each other as bullets from Lynn's machine pistol stippled the water's surface like hail.

The Scorpion ran dry. For a moment Saxon stood on

the brick embankment, yanking the trigger so furiously that the weapon bobbed in his hands, as if he were a kid pretending to fire a toy gun. Its pilot hugging the deck beside his passengers, the tour boat ran into a moored houseboat with a bump and grinding crunch.

Gary Hamilton was wandering in a tight if irregular little circle. A trail of blood ran down the side of his broad, square face from a cut in his forehead. He made small gestures with his hands and talked to himself.

Helen Carlysle was out of the car, showy vast cape swirling about her, staring in white-faced fury at the front bumper of the Citroën, which was well and truly locked with the yellow Japanese compact.

A black Mercedes glided to a halt behind the Citroën. The driver opened his door and stood up behind it. J. Robert Belew regarded Carlysle through Ray-Ban aviator shades.

"Another screwup," he said. Mistral threw her hands up from her sides.

Sirens were beginning to burble in the background.

"Tell Crockett and Tubbs to hustle their hinder parts into the car. If the Dutch pin this one on them, George Bush himself won't be able to get 'em out of stir in this millennium.

"Oh—from now on you can consider this a Langley operation. And that's official."

It was a little suburb strung along the Amstel River somewhere south of town. Mark sat on the grassy banks with his knees up and his head down and spent some quality time just dripping and breathing.

After a phase-shift between one of his "friends"—the ace personas his color-coded powders summoned—and plain-vanilla Mark, his thoughts tended to fragment like a frightened school of fish. It took time for them to coalesce.

Why did I come to this hot, heavy world? was his first coherent thought. *On Takis I was a hero, a prince. I had Tis, and safety, and Roxalana.*

But Sprout wasn't on Takis. Even if she didn't seem a whole lot closer, right this minute.

He picked up the do-it-yourself vest Aquarius's ace strength had made out of Agent Gary's coat. He wasn't at all sure why the shape-changer had hung on to it; usually Aquarius felt total disdain for material things, particularly man-made ones.

In his dolphin form Aquarius wasn't fully human in intelligence, in any sense of the word; the processing power of his brain was largely used up by the environmental interface, hearing and taste and sonar-sense, the orientation of self in four dimensions: up/down, left/right, forward/back, *flow*. Dolphin-Aquarius was a more truly alien creature than any Takisian. At two removes from baseline Mark, as it were, it was difficult to discern his motives. It was tough enough making sense of his memories, incredibly sensual and rich but incomprehensible, like watching a Kurosawa film in Japanese.

Mark suspected the reason Aquarius had hung on to the jacket during his high-speed swim through the canals of Amsterdam to the river was that the thing was stuck on his snout.

There was nothing in the outer pockets but two rubbers and a pair of sodden ticket stubs to WWF wrestling in Madison Square Garden. The inside breast pocket rang all the bells. There was a passport in the name of Hamilton, Gary A.; a case of business cards, soaked beyond recovery, identifying Hamilton as a marketing associate for Pepsico—weren't they big Nixon contributors, way back when?—and a billfold.

Mark opened the billfold. There was two hundred and twenty-three dollars cash, Hamilton's Ohio driver's license—he'd been born in Youngstown in 1963—and one American Express Gold Card.

Mark ran his tongue slowly over his lips, which felt dry in spite of his having just climbed out of the river. He was aware that he'd lit the FREE GAME light on the pinball machine.

Everything depended on how he played this one. His life, his freedom, his chance of seeing Sprout again. *Everything.*

He buttoned the wallet carefully in the back pocket of his khaki pants, walked to the quiet, tree-shaded street, and stuck out his thumb.

*　　*　　*

"This is Captain Leeuwebek," the overhead speaker announced. "We will shortly be landing at Rome International Airport. The sun is shining, and the temperature is a pleasant twenty-one degrees. We will be remaining on the ground for forty-five minutes for routine maintenance before continuing on to Beirut. If you choose to leave the aircraft, please make sure the placard that reads, 'Occupied,' is displayed on your seat. Thank you for flying KLM."

The tall man seated over the wing of the big Airbus accepted a final complimentary glass of orange juice from the strikingly pretty Indonesian flight attendant. She let her eyes linger on him before traveling on. Like most humans, she had a fascination for the *different*, and he certainly qualified. He was at least half a meter taller than she was, for one thing, his unbelievably long frame encased in an obviously expensive three-piece suit, navy with an old-gold pinstripe. His features had that exotic Northern European sharpness; his hair was yellow, gathered into a neat little upwardly mobile ponytail at the nape of his neck. Most of all she liked his eyes; they were the blue of the noon sky over the Savu Sea, and they danced with what seemed genuine pleasure behind the thick round lenses of his glasses.

He was obviously a wealthy and important man. Perhaps he was a Wall Street stockbroker who would soon be indicted for a crime. She didn't quite understand the current American fascination for turning their most successful citizens into criminals while symphathizing publicly with those who refused to work; it smacked to her of certain religious practices on some of the wilder headhunter islands back home. Oh, well; Westerners were all crazy. But at least this one was *cute*.

Mark Meadows looked quickly away from the flight attendant—you weren't supposed to call them "stewardesses" anymore, and he tried to be scrupulous about that sort of thing—so she wouldn't think he was forward. If she had told him point-blank what was on her mind, he would have thought she was trying to humor him, for some unknowable reason.

He sipped his juice and watched the greasy yellow River Tiber wheel below. Beirut was the place for him; he was sure of it. American influence had waned substantially

there the last twenty years. Though the Nur al-Allah fanatics
had been making their presence known of late, it was still a
favorite holiday resort for most of Europe and indeed the
world. Surely the premier party city of Africa would be a
tolerant place, the sort of place a lone American fugitive
could drop quietly from view.

Also, Lebanon had the laxest entry controls in the
Med. The passport photo of young Agent Hamilton didn't
resemble Mark at all, but he figured all blond European
types would look alike to Lebanese Customs. And no official body anywhere in the world looked too hard at a man
in a suit and tie. Lucky Mark still remembered how to knot
one.

The wheels touched down, with a bump and a squeal.
Mark looked around eagerly in hopes of seeing ruins or rus-
tic Italian peasants or something, but like all airports Rome
was built in an area that was predominantly flat and open.
Off in the distance he did see some hills clustered thickly
with houses, some of which may have been villas or may
have been big blocks of cardboard government housing; you
couldn't tell, through the thick ground-hugging layer of
heatwave-stirred petrochemicals.

The Airbus slowed and began to taxi toward the terminal. About two hundred meters shy of it the airplane
stopped. The chief attendant came on the P.A. to announce
that there would be a slight delay for the preceding flight to
clear the gate.

Mark's eyelids began to gain weight as if Hiram
Worchester were playing games with them. His chin
dropped toward the knot of his tie.

A change in the timbre of the conversation around him
brought him abruptly back to himself. He blinked around,
momentarily disoriented, and happened to look out the window two seats to his right.

A little utility car pulling a baggage trailer was just
coming to a stop forty meters from the plane. There was no
baggage on the cart, but there were half a dozen men, who
began to spill off before the vehicle fully stopped. They
wore the white jumpsuits and earmuff-style hearing protec-
tors common to airport ground crew the world over. But
even Mark, naïve as he was, knew that the stubby little

submachine guns with fore-and-aft pistol grips were not standard aircraft maintenance equipment.

He unfastened his seatbelt, stood, and walked deliberately back toward the bathroom.

When the Rome police department's elite antiterrorist unit kicked in the door five minutes later, there was nobody inside.

Chapter Six

Lynn Saxon stormed from the bathroom as though washed out by the thunderous noise of the toilet flushing. "I can't believe these Roman weenies let him slip through their fingers."

Gary Hamilton looked up from his Smith & Wesson FBI-special 10mm, which he had disassembled for cleaning on a copy of *L'Osservatore Romano* Belew had picked up at the airport. "What do you expect? They're Italians."

Helen Carlysle stood outside the open sliding door by the balcony's wrought-iron rail watching the sun dissolve into the brown, toxic cloud that squatted over the Roman hills like a Japanese movie monster. Her hips were canted, her wrists crossed meditatively at the small of her back. The muggy air that crowded in past her like kids back from school and billowed the skirt of her lightweight dusty blue-and-gray dress smelled of diesel fumes, cooling asphalt, and garlic fried in olive oil.

"He's an ace, after all," she said, glancing back. "We didn't do such a hot job holding on to him either."

"Big of you to admit it," said Belew. He had his shoes off and his feet up on the bed. His hands were clasped behind his close-cropped head, and his eyes were closed; everyone had assumed he was asleep.

"Let's see you do better, big fella," Saxon said. He sat down on a chair beside the table on which his partner worked, his butt barely seeming to touch the fabric, as if he were about to bounce right up again. He brushed his right nostril rapidly with his thumb, dropped his hand to his lap to tap his thigh with restless fingers.

48

"Speaking of aces," Belew said, "just what are you doing along on this expedition, Ms. Carlysle? I didn't think the Governor had any use for aces."

"Fucking SCARE saddled us—" Saxon began.

"Hey, we're not prejudiced or anything," Hamilton said hurriedly. "The Director just believes the job can best be done by real people. I mean, normal people. I mean—oh, Jeez, Ms. Carlysle, I'm sorry."

"What dickwit means is that the Director thinks us nats can do the job just fine," Saxon said sourly.

Belew swung his legs over the side of the bed and sat up. "I reckon I can rustle up some forms from the American embassy if you want to file a discrimination complaint against our little pal here," he said to the woman. "They're making insensitivity a crime, back in the world."

Helen turned with a tight, ironic smile. "Nobody seems to care much about insensitivity toward aces, Mr. Belew."

"I guess aces aren't a fashionable minority," he agreed, nodding affably to Hamilton, who was staring gapemouthed at him and Helen alternately, trying to figure out if they were kidding.

"In answer to your question, Mr. Belew, SCARE believed ace talents would come in handy in a hunt for America's most prominent rogue ace. Director Martínez agreed. I'm a civilian contractor, much as you are yourself; my father is . . . was a personal acquaintance of Mr. Bennett."

"That's no surprise. Old Vernon made it a point to be acquainted with everybody who turned up frequently on the *CBS Evening News*, with the possible exception of the Nur."

Her eyes flared. "What's that supposed to mean?"

"I was unaware simple declarations of fact were required to *mean* anything, honey." He stood up and walked over to the table where Hamilton was just fitting the slide back onto his piece.

"You speak of insensitivity," she said in a shaky voice. "I don't think repeatedly throwing my father in my face is very sensitive."

Hands in his pockets, he looked at her. "Don't you think it's time you came to terms with it?" he asked quietly.

Color burned like slap marks on her cheeks. "What makes you think it's any of your business—"

"I don't know why we had to come to this dump,"

Saxon said loudly, flipping a hand at the Art Deco decor. The wallpaper was mauve above the molding. "It's so fucking tacky, it hurts. Aren't there any Hyatts in this town?"

"This place has character, son," Belew said. "There's more to life than Big Macs and *The Cosby Show*."

He unfolded a map of the Mediterranean. "Right now we maybe ought to figure out where our Dr. Meadows is going to be heading from here."

"He's going to Beirut," Hamilton blurted. He looked down at his hands, immediately aware he'd made a tactical mistake.

"Yeah," Saxon crowed. "That's where he bought a ticket to on *your* credit card, Gary. He's headed there on *your* passport. You're his *best friend*, Gary."

"I think we can forget about Beirut at this point," Belew said, picking up an ornate cigar cutter from the dresser. "At least as a near-term destination. He knows it's blown."

"He didn't realize we'd trace his route through Agent Hamilton's credit card," Carlysle pointed out, all business once again. "Why should he suddenly be so sophisticated as to realize we're onto his destination?"

"He's a naïve son of a gun, I'll give you that. But he's behind the times, and as a consequence he's still capable of doing something that's currently out of fashion: *learning*."

"You're sure a hell of an expert on this old fucking hippie," Saxon said.

"Son, I make it a point of knowing my enemy. You talk about it; it's not just words to me. It's kept me alive in places they'd have had your hide drying on a rock."

Outside, the sun had dissolved into bloody-looking drool. Saxon started to his feet, eyes crazy-mad. Hamilton got a big hand on his arm and held him in his chair by main force.

"We're running the problem through our computers in Washington," Hamilton said. "We have a complete personality profile on Dr. Meadows. They'll wargame the possibilities and give us some insight into where he'll head from here."

"Fine," Belew said. "We'll let your pocket-protector brigade play their computer games. In the meantime, let's try

to get a handle on where our quarry is in the real world."
He snipped the end off his right forefinger.

Saxon jerked back as blood squirted from Belew's fingertip. The younger man's face instantly drained of blood.
"Jesus *Christ!*"

Belew pressed the raw tip of his finger against the base
of a gooseneck lamp. It glowed to life. The head suddenly
craned and swiveled to bring its glow to bear on the map.

"Time to cast a little light, rather than curse the darkness," Belew said with satisfaction.

Helen stepped forward with her arms crossed tightly
beneath her breasts. Reflections from the lamp glittered in
her eyes. "You're an ace, too, aren't you?"

"You never told us that," Saxon said sulkily.

"Son, Langley isn't in the habit of telling everything it
knows, unlike certain of our finer government agencies.
Now, pay some attention here. I'd at least like to have some
tentative answers to hand before I have to leave."

"Leave?" Saxon said. "Where the hell are you going?"

"The opera, of course. *The Marriage of Figaro.* They've
got an ultramodernistic set and staging for it. I hear it's a
hell of a mess, but I like to see things with my own eyes."

The old night train to Brindisi. Mark's asleep.

Elite unit or not, the Rome antiterrorist unit had a tendency to mill. When somebody dressed in the same coveralls they and the legitimate ground crew were wearing
dropped into view beneath the tail of the Airbus, all eyes
were locked on the front of the plane, where the first team
was going up a ramp that had been wheeled across the heat-
shimmering pavement. When the figure strolled away, no
one paid any mind.

Escape was what Cosmic Traveler did best, after all.
Mark will have to engage in some creative chemistry before
he can play that ace again.

The train is winding its way across Italy's Apennine
spine. Mark is heading east—where, he isn't sure. He's
mainly on the train because you don't need to surrender
your passport to spend the night on the train the way you do
to spend your night in a hotel.

The night is clear, but that's okay. The rolldown plastic
shade is drawn.

He paid cash for the tickets. He's still using the passport; he figures it isn't quite as hot as the credit card. Most grunt-level Eurocrats, he's noticed, don't look beyond the distinctive American jacket on the document, if they look at it at all. If you look like a North African or a Turkish guestworker, they're liable to want to count the hairs in your mustache to be sure the number's the same as in your passport photo. Americans get treated differently. He's learning, Mark is.

Since he's asleep and all, he dreams.

In his dreams he's a strapping golden youth, barechested, with blond hair flowing to his muscular shoulders. He swings a glowing peace symbol on a chain, and the secret police and jackboots and censors and informers of America's New World Order retreat in confusion. He is the mightiest of Movement aces: the Radical, who fought the National Guard and Hardhat to a standstill during the riots following the Kent State murders and saved the day in People's Park.

Mark *was* the Radical once, which is all the times the Radical appeared. Or maybe he wasn't. See, he isn't sure.

He was a sheltered child of southern California and the military-industrial complex. His father was a war hero and technocrat, his mother a very nice woman who did all the social things expected of an officer's wife and drank perhaps more than she should, a fact Mark didn't realize until much later. He had arrived at the University of California at Berkeley in 1969 as a four-star scientific prospect, recruited during a drive by UCB to improve its standing as a hard-science school.

He had won acclaim and science fairs with high school experiments on the effects of hallucinogenic drugs on cognitive faculties in rats. He came into college with a powerful fascination with the biochemistry of mind and very little experience of life beyond his comic books, his science club, and a crush on black-haired, violet-eyed Kimberly Anne Cordayne, who had been his major heartthrob since elementary school.

He undertook what he considered fieldwork, observing the effects of psychedelics on humans by plunging into the Bay Area subculture at the maximum bubble of its fermentation. One of the first potential subjects his searching turned up was none other than Kimberly Anne herself, now calling herself Sunflower and lovelier than ever.

He had become infatuated, both with Sunflower and the Movement with which she had so seamlessly blended. He himself couldn't quite connect with either. But both seemed to him inexpressibly beautiful, worth any lengths to attain.

He had finally nerved himself to take the logical experimental step of dropping acid himself when the fateful news of the Kent State killings hit. Wandering by the university waiting for the drug to kick in, he had stumbled upon a confrontation in People's Park that was rapidly going critical. That tripped the drug and flipped him right out of his skull; he stumbled backwards into an alley and wasn't seen by a living soul for twenty-four hours.

But out of that alley at the crucial moment stepped the Radical. The National Guard was sent packing and Hardhat humbled. Radical was embraced as a brother by Tom Marion Douglas, the Lizard King, reigning rock 'n' roll ace and master of a somber, driving musical style that was at once cerebral and visceral—Apollonian and Dionysian, as Douglas liked to say.

The Radical led a wild victory celebration, consuming vast quantities of beer and pot and truly epic sex with a violet-eyed lady who called herself Sunflower. Then, at dawn of the day following his triumph, he waved good-bye to his baggy-eyed but still stoned and jubilant admirers and walked into an alley. He was never seen again.

Mark was, though. He staggered out of the alley a short time later with his Coke-bottle glasses gone and his pants all crumpled and a headful of images he would never quite get sorted into coherent memories. His just-friend Sunflower had grabbed him by the arm and wondered loudly how he could *possibly* have missed what might have been the most glorious moment of the Movement. She had seen a Hero, and her eyes glowed like stars.

Mark's faculty advisers, alarmed at the turn his private life was taking, steered him away from his study of psychoactives. He allowed himself to be maneuvered into genetic research, at least in the classroom. Outside the UCB lab, though, he grew his hair long and increasingly gave himself over to a glowing Summer of Love vision of life—an ideal that had never been, and was little more than a gauzy memory in that blood-in-the-streets spring of 1970.

His work in psychedelics continued on an extracurricular basis. He was convinced, somehow, that *he* had been the Radical. Some combination of drug and existing brain chemistry had activated his ace, and for one moment he had been strong and loved and valid. He would recapture that, somehow, anyhow. And Sunflower's eyes would shine for *him*.

He got his doctorate in biochemistry and performed what would prove pioneering work in the field of recombinant DNA. But his heart wasn't in it. The Radical eluded him, and that was the only goal he truly felt.

One summer dawn in 1974 Sunflower had turned up at the door of his apartment in the burnt-out huckstered-out husk of the Haight. Only, her glossy black hair had been cut to a bristly paramilitary brush, and she was calling herself Marshal Pasionara of the Symbionese Liberation Army. A dental emergency had pulled her out of the SLA's hideout in Watts just in time to miss the fiery shoot-out in which Field Marshal Cinque and the others lost their lives.

The SLA's harsh discipline had brought her off recreational chemicals of all sorts, but after four months on the Revolution's far nut fringe she was as weird as if she'd been tweaking on crystal meth the whole time. The live news coverage of flames shooting out of the house she was supposed to be in—and the dark hints in the cell that she was showing signs of dangerous deviation and bourgeois weakness when she left to seek attention for her toothache—had slammed her to reality's cold, hard ground.

To her parents she was dead, to her old Movement buddies she was either a dangerous zany, a deserter from the real revolution, or a possible government *agente provocateuse*—there was anything but consensus about the Symbionese crew—and to the United States government she was a wanted fugitive, though not under her real name or a reliable description. In all the world she knew of only one person who wouldn't judge her, one way or another.

Mark was scraping by on sheer if sporadic brilliance, helping lesser lights deliver on their research grants. Most of his money went for his chemical dream quest and enough marijuana to take the edge off his continual disappointment. But he took her in, and felt only joy.

The first two weeks she was like a fresh-trapped wild animal, all nerve ends. He let her be, even cutting his tiny apartment in two by hanging a Madras print to give her some privacy. Eventually the adrenaline buzz began to recede.

On August 8, 1974, the sixties officially came to an end with the resignation of a Whittier College alum even more notorious than Kimberly Anne and Nancy Ling Perry. Mark and Kimberly killed a bottle of wine—*not* Gallo—and wound up fumbling together on the rump-sprung mattress on the floor on his side of the partition. The divider came down the next day.

The next seven months or so were the happiest time Mark could remember. At dawn on the vernal equinox of 1975 Mark and Kimberly—again calling herself Sunflower—were married at Golden Gate State Park.

After that, nothing seemed to go quite right. Sunflower drifted from cause to cause, cult to cult, at once restless and listless. She began to drink and take pills. Mark retreated further into pot smoke and his search for the Radical. His odd research jobs got odder, not to mention less frequent.

Sprout was born in the spring of 1977. It was another case where partners in a failing marriage shared an unspoken belief that having a child would somehow cement their relationship. As a remedy it was akin to trying to save a crumbling bridge by running more semis over it. By the time Sprout's developmental problem, or whatever euphemism they were using, was diagnosed in 1978, Mark and Sunflower were communicating solely in screams and silences.

The divorce was finalized in 1981. A nasty custody fight was aborted when Sunflower broke down completely at a hearing. She was declared incompetent and institutionalized in Camarillo. Mark was given sole custody of their daughter.

He took her and fled east. As a countercultural pole star, the Village had shone almost as brightly as San Francisco and Berkeley and didn't harbor the landmarks and memories that reproached Mark for his many failures. His father, now four-star General Marcus Meadows, lent him the money to go into business for himself. He opened the Cosmic Pumpkin head shop and deli on Fitz-James O'Brien Street on the southern fringe of Greenwich Village.

He was not, to say the least, a natural businessman. His father established a trust fund to discreetly funnel money into the store. Mark and Sprout got by.

Then, in early 1983, his long quest for the Radical bore fruit. But like Cristoforo Colombo setting forth in 1492 to find a quick way around the world and fall on Jerusalem from behind to liberate it from the paynim, where he wound up wasn't exactly where he intended to go. . . .

Curled up on the fold-down bed, Mark stirs, moans softly. He has the compartment all to himself. He drools a little on the pillow. Outside, the Italian night rattles by.

Chapter Seven

Mark sat there on the bald rock of the Areopagus and let the wind tousle his hair. The sky was a high, thin blue scattered with fat, fraying cotton bolls of cloud. In his mind he saw a couple of satyrs carrying those funky panpipe things Zamfir always plays on late-night ads on cable come out of the weeds to check him out. Life was kind of a Disney flick for Mark, when he was left to his own devices, even though he hadn't imbibed any illicit chemicals—for recreational purposes anyway—since blowing Amsterdam a week ago. He was not an ideal Clean and Sober poster boy.

He sat and stared off at the crisp weeds and Japanese tourists stirring among the white-stone jumble that surrounded the Parthenon, over on the Acropolis. It wasn't anywhere near as large as he'd expected, the Parthenon, even though it was just as lovely as advertised. That was an ideal encapsulation of life: that which was eagerly anticipated turned out to be, at firsthand, smaller than it was in the imagination, and either shabby or—as in the Parthenon's case—somehow fake-looking. It would be the hip and happening thing to blame that phenomenon on television and movies and the easy street-level availability of wonders, designer drugs for eye and mind from the secret labs of Industrial Light & Magic. Sitting up here on these ancient-shaped rocks with the same wind running its fingers through his hair as had run them through Solon's when he was splitting for the coast with the ever-fickle Athenian mob at his heels, Mark had the heretical notion that people had been feeling that way, shortchanged by actuality, since they developed crania larger than egg cups.

Getting here had been easier than he would have imagined. At Brindisi he had gone straight to the docks. There he looked at freighters: not too large, not too clean, definitely nothing that looked as if it were owned by some uptight multinational. Multinationals had books of rules and regulations and suits who prowled to make sure they were followed to the letter. The rules didn't provide for any clandestine passengers, he felt sure.

He didn't even care, particularly, if the damned boat looked as if it would *float*. The Med is not a huge sea, and he had a vial of gray powder left. The were-dolphin Aquarius could swim a long way in the hour of freedom it would give him.

He was looking at ships that flew flags from countries in what he had grown up thinking of as Eastern Europe and was now being called Central Europe, the way it had been when his dad was growing up. He figured Eastern—no, *Central*—Europeans had gotten mightily pissed off at their own governments and might be inclined to transfer their anger to government in general. At least to the extent of not caring too much about the finer points of law.

His third try he got lucky. The *Montenegro* had a Yugoslav registration—which was looking more academic by the moment—and a mostly Baltic crew. The ship had a load of Catalan tennis balls from Barcelona to Piraeus, the port of Athens. The captain would be more than happy to take Mark along for five hundred dollars American.

Mark had no plans to go to Athens. But then, he had no plans not to, and until he settled on a final destination, Athens was as good a waystation as any. He suspected that five hundred American was more than the trip would have cost on a luxury liner. But luxury liners were sticky about things like passports, and their pursers had lists of names of people the authorities would like to talk to in case they tried to slip off for a nice relaxing cruise. Mark was dead sure his borrowed name of "Hamilton, Gary A." would be on them. The master of the *Montenegro* didn't give a particular damn if his passenger called himself Nur al-Allah. Or even if he *was* Nur al-Allah, as long as he behaved.

The Italian authorities were no problem at all. Italian exit controls were anything but notoriously strict, something they had in common with the Dutch ones. Like everybody else the Italians were on the watch for guns, drugs, and undocumented immigrants coming into the country from places with economies still more blighted than their own. They didn't worry much about who left, or what they left with, as long as it didn't look like immobile naked people with very pale complexions under tarps.

The trip was uneventful. The crew seemed genuinely friendly. Half of them spoke some English, and his science-symposium German was enough to get him the rest of the way.

He negotiated with the ship's cook, a wiry and diminutive Macedonian with curly black sideburns who probably wasn't as young as he looked, for a French passport. It wasn't his first choice; when you looked at Mark Meadows, *Frenchman* wasn't the first word that popped into your mind, unless you were from some weird ex-colonial part of the Third World where the only white guys you'd ever seen were Frenchmen. But French papers cost far less than, say, American, by reason of lesser demand, and anyway the cook had the fixings for a French ID on hand.

Even as he began negotiations, it occurred to him that the simplest way for the cook to get whatever money he offered for the papers was to slip him a plate of food dosed with some nice corrosive sublimate that would dissolve his bowels for him come mealtime. He had been sure to let the cook know—untruthfully—that the settled price took him near the limits of his ready cash. And he had been careful not to dicker too long.

In some ways Mark was turning into somebody he didn't exactly like, somebody nasty and suspicious of his fellow bits of star-stuff. He blamed his stay on Takis for that; intrigue was like an extra classical element there: earth, air, fire, water, skullduggery. All the same he slept lightly, didn't venture too near the rail when others were around, and tasted gingerly in case the cook used a little too much lye in the goulash.

The most Mark could say about the passport was that the Polaroid picture of him glued inside it looked rather more like him than the picture of Hamilton in the liberated American one, which he'd handed over to the cook by way of a trade-in. At Piraeus, Customs went over the ship as if they were expecting loose diamonds to have rolled into the

seams in the decking, but passed him ashore without a
glance. He suspected—that nasty Takisian-born cynicism
again—they were really scouting for cumshaw. He had simply shouldered the imitation Vuitton flight bag he'd picked
up before hitting the train in Rome and walked down the
gangplank with an airy wave to them and his Central European pals.

If only all life's problems could be blown off with such
ease.

The papers had stood him to a third-floor—okay,
second—walk-up room in a grimy *pension*, with a sporadic
and unsanitary bathroom on the floor below. The stripy pa-
pered walls of the flat were even more sweat-stained than
the male concierge's undershirt, but unlike the building's
water and electricity, the rats inside them ran day and night.

It wasn't exactly *Rarrana*, the harem of the Ilkazam.
But then it beat Bowery flophouses or the stinking dorms on
the Rox. Or a wet, drafty warehouse on the IJ. Creature
comforts had never mattered that much to Mark.

And the price was right. Mark had sensibly run Agent
Gary's Gold Card to the cash limit before leaving Amsterdam and picked up a few extra bucks selling the card itself
to a hustler on the Brindisi docks—fewer American tourists
got down that way than to Rome, so the market price was
higher. But he didn't know where he was going to come by
any more money for a while, and he had some very expensive purchases to make if he were going to have a chance of
giving the slip to Mistral, her trigger-happy DEA friends,
and the mysterious, mustachioed Mr. Bullock.

He glanced at his watch. It was a throwaway digital
with a plastic band he'd picked up at a vendor's cart over by
the Pnyx. It had a garish image of a little redheaded guy in
a red-and-orange jogging suit leaping skyward on a blast of
flame. It was from Taiwan, and was of course unlicensed.
Mark smiled to himself; he got a kick out of it. It was the
first watch he'd ever worn in his adult life, so it might as
well be a souvenir of sorts.

Time to meet a man. He stood up. His joints made rip-
pling cracks, as if they were on ratchets. The satyrs watched
him with secret grins. He gave them a thumbs-up and
headed off to the northwest.

*   *   *

Mark Meadows once went through a period of intense fascination with ancient Greece—this was during early pubescence, when his hormone-driven interest had been captured by visions of babe goddesses and nymphs in gauzy robes. He still remembered how shocked he was to discover, mainly between the lines, that a good many of those squeezes of old Zeus that astronomers were always naming moons of Jupiter after had been little boys.

Aside from that, he recalled that after the Persians trashed Athens in 479 or so, the city had been rebuilt without any kind of plan. Most of the city these days was Apartment Bloc Generic, and the national government was giving its seat in the Syntagma district in the New Town a bulldozer makeover to bring it more in line with what a capital of the European Community should look like—Mark had the impression sometimes that this whole Unification trip was really just Mickey D's writ even larger. But here in the Plaka the streets of old Athens were still narrow, twisty, and, given the way the Greeks drove, perilous.

As evidence a big lorry with streaked white sides bearing lettering that was all Greek to him had come popping out of a sidestreet and mashed one of those little slab-sided European subcompacts that look as if they're built around a skateboard. The respective drivers were standing in a pothole waving arms and mustaches at one another. Mark squeezed the vial he had palmed a little tighter, sidestepped the argument, and sidled through the crowd that had gathered in hopes the two would come to blows.

Here on the backside of the Acropolis where the tourists seldom went the buildings seemed to lean in various directions without being visibly off-true. Mark wondered if that were another example of the subtle architectural tricks the Greeks had used building the Parthenon, up on top of the hill. Façades were stucco that was showing a tendency to flake off in huge sheets and had probably been gaudy before it faded. The sky overhead was crisscrossed with clotheslines fluttering with laundry like those strings of plastic pennants that used to festoon gas stations along old Route 66 in the sixties—the early sixties, which were really just a continuation of the fifties. Immense chrome Japanese ghetto blasters vibrated on every third windowsill, further endangering the stucco with earsplitting noise that sounded like a cross between rap and belly-dance music. The occasional shopfront was boarded and graffitied; Greece was suffering another economic downturn, which Mark suspected had lasted since Alexander's daddy, Philip, blew into town. Even the people who weren't fighting seemed to communicate at the top of their lungs.

He marveled at just how scuzzy it could be right up against your marvels-of-the-ancient-world. But you didn't go looking to score drugs in the ritzier parts of town unless you happened to belong there. Since Mark didn't look like Anthony Quinn, he manifestly did not.

He looked around for his contact man, a gangly joker kid with green-seaweed hair and teeth even worse than the Greek norm. Jokers were generically less likely to blow you up to the authorities, no matter where you were. It wasn't certain, but scoring proscribed pharmaceuticals was a percentage game.

He took for granted that the odds were going to catch up with him fairly soon. From years of listening to counterculture scuttlebutt he knew that a favorite game of your petty dealers and pushers and hustlers in Third World countries—which Greece to all intents was—was to turn over the occasional foreigner. It kept the cops happy and bought a little leeway, without pissing off the local talent, the people you had to live with—and, more to the point, who knew where you slept.

The nature of his purchases was odd enough to be worth a little extra slack. He wasn't primarily interested in any of the local drugs of choice, not the ancient Mediterranean standby hash or grass, not smack—a favorite with your seagoing trade—and not coke, still in demand by European and American tourists. He was shopping more for psychedelics. In a Med port as ancient and wicked as Athens, or anyway the appendix Piraeus, you could find anything, including acid and psilocybin. But it took time, and money, and made you conspicuous. Mark could not afford much of any of that.

He had also had to blow a major piece of his dwindling roll on fine pharmaceutical scales. The Greek heat was not on the prod for drug labs in any extreme way; homebrewing synthetic dope was not yet a popular local pastime, what with the natural product so readily available. But the requisite equipment wasn't easy to find, even in an age in which the digital revolution had made even precision scientific measuring equipment comparatively cheap and available. It was another datum, another mote of dust on a pile that would eventually bury him unless he moved quickly enough.

A young woman attracted his attention, one of your occasional Grecian redheads, small and pretty, whose lethal Mediterranean Fat and Mustache Chromosome hadn't kicked in yet. She reminded him of some of the women he had seen on Takis. She had such a sweet look that he doubted she actually knew what the English word SEX NINJA written in cursive glitter on the front of her T-shirt meant. He caught her eye, smiled, and nodded.

She smiled back behind her big round shades. Then her jaw dropped, and she moved quickly away.

Uh-oh, said one of the many voices available at the back of Mark's head. He turned.

The two debaters at the accident had opened a door of the squashed subcompact and were taking out Uzis. Their differences seemed to have resolved themselves.

Chapter Eight

So much for jokers not ratting to the pigs. He'd gotten so bad on Takis that he wasn't even much disappointed in human nature.

He looked back the way he'd been going. His two old friends from Amsterdam were just strolling into view in their pastel Mid-Eighties Casual Guy suits. "Hey, dude," the dark one said, "what's happening?"

And then he yelled, "Hey!" for real. It was too late.

Making the transition to one of Mark's alter egos was like coming: the more recently it had happened in the past, the less violently it happened in the present. Back on the Rox when he had taken one of his powders for the first time in many months, he actually burst into flames, destroying the clothes he'd been wearing. This time, though, there were just a few mostly cinematic jets of fire as his molecules rearranged themselves.

"Holy shit," said the beefier narc, suitably impressed, "it's Jumpin' Jack Flash!"

"It's a gas-gas-gas," J. J. Flash said with his patented devil's grin. And a big blast of wind knocked him ass-over-ears into the front of a building.

"Well, shit," he said, trying to stand. "This is getting to be a regular drag."

The last word was sucked away by a miniature tornado, a howling vortex that buffeted him like the wings of angry eagles. J. J. sat down hard. He'd spotted her now, standing across the street in her blue-and-silver uniform with the silly-ass cape, hands on her hips, a smug smile on her ice-princess face.

He could take care of *that* in a hurry. He rolled a hand open and sent a nice hot spike of plasma her way. She dodged, and the striped awning of a tobacco shop that had somehow survived the current depression puffed into flame.

The wind went away. Without standing up he shot a blast between the two Greek narcs who were standing with their guns and jaws hanging slack, right at where he figured the subcompact's gas tank to be. It blew up and sent the Greeks running.

A sound like firecrackers right over his head. Dust stung his scalp as a burst of 7.65mm gouged the front of the building. There was Agent Saxon, soloing on Scorpion again. He really seemed to love that thing.

J. J. pointed a finger at him. "You," he said, "go away." A line of fire leaped out. Saxon pirouetted like a bullfighter. *He's been putting in his time in the gym, anyway.* J. J. thought, *gotta give him that.*

Saxon had not pissed J. J. Flash off enough to burn a hole right through him. Yet. The relatively cool jet caught a corner of the dodging agent's off-white sport jacket. The polyester blazed up nicely. That gave Saxon something to think about other than endangering the public, which was all J. J. had in mind.

Wind hit J. J. like a fist, cracking his head back against the storefront. It struck again and again with a sound like a snapping spinnaker, jackhammering his ribs and face.

"I handled Fireball, J. J.," Mistral called to him. "I can handle you."

Rage blazed white inside him. Fireball was a serial killer Mistral had apprehended in Cincinnati, live on global TV, thanks to Daddy's infallible headline-hunting instincts. He had been thrown in J. J. Flash's face once already this incarnation: in court in New York, when Kimberly Anne's attorney St. John Latham had flashed pictures of one of the psychopath's victims, an adolescent girl, horribly charred. The implication was that J. J. Flash, as one of Mark's friends—no one but Dr. Tachyon knew, then, that the relationship was rather more intimate—might inflict such a fate on Mark's daughter, accidentally or otherwise. The suggestion that he might harm Sprout in any way had burned like a cancer for all the months of J. J.'s captivity in the back of Mark's mind.

Inadvertently Mistral had punched a very bad button. "Where are you, bitch?" J. J. gasped. He battled upright. The wind came back at him, pummeled him against the wall. He looked around desperately. She had to be somewhere she could see him; like most ace powers, hers were strictly line-of-sight. That meant *he* could see *her*. . . .

There. Up the block, crouched behind a low stone wall. He gathered up the rage into a big ball of fire and just bowled it at her.

Mistral ducked. The wind stopped. The fireball hit the wall, flash-heating stones, shattering them. The wall blew up, knocking Mistral backward, stunned and bruised.

More gunfire, again badly aimed. J. J. jumped into the air. Agent Hamilton had his partner on the cobblestones rolled up in his coat; Saxon was only smoldering a little, though he was bitching loud enough that you'd think he had third-degree burns over half his body. More Greeks with guns had appeared on the scene, or at least revealed themselves. One of them was just nerving himself enough to spray the sky with bullets.

"Everywhere I go, people shoot at me," J. J. complained to the air. "I could get a complex."

Instead he split, streaking off up the flank of the big hill. At the top he swung low, scattering Nips with Nikons, and then fancied he could hear the shutters clicking like a cicada chorus behind him. He gave a rebel yell for the benefit of those with camcorders.

He'd always wanted to fly slalom through the pillars of the Parthenon. At least it *felt* as if he'd always wanted to, like a lot of his whims. Instead a big wind hit him from behind and somersaulted him into the frieze, second centaur to the left.

"Ow! *Fuck*." He plummeted toward the cracked marble steps, recovered just in time, darted into the ruined temple, cracking his hip on some scaffolding and toppling a hapless laborer off his platform.

"Be sure and sue the United States government," he called back over his shoulder as he flew between colonnade and interior wall. Talking felt like driving nails through the right side of his ribs. He wondered if he'd cracked some.

Mistral appeared, flying parallel to Flash outside the Parthenon with her arms outstretched like some goddam little girl playing airplane. Her cape billowed like a parachute. A sideblast of wind slammed him up against the wall. He fell to the floor, rolled. He was a small and acrobatic man, but he made a poor landing.

He did manage to get to his feet rapidly and fire a jet of flame at his tormentor. She dodged, laughing, dropped to the block-littered ground.

Mistral gestured. J. J. Flash ducked behind a pillar. She laughed again, high and clear and malicious as a glass razor.

A wind began to blow through the Parthenon. Yellow film wrappers skittered over the blocks. J. J. leaned out and shot a blast down at her from his palm.

It veered away from Mistral, dissipated in the air. J. J. blinked. He'd been known to miss, but he'd never had his fireblasts wander off course on their own.

He fired again. The same thing happened. Mistral showed her teeth in a grin. The bitch was deflecting his fireblasts with her damned winds.

The wind began to blow again along the colonnade, rising abruptly to a howling gale. J. J. dug his fingers into the pillar's fluting. He shot fire, hoping Mistral couldn't parry and keep up the hurricane at the same time.

She ducked. Flame splashed a toppled segment of column. The ancient stone discolored, took on a different texture. He recalled that heat damaged marble, degraded it into plain old limestone or something—Mark would know. *Great. All I need. I'm going to get "defacing ancient monuments" added to my rap sheet.*

A solid-seeming blast hit him in the face, threw him back into the inner wall. The transverse wind started again, and this time it picked him up and rolled him along like a tumbleweed.

As he bounced between pillars and wall, it occurred to him he wasn't making a very good showing. J. J. Flash was not a male chauvinist, but the thought of this spoiled super-WASP ace-baby ingenue kicking his butt was way too much to take.

Mistral's wind blew him right out the end of the colonnade and into space. Still ballistic in his fetal curl, he jetted flame at her. Mistral yelped, a musical sound. The wind stopped. J. J. extended and took off, banking to put the mass of the ancient pile between him and her.

He flew low, dabbing with the back of a finger at the blood-trail streaming from his nose, ignoring shouts and pointing from the ground. Under most circumstances he'd showboat a little for onlookers this appreciative, maybe summon up a flame guitar, a Fender o' Fire, and pretend to play it, always a crowd-pleaser.

Right now he had other things to worry about, more pressing even than image . . . a downdraft forced him low, and he had to concentrate all his energy on quick, evasive flight to keep from going into the dome of an old Orthodox church. A quick glance back: Mistral, flying after him, overtaking him gradually. With her gaudy getup, he realized, he was in danger of being totally upstaged.

"Jesus. This bimbo doesn't give up." He swiveled his head rapidly. He needed to scrape the wind-powered ace off his tail, and he wanted to do as little damage to the locals as possible in the process. That meant looking for a building higher than its surroundings, because flames propagate *up*.

There. Two-story, up on a rocky hill with not much nearby: something that looked like a graveyard out back, a road winding up to the front. The structure looked to be your basic frame and flaking white stucco, with a balcony in front and bars on the windows. There was a loading bay in back, and men were hauling something long and rolled into the back of a panel truck. Looked like a carpet.

Indeed. He streaked past the men, landed on the concrete dock. "Clear out, boys," he commanded. "Your employer's about to collect on his fire insurance."

The two workmen gaped at him with total lack of comprehension. J. J. smiled, and with a quick and deliberately noisy jet of flame fused the black pebbly soil at their feet into glass. That bridged the communications gap nicely. They lit off down the hill at a dead run, knocking over little fence-picket grave markers with plywood Greek crosses and plastic flowers on them as they ran.

The second story seemed to run only along the front of the building; the back was two stories high, piled with rolled carpets. He flew up under the rafters, pulled a couple of carpets down, dropped them in front of the open bay. A palpable cloud of dust and mold blew up into his face, deceptively rich and golden in the backscatter afternoon light. J. J.

felt his nose twitch. *I stay here long, it's gonna mean one major asthma attack.*

He went storming into the front, screaming like a madman. Clerks in fezzes and a couple of customers browsing at carpets stacked on big tables looked up in alarm.

"Out! Out!" he screamed. "Crazy Jewboy alert! Out! *Aaauuuughhh!*"

With a quick puff of flame he melted the iron bars out of the upper half of the door that separated the area behind the counter from the display floor. A second blast burned through the waist-high wooden lower half. J. J. stepped through.

Once again the language barrier had been surmounted. Customers and clerks went flying out of the building like frightened pigeons from a church, one bold soul pausing long enough to make a sign to ward the evil eye before he fled.

Working with wild energy—he had a higher metabolism than a nat, to go with his hyper disposition—J. J. began pulling carpets off the tables and dumping them on the scuffed wood floor.

After a moment he heard the expected challenge from outside: "I know you're in there, J. J. Come out with your hands on your head."

"With my hands on my *head?*" he shouted back. "What, you think I'm in here with a Saturday Night Special in an ankle holster?"

"You know what I mean, J. J. This can go easy, or it can go hard."

He mouthed the words along with her: *This can go easy, or it can go hard.* "You've been watching too many movies, babe." He began to strew the office area with ledger books. "This isn't *Lethal Weapon III*."

"Hear the sirens? The Greek police will be here in a few minutes. I promise you, J. J., it'll be a lot easier on you if you come with me instead of waiting for them to take you."

He didn't doubt that for a minute; he bet these Athinai cops didn't catch little red-haired Jewish boys with tight dancer's butts any too often. He could not in any event afford to play a waiting game with her—when you only exist for an hour at a time, time is never on your side.

But he figured that the daughter of the late Vernon Carlysle, literally groomed to acehood from the cradle and at the moment trying to hold her own with a couple of jocks from DEA, would have her own brand of *machismo*.

"What, you need the natives to make the collar for you? Is big bad J. J. Flash, Esquire too much for the spoiled little rich girl to handle on her own? Your daddy would be *so* disappointed."

The fly-specked glass and wrought-iron bars of a front window sublimated away before a roaring gout of flame. *"If you can't stand the heat, babe, stay out of the kitchen!"*

Silence. He stood behind the counter, drumming his fingers nervously on the top, scored in unreadable doodles by the penknives of bored clerks. That damned wind power of hers was too much for him; if she didn't rise to his taunts, he was going to be in a cold, wet place in one hell of a hurry.

"All right, J. J." From the back of the building. "Just you and me. I'll show you what this spoiled little rich girl does to male-chauvinist assholes like you."

He turned with what he hoped was a sufficiently psycho snarl and blasted a fire-jet at her through the door. She dodged, laughing that snotty little-girl laugh.

The carpets he'd sprawled in front of the loading door caught fire. The dry wool blazed up nicely.

"You'll have to do better than that, J. J.," she called, tauntingly. "What was that about heat?"

"Here." He popped around the door, blasted for the voice. She stood there in the open and didn't even bother to move as her windblast knocked the fire-pulse aside.

"Come on, J. J.," she urged. There were spots of color high on her cheeks, he could see even in the dusty, smoky gloom. "Hit me with your best shot."

He did, giving her two quick blasts, almost white-hot. She deflected them without effort. A buffet of wind sent him sprawling back through the narrow office into the front room.

She stalked through the door with the feral grace of a leopard. The flames behind her made the tips of her light brown hair a fiery corona like the sun at eclipse.

He felt a whirlwind surrounding him, gathering velocity. "Had enough, J. J.?" Mistral purred. "Or do I have to hurt you?"

He blasted fire at her, two-handed. She ducked behind the counter. The whirlwind continued to pick up strength; she didn't need to see *him*, just the air above his head.

"Honey," he said in a quiet voice that barely carried through the roar of flames from the warehouse area, "that partition is wood."

Without giving her time to digest that, he stood and spread his arms. Flame sprayed from both hands. The scattered carpets exploded in fire.

The whirlwind plucked at him with *afrit* arms. He wrenched himself away, stumbled through the front door, turned to torch the wooden posts holding up the porch.

Yellow flames were vomiting out the front windows now. The carpet store was going up nicely.

"I'm trapped!" Mistral cried. He heard a panic crescendo in the voice. It wasn't so superior and self-assured now.

"That's what I meant about heat, babe," J. J. called.

"You're just going to leave me to burn?"

He had to hand it to her—her voice strained, but didn't quite crack. "No. You should be able to blow out the flames, if you work hard enough."

He glanced back over his shoulder. A white Toyota Land Cruiser with a flashing blue light on top was bouncing up the road. More police vehicles wailed behind.

"If not, help is on the way. *Ciao*, babe."

Mark's Roach Motel *pension* was near the top of a hill in a part of town he couldn't pronounce. J. J. Flash couldn't either. He trudged up the hill with his head down, feeling wrung out. Flying and fire-shooting really took it out of you. Also he was beat to shit. Going 'round and 'round with Mistral's ace power made him feel as if he'd been for a blender ride.

His hour was almost up. He was starving, and when he made the transition he didn't come with money in his pockets, otherwise it would have been *souvlaki* time once he ditched Mistral. Mark was going to have a king-hell case of the munchies when he got back.

The locals gave him odd looks and plenty of sea room

as he passed. Everybody knew foreigners were crazy, especially Americans, but the red-and-orange jogging outfit did tend to set him even further apart. But he was a lot less conspicuous arriving on his red Adidas than he would have been if he'd flown in.

Not that it mattered. The bad guys knew Mark and his friends were in Athens now. That meant the time had come not to *be* in Athens anymore.

As if cued by the thought, a voice called out behind him: "Flash! J. J. Flash!"

He turned. The man who called himself Randall Bullock was walking up the street toward Mark's *pension*, wearing khaki pants and an Indiana Jones leather jacket.

"Jesus *Christ*! Can't you assholes give me any peace?" He chased Bullock into an *ouzo* stand with a roaring jet of flame from his hand and took to the air.

He had to recover the extra powders. Mark had blown almost his entire roll to stockpile them, and J. J. was not about to leave them behind.

He streaked up toward the window of his flat. The key was in the pants of his Mark-form. Somehow he wasn't worried about getting in.

And if the local heat had the flat staked out inside . . . he'd just show them what heat was all about.

Chapter Nine

Cool water caresses him like a lover, his sides, his belly, his back. He drives through it with a lover's easy fervor, with rhythmic contractions of the muscles of back and stomach. There is pain in his side where his ribs were cracked when he was the small orange flying human, but in his exalted state he ignores it. He feels at once serene and charged with energy.

He tastes. He tastes his cousins, cleaving the water on all sides of him in a joyous, plunging roil. He tastes the Bulgarian freighter fifteen kilometers to the northeast, making for the Dardanelles and illegally dumping waste; and he tastes the sewage-and-chemical bloom of the land, near at hand on three sides. The taint is evil, more black and bitter than squid-spew. But it does not ruin the fullness of his pleasure, merely increases his disdain for what he is when he is not this.

And even that is small, distant, something his attention is easily drawn from. This form is quick in its emotions, anger and happiness alike. Infinitely changeable as the water all around.

He hears. He hears them around him, these Mediterranean dolphins, small yet fleet. He can barely keep up with them, and he can swim faster than a natural bottlenose. In his mind he has a marvelous image of them in many colors, a four-dimensional tapestry of where they are, where they have been, where they are going, each swimmer a different color, each one's life line a sensuous curve extending to infinity.

He is out of place here, burly silver Pacific creature

73

among lithe black-and-white Middle Sea shapes. But the others accept him, singing to him in their clicks and whistles with eagerness and love and even awe. For they know him, in that way of theirs that knows without much thought. He is at once one of them and one of the droll and sometimes dangerous land beings, a creature long foretold in their songs, belonging simultaneously to their darting, rushing depths and to the arid world above and beyond.

A school of small, furtive fishes darts past below, left, down, and away. Several of his escorts make as if to follow. But they come back to rejoin the chirping, leaping retinue, their wish to be near him overriding their desire to feed.

The Bulgarian freighter has a bent screw; he can hear. The Aegean is alive with craft today: freighters, sailboats, a hydrofoil mosquito-whining toward Lésvos. He knows where each one is, for many kilometers around—even a Soviet Yankee missile boat, a deep, slow drumming, one of the new-generation nuclear subs the glasnost' Russians hope the rest of the world will forget about, that carries in its long, round snout the capacity to sow the earth with temporary suns, brief and bright and deadly.

Some part of him behind his consciousness notes the fact and files it away; his conscious mind has little energy for facts. The torrent of sensory impression rushing in upon him occupies his mind to the full.

Off to the north-northeast he senses land: sonar picture of a small mass, taste and scent of sand and soil and landborne vegetation without the taint of recent human habitation. Something inside him makes him turn his rostrum, reluctantly, toward the island. Soon he will change, first to the being with the form of a landling but the skin and smell of a dolphin and then to the full human, comically pale, skinny, and hairy.

The others shift course, but their song changes, becomes wheedling, cajoling, and their bodies bump against his in a near-erotic way as they try to urge him to turn away. But the human he will become, too shortly, cannot swim, at least as he and his kindred understand it. When the transition inevitably arrives, he must be within wading distance of shore. Or the pale-haired man—and he, and the rest of the beings his own life line is intertwined with in a dance even dolphins cannot comprehend—will die.

The air above is growing dark with approaching eve-
ning; in the west, sea and sky collide in a sheet of copper
flame. He can feel the weariness come upon him, and the
ache in his side throbs deeper, more insistently. It still takes
all his will to keep drawing nearer to the land. The open Ae-
gean water is dark and intoxicant as wine, the songs of his
kindred more seductive than the Sirens'. And a different part
of him, swimming down where light never reaches, would
even welcome the fumbling and frenzy and final darkness if
it meant not having to return to the prison of a landborne hu-
man body.

But he swims for the island, picking up velocity as he
does so until even his speedy cousins can barely keep pace.
His sense of time is not exact. If he misjudges, his kinfolk will
try to help him even in his floundering human form. But
they're as likely to nudge him farther out to sea as in toward
land; they are aware, and their minds are ever-filled with
brilliant, flashing imagery richer than any human can ever
conceive, but they aren't really very bright.

Staring out the window at the traffic and construction
in Constitution Square, the woman in the high-laced sandals
and belted white tunic laced her fingers together and flexed.
Muscles popped out all over her bare arms, and stood out
like flying buttresses on her neck.

J. Robert Belew lit his pipe and puffed happily. The
Greek national ace had curly black hair, flashing black eyes,
olive skin whose natural gloss was augmented by a fine coat-
ing of olive oil. The broken nose added character to her face
without detracting from its striking handsomeness.

Hera would be a thoroughgoing babe, thought the un-
abashed male-chauvinist part of him, *if the rest of her didn't*
look so much like Lou Ferrigno with breasts.

Standing by a wall-sized map of Athens, Mistral gave
him a quick dirty look for lighting up. Her cheeks were
smudged, there were dark scorch-marks on her white cape,
and her trademark uniform was in dire need of dry cleaning. Raised since birth to be overwhelmingly conscious of
her public appearance, she was visibly suffering from her
disheveled state. *More's the pity,* he thought. *You look in-*
credibly cute.

The builders had tried their level best to give the offices of the new police headquarters the sterile, ergonomic look appropriate to the new European Community. The briefing room still stank of sweat, wool, and latakia. He faced her glare with total equanimity. If she had a magnanimous soul, she would think of his fine and subtle Virginia blend as air freshener.

Then the female American ace noticed her Greek opposite number's dark eyes upon her. She lowered her own and turned quickly back to the map. J. Bob grinned around the stem of his pipe.

"—estimates property damage at upward of four million drachmae," Colonel Kallikanzaros was saying beneath his Saddam Hussein mustache. He was a big man with droopy eyes and a face that seemed to have been laid down in several successively smaller slabs. He sat with his big hands propped above the tabletop by arched fingers, as if he were touch-typing. "We have damage caused by excessive and unnatural heat to our single most prized national monument. We have one gunshot wound, treated and dismissed, and two National Police officers with second-degree burns, likewise treated and dismissed. Finally, we have one Bureau of Antiquities employee in a neck brace, who claims an angel of God told him to sue the United States government."

He folded his hands together. "Your fugitive ace Jumping-Jacks Flash suggests more to me a devil, but perhaps the workman felt it would prejudice his case to say that a demon told him to sue."

He was a fine one to be talking about devils. He was an ace, too, or so rumor had it. A shape-changer, though he kept the details of his powers—if any—as carefully obscure as did his German counterpart, the famed counterterrorist ace Wegemer. His name was really a nickname, which referred to some kind of mythological imp or other. Belew had noticed that if you looked at him sidelong, in just the right kind of light, his outlines shifted subtly, took on a disturbing quality, like those pictures made up of microgrooves that changed when you turned them in your hand.

"How the hell did some blue-collar dickweed understand English?" Lynn Saxon demanded. He looked younger without his mustache, which had been the only part of him of any consequence actually burned off in J. J. Flash's attack.

"We've got the dossier, and J. J. Flash no more speaks Greek than my ass can whistle 'The Stars and Stripes Forever.' "

"Jeez, Lynn, that's something I'd like to *see*," his partner said.

"Shut up, Gary."

"Far from being a noxious plant, Mr. Ipiotis is a very skilled worker, highly educated," the colonel said briskly. "He learned to speak English in school, as many of our children do. Our educational system is quite advanced, Mr. Saxon. How many American children learn Greek?"

"Why should they? Who the fucking hell speaks Greek?"

Helen Carlysle had taken a seat at the table. She cocked her forearm and opened her hand as if flicking water off the fingers at him. "Agent Saxon, you are being *highly unprofessional*—"

"Put a rag in it, babe. You don't talk to us about *professional;* you're just a rich civilian on a ride-along, you got that? And while we're on the subject, sweetheart, you're the one who lost him."

Hera turned from the window and growled low in her well-muscled throat. She was not one of the Greeks who knew English, but she could read tones of voice well enough. Saxon went dead pale. Hera had once arm-wrestled New York–born Israeli ace Sharon Cream in London for the title of World's Strongest Lady Ace. The match had gone on eleven hours and sixteen minutes before both parties agreed to a draw. And Sharon Cream had destroyed a Syrian T-72 main battle tank bare-handed in the Golan Heights in 1982. . . .

Kallikanzaros held up a weary hand. Hera colored—she did that readily, and rather prettily to Belew's eye—and walked over to stand with her back to the door.

"Hearts and minds," the mercenary murmured.

"What did you say?" Saxon demanded, glaring at him through his bangs like a crazy man in elephant grass.

"Just an old Special Forces saying."

"Yeah, well, I got one for you, too, old man: 'Grab 'em by the balls, and their hearts and minds'll follow.' "

The colonel cleared his throat. "We gave you our complete cooperation," he said, "and the result has been a complete debacle. The Interior Ministry is in a roar-up. And though our media are better disciplined than yours, enough has happened that we cannot prevent embarrassing questions from being asked in the newspapers and on the television. I must therefore ask what your intentions are now."

Hamilton looked at his partner, who had gotten up and was staring out the floor-to-ceiling louver blinds at the atherosclerotic traffic on the Syntagma. "I guess, hunker down and start scouring the city section by section until we run him down," the blond agent said. "We still got this advantage, that Meadows does tend to stick out in a crowd."

"He won't be here," Helen Carlysle said.

Saxon half turned from the window. Sunset light spray-painted his narrow face with shadow strips. "Look, will you just butt out and let the people who know what they're doing handle this from here on in?"

Hera laced her fingers again and cracked her knuckles. It sounded like target shooting with a nine-millimeter. Saxon jumped.

"It is impossible that he should have left the city," the colonel huffed. "We are watching the roads, the airports, the harbor, everything."

"It's impossible for a man to fly and shoot fire from his hands, too, Colonel," Belew said mildly. "Or change the shape of his body, for that matter."

He flicked his eyes to the American woman. "How do you figure this, Ms. Carlysle?"

She took a deep breath. "He's run every time we've caught up with him."

Belew shook out his pipe and tamped it with a little fold-up silver tool he carried in his pocket. "Not the very first time, in Amsterdam."

Color flamed up on her high cheekbones, but she controlled herself. "He just thought that was a, a fluke, an accident. And it was, in a sense. Once he realized we were going to persist, were going to be able to track him down if he stayed in Amsterdam, he took off. Why should he behave differently this time?"

Belew stuffed some more tobacco in his pipe, put it back in his mouth, and relit it, studying Carlysle the while. She faced him with her head thrown back, flushed and defiant.

"I think she's got a point, gentlemen."

"Oh, horseshit," Saxon said. "Colonel, we want more help. We want to take this town apart."

"Agent Saxon," Belew said, "maybe I should remind you that this operation—"

"Screw you, and screw the CIA," Saxon spat. The colonel's eyebrows shot up. "Hamilton and I are still DEA, and we're still on the case. We're going to do this the right way. Got that?"

Helen Carlysle was visibly knotting with anger. Murmuring low in her throat, Hera crossed to her, put her big hands on the American's trapezius muscles to either side of her neck, and began to massage her with the carefully controlled power of those armor-crushing hands. Mistral's eyes bounced back and forth in her head like tennis balls, seeking escape.

Belew laughed and spread his hands. "Confucius tells us that 'the superior man does not set his mind either for anything, or against anything; what is right he will follow.' Have it your way, boys."

Chapter Ten

Mark sat beneath a cypress tree like *bonsai* on steroids with his knees up under his chin and watched the last fingernail fragment of sun, red and not particularly bright, disappear into the horizon. He shivered, though it wasn't cold. He wasn't even wet; Aquarius had grumpily emerged from the water before returning to Mark-form, and Aquarius' slick delphinoid skin shed water.

He still felt waterlogged, the way he always did after taking Aquarius out for a spin. It was something he had never done that often; there was water all around Manhattan, but not so you'd want to *swim* in it. Besides, Aquarius resented the baseline Mark persona worse than any of Mark's other friends. There was always a chance that he'd take it in mind to just swim way out of sight of land before making the transition back.

It was a risk Mark was taking now, again and again. Ironically the silvery-gray powder that summoned Aquarius was the cheapest and easiest to make of Mark's five potions—four, now. So he had made up an especially large number of doses of it, back in Athens, figuring he might have to try to split via water. The Aegean was ideal for that, dotted as it was with small and mostly uninhabited islands like this one. Aquarius' dolphin-form could swim at just upward of twenty knots—Mark had once gotten Tach out in the Hudson in a boat to time him—and that meant he could island-hop, taking time out as Mark to recuperate.

Jumpin' Jack Flash could fly a lot faster than that of course. But, small as he was, a flying man was not exactly *inconspicuous*. And being J. J. took a lot out of Mark, emotionally as well as physically. Jumpin' Jack lived with an intensity Mark found almost as alien as the mind of Aquarius's dolphin-form. When he was J. J. Flash, it really was like being on a drug trip, a sort of blazing speedball rush.

Mark opened the fluorescent green fanny-pack he'd bought way back in Rome. Aquarius, human or *Tursiops*, was bulkier than Mark; when he made the transition, he somehow sucked up enough ambient matter to make up the difference: air primarily, but also things like personal effects. It was a handy way to carry things.

Inside the fanny-pack were a mess of extra vials of powder, some figs, and a few Mars bars. Mark knew from experience that he had to get his blood sugar up in a hurry after being either Aquarius or J. J. Flash, or get the shakes real bad, plus nausea and dizziness. If Aquarius hadn't scarfed a lot of fish en route, he'd be barely conscious now.

Mark stuffed his mouth with a whole candy bar, realizing suddenly just how hungry he was. He ate some figs, and another Mars bar, and felt better.

But by then the sun was completely out of sight, leaving only a glowing green band across the horizon. Overhead the stars were beginning to open like tiny demon eyes. There were no clouds in sight to cover their malevolent gaze.

Mark burped softly, wiped a chocolate smear from the side of his mouth and mustache, and gazed ruminatively into his pack.

For most of his adult life Mark had sought shelter from the stresses of existence in chemicals. That was why his drug of choice was marijuana. He wasn't interested in the artificial self-esteem of coke—self-esteem was pretty alien to his experience, and he wasn't comfortable with it, and besides coke gave him shooting pains in his chest and made him honk like a Canada goose when he talked—nor in the edge you got from speed. He was mainly into taking edges *off*. He didn't like needles, which mostly let heroin out, and besides he had a basic middle-class hippie prejudice against being a junkie, plus real concern about heavy physical habituation. His use of psychedelics he'd always regarded as experimental.

When he had to say, "Gimme shelter," he'd turned to his old friend Mary Jane. Then Sunflower—Kimberly Anne

Cordayne Meadows Gooding—had turned up suing for Sprout. For the first time in his life Mark had had *real problems*. He faced them cold-turkey. He came off the grass at the suggestion of Jokertown's joker lawyer Dr. Pretorius. He had spent the first couple of weeks after the trial ended drunk, but that was a phase; he had basically spent the last two years clean and sober, as the yuppies say.

He'd scored himself some hash in Amsterdam, but that was mainly because he was bored after the constant fear-and-culture-shock rush of Takis and also because he was *in* Amsterdam, and that was what you did there. It had been dabbling, like a retired tennis pro who turns in a couple of sets occasionally for nostalgia's sake.

Now the night was coming, and he wanted to hide. Not that he could hide completely; there was no overhead shelter except for these scraggly cypress trees. But creative chemistry would offer him shelter—if only a temporary one.

What's the big deal about the stars? he tried to tell himself. *What's to be afraid of?*

The answer, unfortunately, was *death*.

As a kid he'd loved comics. He'd grown up thrilling to the four-color adventures of Jetboy and the Great and Powerful Turtle—no Superman for him; he was only interested in actual aces, even though he understood their exploits were mostly made up by Cosh Comics or whoever held the license. He had wanted, more than anything in the world, to be a Hero, like the ones he read about.

That was the spring which drove him in his long search for the Radical. It was the obsession that had shaped the expression of his personal ace. He had become not one Hero but five.

—And yet, and yet. They weren't *him*. At least, he could not accept that they were. He formed a theory that his "friends" were real, actual individuals, from alternate realities, perhaps—he was a science fiction fan, too, of course—whom he had somehow, unknowingly, abducted and trapped within the recesses of his own psyche. They seemed to buy that explanation too; the Traveler and J. J. Flash were always trying to figure out ways to spring themselves, or at least establish themselves as baseline persona instead of Mark, and Moonchild had the expressed goal of liberating all of them,

Mark included, so that each could work out his or her own karma.

So while each of them performed many deeds that might be called heroic—J. J. Flash fighting in the raid on the Astronomer's headquarters in the Cloisters, Moonchild defeating the gene-engineered Takisian killing machine Durg at-Morakh, Starshine deflecting a killer asteroid set on a collision course with Earth by the unholy alliance of the Swarm Mother and Tach's dashing cousin, Zabb—Mark was adroitly able to escape taking credit for any of them.

Then the last two years happened. Sunflower came back into his life. The custody battle began. Mark not only went off the dope, he did the unthinkable: put the purple tailcoat and top hat out on the curb with the trash and retired Cap'n Trips. One final dose of blue powder had permitted him to escape the courtroom and the friendly clutches of the DEA, but after that he was cold-turkey—on his own.

It had not been easy. He had done things he was not proud of. But he had survived. On the streets and on the Rox. *Alone*. Without chemical crutches of any kind.

The time had come to call his friends back, to rescue his daughter from the living hell of a New York kid jail. But it was different, then. It wasn't J. J. Flash or Starshine or Moonchild acting the hero on their own. Mark was the director, the initiator, deploying his friends like a combat commander his troops.

Of course combat had its casualties. He'd left the woman he loved dead by the side of a New Jersey road, fatally injured by the hand of Tach's grandson, Blaise. And he had left Durg there, too, telling him that he was free, that he belonged now to no master but himself. . . .

Yes, and that was the worst loss of all. He had not understood, though Durg had tried to tell him, that a Morakh could *not* be free, that they were bred to require servitude as they needed air and water. So Durg, the ultimate bodyguard, designed by Takisian genetic scientists to be master of the arts, not just of combat, but of strategy and diplomacy as well, had transferred his loyalty to the best available master.

Perhaps ten million Takisians had died as a result. Payback for the wild card, with interest, if only Mark could think that way. He couldn't.

Blaise had taken Doctor Tachyon's body, with the mind of Kelly Jenkins trapped inside, and with Durg in tow as his adviser, had stolen *Baby* and headed back to Takis. Tachyon, trapped in Kelly's body—impregnated by Blaise's repeated rapes—had gathered his three dearest human friends and gone in pursuit.

Since then Mark had done wonderful things. He. Mark.

He had passed a test his boyhood idol Turtle had failed, stepping aboard the Network scoutship in the White Sands desert. The ship was too small to accommodate the Turtle's shell, and Tommy, for all his proven love and loyalty to Tach, had been unable to leave it behind.

He had flown across the unimaginable distances of interstellar space, and found out spaceflight was mainly boring as hell.

He had taken part in the glittering, bloodstained intrigues of Takis, had helped commit murder, had seen the inside of a *hareem* that made the *Thousand Nights and A Night* seem tame. He had helped a woman—who was also his best male friend—give birth. He had fled with a captive princess across a snow-covered mountain range as mighty as Earth's Himalayas. He had flown on the back of a winged predator the size of a Cessna.

His friends had been there. But he had made the tough decisions.

He had engaged in a wrestling match with Zabb, a Takisian warrior who made Errol Flynn look like a wimp. He had taken part in a desperate commando raid against an enemy castle. He had fought a battle in space.

And he had died.

Starshine, the poet with the wavy blond hair and jutting jaw, so politically correct he was actually solar-powered, was probably the most potent physically-oriented ace Earth had produced—Fortunato was more powerful still, but his powers were of the mind, of a scope and breadth even the Takisians had trouble grasping. Starshine was nearly as strong as Golden Boy, and he could fly through space at the speed of light and fire sunbeams from his hands. He was also a pain in the ass.

He was brave, though. In the battle with the Network he had fought a Ly'bahr cyborg, an alien brain encased in a body like a miniature battleship. He had done what no other being was ever known to have accomplished: defeated a Ly'bahr one-on-one in personal combat.

Unfortunately there were two of the cyborg legionnaires. The second had wrenched Starshine's leg off at the hip.

He died. Up above the world so high, where night always was. Where the stars never shut their eyes.

Mark had survived, somehow, and the magic of Takisian technology had made him whole again. His body anyway. The mentatic magic of Tachyon's sister Roxalana had given him back the power of speech. She'd used a different kind of magic, to give him back something he hadn't been able to identify yet. He was grateful anyway.

But he had not been able to face the stars. The stars that killed him.

He held up a vial. The powder within was black and silver, swirled together.

There was no hiding from the stars now. But night was Moonchild's element. He didn't have enough of the black-and-silver vials to take him all the way through to dawn, even if he wanted to burn them all up. But if he had to face the night, he could at least ease into it.

Besides, Moonchild had the power of self-regeneration, and now that he was over his hunger attack, he was becoming acutely aware of the pain that stabbed him in the side with every breath. It was time to heal the damage Mistral had laid on J. J. Flash in the Parthenon.

If they gave out black belts in rationalization, you'd have a third dan. It was J. J.'s voice, way back in his head. He smiled.

So fucking what, J. J.? He uncorked the vial and tossed its contents back.

On the foreshore the woman dances through the stations of her art. She is small and finely formed. Her black hair falls unbound to her shoulders. She wears a formfitting garment of black and silver; a black half mask is yang to the yin of her face.

She dances the first Ki-Cho, simplest and most bluntly physical of the Poom-Se *forms. She is stretching her muscles after long disuse, blowing the dust from her neuromuscular pathways. She slides her right foot forward and fires her right fist in a middle punch as a* kiai *explodes from the center of her, then cocks her left foot and snaps ninety degrees into a low block. Then step forward, punch, reverse, block, step forward, punch, the ancient dance, and activity and long familiarity begins to soothe the fear that yammers in her hindbrain and makes even her warrior's heart flutter.*

She consummates the first Ki-Cho, *segues smoothly into the next, and next, and then on to the* Tae-Kook *forms, the shadowboxing, in which combat is more realistically acted out. Then, when she is warmed and energized and her body is well oxygenated, she moves on to* Pal-Gwe, *the forms of Law and harmony, the active meditation that reconciles the three* Do: *Heaven, Man, and Earth.*

Rest easy, Mark, my older brothers, *she thinks, controlling her breath so that active calm suffuses her selves.* Now we have nothing to fear from Death. We have transcended, passed through the Flame, stepped through the Gateless Gate.

Don't fear the stars. What can they do to us, who have died and risen again?

The moon comes up, laying a silver path upon the water. Where its rays touch her, her skin tingles and grows warm. The pain in her ribs fades, is gone. All that remains is serene exaltation, and motion, and the wind on her cheek, and the smells of sea and cooling soil and grass and trees, and the moon's mother love.

Mark took a deep, shuddering breath as he came back to himself. *Moonchild sure gets herself a heck of a workout,* he thought. He lifted his head from between his bony knees.

The stars stared him in the face, unwinking.

He looked at the sky for a long time. *I wonder if those three stars in a row down by the horizon are Orion's Belt,* he thought after a while. He had owned a telescope as a kid, a simple little Tasco three-inch refractor, and had been an avid amateur astronomer. But it had been a long time, and anyway he'd never quite been able to get the hang of the constellations.

He wished Sprout were here to see it with him. *When I get somewhere the DEA can't trace me, I'll have to send her a postcard, let her know that I still love her and that I miss her.* If there was any such place on Earth.

He stood up, batted the loose earth off the seat of his pants, and trudged up to the top of the promontory that dominated the tiny island. He needed some heavy-duty sleep, and he didn't want to be soaked in case a tide came in.

Chapter Eleven

What a long, strange trip it's been. . . . Mark had always thought of that old Dead tune as the soundtrack to his life. Even before the last few years, when things *really had* started getting strange. Now here he was, literally *Truckin'*, on a trip in its way almost as strange as the one to Takis in a Network starship: in the dimly red-lit cab of a giant gleaming white Mercedes tractor trailer highballing through the flat Iranian plains on the midnight run from Tabrīz to Tehrān. And on the Blaupunkt CD player was, not Jerry Garcia and company, but Hank Williams, Jr., singing about just who was coming over tonight.

He caught himself on the edge of dozing, glanced over at Otto, his codriver, who currently had the wheel. Otto beamed and bobbed his head. He was a stocky man in probably his early forties, with a ruddy complexion and thinning blond hair. He was shy a front incisor, apparently because of a dispute with an earlier employer. Or maybe even the one he and Mark were temporarily sharing; Mark could just barely make sense out of his Bavarian accent, with its Austrian lilt and sprinkling of Italian vocabulary. The Yugos on the *Montenegro* had been easier to understand. They'd learned the same academic *Hochdeutsch* in school that Mark had.

"Nice rig you got here, man," Mark said. Otto had had English classes in school and seemed to understand it pretty well, but he spoke the language even worse than Mark understood his southern German.

Otto beamed and nodded. *"Ja, ja. Ganz modern."* Which Mark actually understood.

It *was* nifty. Even Mark, no connoisseur of the big rigs, could tell that. It was all ergonomic and streamlined inside, no sharp corners, and it had one of those neat little sci-fi phones that bounced signals off the ion trails left by meteorites, of all things, so you could talk to just about anywhere in the world. Then above and behind the cab you had an *entire apartment*, complete with a bed with burgundy silk sheets and a miniature refrigerator and a TV and VCR and a selection of really startling pornographic videos.

As a matter of fact, since he was off-shift, Mark was fully entitled to be up in the apartment, putting the bed and other modern conveniences of his choice to use. Somehow he preferred being awake and alert and down here, so that he could pop an appropriate powder in his mouth when *Pasdaran* Revolutionary Guard crazies came screaming out of the night with their AK-47s blazing.

There were *risks* involved, though hundreds of trucks a day made the run from Turkey. The situation in Iran was fraying like a cable under tension, giving way one strand at a time without the Ayatollah Khomeini's charismatic presence to hold it intact. The ethnic, political, and religious factions that had been kept down by force of Khomeini's personality—and brute repression—were crawling out into the air again, and most of them had guns. That was why the German trucking company had signed Mark on with few questions asked in Istanbul. Trade went on—Mark was getting the impression that was pretty much true no matter where you were or what else went down.

As a matter of fact Mark had no idea what they were actually hauling in the trailer. Whatever it was, the Islamic Iranian government was eager enough to get its hands on it. They'd been waved across the Turkish frontier with barely a glance. That may also have had something to do with the fact that trucks were lined up for a good eight klicks waiting to cross—and that no matter how hot your zeal once burned for preserving the purity of the revolution, after a dozen years at a border checkpoint your interest in what was in the nine hundred and eighty-seventh truck of the shift was bound to be guttering low.

What blew Mark away was that he was involved in importing stuff into one of the crankiest and most uptight nations on Earth, and it was *perfectly legit*. Well, except for the vials of powder tucked away in his lurid green fanny-pack. They'd be good for a short gig between a wall and a bunch of automatic weapons if he got caught with them.

Hank, Jr. wound down. Otto took the CD out, put it in its plastic box, stuck it back in the rack built into the padded cream-toned dash. He took out another. Mark craned to see the cover. Lyle Lovett: *Pontiac*.

Another collection of adobe houses and bad stucco public boxes ghosted past outside. If anybody was up late, they weren't showing any lights. In 1991 Iran, it paid not to be seen.

If anybody in the village pointed guns at the semi, Mark didn't see.

Coming into Ruhollah Khomeini Airport in Tehrān, you queued up for your official Customs boys in their trim mustaches and tan uniforms. Beyond them *Pasdaran* prowled in pairs and packs, wearing those turtleneck sweaters they love so much and carrying assault rifles. They were not official, but one way or another you had to get past them.

Jacobo Burckhardt Bustamante stood in line for Customs, smiling serenely beneath the impressive sweep of his seal-colored mustache. He was a trim man somewhere in middle age, with graying hair cropped close to his head. He wore a dark silk suit and darker shades. He had a London Fog trench coat on one arm and his mistress Elena on the other. With her fine features, light-brown hair, and long legs you knew she had to have a lot of Italian or German in her, as many Argentineans do. She wore an indigo dress with the bodice cut high by European standards, just showing the first hint of cleavage—enough to titillate, but not enough to enrage, puritanical zealots with guns. The short silver-fox jacket she wore against the spring chill up here on the Iranian Plateau, beneath the lofty Elburz Mountains, set off her color to excellent advantage.

Señor Burckhardt's goons, standing right behind him and the beauteous Señorita Elena, shifting their weight and glaring suspiciously at the ragheads in line with them, were dressed like goons. They might have come from anywhere in the West; in fact the dark, intense one could well have passed for Iranian. His partner was blond, but there are plenty of blonds in Argentina.

The blond one, who was the bulkier of the two, let his eyes slide toward a pair of Revolutionary Guardsmen who stood watching the Customs men open bags on a long table. They carried old-model M-16s slung.

" 'Look, Ma, I just stepped in some Shi'ite,' " he said out of the corner of his mouth.

"Shut the fuck up, Gary," the dark one whispered back. "These boys twig to who we are, they're definitely gonna want to fuck you some before they stick the alligator clips on your balls and the tip of your dick and plug in the transformer from the Ayatollah's old Lionel train set."

"I don't like this," the lovely Elena said. She gave her escort a look before clutching his arm tighter.

Señor Burckhardt grinned back over his shoulder. "Iran is like what the Book of Common Prayer says about marriage: 'It is not by any to be entered into unadvisedly or lightly; but reverently, discreetly, advisedly, soberly, and in the fear of God.' "

"You betcha," the dark goon said.

Their turn came. Burckhardt passed their papers to a plump man in Customs uniform, who glanced at them, pivoted, and passed them on to a lean, dark man in a buttoned trench coat and snap-brim hat who stood behind him.

Snap-brim stepped forward. "Señor Burckhardt?"

Elena and the goons tensed. Burckhardt said, "Sí," quite calmly.

"Of the FMA?" He spoke English.

"Yes. *Fábrica Militar de Aviones.* Of Argentina, as you can see."

The Iranian nodded. "Please come with me."

Burckhardt cocked his arm. Elena hesitated. Her face was very pale. She threaded her arm through his, and they followed the man in the snap-brim hat. The goons walked behind them like kids on their way to school.

Snap-brim led them through a side door. Instead of to an interrogation chamber with tile walls and a drain in the floor, though, it led to a corridor, and then out into the Tehrān night.

A gray stretch Mercedes limo was waiting for them. Snap-brim saw them inside, the goons seated facing back,

Burckhardt and his mistress facing forward. Then he slid in next to the driver and signaled for him to move on.

"I am Ghodratollah," he said. "Welcome to Tehrān."

"It's always a pleasure," Burckhardt said.

They drove too fast through streets that seemed too dark for a major world capital. Sometimes they came to barricades manned by shadowy figures with guns. They always drove through, without slowing and without being challenged.

Ghodratollah and Burckhardt conversed between the two goons, chatting about an airplane FMA built. It was called the *Pucará*, a light two-engine prop job designed primarily for a light counterinsurgency role. Evidently the Islamic Republic was enjoying the odd light insurgency, though Mr. Ghodratollah did not come out and say so. Both men knew a great deal about the *Pucará*.

Eventually Elena and the goons relaxed.

The Mercedes pulled into the circular drive of a building shaped like a giant ring-cake section strung with Christmas lights and stopped. Ghodratollah stayed put while the driver got out and scurried back to open Burckhardt's door.

"Your baggage is in your rooms already. Please enjoy your stay."

"I always do."

Chapter Twelve

Helene Mistral Carlysle, also known as Helen or—currently—Elena, stood looking in wonder out over the sunken dining room. It was huge, and it was packed. A cut-glass chandelier blazed overhead like frozen fireworks.

She had changed to a long midnight-blue gown by a trendy Barcelona designer, a joker called Jordi. She wore a heavy choker of short silver bars. Her wrists were crossed at the small of her back.

Indecently dapper in evening dress, J. Robert Belew stepped up behind her and circled her wrists with his strong brown fingers. She colored. A beat, and then she stepped forward and pulled away.

"Don't start taking your role too seriously," she said. He laughed.

A maître d' in Western tux and oilslick hair materialized and escorted them to a table. The two goons, still wearing the cheap suits they'd arrived in, followed.

"So why do we have to masquerade as cheap muscle?" Lynn Saxon asked as he took his seat.

"Because you won't pass for expensive muscle. Look around, son; what do you see?"

"Lot of fat ragheads eating with their fingers."

"And guarding them?"

"Arab dudes in suits, with necks larger than their heads and bulges under their arms," Gary Hamilton put in hurriedly. He was feeling left out.

Belew nodded. "Indeed. Those are *Husseinis*. What they really are is soldiers of Jordan's Arab Legion, probably the toughest outfit in the Arab world. They're called

Husseinis because everybody in Jordan is named Hussein. Jordanians let their services out as bodyguards. Every raghead who's anybody has them. I'm a paltry foreign infidel, so I have to make do with you."

"I notice you got seated quick enough," Hamilton said.

"Señor Burckhardt is a well-connected infidel."

"What's all this FMA crap, anyway?" Saxon asked. "What does an Argie plane salesman want in Tehrān?"

"Argentina's air force, as most people don't know, is trained by the Israelis. That's why they did as well as they did against the Brits in '82, when most of the Argentinean armed forces were a complete washout. Israel also happens to be one of Iran's number-one suppliers of military matériel and know-how. They can't exactly do it openly, though. Argentinean military-industrial types are natural go-betweens."

"The *Israelis?*" Helen said. "How long has this been going on? The last couple of years?"

"All along. Even when the Iranians held the hostages, and even during our doomed little stab at getting 'em back." He sat a moment, eyes distant. "The real world is an ugly place, my dear."

"But the Israelis are our friends," Hamilton said.

"'At the narrow passage, there will be no brother, no friend,'" Belew said. "Old Arabic saying."

Helen showed a wintry smile. "Somehow I have the feeling Señor Burckhardt has been here before."

"Naturally. Iran's a very interesting area, geopolitically speaking. The Israelis can be very accommodating, when Langley asks nice."

The waiter arrived. Belew ordered for everyone in French.

"What'd you get us?" Saxon demanded sullenly when the waiter left.

"White man's food. Don't worry about it." Belew turned to Helen. "You looked overwhelmed when I came in. I wouldn't guess you're exactly out of your depth in surroundings such as this."

"I wasn't expecting such, such opulence. The Iranian revolutionary government is supposed to be quite puritanical."

"They are. Just as you are yourself."

She glared. "I am not puritanical. I'm only . . . careful."

"A woman for the eighties. Of course, it is the nineties."

The soup arrived. "How come the Revolutionary Guards don't bust in and trash the place, then?" Hamilton asked as the others raised their silver spoons.

"The Iranians have learned a hard lesson that a lot of other revolutionary societies have had to learn, some harder than others. Nobody goes it alone in this world. You need contact with the outside world—you need trade. And that means you have to cut outsiders a certain amount of slack. Otherwise you end up being the Khmer Rouge."

He sampled his soup, rolled it around his mouth, nodded. "This hotel is the Vale of Kashmir. Built in 1984. It's owned by the Sultan of Kashmir. Jalal-ud-din Shah Durrani, grandson of old Abd-er-Rahim Durrani, the Khyber bandit who grabbed the kingdom from the Hindus when the Brits pulled out in '47. Young Jalu is a heavy hitter in these parts, even though he's a Sunni and something of a progressive. He's ethnically Persian, being a Pushtun. Also, he poured a lot of much-needed investment dollars into the country during the war with Iraq."

"So they tolerate a certain amount of conspicuous consumption on his premises?" Helen asked.

"Not all of them." He sipped from a champagne glass. "By the way, by all means try this. It's melon juice from Tashkent, in what used to be Soviet Central Asia. Just recently started importing it. It's miraculous stuff; poets used to write songs about the melons of Tashkent."

"Nonalcoholic, though," Helen said.

"There's only so far you can stretch tolerance. Though if you're discreet, you can get booze served in your room, at ruinous prices. Still, some of the more fanatical locals have been known to take exception . . . notice the tall men in the turbans, standing where they can take it all in?"

The others looked around. "Big bearded sons of bitches," Saxon said, "so what?"

"So they're Afridi, Gilzai, and Yusufzai tribesmen. Your real Khyber cutthroats, the very boys who handed the Russian Bear his head over in Afghanistan. And I mean the very ones; these are all hard-core *mujahidin* vets. The sultan imports them to pull security."

"The ayatollahs are afraid of them?" Helen asked.

"Back in '86 a couple of fanatics—schoolteachers, oddly

enough—tried a trick they used to pull on movie theaters and other places they thought subverted true Islamic values. They brought chains and big jerricans of gasoline. They were going to pour the gas inside, chain the doors shut, and set it all off to sort of *encourage* other sinners."

"My God, how awful. What happened?"

"Afridis caught 'em. Chained them up out front, doused them in their own gas, and lit up." Belew wiped his mouth. "Didn't have much trouble after that."

Helen choked. After a moment Saxon gave an explosive snort of laughter.

"Where's the bathroom?" he asked.

Belew pointed the way. Saxon excused himself. While he was gone, the entrees came: tournedos of beef on toast.

When Saxon returned, he moved more crisply and his eyes were bright. "So even the Shi'ites can be tolerant once in a while." He laughed. "That's a mistake."

"How do you mean?" Belew asked.

"I mean, that's where they lose it. They're history. *Zero* tolerance; that's the only tolerance level for a society that's, that's . . ."

He paused, puzzled, then raised a hand and knotted it into a fist. ". . . Together."

"That's what you have in mind for America?" Helen asked. "A society that's more restrictive than Shi'ite Iran?"

"You got it. See, you're soft, babe, you got a runny core. Just like a woman. That's why you aren't cut out for this work. That's why—"

Hamilton laid a hand on his arm. "Hey. Lynn. Easy does it, man."

"No. Nothing easy about it. We have the ability now; we know what's right for people, we can make them do it. It's our responsibility. All it takes is the *will*."

"The New World Order," Belew said, swirling melon juice in his glass. "High ideals . . . except you never know when you might run into Afridis."

"So what's our next move, Mr. CIA Mastermind?" Lynn Saxon asked, riding up in the elevator after dinner.

Belew smiled at him. "I guess it never occurred to you that we're in the middle of what has to be considered Indian country, and they don't much care for the Agency in these parts. Or doesn't the DEA know about bugging elevators?"

"Jesus, Lynn, will you for God's sake watch your mouth?" Hamilton said. A sweat catenary had formed along his hairline. "We're in this, too, you know."

"Hey, stay out of my face," Saxon said, but without force.

"In answer to your question, we stay loose and wait to hear from my contacts."

"Your contacts," Saxon sneered.

"They have a pretty good batting average so far," Belew said, sticking his hands in his pockets.

"I guess you think that makes you pretty damned smart, cowboy."

"I think it makes me a professional in the intelligence trade. One who makes judicious use of carefully cultivated contacts, which are important tools of that trade. Whereas you, I think, are a mean Nintendo pig who's seen too many Mel Gibson movies."

For a moment Saxon just stood there. Then he snarled and threw himself at Belew. Hamilton got in between them and trapped his smaller partner against the side of the elevator. Belew stood there watching without especial sign of interest.

" 'The superior man is satisfied and composed; the mean man is always full of distress,' " he said.

The elevator stopped on their floor. Belew walked out without looking back. Helen came with him, sticking close.

"We're the professionals here," Saxon yelled at Belew's dinner-jacketed back. "We're the cops. You're just a fucking burned-out Green Beanie playing spy games."

Belew unlocked the door of the suite Señor Burckhardt shared with Señorita Elena. He ushered Helen in, then turned in the doorway.

"Show me," he said. "Prove you're the real cops. Catch Mark Meadows."

"You bet your ass we will, old man."

"Good." Belew started to pull the door closed. Saxon made as if to follow him in.

"Do you mind? You have your own room." Belew shut the door in his face.

"I apologize for the scene," Belew said, turning. "Confrontation does little to aid the digestion."

"That's okay," Helen said. Her posture was stiff, defensive. "I think I need to get some sleep. I'm dead on my feet."

"I can have the maid come make the couch up for you."

She stared at him. "What? I thought—"

"I'm Señor Burckhardt. This is my room; I made the arrangements for it, my firm is paying for it. The bed is an old-fashioned brass one, and I'm sleeping in it. Where you sleep is up to you."

Helen started to say something, but the sheer enormity of what he was saying overwhelmed her. She sat down heavily on the sofa with tears shining in the corners of her eyes.

Belew went into the bedroom, came back with a portable stereo tape player, which he set on the coffee table. "Care for a little late-night listening before you turn in?"

She tried to be polite: "No, I'm sorry, I'm not in the mood for any music—"

He punched the button.

Lynn Saxon's voice came out, slightly muffled: *"Washington on the line, finally. Shag ass over here!"*

She frowned up at Belew. He looked straight into her eyes.

"All right, Mr. Bohart. I've got Agent Hamilton here with me now."

"About this Flash thing—"

"Yeah. Yeah. Meadows was already spooked. We think the Geeks had done something to tip him off—he had the vial in his hand. . . ."

"But Mistral—"

"She just wasn't up to it, you know? Woman in a man's job. What'd you expect? I got no clue why SCARE wished her ass on us. Probably trying to put a spoke in our wheels—"

"If you'd let me finish a sentence, Saxon . . . we were surprised to learn how, ah, how lenient Flash had been with her."

"I don't know what to tell you, boss. The guy's so far gone on drugs, he changes into somebody else . . . I mean, you just don't expect him to walk away and leave anybody, you know, alive in his backfield."

"There's no chance he intended her to die in the fire in the carpet warehouse?"

"He told her he reckoned she could blow the flames out, and the Geek police were coming up the hill to lend a hand. He just wanted her off his case."

"The Director . . . Saxon, are you still there?"

"Didn't want to interrupt you again, Mr. Bohart. Look, if he's concerned about our little civvie ace showing up the Agency, you can tell him from me he's got nothing to worry about. She's strictly out of her depth. We're talking serious bimbo here."

Helen sniffed, and looked at Belew in outrage. He held up his hand.

"—other concern," the man on the far end of the connection was saying. "We're having some real problems here. Another damned limp-dick federal judge came out for legalization two days ago, and the press is getting out of hand. Public support for the War on Drugs is beginning to waver. If this goes too far—"

"I know. I know. The end of civilization as we know it."

"Precisely. A victory for the forces of darkness. There are larger issues involved here, Saxon. The fate of the Agency could be involved. We are in need of serious image enhancement . . . we talked about this before you left. There was a reason we acquiesced to the pressure to let Ms. Carlysle join the team."

"Look, if we need a martyr that badly, why don't you just let me and Gare waste the bitch ourselves and get it over with? This Meadows wimp hasn't come through, and it sure wouldn't give us any problems. We'd make it look good."

"For God's sake, Saxon, watch your mouth! This is an international connection. We don't know who might be listening. . . ."

Belew switched off the tape player and smiled. " 'Distrust all in whom the impulse to punish is powerful,' Nietzsche tells us."

She stood and walked toward the fireplace. "I don't believe it. How did you get that?"

"My dear, remember whom I work for."

She put her head in her hands. A moment later a sob escaped between her fingers. "Oh, my God."

He came up behind her and put his arms around her. This time she didn't pull away.

"They were talking about . . . about killing me."

"You can't make a New World Order without breaking a few eggs."

She tore away then, whirled, tearful and angry. "You think it's funny!"

"Not at all. I think it's appalling. I've been putting my life on the line for my country for three decades. It hasn't been so fine young cannibals like Agent Saxon could erase the distinction between the good guys and the bad." He took her by the upper arms.

"What are you doing in all this?" she asked.

"Helping you—and them—apprehend a federal fugitive. But somebody's playing a deeper game. I thought you should know."

He gathered her body against his, slid his hands down her arms to the wrists, brought them together behind her. He held them there with one hand while the other arm circled her shoulders.

They stood that way for a minute, two. "How do you feel?"

She sniffled. "I feel . . . safe." She looked up at him, blinking the tears from her hazel eyes. "Isn't that silly?"

"Not at all." He kissed her. After a moment she opened her mouth to him.

Chapter Thirteen

The truck park was no-man's land; King's X. Mark only hoped the bearded *Pasdaran* toughs who hung around the gates like wolves respected the ancient sanctity of *base*. He did realize their record in that line was none too good.

He'd run into a snag. Otto and the Great White Mercedes were fixing to turn around and drive back to Istanbul. Mark could go with him or stay here.

Neither was exactly what he had in mind.

Mark walked across the graveled parking lot sipping fruit juice from a bottle. The sky was high and blue and serenely uninvolved. The morning air was cool, almost chill. Off in the distance a tape-recorded call to prayer played from a minaret.

A voice called his name: "Mark! Mark Meadows!"

Tears filled his eyes. *Don't I get any* breaks? He threw his bottle down and without even looking back started to run for the gate. He *knew* what the DEA would do to him; there was at least some question with the Revolutionary Guard.

He ran into something. It seemed to have the dimensions and solidity of a redwood. It said, *"Oof."*

He looked up. He was six-four; he looked up anyway. The man he'd run into had a good three inches on him. He also had a hook nose, a wild beard, wild hair, and a round cap on top of his head that looked like one of those little cushions old ladies put on their divans.

Mark looked left and right. The boy he'd collided with had brought his brothers along to play. His *big* brothers. They wore baggy pants and Western shirts that looked like they'd come from Goodwill and vests over them. They all had knives as long as Mark's forearm through their belts. They did not look well socialized, at all.

One of them wore a red rose over one ear. He grinned at Mark when he caught his eye. He had a gold tooth.

"Mark! Mark, my man. What's your hurry?"

He turned to face his doom. In this case Nemesis took the form of a skinny guy of maybe medium height, with a dirty-blond handlebar mustache, round cherry-tinted wire-rim glasses, and a black straw cowboy hat with a big feather panache plastered on the front that made it look as if a sparrow had run into him in a full-power dive. He resembled the counterculture answer to Richard Petty.

"Frank?" Mark asked in a barely audible croak. "Freewheelin' Frank?"

"One and the same, bro, one and the same." He gave Mark a huge hug, and then, by God, a Revolutionary Drug Brothers Power Handshake.

"So how the hell have you been, man?" he demanded, holding Mark at arm's length. "It's been what? God, fifteen, sixteen years. You're lookin' better than I would have thought possible, you lanky son of a bitch. There's something about you—it's like you're more, you know, *together* than I've seen you before. And there's something else, around the eyes—"

"Just crow's feet, man."

"Oh, I'm forgetting my manners. Mark, I want you to meet the boys: this is Yilderim, and this is Muzaffar, and Qasim, and this is Ali Sher."

Ali Sher was the one with the rose. He grinned again at his name and batted his eyes.

"Uh . . . hi," Mark said. "Pleased to meet you. What, uh, like, what line of work would you boys happen to be in?"

"They're *mujahidin*, Mark," Freewheelin' Frank said. "Afghan freedom fighters."

He took Mark by the shoulders. "C'mon, man. Let's book over to the *chaikhana*, toss back a few cups and catch up on old times."

"So, what've I been doing?" Freewheelin' Frank tossed back his cup of tea and held it out for one of the *mujahidin* to pour it full from the pot in the middle of the table. The *chaikhana*—teahouse—was a disappointment, glass and steel and Formica like every other transport caf in the known world, or at least the world known to Mark. They were crowded into a couple of booths by a window looking out over the yardful of semitrailer rigs. "Well, shit, lemme figure out the *Reader's Digest* condensed version."

Back in the old Bay days Freewheelin' Frank had been Mark's supplier of hallucinogens and prime smokables. About a year or so after Sunflower turned up at Mark's door, he'd dropped from view and been seen no more.

"Well, what happened to me was about what you'd expect: somebody blew me up to the pigs, and I had to roll. Went out to Oahu for a couple years until that got too hot. Then, what? Spent a lot of time in Latin America. Hunted investment insects for a while in the Amazon."

"Investment insects?"

"Yeah. For a while all these West Germans were buying up your collectible bugs as inflation hedges. Nothin' all that rare, mind you, at least not down in the rain forest. But spectacular. Great big green beetles, walking sticks, that kind of thing. Weird old world we live in, ain't it?

"That didn't last. Local authorities wanted to cut themselves in on a piece of the action, namely all of it. Then I just knocked around a bit—ran guns to the rebels in Guatemala, ran pre-Columbian stuff out, mostly to the Japanese. Smuggled emeralds from Colombia—that was all I touched down there, I swear to God; coke lords were getting too crazy to deal with by that point. Fuckin' Bush'll do us all a favor if he cleans out those Medellín pukes, let some Japs or Taiwanese take over who aren't gonna be eat up with dumbass *machismo* shit.

"After a while I got bored with that and decided to head east, young man. I'm doing pretty well, here, too. Asia's full of entrepreneurial possibilities in the import-export line."

He rubbed the bristles on his face. They were almost white down at the point of his chin.

"So you finally decided to hit the hippie trail, old man? The road to Kathmandu. That where you're headed?"

Mark shrugged. "I don't know, man. Seriously."

"I heard you got run out of the old US of A."

Mark didn't see much point in dissimulation. "That's right, man."

Frank leaned forward. "Is it true, what they said on the satellite? You're really an ace—you scarf some shit and turn into all these super dudes?"

Mark licked his lips, looked around at the brave freedom fighters. They were watching him keenly and smelling about the same. Ali Sher smiled again.

"It's true."

Frank leaned back and ran his hand down his jaw with a scraping sound. "Then I got a proposition for you. You seem to be heading east. How'd you like to keep going that way, maybe pick up a little loose change?"

"Doing what?"

"Riding shotgun."

Mark shook his head. "You lost me, man. What do you mean?"

"We—my bros here 'n' me—we're making a run into Afghanistan. It's maybe a thousand mile between here and Kabul." He pronounced it "Cobble." "Now, the Revolutionary Guard, they usually leave us alone, because we're brave Islamic Holy Strugglers and all, and anyway these Pushtuns can kick the shit outta their low-country cousins any old time they want. But you never can tell. This country is fallin' apart, just between you and me and the wall, and every third village got some badass holed up in it with a lot of ex-militia boys with guns, figure they're gonna play *The Wind and the Lion* now that Ruhollah ain't here to hold the center anymore.

"Once we get to the border, we got the DRA, that's the Afghan Army, looking sharp to nail our asses to a board. And they got nasty Mi-35 Export Hind helicopters flying around, and they still got more than one or two Spetsnaz—that's Russian Green Beret—caravan hunter teams wandering around the countryside looking for *dushman*s, that's bad boys like us. So having along a little friend who can fly and shoot some serious fire from his hands has the potential to come in *mighty handy*."

"What're you carrying?"

"Well, the boys themselves. They been on furlough, kind of. Plus we got some antiaircraft and antitank missiles. Russian stuff—buy it offa the *Morskoye Pekhota*, Naval Infantry boys attached to the Black Sea fleet. They'll do anything for hash oil and Traci Lords videotapes."

"But I thought the Russians had left Afghanistan," Mark protested.

"Most of 'em have."

"Then what're the freedom fighters fighting against?"

"My man Dr. Najib. The dictator. Soviet puppet with most of his strings snipped."

"I've heard of him. But the TV news always said he was a moderate. Really interested in, like, trying to reform the country."

"He's got him some funny notions about reform. He broke into the big time as a professional torturer for KhAD, the Afghan secret police. He's really into *medical experimentation* too, if you know what I mean. Can you say, Dr. Mengele? Sure. I knew you could."

"I don't know, man. I don't want to get mixed up in a war or anything."

"Peace, Love, Dope forever, huh? Well, shit, man, I gotta say I respect you for it. These days it's War, Hate, and Just Say No. Teach it to the kids in school."

Actually it was that Mark had just *been* in a war, and it was pretty bad, and he didn't want to get mixed up with another. He didn't say anything about that. He didn't want Frank to think he was *completely* crazy.

"Still, man, think about it—where you gonna go? You surehell can't stay here. You want to get where the DEA can't lay a glove on you, right? Try Afghanistan. Or if that's a little too intense, I can pull a few strings and you can just keep trucking into India."

India. Now, there was an idea. There was a place he could really *use* his talents, use them to help other people. He could help them manufacture cheap antibiotics to fight disease, safe, biodegradable insecticides to save their crops. Some of those maharajahs were incredibly rich, rich as any oil sheik. Maybe he could get one to spring for a research facility, really get some work done.

Maybe he could find a guru, too. India was a very spiritual place. The Maharishi came from there, and Meher Baba. Maybe it was time to cultivate that side of his nature.

"How about it, man?" Frank asked. "You stay clear of

the one or two kingdoms the U.S. has in its back pocket and they'll never touch you. What do you say?"

"I'll do it."

Frank jumped up and threw his hat in the air. "All *right*! Come on, boys, saddle up—we got us an ace in the hole."

The Revolutionary Ministry of whatever it was had let them have a car to drive around in. It was an '87 Toyota Camry in a shade of blue nobody could ever remember seeing before. It ran well.

J. Bob Belew walked slowly across the truck park. The setting sun stretched his shadow clear to the perimeter fence. He slid in behind the wheel and slammed the door.

"Straw boss says a man matching Meadows' description was here, all right. But he left three, four hours ago with another American he met here. They say they headed north, as if they were planning to cross the Elburz, for what that's worth. Which is probably nothing."

He started the engine. "Does that mean we've lost him?" Helen asked from the passenger seat.

"For the moment."

Helen Carlysle set her mouth and gazed out the window at the distant blue Elburz. In the back where they thought he couldn't see, Lynn Saxon shot his partner Gary a thumb's up.

In front, where no one did see, J. Bob Belew smiled. All to himself.

It was dark on the windswept Iranian Plateau. It was getting extremely cold in the bed of the canvasback truck grinding up the endless grade toward the Roof of the World, even though one of the *mujahidin* had given Mark a sheepskin coat that smelled as if the sheep was still living in it, and possibly several other animals as well.

He pulled the coat closer about his skinny frame and tried again to find a comfortable position in which to rest his butt on a lot of wood crates marked in Cyrillic letters. In the near-total blackness he could see the glimmer of starlight on eyeballs turned expectantly toward him, a vagrant gleam from Ali Sher's gold tooth.

They'd pretty much played out "Give Peace a Chance." In fact the Afghans didn't look as if there were anything in the world they were less ready to give a chance to than peace, unless it was a Soviet armored column. But that hadn't stopped them from singing about it with a will. Now they want more.

"I know you probably don't drink, either," he said, "but try this anyway: *Ninety-nine bottles of beer on the wall, ninety-nine bottles of beer . . .*"

Chapter Fourteen

"Dr. Meadows," the tall, sleek, dark-skinned man in the blue turban said, "we have satisfied ourselves as to your bona fides. You have a most impressive résumé. I must admit, however, that it surprises me that one of your qualifications should have spent the last several years as a merchant and restaurant operator."

"Uh," Mark said, brushing his nose with the thumb of his closed right hand. He had an answer ready for that one. "Burnout, man. I just couldn't take the pace any longer. Like, New York, y'know? But I'm ready to get back to work now."

He also had a blue vial stashed away in his right fist, ready to slam down at the first hint of trouble. He wasn't trusting *anybody* these days. Another sign of his moral corruption.

Mr. Singh nodded, one of those extremely precise nods that make you suspect a person has click-detents in his cervical vertebrae. "The Maharajah is definitely willing to consider accepting you into his service." He smiled. His teeth were too white for his own good. His English was mellifluous, steady, and Oxonian, not the singsong high-pitched whine of most Indians Mark had tried to converse with. In his dark European-style business suit Mr. Singh looked as if he played a lot of handball or found other means of keeping himself trim.

Mark leaned forward in his chair, his heart jumping around in his ribcage. Visions of himself as Mother Teresa danced in his head. "I can start you out on production of certain basic antibiotics right away. From there we can move to simple gene-engineering stuff like making *E. coli* create insulin—kids' stuff, anyone can do it. In a couple of years, given the current state of the art and the availability of biotech equipment, we start doing *original* work. It's time somebody made a real move with monoclonal antibodies, or if your maharajah wants to be *ambitious*, he can shoot for the whole enchilada: creating a countervirus that will attach to the gp120 sequence on the protein coat of the AIDS virus—it never changes, no matter how the virus mutates, 'cause without it, it wouldn't still be AIDS."

Laughing, Mr. Singh held up his hands. He had a rich, deep laugh. "Dr. Meadows, please. Your enthusiasm does you credit; no doubt you will accomplish many great things for our people."

Mark stopped with his face hanging over the huge mahogany desk. He was practically panting with eagerness. He had had no idea until this instant how much he really wanted to get back to *work*.

It's Sprout, he thought. *When I get settled here, I can bring Sprout over, settle her down in a nice bungalow....*

"But we must first concern ourselves with practicalities," Singh said. Mark's heart folded its wings and fell to the floor of his chest like a buckshot dove. No joy had ever come into his life from speeches with the word *practicality* in them.

"Haryana is a poor state, Doctor. We lack the enormous wealth of Kashmir to the north. It is a substantial drain upon our resources to keep ourselves in a state of readiness to resist any encroachment from the Punjab or Uttar Pradesh. You will have your fine research laboratory, but first we must discuss our immediate need for revenue enhancement."

He leaned his fine turbaned head forward. "Now. What would it take you to begin producing the drug *rapture* for export?"

In the main square of Ambala it was hot as hell. The seat of the Maharajah of Haryana was practically in the Himalayan foothills, but it was still about 103 in the late morning, and the heat hit the pavement and bounced up into your face and stomach like medicine balls.

He walked around two sides of the square to a little sidewalk café with parasols. He bought a copy of a newspaper and sat down thankfully in the shade, ordering a bottled fruit juice from the bowing waiter.

You told him you'd think about it? There was no mistaking J. J. Flash's voice, blaring out from the cheap seats of Mark's mind. *You're a total schmuck. These little vest-pocket princes and their grand viziers are the only law west of the Pecos, and they aren't used to being told you'll "think about it." You tell them, "Yes, O great and powerful Lord of All Creation, I am your eager and obedient slave." Then you run like a bunny.*

He found himself sweating from more than the heat, which was more than enough by itself. *At least I had sense not to turn him down point-blank.*

Oh, Flash said, impress *me. You're just dumb, not suicidal, is that it?*

Maybe if Mr. Singh had hit him with a proposition to manufacture a different drug, Mark would have responded differently. Despite the attempts of the government and media to demonize them, the major recreationals weren't very dangerous. As a general thing they had fewer side effects than a majority of prescription drugs, and all of them were physically less harmful by a long shot than legal drugs like alcohol and nicotine. And Mark had no reason in the world to love America's drug warriors.

But rapture was one of those synthetics that crop up when the government actually does manage to put a temporary squeeze on the importation of recreational drugs. Unlike heroin, say—which, according to the DEA, has *no* clinical side effects—the synthetics, the "designer drugs," have unpredictable and frequently horrible side effects, commonly including things like neurological dysfunction and death. Mark wanted no part of that.

But even if Singh had offered him his own marijuana plantation, Mark probably would have felt miffed and recalcitrant. He wanted to do real work, wanted to be a *scientist* again. On Takis he had seen just what biochemistry and bioengineering could accomplish. Earth's technology was ready for a revolution, a nanotechnological upheaval that would produce plenty and prosperity for all humans while not only eliminating pollution but actually providing the means to repair the damage Man had done his planet. *That* was where Mark wanted to be.

A sacred elephant was wandering across the plaza with a mahout on his back. Japanese tourists stood snapping pictures as devout locals ran up to touch its trunk. Mark reached into his shirt pocket and took out the head of the rose Ali Sher had been wearing behind his ear. It was definitely the worse for wear, and getting black around the edges.

When they'd finally parted company at the mouth of the Khyber Pass, Ali Sher had wept like a baby and kissed him on the cheeks. He had wanted to do considerably more, he had made clear, but there was a limit to how understanding even Mark was willing to be. Freewheelin' Frank had given him a thousand bucks American for his escort services and said that any time he wanted to go into the caravan line along the old Silk Road, he should look him up. Ali Sher had broken the head off the rose he wore behind his ear and given it to Mark to remember him by.

A bus honked at bicyclists. Mark sighed. India was not shaping up to be the way he'd imagined it. The gurus weren't interested in you if you didn't have your Gold Card. And riding into town at dawn two days ago on the Delhi Express from Amritsar, Mark had looked out the window to see the fields covered with hundreds and hundreds of locals, hunkering down for their morning constitutional. It looked like the whole cast of *Gandhi* taking a communal crap.

Mark had never bought into the *dirty hippie* part of the sixties trip. Sunflower used to say he was anal retentive, back in their Bay student days—though she'd turned into Ms. Clean quick enough, once she actually moved in with him. Mark was too much the biochemist not to have a handsome regard for hygiene. It didn't seem like a number-one priority here.

He sipped his juice and opened the paper. It was a copy of the *Haryana Times*, written in this funny stilted Babu English. The first thing he saw was an article on Vietnam.

" 'We suffered forty years of war,' said Mr Tran Quang, a cultural and ideological spokesman for the Central Committee. 'More than other countries we need friendship.' "

Vietnam. They were still holding out, holding on to the socialist dream. It was tough on them; the Soviets were telling them they had to go it on their own from here on in, according to the article. Even wanted the Viets to start paying them *back*.

Most of the world had turned its back on communism, Mark knew. In fact, most of the world seemed determined to forget there'd ever been such a thing in the first place. Mark guessed maybe it hadn't worked so well.

But he remembered the old days, *Ho, Ho, Ho Chi Minh/NLF is gonna win*, Bonnie Raitt dedicating her second album to the people of North Vietnam. There was something stirring in Vietnam's defiance, something grand. Something that *spoke* to the old hippie in Mark.

And then he saw it. "Mr Tran announced that the Socialist Republic is opening its doors to all the people across the world who have been touched by the wild card virus. 'When all the rest of the world is turning against the aces and jokers,' he said, 'we welcome them. We invite them all to come and enjoy the benefits of life in our progressive republic.' "

Mark laid the paper across his thighs and for a while just stared out into the heat shimmer. Then he stood.

A couple of tall bearded guys in turbans, Sikhs most likely, had been loitering half a block from the outdoor café. When Mark stood, one of them touched the other on the arm. Very discreet motion, but Mark caught it anyway.

He turned and walked directly away from them. As he came up alongside a parked Hyundai, he glanced in the wing mirror. Sure enough, they were following him.

Obviously the maharajah thought he was too priceless a pearl to be permitted to slip through his fingers. It was flattering in a way. He turned a corner.

The two Sikhs broke into a run. Just as they reached the corner, a giant Pushtun came around it. He stopped a moment, glared at each of them in turn. They stood their ground—Sikhs don't give way to any scabby Khyber trash, even when it looms half a head taller than them—but they shared a look of frank relief when he grumbled and went his way. They hustled around the corner in pursuit of Mark.

"What buttholes," Ali Sher said in the voice of Cosmic Traveler. He grinned in his beard, stuck the dead rose over his ear, and walked off toward the train station, whistling Frank Sinatra's "My Way."

Part Two

ICE CREAM PHOENIX

Chapter Fifteen

The former American embassy compound had a washed-out look to it. Mark attributed it to the blinding sunlight of afternoon, and not the flaking stucco and missing roof tiles. Summer monsoon was late to hit the Mekong Delta this year. It made everything look oppressed and gritty.

The Wild Cards Affairs office was in a bungalow off to one side, seemingly shouldered there by the huge embassy building proper, which was currently headquarters to the Vietnam State Oil Company. "I'm Mark Meadows, Ph.D.," Mark told the plump and horn-rimmed woman behind the desk. "I'm an ace."

She beamed. She had started out beaming, and she didn't stop doing so. "That is very nice," she said in chipper musical English. "The Socialist Republic of Vietnam welcomes all victims of the wild card who seek refuge from the unconcern and persecution of the capitalist world."

That nasty, Takisian-born part of him thought that latter statement had the flat copper tang of a memorized speech. Mark wished he could do something about that cynical streak.

The woman wore a lightweight dark dress with flowers printed on it. She was the first person he had dealt with in any official capacity since arriving in *Cong Hoa Xa Hoi Chu Nghia Viet Nam*, if he had all the syllables right and in the right order, who wasn't in a uniform. He found that reassuring, a humanizing touch. He knew that the revolutionary socialist world, or what was left of it, had been getting some

117

bad press of late. All those uniforms had caused the unhappy suspicion there might be something in it.

"I'm a biochemist," he said. "I, uh, I don't have copies
of any of my diplomas or anything. But it would be easy to
verify."

"First you must have a blood test, to show that you
have the wild card," she said, squaring a stack of papers.

"Yeah. Fine. But, like, I have some skills that could be
very useful, and I'd like to use them to benefit the jokers."

She beamed. "First the blood test."

"Roll up your sleeve, please." the orderly said in English. He wore a tan tunic that reminded Mark forcibly of a
Nehru jacket, over doubleknit blue-herringbone bells. Mark
thought of 1971 with a nostalgic twinge.

Mark was sitting in an uncomfortable straight-backed
wooden chair that must have been sold to the former Republic of Vietnam as surplus by the California public school
system, because he was dead certain he'd sat in it in elementary school in 1958. It made it natural to do as he was
told. Still obedient, he knotted a length of rubber tubing
around his biceps and gazed raptly around at the posters on
the walls, some of which showed obvious doctors in white
coats exhorting peasants in conical straw hats, and others
dudes in pith helmets waving guns and yelling. He wished
he could understand what they said. He wanted to, like, get
with the program.

Then he noticed the orderly picking up a syringe that
had been lying beside the rusty sink, drying on a square of
gauze. It had obviously been used before. More than once,
Mark guessed.

"Make a fist, please," the orderly said mechanically, advancing and waving the hypo in the air.

Mark gave it the fish eye. "Don't you, like, have another one of those?" he asked. "A *newer* one?"

"We are a poor country," the orderly said peevishly.
"We cannot afford luxuries such as extra hypodermic needles. If your government sent us aid, we would be able to
provide such services. Give me your arm, please."

Oh, no. When Mark had blown America, the public was
still being megadosed with AIDS hysteria, courtesy of the
government and complaisant, sensation-loving media. Mil-

lions of people imagined themselves at risk who were in more danger of being hit by a meteorite.

On the other hand, if you *really, truly* wanted to contract HIV, getting stuck with a well-used hypodermic needle in the depths of the Third World was an excellent way to go about it. If only this were Haiti, it would be perfect.

Mark jumped up and backed away from the man. "I'll write my congressman just as soon as I get out of here."

The orderly stopped and folded his arms. "If you do not have the blood test, you cannot register as a wild card. Then no food, no ID, no place to stay in Saigon. *Giai phong.*"

"Maybe if I, like, kicked in a couple bucks, I could get a new needle?"

"It is against regulations."

Mark sighed. "Look. You got a scalpel anywhere? I can draw my own blood with that. I'm not afraid to cut myself."

The orderly looked mulish. *Or I could bounce your jug-eared head off the counter a few times, you crummy little jackboot quack*, a voice said at the back of Mark's head.

J. J.! he thought, shocked and appalled. Since Starshine died, he had noticed it was harder to keep down the Flash's antisocial impulses. The two seemed to have counteracted one another.

The orderly was staring at Mark's face His own was the color of wood ash. "Very sorry," he said. "Of course I will find a scalpel at once. Of course."

"Why, thanks, man," Mark said, thinking, *See, J. J.? Give peace a chance.*

For some reason J. J. Flash just laughed.

He left the bureau with a piece of official paper announcing his status as a provisional ace and wild card refugee—on his own recognizance, so to speak, pending the test results; a booklet of ration coupons with pictures of sainted Ho printed on them in blue; and another form assigning his quarters in Cholon, the district of Ho Chi Minh City set aside for wild cards, with instructions on how to get there scrawled on the back.

Walking into daylight was like walking into a wall, a phenomenon he was getting used to in South Asia. He paused a moment, letting his eyes adjust.

When he started across the yard a whistling scream

drew his eyes up into the dazzling pale-blue sky. An airplane was passing over with its flaps and gear down, heading for a landing at Tan Son Nhut, a fighter, lean and predatory with delta wings and twin tail fins. He felt a weird sense of sideways nostalgia, of adventitious *déjà vu*: his father had often flown fighters into that very base, more than twenty years ago. Despite his years of professed pacifism, Mark easily recognized the airplane as a MiG-29, one of the latest generation of Soviet military aircraft—he had always harbored a secret, guilty fascination for warplanes.

As he left the compound, some skinny brown kids in shorts threw stones at him, shouted obvious insults at him, and ran off, their tire-soled Ho Chi Minh slippers clacking against their feet like motorized novelty-store dentures.

Fortunately their aim was bad. Watching them go, Mark shook his head sadly. "They sure must still hate Americans around here," he said. Not that he could blame them.

Some of Cholon looked pretty good—more prosperous than the rest of what Mark had seen of Ho Chi Minh City, and more lively. The wild cards quarter wasn't in that part.

He felt self-conscious sitting in the shade of the little fringed awning on top of the *cyclo* bicycle cab, resting while the driver pedaled his heart out in the sun. It didn't seem consistent with socialist equality. All the same a lot of putatively good socialist Vietnamese seemed to be riding around in the things, so who knew?

Mark wasn't really a socialist, when it all came down to it, and actually didn't know vast amounts about the doctrine, though people who spoke in Capital Letters had frequently tried to explain it to him—or at least lectured about it. He just knew in a vague Summer of Love way that it was a Good Thing.

Besides, the shade gave relief from the pile-driving force of the sun, and their wind of passage even kicked up a bit of a breeze.

The stucco began to flake off the façades and trash to pile up in the gutters, and Cholon began to look more like the rest of Ho Chi Minh City. He gathered he was getting closer to his destination.

The *cyclo* stopped abruptly, *bang* in the middle of a

block and the street. A little decaying orangish Trabant screeched its brakes and veered around them with a fart of exhaust and a trail of what Mark was fairly sure were Vietnamese obscenities.

"This it, man?" he asked dubiously.

"This far as *I* go," the driver said. For all his exertion he wasn't breathing heavily. *Cyclo*-driving must be great aerobic exercise. "This place Number Ten."

"Oh." He paid the guy off in a fistful of the flimsy *dong* they'd given him at the Wild Cards Affairs office, hesitated, and handed him a buck for a tip. "You might be tempted to head into Commie-land at some point," his buddy Freewheelin' Frank had explained when he paid Mark off. "Good old greenbacks are good as gold there, and a whole lot easier to carry."

He must have been right. The *cyclo* driver cranked his eyes left and right, snatched the dollar out of Mark's fingers, and instantly made it disappear—a good trick, since the sleeves of his black Harley Davidson T-shirt only came halfway down his skinny biceps. Then he whipped his cab around and went pumping off the way he had come. Mark shrugged and continued afoot.

About the first thing he saw was a joker child with the body of a big green-black beetle and the face of a four-year-old girl. He smiled and nodded at her. She clutched her ragdoll to her chitin with the upper two pairs of legs and stirred her wingcases with a noise that reminded Mark of his childhood trick of fixing a playing card to the frame of his bicycle so the spokes would snap it as he rode, and stared at Mark as if he were the most terrifying thing she had ever seen in her life.

"But look here," Mark said, sticking his sheaf of official papers under the woman's nose. "My *Ho Khau* form is all in order. See? It says I have a room here."

He pointed to the number over the doorway, then pointed to the form. It was fortuitous that the building *had* a street number. Few buildings he'd passed did. For that matter, few of the places on this block deserved the name "building"; they mostly ran to shanties slapped together out of plywood and corrugated tin.

Mark's assigned domicile was whitewashed brick,

which he gathered meant it was a survival from French Colonial days. The stocky concierge, or whatever she was, obviously had no intention of letting him into it. She stood there expostulating in no language he knew and waving her little pudgy fists and turning red until her face looked like a beet with a bandanna tied on it.

Culture shock was starting to set in, and some good old down-home paranoia. Mark was a stranger in the strangest land yet—okay, maybe it wasn't stranger than Takis, but as far as Earth went, it was pretty alien—and he had been given to believe things worked a certain way, and here they weren't working *at all*. The smiling woman at the Wild Cards office had handed him his papers and permits and said everything was taken care of, and he just naturally expected things to proceed with smooth scientific-socialist efficiency. And here was this woman yelling at him in a street full of jokers, refusing to let him into the living quarters assigned him.

He was tired and beginning to feel that traveler's panic of not knowing where he was going to *stay*. And maybe some of his socialization had died with Starshine. Because, much to his own surprise, he shouldered abruptly past the noisy woman, went stilting down a dark hallway that stank of urine and less nameable aromas on his great gangly Western legs, clutching his papers in his fist and peering at the faded numbers painted on the doors.

His papers matched one on the second floor. He knocked. He prepared a speech in his mind: *Look, I'm sorry. There's been some kind of misunderstanding. The government assigned this room to* me. . . .

The door opened. A tiny woman dressed in black peasant pajamas stood there, so gaunt her cheeks looked like collapsing tents and her arms and legs like sticks. Her eyes were huge, and they widened in terror when they saw what was standing at her door.

At least a half-dozen children and a couple of ancient women sat on the floor behind her, staring at Mark with fear in their dull eyes. One tiny stick-figure child—a boy, he thought in a horrified flash—staggered against one of the old women, who wrapped him in her meatless arms. He had a bandage wrapped completely around his head, brown with old dried blood.

"I—oh, Jesus, man, I'm sorry—I—" He whirled away from the door and went race-walking back down the corridor, his brain spinning.

The concierge was laying for him at the foot of the stairs with a Bulgarian-made push broom. She uttered a piercing screech and whacked him in the head with it. Horse hairs flew in a cloud around his head. He raised his arms to defend himself. She hit him again, at which point the head fell off and cracked him on the crown. He retreated in a hurry, hunched down with his hands over his head as she belabored his back with the broomstick, cawing like a triumphant crow.

In the hot, stinking street again, heart pounding, brushing horse hairs from his shoulders like dandruff. He started walking, not sure where he was going.

A kid of maybe fourteen fell into step beside him—it was hard to tell exactly; between genes and doubtful nutrition most adults around here seemed child-sized compared to Mark. But though the youngster was dark, a glance told Mark he wasn't Vietnamese, or any kind of Southeast Asian probably.

"You American, yes?" the boy asked.

Mark bit down hard on hysterical laughter. He was blond and white and two feet taller than anyone else on the street. He looked as if he had arrived in a UFO. In fact he looked more alien than when he *had* arrived in a UFO, when the living ship *SunDiver* dropped into Holland for a touch-and-go on its way to deliver Jay Ackroyd and his sharp-tongued war bride, Hastet, back to the US of A.

"Yeah," he managed to say, with only a giggle or two escaping his mouth like Lawrence Welk bubbles.

"You are joker?"

Given what the nats looked like around here, he could make a case for it on his own merits. But he was feeling waves and waves of guilt crashing down on him for disturbing the desperate people in "his" room. He waved the handful of papers still clutched in one hand—a little tattered from the Bulgarian broom attack—at the boy. The imprint of the Wild Cards Affairs office at the tops seemed to satisfy him that Mark was one of *us* and not *them.*

"My name is Ali," he said proudly. "I am from Dimashq."

"I'm Mark," Mark said, the conversational idiot taking over. "Like, what brings you here, man?"

The boy hiked up the long tails of his Western-style man's shirt, which he wore hanging over his shorts. There was a fistula in his skinny side you could roll a bowling ball into. Wet, shiny red-purple things writhed in there like eels.

"I am joker," he said, not without pride.

Mark swallowed. It wasn't the deformity itself; he'd seen as bad just a-walkin' down the street this afternoon. Syria was the heartmeat of Nur al-Allah's bad-crazy Muslim fundie movement that claimed jokers were cursed by God; more than three hundred jokers had been massacred in riots in the joker quarter of Damascus—Dimashq—not ten days ago. The boy was awfully damned lucky to be here, squalor or no.

The boy dropped his shirttail. "You look troubled, Mark my friend from America."

"Well, I just got here, and I got assigned these living quarters. And I went to the address they told me, and the place I'm supposed to live in has all these people in it. Must be a whole family in there. I've got to talk to somebody. Get this straightened out."

The boy spat. "Squatters. Refugees from fighting in the countryside. Everybody wants to live in Saigon *giai phong*. I will take you to someone who will make it right." He puffed out his chest importantly and led off down the street.

They went two blocks, Ali proud, Mark ducking his head between his shoulderblades in a doomed attempt to be inconspicuous. They turned a corner and a burst of automatic-weapons fire cracked out right in front of them, followed by the slap of muzzleblast shocks hitting the building fronts.

Mark grabbed Ali by the arm and dragged him into a recess between two more or less solid-looking structures. He was getting to be an old hand under fire. Hell of a note for the Last Hippie.

Ali squirmed. "What are you doing?"

"Trying to keep you from getting shot."

Ali pulled free. "There is no danger. They fire only into the air." His body language said *he* knew a little something about being under fire too.

Mark was becoming aware that he was standing in

somebody's front yard, as blank joker faces stuck out of the lean-to jumble set back from the street between the larger buildings. Ali stepped right out into the street. Mark peered cautiously after. The loose horse hairs were starting to itch down inside his shirt, and he remembered he was allergic to horses.

Another burst crashed. Mark flinched but willed himself not to duck. Men in khaki shorts and pith helmets were herding people out of a building down the street, slapping and kicking and firing Kalashnikovs into the air to keep them moving.

"See?" Ali said smugly. "It is the People's Security Force clearing out squatters. They think they can come here and take the housing the government gives to jokers."

The PSF troops were bundling the squatters into the back of a big black step-van. A young man suddenly broke away, went running down the street, thatch of stiff black hair bouncing to the rhythm of his stride, elbows flailing.

One of the men in the pith helmets pulled an AK to his shoulder and fired. Dust flew from between the young man's shoulderblades. He fell on his face, skidding several yards on the sidewalk. The security man fired again. Screams answered, as if his bullets had found other targets.

Ali showed Mark a smile full of white, well-tended teeth. "Nat dogs. They deserve no better, yes?"

Chapter Sixteen

The hunt for Mark Meadows stalled out in Bangkok, on the pool deck of the Oriental Hotel. The dogs, however, were not as idle as they looked.

"This isn't gonna work, Lynn," Gary Hamilton said. He had a mostly peach Hawaiian shirt on over khaki shorts and flip-flops. He sat on a big plastic chaise longue, keeping carefully within the umbra of an umbrella, applying thermonuclear-blast-protection-factor sunblock over every inch of his large body and worrying.

"What's not gonna work?" his partner demanded. Lynn Saxon sat cross-legged right up on the pink pavement by the pool. He had a headset clamped on his dark hair and a little black box well equipped with blinking lights and digital displays resting next to his skinny, hairy haunches. He wore matching Hawaiian shirt and shorts dominated by an explosive shade of magenta. The Aussie tending bar in the little strawtop cabana over on the other side of the pool had opined that looking at Saxon gave him a whole new grasp of the phrase *technicolor yawn*. Unlike college-boy Hamilton, Saxon had never been a member of any beer-drinking fraternities, so he felt vaguely complimented by the remark.

Rubbing thick white zinc-oxide cream on his nose, Hamilton glanced sideways at his buddy and inhaled a snort of laughter. He had been fighting off the giggles all morning. He didn't see Lynn get zinged much. It was especially great when he didn't even *know* it.

"Just sitting around listening to Belew's phone in case he happens to get a call telling him where Meadows is hanging out," Hamilton said. "What good is this doing us?"

Saxon was hot, wired, and running, flipping those channels on his Black Box and alternately ogling the women of various colors in their French thong bikinis and shrieking curses at them if they splashed too near to his sensitive electronic equipment.

"Listen, bud," he said, talking fast and emphatically. "Do you have any idea, any idea *at all*, where this puke Meadows is?"

Warily, Hamilton shook his head.

"Right! Neither do I, neither does Washington. It's been good old J. Bob all along who's been steering us after him. I mean, we gotta admit, when he's right, he's right. Right?"

"Right. Er, yeah."

Saxon bobbed his head. "Okay, now. When we found out Meadows was headed east with the gunrunners, we all agreed he was going to try to set himself up in charge of a drug lab for some big Asian operation, probably in the Golden Triangle. Now, we've been sweltering in this combination steambath and sewer two whole days now, and J. Bob has been running around playing Secret Agent Man and slipping the old Spam Loafski to Mistral, while all we do is sit by the pool sipping Mai Tais, playing with our wingwangs, and praying for the Eurasian babes to fall out of their swimsuits. You following this?"

In fact the very different personalities of Belew and Helen Carlysle had caused both to be extremely discreet about their nascent affair. But Saxon had noticed that the two had begun to adhere into a mini-bloc opposed to him and Hamilton. Carlysle had certainly shut Saxon down in no uncertain terms, and what that added up to for Saxon was that either Mistral was getting it from Belew or she was a dyke. She hadn't exactly dropped her drawers in response to Hera's come-ons in Athens. That left one possibility. QED.

"I suppose you think Belew is in cahoots with Meadows," Hamilton said sullenly.

Saxon flipped his shades up on top of his dark hair and gazed at Hamilton for a long moment before flipping them down again. A corner of his mouth worked. Hamilton wanted to yell at him. Saxon did that with his mouth when he was being clever. Hamilton *hated* it when he was clever.

"Well-ll," Saxon said, "I guess we can't entirely *discount* that little possibility, now, can we? I mean, he *is* with the Company after all, and who set most of these ethnic-army drug lords up in business in the first place? Can you say, *C-I-A?* Sure. I knew you could."

At that point a five-foot-tall woman with red hair hanging to a perfect butt and green eyes shaped like almonds dove off the board. Water droplets hit Saxon on the hand and cheek. One splattered on the precious Black Box.

"Hey, you stupid cunt!" he shrieked when she surfaced. "Watch out what the fuck you're doing!"

Treading water, she glared for a moment, then laughed and dog-paddled away, her mostly naked rump protruding slightly from the water and just working away. "Stuck-up bitch," Saxon snarled. "If we were back in the USA . . ."

Hamilton cleared his throat.

"Oh. Yeah." Saxon rubbed his upper lip where the stubble from his returning mustache itched him. "So anyway, the real deal with our friend J. Bob is that this is his old playground, and he knows a lot of the big kids on it, and he knows a lot of the little ones too. If Southeast Asia really is where Meadows has gone to ground, you and me and the dink shining shoes over there all know J. Bob's gonna sniff him out first."

"So? Why does that mean we have to bug his phones?"

Saxon quit fiddling with his knobs long enough to reach up and feel his partner's forehead, then pinch one cheek and lightly slap it. "Are you running a fever? Has your little brain overheated? Wakey, wakey, Agent Hamilton." He laughed at the way Hamilton jerked his head back and batted ineffectually at his hand. "Were you asleep last time we talked to Washington? The fucking media finally figured out we didn't win just 'cause Bill Bennett said we did when he cut and ran. The Agency needs a win, here; it is definitely not policy that the frapping Company should get to collar the biggest-ticket ace fugitive in the history of the U.S. of A."

"So you figure somebody's going to call right up to Belew's room and finger Meadows?" Hamilton said sullenly.

"I figure he's been putting out feelers, and *somebody* might get back to him, if only to set up a meet. Who knows? Maybe he'll do a deal with the Muang Thais or the Shan

United Army. Sell 'em a couple juicy DEA agents in exchange for Meadows."

Hamilton paled.

"Besides, I don't expect somebody to just call up to his *room*. That's why I got all the phones in the lobby wired too—"

"Oh, shit." Gary grabbed Lynn's shoulder and pointed. Mistral was just emerging from the hotel lobby, moving tentatively as she came down the broad white steps to the pool, as if the fierce noon sunlight was a wind she had to walk against. "Jesus, put that stuff away."

"Why?" Saxon demanded. "She's a playgirl, not a cop. What does she know about surveillance equipment? We'll tell her it's a magic ace detector we just got from the Governor by Federal Express."

She stopped across from them in the terrace that ran around the pool, tentative as a forest creature. She wore a lightweight dress to mid-calf, smoky gray with little abstract dabs and slashes of mauve and midnight blue in it, set off with just a couple of streaks of silver, for contrast. It was sheer enough that you could see her bra and panties through it. She was wearing her ace suit less since she'd taken up with Belew. Maybe it was the humid Southeast Asian heat.

Helen Carlysle had spent some discreet time in the sun. Her limbs shone like polished hardwood. She had lost weight; the summerweight dress had a tendency to hang in places. But the slight loss had sharpened the definition of her collarbones and her slim, long neck, added a touch of romantic concavity to her cheeks, made her eyes looked huge and haunted in the shadow of her silver straw hat.

A gentle, stinking breeze off the Chao Phrya River ruffled her permed hair. She was a great-looking woman, there was no doubt about that.

"Too bad she doesn't have enough tits," Hamilton said sadly.

"More than a mouthful is wasted," Saxon said. He clutched at the side of his head and teetered way to one side. "Whoa! We got something here."

"What?"

"*Shh!* The Man Himself is on the line." He listened, a

nasty predator's grin spreading gradually across his lean, dark face.

At last he nodded, peeled off the headset. "Okay," he said, "we're good to go. J. Bob's meeting his man in half an hour. And he did, too, call him in his room, so there."

He grabbed his Black Box by the little plastic carrying handle. Mistral caught sight of them as they stood up in a hurry. Saxon gave her the thumb-and-pinky Hawaiian hang-loose salute, and they booked.

The women were out buying fish, vegetables, and fruit from the vendor-boats on the *klongs*, canals. As Belew got nearer the Menam Chao Phrya, the wares being cried took on a more exotic flavor.

Bangkok was not an eighties kind of place. It was prob-ably not going to be a nineties kind of place, either, but the decade hadn't really set its style yet. The delicate called *Krung Thep*—Bangkok—the "Cesspool of the Orient." It was noisy, loud, nasty, and bright, whether by day or by night.

There's a hoary cliché about places in the East where anything is for sale. In Bangkok it's all for sale *cheap*.

J. Bob Belew liked the place immensely.

Through a day whose humid heat was so thick you practically needed a machete to get through it, he negoti-ated thronged and hyper streets down to the waterfront dis-trict. Nearer the river, broad avenues became narrow, crowded with bodies in motion, and the cries of beggars, peddlers, and pimps warred with Moroccan-roll, Vanilla Ice, and that Chinese popular music that sounds like the themes of old cowboy movies for the top niche in a whole vibrant ecosystem of noise. The white-boy rap was cranked so that all you could hear was the jackhammer bass, which was probably a blessing.

Belew wore baggy-cut khaki Brittainia trousers, Nike athletic shoes, a cream-colored polo shirt, light-tan jacket, dark-green Ray-Bans. He moved like a man who walked these cracked and littered streets every day of his life.

It was not the best part of town he was going into, nor the safest, and the muggers were even better armed than the ones in Central Park, if not usually so bold. That was why he wore a Para Ordnance 10mm in an inside-the-pants holster down the back of his trousers. *That* was why they were cut loose, in contradiction of Belew's customary fashion statement.

The Para Ordnance Ten was basically the same thing as the old Colt Government .45, but muscled up to take the hot 10mm cartridge. It also had a magazine capacity of fifteen rounds, unlike the old Colt, which held seven. That made for a mighty hefty grip, but Belew had big hands for his size. For all that the Para was a largish chunk of iron, it suited him well, and felt very good. The feel of a piece of equipment was very important to him.

The fore-end of the Ten in its Cordura holster did tend to kind of gouge him between the tops of his buttcheeks as he walked. That was the price you paid for concealed carry. You did not want to wear a shoulder-rig in the Tropics: Rash City.

An *open* display of ordnance was conspicuously not a good idea. The Thai Army had taken over again in late February under the direction of a general with the—to Belew anyway—immensely satisfactory name of Suchinda Krapayoon. Though the less resplendently named General Sunthorn Komsongpong was the front man for the junta, Suchinda was known to desire to move from being the brains behind the throne to the butt seated on it. The coup—the seventeenth, successful or otherwise, since 1932—had come in on a law-and-order theme. Since Western governments did not want their citizens armed, what could be a better way of demonstrating the junta's commitment to the rule of law than rousting gun-slinging Westerners in approved Southeast Asian style?

The prohibition, of course, did not extend to the Army, the various police agencies, or the paramilitary Thai Rangers. These latter bad boys, in their characteristic Victor Charlie black pajamas, swaggered in bands through the waterfront district with the slings of their Kalashnikovs hung around their necks along with their trademark sky-blue neckerchiefs. Belew gave them room but little thought, as an experienced jungle traveler would a cobra sunning himself on a trailside rock.

The bar was called the Headless Thompson Gunner. It had a cute neon sign with the outline in blue of a big combat-booted dude with no head blazing away with an old drum-fed Tommy 1927 A-5, the same gun all the Feds back home—having discovered the hard way in numerous shoot-outs that, beyond being a shitty handgun round, 9mm was also a shitty submachine gun round—were lugging around in spite of its enormous weight. The sign even had a flicker-ing red-neon muzzle flash, Belew wished the place would open a franchise in Manhattan. It would make the Park Ave. set soil themselves.

It wasn't really pitch-black inside, but after the dazzle-bath on the street it seemed that way until Belew's eyes sorted themselves out. He took off the Ray-Bans and tucked them into his jacket pocket to speed things along.

On a rat's-ass little stage to the left of the door a couple of listless babes gyrated to Madonna, lit by cyan and ma-genta spots that made them look more like tropical fish than go-go dancers. Both of them wore bikinis. For a town where everything was for sale, Bangkok had its surprisingly prim side. You *could* see anything your deviant heart desired, if you were willing to pay, but not walking in flat off the street. Even down in the gut of the Chao Phrya slum.

As he got his bearings, Belew listened to the music. It was not really his kind of sound—if he had to hear modern music, he preferred speed metal—but it brought back pleas-ant memories. Madonna was a dear girl, sweet and genu-inely vulnerable behind her sex-bitch-goddess onstage persona. Still, José Canseco probably fit better into her life-style. . . .

"J. Ro-*bear*! *Mon dieu*, fuck me, it is good to see you!"

It sounded like a man trying to bellow with a mouthful of pebbles, and it gave you a major clue why Demosthenes failed to keep the Macedonians out of Athens. Still squint-ing, Belew saw an oblong oasis of relative light that was the bar, and outlined against that light a hulking shadow.

Grinning, Belew threaded toward that shadow between tables of serious drinkers, who all looked like pirates off the South China Sea and conceivably were pirates off the Chao Phrya. He held out his hand to have it engulfed by a vast black-furred paw. The barkeep and owner of the Headless Thompson Gunner was an enormous lumpy man with a square, scar-tracked face beginning to sag at the jowls, a nose like a bad potato, large and basset-soulful eyes, and, despite the hot humidity that filled the bar along with smoke in defiance of the creaking ceiling fan, a toupée stretched across the top of his head like black-dyed roadkill.

He was, of course, named Roland.

He claimed to be the inspiration for the Zevon song, which was to say the least unlikely. For one thing he wasn't a Norwegian. For another there was the inconvenient matter of him still being in possession of his head—which, as his old black-war buddy Belew loved to remind him, no sane man would pick for himself and thus was surely the one he had been born with, QED.

"So how are things, you ugly Walloon ape?" Belew asked, reclaiming his hand, which his sometimes comrade-in-arms had tried yet again to crush and, as always, failed.

"Well enough," Roland rumbled. He tipped his large head toward the stage. "If *they* don't cause trouble."

They were four Thai Rangers knocking back brews and raising a general hooraw. They had checked their AKs at the door—four men with assault rifles were not stud enough to *force* their way into a Chao Phrya bar—but the dancers kept giving them apprehensive looks.

"They are either on furlough from the northwest, raping the Karen of their teakwood at the behest of the army of Burma—*pardonnez-moi*, Myanmar—or from the east running guns to the *Khmers Rouges*. If you wish to know more, you must ask them yourself—do you still drink nothing stronger than fruit juice?"

Belew nodded. "Still."

Shaking his head at Belew's foibles, Roland poured him a glass of apricot juice. He had gone into the Congo as a Belgian paratrooper in 1960 and gone back as a mercenary under Schramme to fight the murderous Simbas in 1964. Since then he'd bounced around the Third World, from the Yemen to Nicaragua to Syria to splintered India, fighting mostly communist and communist-backed insurgents. Ten years ago, pushing fifty, he had bought the bar and retired.

He pushed the glass at Belew. "How the times change," he said with a sigh. "When I quit, I was convinced the Soviets were winning, slowly but surely."

He shook his head and laughed. "How quaint that fear seems now, when it is a good morning for *Monsieur* Gorbachev if he awakens to find he still has Moscow."

Belew raised his glass. "To changing times." Roland poured a splash of cognac in a glass, and both men drank.

"But *plus ça change, plus c'est la même chose* did not become a cliché for no reason," Roland said, setting down his empty glass with a solid thunk. "Perhaps history has ended, as one of your people has written, but whatever is taking its place still offers employment to such bad men as you, it seems."

Belew grinned. "And so it does. And bad men like me still have need of bad men like you." He leaned across the bar. "Roland, I need your help. Right now. The risk is high. So is the pay."

Ten minutes later J. Robert Belew emerged from the Headless Thompson Gunner. As the sunlight hit him full in the face, he paused long enough to put his Ray-Bans back in front of his eyes. Then he took off down the street like a man on a mission.

Half a block in the other direction, nearer the Menam Chao Phrya, Lynn Saxon and Gary Hamilton sat under the gaudy fringed shade of a *tuk-tuk* motorized-tricycle cab. Saxon had added a Panama hat with a band that matched the rest of his ensemble. He looked like an upmarket drug mule who thought he was on the fast track to middle management but was actually being cultured to take a fall. Hamilton was carrying some extra marble to his beef, and in the wet Chao Phrya heat was sweating as if it were a medal event in the Goodwill Games.

As Belew receded from them without a backward glance, Saxon held up his hand.

"Did I not tell you?" he crowed. "Did I not?"

"You did." Grudgingly, Agent Hamilton slapped his palm.

"All right, then," Saxon said. He pulled his Sonny Crockett Bren Ten from its waistband holster and pulled back the slide to check the load. "Let's rock and roll."

Chapter Seventeen

The young woman slowed way down on her 50cc Suzi scooter, scoping Mark over the tops of the white heart-shaped shades she was wearing despite the fact that night had settled in to stay on Ho Chi Minh City's main drag. She wore a sleeveless denim vest patterned in swirls of studs, blue denim gloves clear to the elbow, and white capri pants. She caught Mark's eye, bobbing around up there in the ozone, gave him a phosphorescent smile, and putted away.

He watched her rump recede, caught himself, and felt like a male chauvinist. But it had been a long time for him. He thought of Tachyon's sister, Roxalana. She was back on Takis. One more reason to question his decision to leave.

Naturally Jumpin' Jack Flash had gotten to her first. It didn't seem fair somehow.

Hey, can I help it if I'm the one with dangerous charisma? came the sardonic voice from the back of his mind.

"Hey, man, You like?"

"Huh?" Mark said intelligently. He blinked his way back to reality, such as it was.

A pair of Vietnamese dudes in shades sat fore-and-aft on a 100cc Honda scooter. The pillion rider nodded after the woman on the Suzuki. "You *like* her, man? She number one."

Mark blushed. He was completely unprepared for this kind of situation. Either they were trying to engage him in some sort of thigh-slapping male-chauvinist ritual, hooting after the hapless woman like New York construction workers, or they were her brothers, bent upon cadging an admission from him that he liked their sister so that they could set upon him and stomp him silly. Only Mark, at least a foot taller than either of them and carrying some of the most powerful aces the world had ever known in a back pocket of his faded Levi's, would worry about that.

So he smiled like a goon, bobbed his head and kind of waved, and walked on. Behind him the dudes on the bike shrugged and zoomed past him into the people flow.

Dong Khoi Street ran wide and only slightly seedy from the city center to the Saigon River. Mark had found the Wild Cards office closed when he straggled back from Cholon. It had been a relief; he still couldn't see himself turning the men with their pith helmets and Kalashnikovs on the wretched family of squatters huddled in "his" apartment. Even if young Ali thought he was a wimp.

That left him loose, to say the least, and what motion there was in Ho Chi Minh City after dark tended to flow down Dong Khoi and back up the parallel Nguyen Hue Street, so he let his bootheels wander down that way too.

This wasn't the loud, bustling, boisterous, decadent, and dangerous Saigon of the movies. But then, those movies were filmed in Bangkok these days, or Manila.

. . . Another young woman was giving him the eye, this one with her long hair piled and pinned atop her head. As Mark noticed her, she flashed him a good many white teeth and accelerated.

"Hey, man! Yo, *My*, that girl fine, yes?" Mark looked around. Two more guys on a motor bike—and he found something else to feel a guilt twinge at, that the only reason he could tell these two from the last was that their scooter was different. He grinned and shook his head—*no comprendo Inglés*—and moved on.

There were people enough, kids cruising past on those farty little scooters like the ones who kept accosting him for whatever unknowable purpose, pedestrians, tourists looking big and ungainly. A café or two was still open, a few shops selling curios, cigarettes, lottery tickets, and maps to the famous former Viet Cong tunnel complex of Cu Chi in what was now the northern suburbs, which the government was touting big-time as a tourist attraction.

There was even a nightclub or restaurant called Maxim's, with bright lights and swing music pouring out the front. Mark took a peek inside, but all he saw were suits and evening gowns. It jarred his image of life in a communist country almost as much as the lottery tickets had.

But the whole scene was, like, subdued. Ho Chi Minh City seemed to be holding its collective breath, waiting, for what he couldn't tell.

Maybe it was the rain.

As he was walking away from Maxim's, a kid came up to him. Mark glanced at him with unafraid eyes—maybe Takis was starting to wear off some, after all. At least this one wasn't riding a scooter.

The boy was tall for a Vietnamese, and then Mark realized with a shock his skin was the color of chocolate. Much darker than any Vietnamese he'd seen.

"Give me some money," the boy said. "I'm hungry."

Stunned, Mark reached reflexively into his pocket and pulled out a couple of wadded *dong* notes. The kid accepted them, grunted at them, made them vanish, and shuffled away.

They were all over him then, big-boned kids, round-eyed kids, kids with dark skin and frizzy hair, adolescents and young adults, saying, "Take me to America," and "Give me money," and "My father was American."

It didn't take long for him to realize that if he tried to help them all, he'd soon be flat himself, and him without a roof to sleep under tonight. Hands on his pockets, feeling selfish and horrible, he lurched away as fast as his long legs would carry him.

After a few paces the youths gave up the listless chase and began to drift back up the street in search of better-heeled Americans to guilt-trip. The experience left him feeling eerie and disconnected, left his head ringing. He was suddenly very, very homesick for Sprout.

In that frame of mind he heard a familiar voice singing—chanting, really—to a dry and sinister backbeat.

> "I'm a joker, I'm insane
> "And you can not say my name—"

He gravitated toward the saloon-style doors through which the sound slithered, snakelike. As he reached them, the voice rose to a screaming crescendo:

"I am the serpent who gnaws
"The roots of the world!"

Familiar, but dead. The voice belonged to Thomas Marion Douglas, lead singer for Destiny. He had been one of Doctor Tachyon's successes with his early trump vaccine. More or less. The return to nat status had finished Douglas off twenty years ago.

Mark had briefly known him. Or maybe he hadn't.

He peered inside. The bar was poorly lit—but then, the next well-lit bar you go into will be the first, now, won't it? It did not take his eyes any time to adjust, but it took his mind a while.

The walls were plastered with posters, giant icon heads, Elvis and the Beatles and Janis and Jimi, Peter Fonda on his bike with his Captain America colors, Buddy Holly before the wild card. Tom Douglas as the Lizard King, going down beneath a wave of cops in New Haven. Richard Nixon flashing V-for-victory, Martin Luther King having a dream. The Grateful Dead. A single-sheet for Peter Sellers in *The Party*. There was a pool table and a lighted Budweiser sign behind the bar and a TV up on the wall playing *SportsCenter* to no one in particular.

Dominating the scene was a truly humongous poster behind the door: Humphrey Bogart in regulation fedora and cigarette, eyes crinkly and wise. And the voices from the gang at the bar were *American*.

Mark had felt more than a few flashes of dislocation of late, mainly because no other earthling in history, except for Jay Ackroyd and Kelly Jenkins, had ever been as *dislocated* as he had. But that old devil culture shock had been creeping along behind him on muffled hooves, lo these many months, and at the sound and smell and sight of so much that was so *American*, he stepped right up and sandbagged Mark behind the ear.

He staggered. He almost went down. He had to take a step back, take a deep breath, reassure himself that this was real, or that he was.

He glanced up. Visible over the door in spillover light from within were the painted words RICK'S CAFÉ AMERICAIN.

What else could it be? he told himself, and walked on in.

He bellied up to the bar, and the words "Hi, guys!" burst out through his shyness, propelled by loneliness and the longing for homelike things.

Conversation died. Faces turned to him. He realized then that many of those faces diverged pretty widely from the human norm. It made no particular impression on him. He had no problem with jokers, and besides, these were *Americans*.

He looked at the bartender. He was a joker, too, a squatty little guy with warty slate-gray skin, stone bald, with a line of fleshy spines running from the top of his head down his back to the tip of a short, heavy tail. He didn't seem to be wearing anything but a grimy barkeep's apron.

"I'd like a Pepsi," Mark said.

" 'He'd like a Pepsi,' " a voice echoed. Mark had done enough time in the schoolyards of his childhood to be all too familiar with that mocking tone. He blinked around, wondering what he'd done.

He was beginning to register a few details his initial rush of homesickness had obscured. Like the poster of Bloat on one wall, like an obscene parody of Buddha. The stern visage of General Francis Zappa affixed to the dartboard with a fistful of darts through his prominent nose. Most alarmingly, the poster of the Turtle floating above the battle lines in Czechago with a peace sign painted on his shell had been crossed out with emphatic slashes of red paint.

A pair of left hands gripped Mark's biceps and spun him around. He found himself looking into a round, malevolent Charlie Brown kind of face, with neutral-colored hair roached up in a butch cut and round wire-rimmed glasses of the kind the kids all called Lennons—what Mark himself was wearing. The overhead light pooled in the lenses and hid the eyes behind.

"You stink like a nat," the round-faced man said, "and you *look* like some kind of hippie."

Mark had been letting his hair grow. He took a breath that was like dry-swallowing aspirin.

The man confronting him folded two sets of arms across his chest. Muscles rolled like billiard balls in the biceps. Below the lower set of arms were two sets of bulges that suggested more pairs of arms concealed under the tan T-shirt.

The sound system was cranking "Sympathy for the

Devil," which Mark didn't think was propitious. "You don't belong here," the round-faced man said.

"Yeah," said a man with a fierce bird's head, white-crested and short-beaked. "This is *our* bar, nat."

"Cut him some slack, Luce," said a man who stood behind the man in the Lennon glasses. He loomed above the rest, at least Mark's height, six-four. He had square-cut brown bangs and dark-prince good looks, though his height and the length of his face and lantern jaw gave him the appearance of Lurch's ingenue brother. He wore a tweed jacket buttoned over a black T-shirt.

He reached over the caterpillar man's top shoulder with a huge, horrible green-on-green-mottled spiky lobster claw, placed the tip under Mark's chin, and tipped Mark's head up. Porcelain-hard spines dug into Mark's flesh.

"W-why did you do that to Turtle's picture?" asked Mark, partially emboldened by the intercession.

Luce's four free hands shoved him in the chest. Hard. He stumbled back away from the claw.

"Are you stoned or just stupid?" Luce demanded. "He sold us out, man!"

"What are you talking about? What did he do?"

Luce looked around at his buddies with an exaggerated expression of disbelief. " 'What did he do?' " he mimicked. "What did he *do*? He only wiped out the fucking Rox. He's only the biggest joker-killer in all *history*, you nat piece of shit! Where have you been, some other fucking planet?"

Well, yes, Mark thought. His lips began to spill denial: "Turtle would never do anything like that, there's got to be some mistake—"

A chuckle fell across anger and exculpation alike. "He doesn't really get it," the tall man said with a lazy smile. "He burned his brain out on drugs a long time back. Just look at him."

His friend's calm voice seemed to drain Luce of rage. He blew out a disgusted breath. "He doesn't look like an objective socialist," he said cryptically, and turned his back. "He's bogus. Get him out of here."

More hands were laid on Mark—purple hands, feathered claw hands, a pair of hands shiny with what looked like mineral oil. He expected the bum's rush back to the street, but instead they propelled him away from the bar, in the general direction of the saloon-style doors.

He figured he had received a pretty clear message, though, so he kept walking that way. He was almost out when a boozy voice hailed him from the dim depths of the bar.

"Where's your hurry, mate? Come along on back. I'll set you straight right quick."

Chapter Eighteen

Heat lightning flashed and grumbled over the Thonburi slums across the Menam Chao Phrya. Sitting in the quietly opulent dining room of the Oriental Hotel, Helen Carlysle set down her wineglass and looked out the floor-to-ceiling windows, out over the terrace toward the river, where the bow-and-stern lanterns of barges bobbed like fireflies.

"I wonder where Lynn and Gary are," she said.

Belew sat back with his arm cocked over the back of his chair. "On a plane for Ankara," he said, and sipped wine.

She looked at him, her eyes huger than usual. "What are you talking about?"

"They packed up their gear and flew out a couple of hours ago."

"What on earth are they doing?"

He smiled into the wine he swirled in his glass. "Following leads, I expect."

"But why—why didn't they tell us?"

"'The gods love the obscure and hate the obvious,' the *Brihadaranyaka Upanishad* tells us. One assumes they had their reasons." He set his wineglass down and signed for the waiter. "Here, you'd best eat something, child. You need to keep your strength up."

Monsoon arrived that night, blowing sheets of rain and white pulses of lightning before it. Belew and Helen made love in her room with the French doors to the balcony wide open, the curtains snapping like banners, the rain splashing across their naked bodies in raw, stinging gouts.

Belew had been the gentlest lover she had known in

142

her limited experience, and far and away the most skillful. Tonight he was wild, obsessed, and the things he did left her shaking and breathing in short, desperate gulps, sure she could not endure any more. But she could; and he drove her again and again to the point of pure overload.

Deep in the night, with her hands twined in fists around the silken bands that bound her wrists to the brass bedstead, she felt his lips go away from her. She moaned, and reached with her hips, and then looked up to see him kneeling Buddha-like between her smooth outstretched thighs, and lightning silvered her skin and his as he quoted again from the *Upanishads*.

" 'This Self is the honey of all beings, and all beings are the honey of this Self,' " he said, and lowered his face into her once more.

"You may wonder," the man at the corner table boomed as Mark threaded his way past the pool table, "why I'm not off in Manila running Flip whores like all the other expatriate Ozzies." He frowned. "Often wonder myself. Habit, mostly, I suppose."

Mark, who was wondering no such thing, stopped by the round knife-scarred table and dithered. "Sit down, sit down. Christ, you make me nervous."

Mark sat. He glanced toward the bar. The dozen or so American jokers there seemed to have forgotten about him. He turned his attention to his host.

He was a vast man, not fat, just big and broad, with a baggy appearance, as if he were losing a grip on his substance, losing cohesion, and was in the process of gradually pooling around his own ankles in the heat. A white linen suit, rumpled and stained, seemed to give him what shape he had. His head was large and square and running into jowls. His eyes were small and blue and set close to a red lump nose. His hair was graying blond, combed over a broad, bald crown and stirring gently in the downdraft from a ceiling fan.

"I'm Freddie Whitelaw," he said, offering a large, damp hand. "I'm a journalist of sorts. What might you happen to be?"

"Mark Meadows. I'm an ace."

Whitelaw settled back in his chair. "Damned lucky on

you you didn't say *that* to the boys at the bar. Things might have gone hard with you. They like aces even less than they like nats."

"Uh, like, who are they?"

"The New Joker Brigade, being recruited to make the Socialist Republic safe for socialism—its two-point-nine-million-man army not being up to the task, apparently. What are you drinking?"

"Pepsi."

Whitelaw's face crumpled in distaste. "Never touch the stuff. God knows it's probably safer than the water. I never touch that either. Waitress! Another gin over here, if you please. And, God help us all, a Pepsi."

"So, why don't, uh, why don't they bother you?" Mark asked. "I mean, you're a nat . . . aren't you?"

"Too right. The reason they don't bother me, my boy, is that I've been here longer than they have. Since '68, in fact."

"In this bar?"

"Much of the time, boy, much of the time. I got here just in time to cover the NLF attack on the American embassy that kicked off the Tet Offensive—not that it was Rick's then; he took it over just a year or so ago, after the government launched this wild card sanctuary scheme. Do you know what? I found that a bar's the very best place to cover a war. Walls tend to keep the bullets off, and sooner or later you hear everything that's to be heard. Damn sight sooner than the American command, I'm bound."

"Weren't you afraid that somebody would bomb the place, man?"

"Heavens, no. NLF drank here too. *Don't shit where you eat*'s a universal principle, my downy-cheeked lad. Besides, the Front was fairly careful to take good care of me; I was on the side of the angels as far as they were concerned. Rising star of the radical press I was in those days, wasn't I just? Always crawling through those wretched Cu Chi tunnels on my hands and knees with Bob Hope afflicting the Yanks with his ghastly jokes right over my head, dashing off to Hanoi to have my photo taken with Jane Fonda, that sort of thing. Those were the days."

The waitress arrived with their drinks. She was a very attractive joker woman, not much taller than the locals, covered with fine golden fur, with pointy ears sticking out through her red-blonde hair, whiskers, and a bushy, tawny tail springing out the back of her short skirt.

"Thank you, Sylvie. You can put it on my tab, there's a love."

She put her hands on her hips. "Rick says no credit," she said in a Scandinavian accent.

"Bloody hell. I've lost my religion; I'm good for it." He dug in his pockets, tossed a handful of coins and bills at her. She scooped them up, curtsied, and left.

"Saucy little minx. I wouldn't mind cleaning *her* fur after the manner of a cat, I can tell you that much." He fixed Mark with a boiled-onion eye. "So, what do you think of our triumphant socialist paradise?"

"Um," Mark said. "They—they've cleaned up the streets. Gotten rid of the pimps and the prostitutes and all."

Whitelaw slammed his hand on the table and guffawed. "You think so, do you? You Yanks! Your naïveté is always so disarming."

He leaned forward and breathed gin across Mark. "Listen well, my ingenuous boy. Just because one doesn't see the Saigon tea—what your media used to call B-girls—any more, just because one doesn't encounter the 'me so horny' sucky-fucky types immortalized in *Full Metal Jacket* and that rap song the new head of your DEA hated so much, does not mean that prostitution has been vanquished. It's alive and well and flourishing on Dong Khoi, just as it did when it was called Tu Do, Freedom Street."

Mark stuck out his underlip rebelliously. To his dismay he had not yet seen much to like in the Socialist Republic. But it did not seem right to just sit by and listen to Whitelaw bad-mouth the place.

"Where are they, man?" he demanded. "I didn't see any."

Whitelaw sat back smirking in triumph. "Oh, I'll just wager that you *did*. Did any young ladies on motor scooters happen to slow down and give you the obvious eye?"

"Yeah," Mark said guardedly.

The Aussie nodded. "And did a pair of young men on another scooter promptly stop beside you to ask if you liked the aforementioned young lady?"

"Oh," Mark said.

"You are learning, my lad. The communists haven't eradicated vice. They've just made it damned inefficient. Like all the other circumstances of life here in Saigon *giai phong*."

"Like, what does that mean, *giai phong*? I thought the town was called Ho Chi Minh City now, but everybody calls it Saigon, and then they tag *giai phong* onto the end, like some kind of religious thing or something."

"You might call it a superstitious thing: *apotropaic*, designed to avert evil—a wonderful word, and God bless you for giving me the pretext for using it. *Giai phong* means 'liberated.' People tack it on when they call the place Saigon to keep from getting in trouble. Nobody but government employees and foreigners calls it Ho Chi Minh City."

Mark sat for a time and nursed his Pepsi and thought about things. He wasn't coming to many conclusions.

"Well, what do *you* think of the revolution here, then?" he finally nerved himself to ask.

"It sucks. It's dirty, inefficient, repressive, regressive, and in my humble opinion is getting ready to blow sky-high. And no, I *won't* keep my voice down. They'd never dare send me to reeducation camp, or even disappear me; I may be a sodden old lush, but I was a damned good journalist in my day, howbeit a soul-purchased one. I know where skeletons are buried all the way from here to Hanoi."

Mark frowned. "Come on, surely it isn't that bad. I mean, look what they're doing for wild cards—"

"Cramming them into a ghetto in Cholon. Recruiting the able-bodied to herd peasants into New Economic Zones, which is a fancy word for *concentration camps*—just like the New Life Hamlets of the late, unlamented South Vietnamese regime. Making propaganda cat's-paws out of the lot of you—"

The double doors opened. Whitelaw broke off and settled back to watch as a big man in a poor-fitting suit entered with a drunkard's shuffle. He had a shock of thick blond hair. His collar was open around his thick neck, and he wore no tie.

The Joker Brigade boys paid him no attention until he came up to the bar and dropped great hairy hands on the shoulders of Luce and his looming buddy with the claw.

"I . . . am *friend*," he announced in a thunderous Russian voice. "I love much American. I love much American joker. We all capitalist *tovarishchy* now, *da?*"

Luce turned to him, round face purpling with fury. "You're a traitor to socialism, is what you are. You're bogus, man. Bogus!"

The tall joker pivoted and drove the tip of his claw into the Russian's midriff. The Russian doubled. Luce clasped his top pair of hands and clubbed him to the floor. The other jokers all clustered around and kicked him until he crawled, moaning, out the door.

"Give Peace a Chance" came up on the box.

The jokers went back to the bar, Luce dusting two pairs of hands together in satisfaction. "That was righteous, Brew. Stone righteous."

"I always thought of myself as a teacher," Brew said, buffing his claw with a bar rag.

"Yeah. You really taught that fucker good," said a purple-skinned man with what Mark thought was severely reduced cranial capacity.

"Never a dull moment when the boys are in town," Whitelaw commented. "Pity they're heading back up-country in a few days."

He tossed off the last of his gin and leaned his elbows on the table. "So tell me, Mr. Mark Meadows. Just what kind of an ace are you?"

Chapter Nineteen

When Helen Carlysle awakened with Thai daylight blasting through the open French doors like laser beams, she was alone. On the pillow beside her where Belew had lain was a note:

> *Don't think ill of me, my child. What I do now, I must do. And what happens next will be for the best.*
>
> *This was never a game you were meant to play in. "Heaven and Earth are not humane," Lao-tzu says. "They regard all things as straw dogs." Go back to your world; fly happy, high, and free. Forget the past, and all else which lies beyond your power to affect. And try—if I may beg a favor—not to think too harshly of me.*

Beside the note lay a single red rose.

She rose, walked nude into the bathroom, spent a very long time washing her face. She took a light robe off its hangar and put it on. Then she came back into the bedroom and sat in a chair by the French doors, letting the smell of sun on wet pavement wash across her on the morning breeze.

She was just sitting there wondering whether to cry or not when the phone rang.

O. K. Casaday was a tall man with a tropical-weight suit hung on broad shoulders and a large and extremely round

head with a fringe of yellow-white hair set on top of a granite slab of jaw. His eyes he hid behind amber shades.

On the phone he had introduced himself as being
"from the embassy." Now he sat across from Helen on the
terrace in the shade of a parasol with his long legs folded
and drummed his fingers on the white tablecloth as if she
had called him here to waste his time.

"Did you call the Governor to confirm my bona fides?"
he asked.

She nodded.

"And did they tell you I was in your chain of command?"

"Yes."

He bobbed his huge head. It reminded her of the
spring-mounted heads of those stuffed puppies in the back
windows of cars. She started to giggle, clamped down on it.
She had a public image to maintain. She was still her father's daughter, even if she'd killed him.

"Are you all right?" Casaday asked, frowning irritably.

She sipped iced water from a cut-crystal goblet. "I'm
fine."

"The first thing I need to know is, where the hell are
those bozos from the DEA?"

"They're gone," she said, drawing pictures in the ring
of condensation the base of the glass had left on the table.

Casaday's shades almost fell off. "Gone? Where the hell
have they gone off *to*?"

"Bob said they went to Ankara. In Turkey."

"I know where Ankara is. Jesus Christ. Whatever possessed those morons to—"

He stopped, swung his head full to bear on her. She
still couldn't see his eyes, but she could feel their awful
pressure. "Bob said. Bob *who*?"

"Belew. J. Robert Belew." She smiled faintly. "To use
your phrase, I guess you could say he's with the embassy
too."

"I guess *not*!" Casaday exploded. "What the hell did
that crazy cowboy sonofabitch have to do with this investi-
gation?"

"He was with us from the outset. He was the one who
got us this far." *Why am I defending him?* she wondered. *He
abandoned me. Like every other man I've . . . cared for.* Yet

he had never promised more than he had delivered, and he had delivered, in his own way, quite a lot.

Casaday had gone dead pale beneath his Southeast Asia Incipient Cancer Tan. "What did you say?" he asked.

"He was with us from Amsterdam on. He was our CIA contact. He took charge of the team, after Saxon and Hamilton messed up two straight grabs on Meadows."

Casaday took a deep breath and shook his head. "I don't know how the fuck stupid you are. Belew is not with Central Intelligence. He had nothing to do with this case. *Nothing.*"

She was glad of his rudeness, his masculine contempt; it helped her pull together. "Mr. Casaday, I am handling this case under contract to the Drug Enforcement Agency. DEA was satisfied with his credentials. It was neither my place nor my right to question his assignment to the team. Now, I would appreciate it very much if you would retract calling me stupid."

"Christ, is this bimbo for *real*?" Casaday murmured under this breath.

A wind began to rise out of the Chao Phrya breeze like Godzilla from Tokyo Harbor. Parasols whipped on their staffs, women cried out as their skirts flew up, a waiter exclaimed as his tray was sucked from his hands in a clatter of breaking china.

O. K. Casaday's tie wound itself around his throat, seemed to be dragging him up out of his chair. It was not tight enough to strangle him, but try as he might, he could force no air into his lungs.

"I am not a bimbo, Mr. Casaday," Mistral said, smiling sweetly. "I am a fully accredited agent of the United States government. I am also an ace. Now, would you like to apologize for your rude and completely uncalled-for personal remarks, or shall I leave you breathless until you lose whatever brain cells you may have remaining?"

Casaday started frantically nodding his head, then shook it just as vehemently. One of the parasol spokes above him gave with a musical ping.

"Which, Mr. Casaday? Does that mean you'll apologize?"

He mouthed the word *yes.*

The whirlwind stopped. The parasol quit flapping.

Casaday fell back into his chair. Immediately he began tearing at his necktie.

Mistral waited primly until he'd cleared himself an airway. "You had something to say to me, I believe?"

A tendril of wind brushed his face. "Yes! I apologize! I'm sorry. Jesus. Believe me, I'm sorry. I take back everything I said about you."

"Very good, Mr. Casaday. I will probably find it unnecessary to file a sexual-harassment complaint against you when I return to Washington. Now, please explain the situation concerning Mr. Belew to me."

"Belew is what we call a cowboy. He's ex–Special Forces, served several tours in 'Nam during the war. Since then he's done a lot of contract work all over the world, for Central Intelligence and free-lance."

"He seems eminently qualified," she murmured. "I see no reason anyone should have questioned his credentials."

"He's a nut, Ms. Carlysle. He thinks he's the last knight in shining armor and he still sees communists under the bed. More to the point, he is not currently in the employment of the CIA. *He has no authorization.*"

There was a time, not long past, when she would have crumpled under the weight of Casaday's revelations. Now she was . . . amused. *I'm beginning to heal*, she thought. She knew who had helped her begin the process.

Helen Carlysle lifted the rose from her lap and twirled its thorny stem in her fingers. "The last knight. Yes, Mr. Casaday, I can see why *you* would have contempt for him."

"Yeah," he said, believing she agreed with his assessment. "He was playing some kind of zany game of his own. He was never on this case. And now—please don't do anything rash here, Ms. Carlysle—now you're off it too."

She looked at him.

He pushed a yellow Western Union slip across the table at her. "You'll find one just like this waiting for you at the front desk. It's from the Governor, and it confirms what I've said.

"Go on back home and spend your paycheck, Ms. Carlysle. Or enjoy beautiful Bangkok a few more days—just as long as you don't start asking any questions. With all due respect for your professional qualifications—and believe me,

I do respect them—you're out of your depth in the phase this game has entered now."

He shook his head. "So are Heckle and Jeckle from the DEA. I wonder what on earth *happened* to those dipshits, anyway?"

At Ankara Customs the neat, swarthy men in tan uniforms and peaked caps that seemed as wide as their shoulders glanced at Saxon's and Hamilton's passports and the holders open to show their DEA shields and murmured, "Please follow us."

The Americans exchanged glances. Saxon shrugged. They followed. Saxon muttered, "We have nothing to worry about. It's all in the bag; we're DEA," to his partner out of the side of his mouth. Hamilton hitched the shoulder strap of his overnight bag up higher on his shoulder and did not look convinced.

They were led to a small room. Though there were only two people in it, it seemed pretty well full already. The man in civilian clothes, fedora, and dark sunglasses didn't take up much space, but the dude standing beside him—in baggy cloth-of-gold pants, blue-and-red vest over hairy bare chest, and an enormous turban on his head—definitely constituted a crowd of one. Especially since his hygiene seemed a little on the questionable side; it was *close* in here.

"Check out this geek with the sofa cushion on his head," Saxon said from the corner of his mouth. He had made a little trip to the bathroom just before landing, and he was feeling fine. Hamilton shushed him frantically.

"I am Colonel Nalband," the man in civilian clothes said. "This is Yaralanmaz, our Turkish national ace. His name means 'invulnerable.'"

Yaralanmaz nodded his extensively turbaned head. "We're honored," Hamilton said.

"Yeah," Saxon said, grinning hugely. "Honored."

His grin shattered when the two uniforms started dipping gloved hands into the pockets of his off-white jacket. "Hey! What the fuck's going on here? We're DEA, damn it. This is bogus, man. Completely bogus."

One of the two uniforms fished out the gold card case Saxon carried but never offered anybody cards from out of his inner pocket, cracked it, glanced inside, and passed it to Nalband. Nalband held up a tiny plastic vial with a bit of white powder drifted at the bottom.

"What might this be, Agent Saxon?"

"Hey, just a sample, you know?" Saxon said, suddenly all smiles again, holding out his palms and being an open, candid guy. "Sometimes we need to, you know, compare, so we can trace the routes the shit's being carried along—"

"Indeed?" the other uniformed Customs officer said. "And is it necessary to carry so very much of it?" He pulled his hand out of Hamilton's bag, which lay open on a table. He held a taped glassine packet crammed full of white powder. "There must be two hundred grams here, Agent Saxon."

Hamilton turned dead white. "That's not m-mine!" he exclaimed.

"It's not mine either," Saxon said, goggling. "Fuck *me*."

Colonel Nalband shook his head. "We were warned you would be trying to smuggle cocaine into the Republic of Turkey. This is a very serious matter. Very serious indeed."

"This is *bullshit*!" Saxon shrieked. "This isn't our shit! We've been set up. And anyway, we're the DEA! You got no fucking *right*—"

"We have every right to interdict criminal activity," Nalband said solemnly. "And when you try to bring drugs into our country, you are nothing better than common criminals."

"You towel-head sons of bitches!" snarled Saxon, and leaped at Nalband.

Yaralanmaz stuck out his hand and pushed against Saxon's sternum. The American flew up into the air and crashed against the wall, his head almost to the dropped ceiling. He hung there for a moment like the Coyote flattened against a cliff by more Roadrunner perfidy, then slid down into a heap.

Nalband produced a compact square-snouted Glock pistol from inside his coat and pointed it at Hamilton. Hamilton held his hands up and said, "No problems." The uniforms cuffed his hands behind his back, then hauled Saxon to his feet and cuffed him too. They had to hang on to him to keep him from sliding back down on his butt again.

"You have undoubtedly heard much of our Turkish prisons, gentlemen," Colonel Nalband said. "Doubtless you will find your stay in them instructive."

Yaralanmaz smiled. His teeth were stained the Turkish national brown from tea and cigarettes. He reached out and tweaked Hamilton's cheek.

"You're cute," he said in a voice like a boulder rolling down a mountain. "You and me will be *good friend*."

Mark accepted the invitation to stay in Whitelaw's flat, which was filled with stacks and stacks of pamphlets and periodicals slowly melting together in the humidity. He still haunted the joker section of the old Chinese quarter Cholon—the joker ghetto, Whitelaw called it—searching for some way to make himself useful.

He was elated to discover there was a clinic in the area. He felt sure it must mirror the function of Tach's Blythe van Rensselaer Clinic in Jokertown. He would certainly find a place there. He would have much to contribute, both his own biochemical expertise and practical advice from watching his friend the Doctor at work. This clinic was operated by the government, so it would undoubtedly be well funded, well run, and open to all.

What he found looked more like the flophouses he knew too well from his early days on the lam in New York than a hospital, and smelled that way too. And the clinic didn't even have any *jokers* in it. It was mainly filled with babies with birth defects and women who had received hysterectomies and were undergoing chemotherapy for choriocarcinoma. They all came from the southern provinces, which had been heavily dosed with Agent Orange defoliant by the Americans during the war. The intense and articulate doctor who took Mark on a tour bitterly drew the obvious connection.

Mark was saddened by the anencephalic babies and the young girls lying two to a bed or on blankets on the floor, most of them bald from the chemotherapy. But he was already familiar with the problem and the possible effects of Agent Orange.

"What about the jokers?" he asked. "There are already thousands of them in Cholon. They have special needs too."

"It's you Americans!" the doctor yelled at him, her

glasses almost flying off her face. "You deny us aid! That's why we don't have the facilities to care for everybody!"

He beat a hasty retreat out onto the sidewalk and the rain.

The men in pith helmets were waiting for him.

Chapter Twenty

A fist slammed into the side of Mark's face. He felt his cheek split. His head snapped sideways until the tendons of his neck stopped it. His brain just kept spinning.

Mark had seen lab rats, picked up inexpertly, frantically propeller their tails in circles. Unless they had their semiprehensile tails curled around something, they felt unmoored, unsafe. Mark felt that way now inside his own head.

Gotta keep conscious, he thought, though he knew deep down that keeping or losing consciousness was a symptom, not something in his control. If you go all the way under after blows to the head, it's a *bad* sign; it usually means there's some crockery broken in there, the movies notwithstanding. Subdural hematoma: brain implosion time.

"You should truly thank us for our grandmotherly kindness," an astringent voice said in precise Vietnamese-accented English, from beyond the blaze of lights that was going to be all Mark could see once he got his eyes open again. "Minh is really being quite gentle with you, comparatively speaking. We have among us as guests citizens of the former People's Republic of Germany who, betrayed by their countrymen, find themselves unable to return home. They are experienced in interrogation, and they have a good deal of frustration to work out."

A pause for a movie-torturer drag on the cigarette Mark could smell. "You don't want to meet them, let me assure you."

Well, you've gone and done it this time, a disapproving

156

voice said from the roaring ringing depths of his skull. *I've always known it would happen.*

It was just Mark's luck that being to all intents and purposes fucked would have the effect of producing in the conspicuously cowardly Cosmic Traveler a curious calm, so that instead of cowering in the back of Mark's head and yammering in terror, he criticized.

Mark tried to hold his head up, but it dipped and wobbled like a kite in the wind, so he let his chin drop to his bare chest. "I don't even know what you want from me," he said through swollen lips.

"The truth." This voice was vibrant, passionate, and All-American. "Who sent you here?"

"Nobody."

Wham. Lights flashed, buzzers went off. The guy with the ham hand must have won a free game with that one.

"That's ridiculous," the All-American said earnestly. "You can't seriously expect us to believe that. Now, let's take it from the top: Who are you?"

"M-Mark," he managed to say. "Mark Meadows."

"What are you?"

"I'm a biochemist. No, don't hit me again—I—I'm an ace too."

"And what were your powers?" the Vietnamese asked.

"I called myself Captain Trips. I had . . . friends."

"If you're Trips," the American said, "where are your potions?"

You had to play it smart, didn't you? the Traveler's voice sneered. *You left us behind.* We're safe here in Vietnam, *you thought. . . .*

Well, so he'd fucked up again; it wasn't as if it was a new experience or anything. He really did figure he'd be all right stashing what remained of the powders he'd whipped up after his Athens score in Whitelaw's digs, and he was wrong again. On the other hand, God alone knew what the minions of the notoriously bluenosed Socialist Republic would be doing to him now if they'd caught him with a fanny-pack full of the most outlandish concatenation of outlaw pharmaceuticals they'd ever seen.

He shook his head. "Don't . . . have any. Gave it up."

A deep chuckle in the voice that belonged to the American. He felt breath on his face, lightly flavored with anise, for God's sake.

"If you are the notorious American ace," the Vietnamese voice hissed in his ear, "who sent you here to spy on us?"

"Nobody, man! I keep telling you. I'm—just—a refugee—"

Time for another allegro for face and fists, fortississimo. *This is another fine mess you've gotten us into,* the Traveler put in between beats of the beating.

For Christ's sake, Trav, J. J. Flash responded, *show some originality. Meadows at least has the sense to play dumb, and God knows he's got practice....*

Do not be cruel, came Moonchild's voice, black silk and silver. *Are we not all one?*

Great, Flash said. *Just what we need: inscrutable Eastern wisdom. If the East's so goddamn wise, how come its anointed representative is doing a bang-tango on our corporate head?*

... Mark became aware the debate was no longer being accompanied on percussion. And there were voices speaking outside the bruised box, his skull.

"—all bullshit, Vo, I'm telling you," the All-American was saying confidently. "He's no ace."

Mark heard a click, smelled a cigarette coming alive, coughed. "We still await the results of the blood tests, Colonel," the Vietnamese interrogator said.

"No, no, no," the All-American said confidently. "I know aces. They're arrogant bastards. No ace would put up with this kind of treatment, I can promise you. Besides, this Captain Trips character is known to be a major druggie. This guy isn't holding squat."

Mark could feel the wind off his headshake. "He's not Captain Trips. He's some random hippie burnout on the run."

A smoky sigh. "As you say, Colonel Sobel. I bow to your superior experience. Very well, Minh: get rid of him."

And just like that he was out on the sidewalk again. Oh, they threw some water over him before they threw him out, and they threw his shirt at him as he stood swaying on the sidewalk in front of the former French villa, blinking in the hot rain and feeling the eyes of passersby all over him.

It could have been worse, he assured his various selves, as he struggled his arms into the sleeves and started buttoning his shirt up crooked. When Vo had told his silent partner with the heavy hands to get rid of him, Mark assumed that meant he was going for a swim in the Saigon River with a brand-new smile beneath his chin. Sometimes it was a relief to be wrong.

"Oh, mama," Flash crooned, *"could this really be the end?*

"To be stuck in Ho Chi Minh City with the Bangalore Blues again."

" 'Bangalore?' " Mark asked aloud. The pedestrians and bicyclists streaming nearest him glanced at him and streamed a little quicker. It was not propitious to tarry near those encountered bloody-headed and talking to themselves in front of this particular address. "I thought that was in India."

You got bangs galore back inside there, wouldn't you say?

Funny, Flash. Real fucking funny.

Oh, dear, Moonchild thought. *I believe we're going to throw up.*

Colonel Vo Van Song, People's Public Security Forces, drew smoke through his black-lacquer cigarette holder. He turned in his chair to gaze out the blinds at the broad, tree-lined avenue outside, and let the smoke out.

"So he is the ace called Captain Trips, after all," he said.

Folded into an uncomfortable French wooden chair, O. K. Casaday grinned. "Don't be too hard on our boy Charles. He's a halfwit, sure. But who'd know Meadows is a real ace just from looking at him?"

Colonel Vo turned to regard his visitor. He had large black eyes, sad and heavy-lidded. His cheeks were hollow, so that the cheekbones formed a tau with his jaws. He had a mouth very reminiscent of a carp's. Jocularly pointing out the resemblance in the mess was not a way for young officers to secure rapid advancement in their careers. Colonel

Vo believed in the axiom *better police for a better police state*, and he believed surveillance begins at home.

Vo and Casaday went back a long way. They had been actual antagonists, back in what both of them, ironically, thought of as the good old days—when they were not so tightly bound about by rules, unlike today, when you had to file a request form two weeks in advance to take a leak.

He had started out as an up-and-coming battalion political officer in a division working the wrong side of the DMZ. It was a job he hated. You faced the same risks as the grunt riflemen, but you got extra headaches. Lots of them.

To be sure, he enjoyed the sinister powers attributed to commissars in Western popular fiction. But the popularizers didn't tell you the *downside*. There were the constant political meetings and self-criticism sessions he had to run, for example, which, not being a complete imbecile, he found as boring as everybody else in the PAVN. He also combined the roles of chaplain and guidance counselor, which meant that everybody in the battalion who had a problem whined about it to *him*. Finally, he was responsible for the performance of the unit in combat as well as out, which meant that his neck was at risk from the blunders of the actual unit commanders, whom he found to be a succession of alternately glory-hungering psychotics and dolts who didn't know which end of Vietnam Hanoi was in.

His own indoctrination had not adequately prepared him for this.

His luck came in at the battle for Hue in 1968. His battalion got chewed up with great revolutionary panache—its current commander was the psychotic type—and he himself took a shell fragment in his shoulder from one of his own side's 130mm field guns—the battery commander was a dolt. It was what the Americans would call a million-dollar wound. It wasn't all that serious, though it hurt like a bastard the first few weeks, and it impressed the higher-ups enough to win him the transfer to Intelligence he'd been maneuvering for.

After some more training, he spent the rest of the war in the south, living undercover, playing spymaster, and generally having the time of his life. Much of his effort had gone into setting up loyal South Vietnamese so that the joint CIA and Special Forces Phoenix program would assassinate them for being part of the NLF infrastructure. O. K. Casaday had been with the Phoenix in those days.

He'd had more hair then.

"It will presumably be more difficult to enlist Dr. Meadows' willing participation," Colonel Vo murmured.

Casaday barked a laugh. He barked everything in fact. He reminded the slim, precise colonel of some kind of great ungainly Western hound.

"Now, Colonel. Sobel may not be the swiftest runner in this foot race, but give the devil his due: he's a charismatic son of a bitch. Some of those monsters of his are right off the Rox, and they think the only good nat's an entree. He's got them eating out of his hand. He can bring Meadows around."

The mirth left his face and he gave Vo a stare hard and flat as a basalt slab. "He'd better, Vo. And if there's any little thing you can do that might give him an edge in recruiting Meadows, you might give serious thought to doing that little thing. My superiors feel Meadows is too prize an asset to let him just slip through their fingers. And with the Soviets withdrawing aid, and the Chinese openly arming your nut-cutting enemies the Khmer Rouge, and your own rebels running wild out in the Delta and up in the Highlands, this is not a time to be losing influential friends, is it, old pal?"

There is something almost refreshing about the American lack of subtlety, Vo thought. Still, Casaday was doing little more than retailing the unattractive truth. The money and power of the group Casaday represented were vital to the survival of the Socialist Republic. They also had come to form the matrix in which Vo's own power structure was implanted.

He sighed smoke through his nostrils. "I will see to it, Mr. Casaday. You are perfectly correct about Colonel Sobel's powers of persuasion." Sobel's silver tongue had been vital in bringing his own superiors around, money or no money. Vo's masters liked wild cards little better than Casaday's did, though they were nowhere near as hipped on the subject.

Casaday grinned and bobbed his huge head. "Great. It'll be good to get a major ace on board. Most of these monsters don't have much firepower, unless you count the ability to make their enemies puke their guts up."

"Much as I hate to raise continual objections," Vo said, "I must also point out that Colonel Sobel is recruiting a new *joker* brigade. Dr. Meadows is no joker, and it's my understanding that Sobel's recruits care little enough for nats, much less nonjoker aces."

"Do I have to handle everything around here?" Casaday threw up his hands. "This all seems simple enough to me. The party line is, Meadows is a fugitive from American nat injustice, just like all the other pusbags. If the Establishment will lean that hard on a blond and blue-eyed nat like him, who knows what they'll do to jokers who look like detached hemorrhoids? You sell that line to Sobel, he sells it to the monsters. You play it right, it'll motivate 'em to fight *harder*."

He rose, sauntered to the window to loom down at the passersby teetering their bikes through the rain, holding black umbrellas overhead with one hand, their wheels spraying mud in their wake.

"What a hoot," he said. "Sobel and his crazies think you're empowering oppressed wild cards here. Little do they know we're setting them up to take a big fall. And *you* get to use them for expendable muscle, into the bargain.

"This is a beautiful goddam scheme, Vo, just beautiful. We can't lose here. We just can't lose."

Chapter Twenty-one

"No," Freddie Whitelaw was saying, "they weren't abusing you for being a Westerner. If they were going to do that, they'd have called you *Lien Xo*, don't you see?"

Mark eyed him through the mid-afternoon murk of Rick's Café Americain. The boys from the New Joker Brigade had not begun to filter in yet from wherever they spent their mornings after Rick shut down at dawn. Rick himself was puttering behind the bar, polishing glasses and occasionally scratching at his fleshy spines. None of his all-joker staff had arrived. The ceiling fan redistributed the thick, muggy air, but it took a determined imagination to feel cooled by it.

"What does that mean?" Mark asked the Australian. He was nursing a bottled melon-juice drink imported from Tashkent, in the Soviet Union. It was quite good.

" 'Crooked allies,' more or less. It actually refers to Russians. Over the years they've come to apply it to round-eyes in general. Just another legacy of their revolution, you might say."

"Oh. Well, what did what they called me mean, then?"

" 'Devil.' They saw you coming out of the Wild Cards Affairs office by the embassy and reckoned you were a wild card, mate—which indeed you are. So they chucked rocks at you and ran."

Mark's brows contracted in a look of pain. "But, *why*, man? I mean, Vietnam is a *sanctuary* for wild cards. We're supposed to be *welcome* here."

"That's the official government line—and, my son, if you suspect the government of genuine humanitarian mo-

163

tives, you're overdue for further disappointment." He laughed and shook his great head, jowls waggling. "But no matter the official line on wild cards, the hearts and minds of the people are rather hard to order about—as you Americans have reason to remember. Asians don't as a rule like people who look different than they do; they're a lot touchier than even your more bigoted Westerners on that score. Wild cards tend to be a *lot* different, but still essentially human in form. That riles 'em the more, don't you see?"

Mark shook his head. He didn't see. For most of his life he had been told that America was the most racist society on Earth. He had also been told it was the most violent society on Earth. The reality of the Third World—where the single politician most widely and universally admired was Adolf Hitler—hit him like a freight train. It was, in truth, like Takis, but grubbier.

Even Europe, older, more cultured, infinitely more supercilious Europe, was little better than America. Violence against wild cards was less common there—or at least less open. But he had gotten the impression that the same hatred and resentment seethed there, held below the surface mainly by traditions of sullen subservience. The new European Community demagogues were far different creatures than Leo Barnett; they spoke of justice for all, wild cards included, but when Mark tried to translate their caring rhetoric into images, what kept springing to his mind were concentration camps.

The defect, he had long since decided, must lie within him. Too many social commentators had extolled the virtues of the Third World as opposed to the decadence and materialism of America. The death of Starshine had robbed him of his idealism, he feared, and that was why he was blind to those virtues.

He sighed and was about to comment on the death of his ideals, when the saloon-style doors swung open and Luce and Brew came in, looking oddly subdued. They were followed at once by a tall man in khaki PAVN walking-out dress. He topped the ensemble with a billed American-style officer's cap and Douglas MacArthur sunglasses, and he carried his fine head at a chin-jutting angle.

For some reason Mark grew cold. Voices began to yammer deep inside his mind.

"Uh, Freddie," he whispered, "who's the dude with the scrambled eggs on his hat?"

Freddie showed him a loose, lopsided grin. "Why, that's himself, of course. Colonel Charles Loyalist-Without-a-Cause Sobel."

For a large and habitually inebriated man Whitelaw had good reflexes. He caught Mark's sleeve before the American was halfway out of his chair. His grip was very strong.

"For God's sake, man, calmly, calmly," Whitelaw said, mopping his expansive forehead with a handkerchief so mottled it appeared to sport a desert camouflage pattern. "You look as if aliens had just abducted you aboard their starship."

"No," Mark said firmly, his eyes never leaving Sobel, "that happens to me all the time. It's no big deal. Getting rousted by the fuzz and beaten up in some cellar—*that* really shakes me, man."

Whitelaw gave him an eye like a sacred carp's, which Mark did not notice.

"You've nothing to be afraid of, man," Whitelaw settled on saying. In their several days' association the expatriate American had displayed a propensity for saying in an offhand way things which were decidedly unsettling even for a journalist with upward of twenty years' experience in Southeast Asia. Despite his journalist's instincts—which gin and years of party-line subservience evolving gradually into encompassing cynicism had not entirely dulled—Whitelaw was not certain he always wanted to know exactly what Meadows was talking about.

Mark was still struggling feebly, restrained more by the need not to draw attention to himself than by Whitelaw's grip. "You said he wouldn't come in here!"

"That's not what I said. I said it didn't *matter* where you were, because if the estimable Colonel Vo of the PPSF wanted your skinny Yank posterior, he'd send his bully boys to fetch it back no matter where you were; you're not precisely *inconspicuous*. So you are as safe here in the comparative cool of Rick's absorbing the benefits of my extensive experience as anywhere else."

Mark allowed himself to be pulled back down in his chair. "But to have *him* here—"

"The same things I said about Vo apply, my nervous

young son. In the matters at hand, Sobel's will and Vo's are one. They are like"—he held up crossed fingers—"this."

"Well . . . okay. If you say so, man." His tone made it clear that it would all be Whitelaw's fault if Sobel set his pit-bull jokers on him.

As Mark was nervously eyeing the bar, where Sobel, Brew, and Luce had been joined by the feathered man, the joker with the purple skin and hair, and the one who seemed constantly to drip with oil, the television suddenly drew his eye.

He swallowed. There was the red-bearded face of Thomas Marion Douglas. Except it wasn't; it was Kurt Russell, starring in Oliver Stone's new film *Destiny*. He was onstage, dry-humping the mikestand in his trademark leather pants before throngs of screaming fans. And suddenly his head and shoulders blurred, became the king-cobra hood of the Lizard King.

And there it was, the inevitable confrontation in People's Park: Douglas bending the barrel of a .50-caliber machine gun mounted on a National Guard armored personnel carrier—Douglas struck down from behind by the wrench of the ace called Hardhat, played by Charles Bronson—the wrench upraised again, abruptly entangled by a golden peace symbol at the end of a golden chain. A quick cut to Jeff Fahey as Douglas' unexpected savior, the radiant golden ace, the Radical.

Which was to say, Mark Meadows in his first drug-induced ace persona.

He was sitting there feeling dislocated again when a sense of *presence* invaded the table. Both men turned to see the colonel himself looming over them.

"Comrade Whitelaw, Dr. Meadows," Sobel boomed. "May I sit down?"

"Certainly, Colonel," Whitelaw said as Mark looked daggers at him. "Be our guest. Take a load off."

Mark clamped his lips shut. There was nothing to say, and he didn't want Cosmic Traveler saying it.

He could feel both the Traveler and J. J. Flash ripping at him for leaving his powders back at Whitelaw's digs again. But his "friends" could only protect him for an hour at a time, and if he summoned them too frequently, the physical and psychological aftershocks became severe in a hell of a hurry. If ever he used the powders to escape an official arm of the Socialist Republic—which the American Sobel, somehow, was—he was a fugitive again. And he had no place left to run.

If he was unsafe in this official preserve of the wild cards, he had decided, he would simply have to face his fate.

Which was now settling itself in a chair with its back turned toward the table and its arms resting across it—a jarringly folksy touch in one who cultivated such frosty military dignity.

"Dr. Meadows," Colonel Sobel said, "I owe you an apology. If you ask Comrade Whitelaw, here, he'll tell you how rare that is."

"Almost unheard of," Whitelaw intoned, with an undertone of irony that Mark caught but which seemed to elude the colonel.

Sobel nodded grandly. "We simply were unsure who and what you were, Doctor. If you were what we were afraid you were, you would pose an intolerable threat to the revolution here. You understand that, surely?"

"Sure," Mark lied.

"The Wild Cards Bureau has your blood tests back. We're satisfied you're who you claim to be. I understand you're looking for a way to serve the revolution, son."

"Uh, I'd like to be of help to the Republic somehow. I'd like to help the jokers—"

"I'm here to offer you the opportunity to do just that, my boy. What better way than by lending your unique talents to our New Joker Brigade?"

Mark blinked. "But I—I'm not a joker. Sir."

"No. But we're not prejudiced." Mark knew damned well better than that, but he was also not about to interrupt Sobel in order to contradict him. "We're fighting for the rights of all wild cards; we're making our first stand here, and in the end we will rise up and take the world by storm. We also offer a chance to atone for our collective guilt as Americans, for our rape of this land and its people, and our crimes against their great revolution."

Mark's throat was dry. Sobel's words buzzed in his head like bees, like the head rush from a whiff of coke. Face-to-face, the man had a compelling quality, an emanation that swept objections away.

"I'm a lover, not a fighter, sir," he managed to stammer.

"I understand you were a peacenik, boy. And God knows you were on the side of the angels, opposing America's making war against the righteous revolution here in Vietnam. But *la lucha continua*, boy, especially now with the forces of reaction apparently triumphant on every side: we're in a war, a just and historically necessary war. Under these circumstances pacifism is bourgeois decadence. It's a luxury the committed can't afford."

"Oh, wow," Mark said.

Sobel leaned away from the chair back with an indulgent chuckle. "Besides, I understand some of your 'friends'—perhaps I should call them *comrades*, eh?—"

In a pig's ass you can call me *comrade*, J. J. Flash thought furiously, with Traveler a beat behind.

"—have been known to show a pugnacious streak, have they not? You've struck blows in the good fight before, my boy. Why not join us, where those blows can do some good?"

"Now, Colonel," Whitelaw drawled, "surely you're aware that in order to exercise his powers, the ace known as Captain Trips made use of certain chemicals whose very possession is looked on most unkindly by the Socialist Republic. Dr. Meadows is a man intent on living fully within the laws of the Republic. You wouldn't be trying to set him up, now, would you?"

"What are you driving at?" Sobel demanded. Mark could feel the officer's glare through his glasses.

Whitelaw bore its full force with fine alcoholic insouciance. "I don't think Dr. Meadows can take your offer very seriously without a few guarantees as to his legal status, Colonel."

Sobel barked a laugh. "You're not trying to *bargain*, here, are you, Whitelaw? I know your political credentials are beyond reproach, but you're still a damned journalist."

"Yes, and I know you still blame journalists for making you lose a war you claim should never have been fought. You Yanks are a complicated lot, Colonel. As for me, let's say that Meadows is an innocent—though he's not a fool, and you judge him so at your risk. Innocence is a rare commodity in this bad old world, Colonel. By trying to keep innocence from injury, I'm looking to atone for a few sins of my own, perhaps."

"But you've always been a loyal friend of the revolution," Sobel said uncomprehendingly.

"Precisely."

Sobel shook his head, shedding Whitelaw's words like water. "Dr. Meadows, this isn't like back home, where the bourgeois bleeding hearts are always interfering with the doing of what's right. If you join the revolution, in the form of my Joker Brigade, what you do in service of the revolution is your glorious duty, not a crime. If you're an ace, we want you. We *need* you. What do you say?"

Mark took a breath. "I'll have to think about it."

Sobel's mouth tightened. He was not a man accustomed to being put off. He relaxed with a visible effort.

"All right. Hell, I understand. You know this isn't the kind of commitment to be entered into lightly. I respect that."

He rose. "I'll be in town for a day or two yet. If you come to a decision"—he pointed with his head—"the boys at the bar know where to find me.

"But just remember, if you're serious about helping the cause of the wild cards, not just here but around the world, this is your best shot at it. Gentlemen."

He nodded to Whitelaw and walked away. He paused to speak to Brew and Luce and the others and left the bar.

"Bloody hell," Whitelaw said. He signaled Rick for another gin.

"So, like, what do you think?" Mark asked. Brew and Luce were looking at him appraisingly, and without any real obvious friendliness.

"It's not my decision, cobber," Whitelaw said.

"I know that, man. But I could use, like, some *perspective*."

Rick arrived with a tray bearing a gin and another Tashkent melon drink. He set the glasses down and left without speaking. Whitelaw sighed.

"Fair enough, mate, fair e-bloody-nough. Turning down our friend the colonel is not a decision to be taken lightly either; as I think I mentioned, he and Colonel Vo of the not-so-secret police are thick as thieves. And you've been rattling around Saigon—sod a bunch of *giai phong*—for days now trying to get the government to give you something to *do* for your fellow wild cards. Well, old son, I think you can regard this as a clear and unambiguous signal of what it is the government has in mind for you to do."

"Which means—"

"You've got damn-all of a chance they'll give you any kind of Cholon Jokertown Clinic, unless you can convince the American government to pony up some serious loot— unlikely in view of President Bush's avid desire to bestow a hundred billion dollars to keep Comrade Gorbachev the Tsar of All the Russias, not to mention your own status as a federal fugitive."

"So you think—"

"I think you'd be bloody daft to go marching off with Colonel Up-the-Revolution Sobel and his merry men. On the other hand, I can't say it would be right sane to tell him to piss off, either."

He leaned his thick forearms on the table. "If that strikes you as ambiguous, lad, then welcome to the real world."

Whitelaw's flat was in a gerrymandered old French villa in a rundown part of Saigon *giai phong*, not that Mark had yet found any parts that weren't. Mark was wandering in the general vicinity and the rain, with a newspaper held over his head. A procession of ancient black Chevies, huge and bulbous, cruised solemnly by. Mark caught a glimpse of a timidly lovely woman in Western bridal white in the back of one.

He was having what you call your crisis of conscience.

If Starshine had still been alive, Mark would have said yes to Sobel in a second. Starshine had constantly been after Mark to use his skills in the service of social justice and had taken whatever opportunities he got to crusade against a world of ills. Mark had of course begun the whole psycho-chemical quest in order to become a fighter for the good, to walk once again the path of the Radical. But once he'd succeeded, if not exactly the way he wanted to, once his "friends" had started to manifest themselves, he had found it wasn't quite that simple to save the world. Much of the world didn't really want to be saved, and it was hard to bull your way in there and save it anyway without lots of the wrong people getting hurt—nor was Mark, the Last Hippie, comfortable with the notion that there were right people *to* hurt. And Starshine had proven, by his occasional one-hour flyers at stamping out injustice, that there wasn't necessarily all that much even the most powerful metahuman could do.

By himself, anyway.

The crusading part of Mark was gone, now, though, the tough-love part determined to save the world despite itself. So Mark had thought. Yet Sobel's words had struck *something* within the soul of him and made it ring like a great brass bell.

An iron core of stupidity is more like it, Jumpin' Jack Flash told him.

He shook his head, which caused the paper to buckle, dumping a load of water stained black by printer's ink down the back of his neck. Sobel was right in a lot of ways. The world was turning savage toward the wild cards, anyone could see that. Mark's own flight, across space and across the Earth's own tortured surface, was proof of that.

But Mark couldn't help remembering—with a little help from his friends—words of old songs, words about money for people with minds that hate, and how revolution was just power changing hands. Did he really want to buy into everything Sobel was saying? Wasn't there some other way to help the wild cards?

About then he looked down the street to see a man walking toward him. A stocky man who, while much shorter than Mark, stood tall among the Vietnamese pedestrians. A man with a dark-blue polymer rain jacket around his square shoulders and a New York Yankees cap on his square head, shedding the rain from his fine waxed seal-brown mustache.

A man Mark Meadows recognized as Randall Bullock.

Mark wasn't carrying his vials of powder, but he had much the longer legs. He turned and made good use of them.

Two hours later he was huddled in the back of a venerable American deuce-and-a-half with a half-dozen damp and apprehensive jokers, listening to the monsoon beat on canvas as the truck ground north toward Fort Venceremos, the Joker Brigade's stronghold at the base of the Central Highlands.

Chapter Twenty-two

This is another fine mess you've gotten us into.

Mark Meadows sighed, dug the point of his shovel into red clay still slimy from the rain that was giving them a brief respite, and leaned on the handle.

Quit your bitching, Jumpin' Jack Flash said in his mind. *You make a pretty ridiculous Oliver Hardy, Trav. It's not like we're doing the actual digging.*

It's our body becoming unduly exhausted, our body being callously abused, the familiar and seldom welcome voice of Cosmic Traveler persisted. *Look at your hands, man. They're a mass of blisters.*

I can heal them. It was Moonchild, her thoughtstream cool and soothing as the waters of a stream. *It is my power to heal us.*

Yeah? Traveler thought savagely. *God knows what kind of horrible infections there are in this cesspool. You can heal wounds, you addled Asian bimbo. You aren't Ms. Immune System. . . .*

"For God's sake," Mark said aloud, "will all of you just *shut up?*" From the furthest recesses of his mind he could detect the formless surge and mutter of Aquarius. He was lost in his dolphin-dreaming again, which was fine with Mark: Aquarius would disapprove of what he was doing now, on the grounds that he disapproved of *everything* landlings did. At least Mark didn't have to hear about it.

Starshine, on the other hand, would have unleashed a tirade about the inherent nobility of manual labor and damned them all as spoiled materialists; for once Mark would have welcomed his bombast as he raked the Traveler roundly over the coals ... he felt an emptiness within, a sense of teetering on the edge of some abyss. It was a mystery to him, and no less to the mind doctors of Takis with their accumulated millennia of lore and experience, how he could have survived the violent death of one of his "friends." He had the feeling, when he permitted himself to dwell on it, of living on borrowed time, living within his own bubble of virtual reality that might contract back to nothingness at any moment, taking him—or at least his mind—with it.

—A hot drop of rain struck him on the cheek. Well, he hadn't done a black-hole dive over the event horizon just yet. The others attacking the earth with pick and shovel and filling sandbags with the excavated soil were all jokers and had yet to speak a word to him, civil or otherwise. The way they were eyeing him now suggested they didn't appreciate him taking a break with most of the bunker left to dig and the monsoon rain about to squat on them again.

He smiled and bobbed his head foolishly at them, grabbed his shovel, and bent to work. He made himself ignore the pain in his shoulders and back and knees. The voices in his brain he just tuned down.

Fort Venceremos didn't look much like a fort to Mark. It looked like a movie set. It consisted mainly of ranks of olive-drab tents and sandbagged bunkers that were, he gathered, slowly spreading outward from the parade ground in the middle, with its podium and its flagpole flying the yellow-star-on-red-ground flag of the Socialist Republic. Paddy land surrounded the fort's wire-tangle perimeter, pool-table flat and well-drowned with the monsoon. Hills several hundred meters high, perfectly conical and an almost painfully intense green, stuck up seemingly at random from the midst of them. When the truck clattered in through the wire, the clouds had broken briefly to let some orange sunset beacons flash through the ramparts of the *Giai Truong Son*, the Central Mountains to the west, and set the sides of the hills alight.

Off to the north, according to the conversation Mark overheard—none was directed toward him during the entire day and a half they'd spent grinding up the coast on Highway One—lay Da Nang, its giant American-built airbase still intact and still jointly occupied, despite the general collapse of the USSR's overseas empire, by Soviet Frontal Aviation as well as by the Vietnamese. A few klicks behind them lay the coastal town of Tam Ky.

The ride up from Ho Chi Minh City had been frequently punctuated by bouts of waiting in the red laterite that sloped the paved highway, while military convoys rumbled past in the rain and the deuce-and-a-half sank to its hubs again. Mark's dozen joker fellow passengers were all Americans—with the possible exception of a pair who said nothing and, by the look of them, might not have been able to—and none of them was familiar, from Rick's or elsewhere. The ones who could bitched mightily at the delays, at the way their hosts failed to appreciate the sacrifices they were willing to make on their behalf, and especially when it came time to push the truck out of the mud and onto the cracked blacktop yet again.

Mark willingly if ineffectually took his place at the bumper and heaved. Of his remaining friends the only one strong enough to be a lot of help probably wouldn't, so Mark figured their identities as well as his should all better just be kept quiet for the moment.

After allowing the weary mud-caked passengers a brief and unpromising look at their new home, darkness and the rain descended pretty much simultaneously. Mark was processed with the rest, assigned temporary quarters, and sent off to the mess tent, without a single friendly or even neutral word or glance—except from the quartermaster clerk, a bespectacled black with a cone-shaped body and no perceptible legs, who pushed himself around the raised-plank floor of the Q.M. tent on a cable-spool end mounted on casters, and was almost tearily grateful that Mark would not require any alterations to his issue fatigues.

Fashionably attired in American O.D. trousers and blouse of unguessable age, which left his ankles and wrists well bare but, of course, bagged substantially at belly and butt, Mark sloshed off toward the mess tent. The meal was tough boiled pork and rice, dished up by jokers who were sullen even to their fellows and who seemed to have been chosen for their unappetizing appearance. Mark didn't exactly think it was a balanced meal, but he didn't complain. He sat by himself and ate with good appetite, as befit a man who'd done his time in the chow lines of innumerable midnight missions, and then went off to the flooded tent he shared with a joker who glared wordlessly at him from a face like a giant bristlecone as he came in.

On the whole, he decided, squishing around on his cot trying to get less uncomfortable, being in the New Joker Brigade was a lot like being on the Rox. Bad accommodations, bad food, and nobody around who didn't hate him on sight: perfect. There was even the lingering feeling of being under siege, though all those tanks they'd passed on Highway One—that had passed them, really—riding on the beds of semitrailers with their long guns trailed and covered, were ostensibly on *their* side this time.

At least there were no roving bands of psychopathic kids who could flip you out of your body and into God knows what on a whim. And there was no Blaise.

Blaise. . . . The sun had probably gone down long since, but here with the monsoon sweeping inland off the South China Sea it was still hot. The thought of Tachyon's grandson did what the night and rain could not: cooled him to the marrow.

Blaise the beautiful boy, Blaise the prodigy of mental power. Blaise the sociopath, murderer, and rapist, who had committed crimes unimagined on Earth or even on Takis, where they had even more practice at that sort of thing. Blaise the Hitler wanna-be, who had come within an ace— two aces and a Takisian prince trapped in an Earth woman's body, to be more precise—of conquering Takis. Not with his unprecedented mind powers, but with a handful of political clichés so threadbare they didn't even try them on at Berkeley anymore. Psi-power giants Takis had known and dealt with before, but its ancient culture lacked any antibodies to everyday Earth demagoguery.

He thought of K. C. Strange, and he thought of Roxalana. Women who, God knew why, had found something in him worth loving and nurturing amid alien surroundings—on the whole, he thought, it was pretty much a toss-up between Takis and the Rox for *alienness*.

He thought of Sprout, his lost daughter. He wondered what she was doing. It was morning in California, probably—he was doing well if he knew what the time was where he was at any given moment. She would be getting up and dressing herself with her persnickety little-girl care,

and combing her golden hair—long when he'd seen it last—
and getting ready to go off to the special school Mark's father was sending her to.

Will I ever see her again? he wondered. And then,
much worse: Should *I?*

For all their differences Mark's father was a man of
ironclad character, with both the advantages and disadvan-
tages that entailed. He had promised Mark that Sprout
would receive the best of care, and Mark knew that this
would happen.

Mark had always spurned materialism and the pursuit
of gain. Of course that was before spending weeks on skid
row and months on the lam. It was easy to sneer at comfort
when you weren't lying on a soaking-wet cot with the monsoon pounding on the canvas over your head and dead bugs
and lumps of Christ-knew-what bobbing around in the
ankle-deep water.

Maybe Kimberly Anne, his former wife, his lost beloved Sunflower, had been right all along. He had always
given Sprout all the love in the world, no one could say otherwise. But Beatles songs notwithstanding, love ain't all you
need.

General Meadows could provide the child material security and comfort greater than anything her father had ever
been able to offer her. But he would also see that she did
not lack *love*, and the knowledge that she was wanted.

She's better off where she is, Mark thought, and shifted
miserably. On the other cot his tentmate grumbled and blew
like a surfacing walrus. *She probably doesn't even think
about me anymore. . . .*

He wandered away into sleep. In the morning they
blew him out of bed with a tape-recorded bugle and handed
him a shovel.

The rains fell back to regroup in late afternoon—not
their usual pattern, Mark gathered. To his surprise the Joker
Brigaders turned dark looks to the semiclear skies. He himself would've felt like singing from the sight of open sky and
the sun just falling down into clouds that seemed to have
been poured across the western mountains like cement, except that he barely had the energy left to hold up his head.

Chow tonight was rice and fish parts. Mark's messmates bitched considerably about the fare. It tasted *just fine* to Mark.

After dinner jokers wearing red armbands chased everybody out into the red mud of the parade ground for political education. "Goddamn," he heard a joker say whose head was covered with skin folds like a Shar Pei's. "It ain't enough we have to dig in the rain. But then the storm goes away the minute we knock off and we have to haul our sorry asses out here to get lectured at."

Instantly two large and menacing young jokers appeared to either side of the complainer. "Showin' signs of antisocial tendencies, are we, bud?"

"Bourgeois tendencies," the older of the pair said.

"Whatever. Sounds like you're in need of a few good self-criticism sessions, help get your mind right."

Mark moved away quickly, feeling cowardly for doing so. He thought the man was being unfair, complaining like that—they'd all volunteered, after all, and Mark reckoned it was standard Midnight Mission rules: you want to eat the soup, you got to hear the sermon. All the same, he wasn't eager to find out just what *self-criticism sessions* were all about.

For once, you're acting sensibly, Mark, Traveler's voice said in his skull. *My, those two were quick off the mark, weren't they?*

Mark's spirits sank into his muddy boots. The Traveler approved his actions. Now he *knew* he was chickenshit.

The clouds still clustered thickly overhead, blotting most of the stars. Mark had come to terms with the night and the stars, back on that Aegean island where he'd had no choice but to confront them. Sort of. He still was not heartbroken when overcast hid the stars.

They assembled in ranks facing the podium, several hundred strong—Mark had never been good at estimating crowd numbers. Mark thought he could make out a substantial split in the social structure. About a third of the crowd had at least a foot on the lower rungs of middle age, or were right up on the ladder, like Mark himself. The rest were young and intense, though in a lot of them the intensity showed in the way they joked and grab-assed with each other.

Then there was Mark. Here and there a man who'd

pulled extreme height out of the wild card deck stood above
the rest, one nearly ten feet tall and covered with what
looked suspiciously like rough bark, and green leaves instead of hair; another, seven feet tall and even skinnier than
Mark, his skin covered in giraffe dapples, but dark purple on
mauve. Mostly though, Mark towered above this mob as he
towered above most. Which made him a conspicuous minority of one, the only nat in sight.

Until Colonel Charles Sobel appeared, marching from
between the tents as if he were headed to shake hands with
Black Eagle himself, trailing a retinue like the late, great
Emperor Bokassa's cape. He mounted the podium and took
his place behind the lectern. Brew and Luce, Luce in his
customary T-shirt with the extra armholes and Brew dressed
as if he were headed out nightclubbing after the camp
meeting was done, took positions flanking him on the dais.

"Be seated, comrades—and I'm proud to use the term."
Sobel's voice rolled out of the speakers like warm motor oil.
"Don't worry, you don't have to sit at attention."

That provoked a ripple of laughter, probably from guys
in armbands, the cynical J. J. Flash facet within Mark
thought. From somewhere in the audience a voice rang out,
"How about sittin' in chairs?"

Luce thrust his round face forward. "The revolution
isn't about your personal comfort, buddy," he snarled.
"That's bogus. If you can't stand a little inconvenience,
maybe you better start walking back to your white-bread
world to be a doormat for the nats again—"

Sobel held up a hand. "Here, Lucius, I've got it. I understand a lot of you men—and you are *men*, more so than
the nats who look down upon you—are new among us. You
maybe aren't sure what you're doing here. What's expected
of you, what you can expect.

"I can answer both questions simply enough. What's
expected of you? Everything you've got. To give less than
maximum effort is to sell out to the oppressor.

"As to what to expect, one word will suffice: *victory*."

The applause was fuller-bodied this time, and at least
some of it was sincere. Mark still heard scattered catcalls,
saw guys making jackoff gestures.

The Colonel stood with his hands resting on the podium, smiling over his jutted chin, waiting for the noise to

dwindle. "I look out this evening and see many new faces, many recent recruits to our cause. I know my words strike some of you as empty rhetoric. All your lives you've been bombarded with empty promises from politicians and glossy Wall Street come-ons. You've earned your right to skepticism, no doubt about it.

"Now, I'm a pretty fair country speaker"—the armband boys laughed dutifully, though Mark wasn't sure what the joke was—"but I also know how closely I fit the profile of the Oppressor: a white, a nat, a man. An authority figure. But there is one among us—one of *you*—whose gift it is to show you the truths which underlie my words.

"Comrades, it is with pride I present to you—*Eric Bell!*"

Much of the crowd erupted in cheers—the watchful old-timers, Mark saw. His recent ride-mates just stood there with *oh, please* expressions on.

A person stepped up onto the platform from behind. Smiling grandly, Sobel stepped back and nodded him to center stage, out front of the podium. He was slender, dressed in a Bruce Springsteen T-shirt and jeans, and by the way he moved, he was way young. But his face was horribly disfigured, a brutal animal jut of muzzle and brows.

He held out his hands. The crowd fell quiet, even the cynical new arrivals, leaving the Wurlitzer automatic accompaniment of the little generator that powered the P.A. *thump-thumpa*-ing along in the background.

It was as if somebody had dropped a movie screen just behind Mark's eyes. He saw an island by night. On that island was a fantasy castle, a wonderland of towers and domes and battlemented walls. But a giant had come to fairyland and stomped it proper; the towers were fallen, the glittering domes crushed.

Then Mark took in the surroundings, the dark clifflike shapes on the land surrounding, sprayed with myriad lights. The skyline of Manhattan. *My God, that's the Rox!* Mark thought. *But it's so changed.*

It was about to change again. Gleaming white in the moonlight, a mobile cliff of water rushed down the Hudson. Straight for Ellis Island.

Floating above the wave was Turtle's unmistakable battleship-plate shell.

A moan rose from the crowd as the *tsunami* struck the Rox like God's own bulldozer. Upon the face of the waters lay chaos. Below them, nothing could still live.

"Look," the young man said in a voice that didn't need an amplifier. "*See*. As I saw. Bloat sent me away from the Rox, away from my comrades, my fellow jokers, though I begged to be allowed to stay and share their fate. He sent me away so that I could see this thing done—and so that, through me, you could see it too."

The crowd was raging, screaming, shaking fists and less conventional appendages in the air. Mark hunched his head between his shoulders and wanted to vomit. All he could think of was the half-remembered words from the radio cast of the *Hindenburg* disaster—"Oh, my God, the humanity, the humanity!"

—That wasn't true. For all his horror and shame there was room in his guts for the realization that his unaltered human appearance marked him in this crowd, as if three sixes glowed upon his forehead.

"But that was not all Bloat wished for me to show you. My friends, I do not come to ask your pity," the young man said. "I don't even come to ask for your anger. I ask of you just one thing. In the word of the immortal John Lennon— *imagine.*"

"A better world," Sobel intoned. And Mark saw—*a better world.*

A city loomed in the distance, across a techno-horror landscape of dead cars glistening like chrome beetles in the sun, with tall stacks violating the sky in the background, dark smoke for come.

He was aware of Sobel's words blowing through his brain like the finest Thai stick, but they left no mark. As he watched, the jumbled car bodies faded, vanished, leaving a field of purple and yellow wildflowers that rippled like a flag. Then the stacks disappeared, and redwoods stretched sunward in their place. At last the steel-and-glass towers of the city shimmered and were gone, leaving a small thatched-hut village on a hill. Healthy tan-cheeked people worked in gardens and carried water up the hill in wooden buckets. Looking closer, you could see they all were jokers, happy, free, and unafraid.

It was so beautiful, he could barely breathe. He felt his eyes fill with tears.

Rain struck his cheek, warm as spittle. He blinked, and once again he was seeing the close-packed ranks of jokers and a sky beginning to congeal again with night and storm.

"That's the true legacy of the Rox," Eric said. His voice seemed a whisper, but it carried to the roots of the distant mountains.

"You've seen the vision now that we're all striving for," Sobel was saying. "All the people in harmony, with the Earth and with each other, striving shoulder to shoulder for the common good, not selfish gain."

Sobel had more words to say, but they were anticlimax. When the session was over, Mark thrust himself forward, risking the wrath of jokers aroused by the vision of the Rox's destruction in his fever to speak to the boy they called the Dreamer. Fortunately the audience was still sluggish, coming out of its dream-state.

He reached the podium as Eric came off it and started to walk away, surrounded by admirers. "Wait!" he shouted desperately. "Wait, I've got to talk to you!"

Eric turned. "It's a fucking nat," somebody said in disbelief and disgust.

Mark bulled through to the boy. "That vision you . . . you showed us," he said. "Was it real? Did it happen that way? Was Turtle—"

The contempt in the young joker's eyes hit him like a blow. "You think I'd use my gift to *lie* to the people?" Eric asked.

"No—I mean, I'm not saying it isn't true, I just can't believe that Turtle would do anything like that."

"Who cares what a nat believes?" Eric asked, and turned away.

Mark tried to keep after him. A kid reared up in his path. He had a Mohawk of white spines like porcupine quills. His mouth was a gape that stretched almost back to the hinge of his jaw, barred with four vertical strips of flesh. A ragged vest left his skinny chest bare. I LOVE THE TASTE OF NAT BLOOD was burn-scarred across it as if by a soldering iron.

"Give it a *rest*, you old nat fuck," he snarled.

Hands held helplessly out to the sides, Mark fell back. Eric and his retinue disappeared into the night.

"My, my," a voice behind him said. "The attitude these kids show."

Mark turned to find himself staring at a man-sized gold lizard. It blinked huge and beautiful topaz eyes.

"Impressionable bunch too," the lizard said, taking a cigar from its mouth and extending a hand with three pad-tipped fingers. "Mark Meadows. Small world. How the hell are you?"

Chapter Twenty-three

"Yeah, man, it's true, as far as it goes. Happened about the way you say Eric showed it—don't get his mental sound-and-light shows, myself. Turtle wasted the Rox with a tidal wave." Croyd Crenson poured himself a cup of tea from the chipped green enamel pot in his bunker. The light of the single kerosene lamp made his fine scales shimmer like Elvis' coat. "Of course the Feds shelled the place pretty well in advance. But yeah, Turtle did it."

Sandbags piled on the bunker roof absorbed most of the fury of the rain, dulling its noise to a white-noise background murmur. Seated on a splintery wood crate, Mark sat with his head between his knees and just tried to breathe without throwing up.

"Lose some friends?" Croyd asked.

"Not many." He looked up. "I wasn't real popular on the Rox. Bloat, though—he was a good man. He and his people deserved better. But Turtle"—he shook his head—"I can't see him committing genocide."

"He had his reasons. The jumpers were way out of hand. Things were getting pretty scaly toward the end, if you'll pardon the figure of speech."

"Yeah," Mark said. And there seemed no more to say. He was still shocked to the core by what Tommy had done. But Tommy had made the decision, and would have to live with it the rest of his life. Mark would not condemn him until he knew his side of the story.

Croyd's apparent detachment bothered him a little. But that was Croyd. You didn't live the way Croyd did without being wrenched somewhat loose from the world around you.

"So," he said, casting about for conversation, "what are you doing here in Vietnam, anyway?"

" 'Bout the same thing you are, I guess: traveling for my health." Croyd winked a big topaz eye and puffed on his cigar. "I made some bad career calls, and then things started getting generally *interesting* in the Big Apple—interesting in the Chinese curse sense, what with the War for the Rox and all."

He leaned back, using his tail as a prop—his reptilian hindquarters were ill suited for sitting in a chair. Mark looked at him holding his saucer with one hand and the cup with another, third and last finger daintily extended, and had to cough to keep from going into a giggling fit. *Things are happening too fast in your life.*

Croyd regarded him from beneath lowered horny lids. "I'm surprised you don't know all this about Turtle and the Rox and everything already. It's not as if it wasn't plastered all over the newspapers and TV and everything. They even had one of those one-week-wonder paperbacks by General Zappa, called *Triumph Over Terror*. Kind of hard to miss. Then again, you did kind of drop off the face of the Earth for a while, there, friend."

"Literally. I was on another planet."

"I thought you gave that shit up."

"No, no. You don't understand, man. I was on *Takis*."

He told him the story, leaving out certain details, such as Starshine's death. He didn't trust himself to talk about that, and somehow it seemed too personal to share. Croyd and he were friends of long standing, but the fabric of both their lives was so woven that they never had gotten exactly *close*.

"So Tach got his body back, and is gonna get a new hand, and got to be king of the Alakazams or whatever you call 'em." Croyd shook his head in wonder. "Regular fairy tale."

He froze, stared down. A huge horned black beetle was making its way across the wooden shipping-pallet floor of his bunker.

"Excuse me a minute," he said, setting aside his cup. "You might want to look the other way, here, pal."

Mark shrugged him off. Croyd got down on all fours, peering intently at the bug. Then his lipless mouth opened and a pale tongue whipped out and back, and there was no more bug.

"Mmm," Croyd said, resuming his tail-rest seat and picking up his cup. "Breakfast of champions. I tell you, man, I must be working out my insect-eating karma—you're an old hippie, you're into that karma shit, right? I was a bug-eater last year, too, during my giant-pink-bat phase."

He shook his head. "On the other hand, if you have to do a turn as an insectivore, this is definitely the *primo* place on Earth to do it in. Bugs everywhere, huge fuckers like that one, and *fine*—man, are they fine!"

He looked at Mark. "Say, that didn't gross you out at all, did it?"

Mark shook his head.

"Shoot, *that's* rare. My gustatory habits are a big reason I have this lovely bunker all to my lizard lonesome. Great word, *gustatory*. Picked it up ten, eleven years ago, and damned if I don't think this is the first time I ever found a way to slip it into a sentence."

"Happy to be of service, man."

"And you tell me the good Doctor had a baby. I'll be Goddamned. I don't envy a kid growing up with her mom and great-something grandpa being one and the same." He sipped his tea and smacked his lack of lips. "Then again, I don't envy anybody having Blaise for a dad either. What happened to the sleazy little psycho, anyway?"

"Tach's cousin Zabb killed him, during the final fight for House Vayawand."

Mark was lying like a dog. He knew perfectly well what had happened to Blaise Andrieux—had seen it happen in reality, and saw it again in rerun about every third night, when he woke up sweating and pale. The story of Tach's return to the planet that gave him and the wild card virus birth was also like a fairy tale in that its ending held a twist of grotesque horror.

For the first time in all the years he and Tachyon had known each other, Blaise's fate had really struck Mark in the face with the truth of what his best pal had told him all along: genes notwithstanding, Prince Tisianne brant Ts'ara of House Ilkazam was *not a human being*.

"So why is it that you didn't see Eric's visions?" Mark was desperate for a change of subject.

Croyd shrugged, which almost pitched Mark headfirst into the giggles. "Lizards don't dream—something about the reptile brain. I never see anything when old Eric does his thing. I don't think I'm missing much."

Mark shook his head. "It was beautiful. I saw—"

Yeah. You saw fields and forests and birds, oh my. Strawberry fields forever. Banal City. It sounded a lot like J. J. Flash.

Mark shook his head. "Words can't describe it. But it was beautiful—as beautiful as anything I've ever seen in my life."

"Yeah, all the faithful sit there with that pole-axed look, drooling gently in their laps. I'm glad my most recent draw from the wild card deck spared me that. Never been much of the True Believer type." He gazed at Mark over the rim of his cup. "Ever read the Hoffer book?"

"Yes," said Mark, feeling pissed-off and chagrined at the same time. Part of him said Croyd was a cynic, the kind of scoffer who made the world what it was. Another part said Mark was a mark. *If only Starshine wasn't dead, I wouldn't have all this trouble believing in the perfectibility of humankind.*

Croyd was staring down at his cup as if there were a bug in it. Or rather, as if there *weren't.* "Trouble with this stuff is, it starts tasting like boiled weeds after a while. Maybe because it is."

He tossed cup and saucer over his shoulder. They bounced off the rough planks with a clatter and fell into the mud-red water that had accrued beneath the pallets. He went to a neon-green-and-white Coleman cooler by one wall, opened it, took out a couple of bottles.

"Time for a little of that good old *Giai Phong* beer. The beer that made Ho Chi Minh City famous."

Mark made a face. "It tastes like formaldehyde."

"That's what it's famous for." He stuck both tops into his horny mouth and popped the caps off.

Mark accepted his beer without qualm. Maybe life on the Rox and in the back of a *mujahidin* arms-smuggling van and other interesting places had wrung the squeamishness out of him. Or maybe that was another hole where Starshine used to be.

Croyd hoisted his bottle. "Here's to good friends. Here

we are in damn near the last commie country on Earth,
waiting for the monsoon to wash us into the South China
Sea, in a camp full of refugees from New York's
bloodthirstiest joker street gangs and run by a crazed Nam
vet. I say that's worth drinking to."

He drained his bottle and tossed it in a corner. "So. You
might as well crash the night here. Hell, you might as well
move in. Most of these boys don't have much conversation,
if you get my drift. The young ones strut around trying to
see who's got the biggest balls, and the old ones spend all
their time spouting slogans and bitching about how all the
rest of us don't appreciate all they did for us the *last* time
they were over here."

"I don't want to be any bother, man," Mark said into his
own beer.

"Hey, no bother. I'm not exactly afraid you'll keep me
up with your snoring."

Mark eyed him guardedly. "So, like, how long has it
been?"

On the street they called Croyd the Sleeper. He was an
original, who got caught in the open the day Jetboy made
his final *faux pas*. Since then every time he laid him down
to sleep, he slept for a *long* time—and woke with a brand-
new face and form, not to mention a brand-new set of ace
powers. Actually, that didn't always happen—sometimes he
drew an unadulterated joker. He had, obviously, never yet
drawn a Black Queen. A few years ago he had gotten something stranger: the power to produce an *infectious* form of
xenovirus Takis-A in his own body, one that could even re-
infect people with expressed wild card traits. He had caused
a hell of a stir until he eventually nodded off.

When Croyd woke up, he usually had no trouble staying awake for a while, a period ranging from days to weeks.
When he started to sag, though, he frequently found himself
none too eager to drop back to dreamland. He might have
an especially useful or entertaining form, or unfinished business, and his wakeup-call surprises weren't always any too
pleasant—and there was always the possibility of that Black
Bitch slipping out of his personal wild cards deck.

That was the main way Mark had gotten to know him,
in his own capacity as overqualified street pharmacologist.
When Croyd's eyelids started drooping, he started gobbling

pills in record quantities. After a time they began to affect him—as his sometime speeding buddy Hunter Thompson put it back in the sixties—the way the full moon affected a werewolf.

For his own research Mark kept a stock of powerful and rare stimulants on hand, and Croyd knew him as a man who didn't like to leave a buddy strung out. For his part Mark had experimented to come up with some speed-analogue that would not, in time, turn Croyd into a raving psychotic. But even if drugs aren't the irredeemable Devil Things the Just Say No crowd claims they are, there is a payback to overdoing anything—eating, breathing, and sleeping, no less than amphetamines. No-comeback speed proved just as elusive a goal as reviving the Radical had been.

Mark had a good reason for asking Croyd how long he'd been up this time. If the Sleeper was about to start rolling those big yellow candyflake eyes and raving that invisible creatures were gnawing on his legs, Mark wanted to be, you know, *prepared*. And there was a still-outstanding matter of what if any powers Gordon Gecko Croyd possessed. He was not too discriminate when the amphetamine psychosis had him.

Mark clutched a vial of blue-and-black powder swirl in a pocket of his trousers, just in case. If he was into the pill-gobbling stage, Croyd could be *very touchy*.

But Croyd just laughed. "Weeks and weeks. Been here six weeks. Woke up like this in the hold of a Yugo freighter. Crew was too strung out over all the ethnic tension back home even to be scared of me. I've been like this ever since, and nary a yawn."

He held up a sucker-tipped finger and winked conspiratorially. "You see, old man," he said, "that's my power this go-round, my current ace-in-the-hole. I like this form just fine, for now—it's kind of relaxing, being a skink—and I don't have to worry about losing it and coming back as Snotman Part II, because *lizards don't sleep*."

And while lizards don't have lips, either, he managed to grin hugely as he sat back on his gold-lamé tail.

"Oh," Mark said. And he was thinking, *I'm not a herpetologist, but I don't think that's right*.

He decided it wasn't his problem. He went to the bunk beside the trench wall, which was stabilized with tree trunks from the mountains, sat down, and began to take his boots off. Right now he wished he could take Croyd's next six-month snooze *for* him.

Croyd went to the door, craned his head out. A rain-drop exploded on the tip of his snout, between the widely spaced nostrils. "It's a good thing I'm not actually cold-blooded," he said, " 'cause this is real prime-time for me."

"What?" Mark asked, lying down and pulling an army blanket up his long legs.

"Hunting. They all come out at night, just like the song says."

"Album title. What does, man?"

"I'm going hunting. Lot of big bugs out, a night like this. And every once in a while I come across one of these big-ass Vietnamese rats—"

"I'm sorry I asked."

Chapter Twenty-four

"All right, ladies, drop your rucks and take ten." The sergeant eyed the squad in disgust. "Maybe we better take twenty. Don't want any myocardial infarcts."

"That's sexist," complained Eraserhead. His weak arms stretched like warm wax as he lowered his backpack onto the paddy dike. "Calling us ladies. It ain't politically correct."

"Out here in the bush, what I say is by definition politically correct, dung-beetle. Do I make myself clear?"

Everything was green, green to the point of being painful, from the stinking water all around them to the conical hills that poked up out of the flats at intervals, like models from an HO railroad set. Out in the monsoon-flooded paddies the farmers were at work, their conical straw hats bobbing. None turned toward the party of strangers that had stumbled into the midst of their world, any more than they heeded the aircraft swarming in the sky above Da Nang to the northeast. Such things were not novelties.

The joker called Spoiler slammed his own pack down. He was a tall kid, tough as a rawhide thong, whose nostrils were shrouded by a shelf of cartilage and bone and whose skull shelved way out in back. As always his anger made Mark wince.

"You son of a bitch!" he shrieked at the sergeant. "The days of slavery are over!"

He came forward with his skinny chest stuck out as if to overpower the sergeant that way. He wore a T-shirt with BURN NATS NOT OIL stenciled on it. Attempts to enforce uniformity of dress on the Brigade hadn't met much success,

191

especially since most of their uniforms were cast-offs and hand-me-downs. Their headgear ran from gimme caps to floppy K mart boonie hats. Scuttlebutt said the Republic couldn't afford to give them helmets.

"Fucker!" Spoiler yelled at the sergeant. "Fucking nat-lover! You oughta be necklaced. We oughta see your head burn, you fuck!"

About then he got inside the sergeant's personal space. The sergeant extended two hard brown fingers and poked them into Spoiler's solar plexus.

The young joker doubled and sat down hard, gasping like a carp. "Get back to your ruck, seedbag," the sergeant said. He turned his back on Spoiler and walked away.

Mark was down with his back to the bole of a palm tree and his insides weak and wavery, from heat, fatigue, and re-action to the ugly scene. Each little wavelet out on the flooded paddy was a tiny laser beam firing white death through Mark's eyes to the top of his skull. He had gone from chilly Takis to the high latitudes of Europe. The wet Vietnamese heat hammered him like mallets. He almost missed the monsoon rains, which had momentarily re-treated.

The sergeant plopped down next to Mark. He had a snouted face with a damp nose and sad eyes that turned down at the outside corners. He shook his head.

"That was bad," he said. "Shouldn't have to touch a man to discipline him. That's my fault, but shit. Kids were never like this, back in the old days. Don't know what's hap-pening in the world."

Spoiler was getting his air back. He sat up squealing. "He hit me! He hit me! I want a court-martial."

"You not back in your white-bread nat world now, white boy," called a joker with his Demon Prince rank tat-tooed on his right hand. "You got no Bill of Rights."

"It's not *my* nat world," Spoiler snarled. But in a sub-dued way; he sensed the consensus going against him.

"Dink officers hit their men," said Slick, wiping his forehead. He was one of what the young recruits called "politicals"—older jokers, mostly but not all ex-Brigaders. Like Brew and Luce and the rest of the Rick's crowd, Slick had no prior military experience. "Do it all the time, in the artillery camp next door. Discipline." He flicked his fingers, spattering the brown shit-scented water with droplets that flattened into disks reflecting the light in rainbow colors.

"Discipline?" Eraserhead wheezed. "What we need discipline for? We're the good guys."

"Nobody ever threatened noncoms, back in the old days?" Mark asked. "That's not what I heard."

"Threaten? Hell. We did more than that. One time there was this nat second lieutenant, fresh out of the Point, and he. . . . No. That's ancient history." The sergeant hung his head between his knees and was quiet a long time. Mark offered him a drink from his canteen.

"I don't know," the sergeant admitted. "Maybe I'm kidding myself. But the kids these days seem sharper, harder. Meaner than we ever were."

"It's the routine," Mark said. "It's pretty tough on everybody, man. All this training."

"Tough? *Tough?*" The sergeant laughed in disbelief. "This is nothing. Compared with Basic, this is a walk in the park."

"Yeah. But at least, like, you *had* Basic. Some kind of training. These kids are coming in cold. . . ."

"Yeah, and they got a bunch of old out-of-shape farts to try to warm 'em up." He looked at Mark. "You never even went, did you? What, were you a draft dodger or something?"

"Student deferment. Like, I would've gone to Canada, though. Or jail."

The sergeant looked outraged. "That's chickenshit, man."

Yeah? How many times have you *died in action, bunky?* Flash wanted to know. Mark blinked at the sergeant.

"Wait a minute. Here you are over here ready to fight for the North—uh, the Vietnamese. And here you're telling me I'm chickenshit for not fighting *against* them?"

"That's different. That was then. This is now."

"That's some answer," Mark and J. J. Flash said in unison.

"Well, at least I was over here with my ass in the grass. I knew what it was like, knew what was *really* going on while all you protesters at home—"

"Well, I'm *really* here now, man. And *I* didn't switch sides."

The sergeant glared at him. For a moment Mark thought the guy was going to hit him. *Whoa! I never* used *to talk like that.*

The air and anger went out of the noncom in a rush. "Maybe you got a point."

"I'm sorry, man, I didn't mean—"

"No. No. You're right. It's a pretty fucked-up set of circumstances. I came over here in '71 to serve my country. Country never did nothing for me up until then but say, 'Drop 'em and spread 'em for the whole nat world, joker.' 1971. Shit, by that time we'd lost already; fucking Nixon had thrown in the towel. Nothin' left to do but hold a few more sessions on the shape of the table and have a whole lot more good jokers die. Yeah, and nats too."

He had to pause, then, because a shadow flashed them and flattened them with a powerful roar. The young ex-Demon Prince with fins on his head like an old Chevy yelped and jumped into the water, to the jeers of his buddies. Mark glanced up to see a MiG-27 Flogger strike plane low, smoking south under full military throttle. He wondered where it was going, loaded down like that.

"When I heard the Colonel was coming back here," the sergeant went on, "trying to pull the old Joker Brigade back together again . . . I mean, Sobel, he was always different. He never treated us like we was *The Dirty Dozen* recruited out of old horror movies. He treated us like we were *men*. He made us feel clean and brave. He made us feel like—like heroes."

He accepted another hit from Mark's canteen. "It all started coming back to me then. What we'd done—what the war had done—to this country, these people. And what the nats had done to *us*, before and after. And I looked around, man, I saw this Leo Barnett smilin' away on the tube, and I saw my man Gregg Hartmann going down in Atlanta with Dr. Fuckin' Tachyon's knife sticking out of his back, and then all this shit hit with the Jumpers and the Rox and everything, and suddenly it looked like it was going to be open season on wild cards any old time. And then here was the Colonel, 'way down yonder in Vietnam, sayin' come to me, I'll let you be free. Let you feel like men again."

He looked at Mark. "Guess even you aces started feelin' it come down hard. You're the first ace I ever met didn't look at me like I was dirt. That or the freak poster-child for the Cause of the Week."

He put his head close to Mark. "Lot of the boys been giving you some pretty hard looks because you ain't just a nat, you're an ace," he said in a low voice. "Reckon that ain't news. But you're right, man. You're here now, with your ass in the grass. You ain't even a joker, but you're layin' it on the line right along with the rest of us. Guess that makes you okay—in my book, anyway."

He stood with an audible creaking of joints. "Even if you wouldn'ta lasted five minutes back in the old Brigade. But then, neither would anybody else in this chickenshit outfit, my sorry ass included. All *right*, everybody, naptime's over. Time to saddle up and *go*."

As Mark was struggling to raise his pack—he'd just gotten used to the lighter gravity on Takis, that was it—Spoiler sidled up next to him.

"Sucking up to the brass," he said *sotto voce*. "Don't think we don't notice . . . *nat*."

Mark looked after him as he joined the file tramping off along the paddy dike. *It's so nice to be appreciated*, he thought.

The night's sticky-hot embrace had healed the blisters on her feet. As she moved through her *kata* her limbs warmed, and the aches of the day's trudging vanished. Deep in the core of her she could feel Mark's guilt at taking the easy path, copping out from the pain the day's exertions had earned.

The weariness stayed with her; her wound-healing ability couldn't lave the fatigue poisons from her tissues any faster than normal. But she knew how to use the tiredness, softening the hard and angular *tae kwon do* movements until they were almost *t'ai chi*–like in their fluidity.

"I thought it was the right-wing types who always said, 'If you want peace, prepare for war,' babe," Croyd said. He was lying on the sandbags piled atop his bunker. The storm lanterns he'd set out to draw bugs flanked him, so that he looked like a guardian on a library's steps in some town whose civic taste ran more to lizards than lions.

"You doubt these people are committed to peaceful means?" Moonchild asked. Her breathing was regular.

"When we—when Mark went on patrol today, his squad did not carry weapons."

Croyd tipped his head up and blew smoke at the low clouds. "Does that mean the New Joker Brigade stands for Peace and Love, or does that mean Sobel doesn't trust the new boots with guns yet? Some of these boys seem a touch on the psychopathic side, to tell you the truth."

"They have the passion of the young," Moonchild declared.

"Yeah. So'd the Khmer Rouge. And speaking of the passionate young, babe, you're about to acquire an audience."

A crowd was drifting their way like sand blown across the parade ground. There was no television in Fort Venceremos, the food was fish heads and rice, and beer was strictly rationed—though Croyd always managed to have plenty in his cooler. Game Boys were outlawed, as were foreign magazines other than the *Daily Worker*, which Mark had never been able to read, and also of course marijuana and other illicit highs. With no Bill of Rights or even Uniform Code of Military Justice to inhibit authority, plus a widespread network of informers doing business as good little *kiem thao* self-criticism group elves, the miniprohibitions seemed generally successful—so far. The marked lack of down-time diversion beyond *kiem thao* and study resulted in a whole lot of fights, it seemed to Mark. Maybe he was just unused to military life.

Even the government radio was down, more or less. For some reason it had played nothing but off-key martial music all day. Not even Luce could muster much enthusiasm for it. The boys were attracted to activity like fat juicy bugs to Croyd's lanterns.

"Hey! Look at that. It's a babe!"

Catcalls and whistles followed. "Hey, guys, that's sexist!" Eraserhead's voice cried, followed a second later by a meaty *thump* and a "Hey! You hit me!"

"Yeah," another voice said. "Now pipe down or I'll tie you in knots, you little narc."

"How 'bout a date?" somebody else yelled.

"She's not for the likes of you lowlives," Croyd said.

"Yeah? What, she goes in for big lizards?"

Moonchild ignored them. She was serene.

"What's she doing?" the joker called Ent asked in his piping voice. "Dancing?"

"Doing *kata*," said Studebaker Hawk. He was the kid with fins on his head. "Karate practice."

"It's dancing," scoffed Spoiler, "unless you just want to call it bullshit."

"No, look at her, Spoiler," the Hawk urged. "She's real good."

"She *looks* good," Spoiler said, "but it doesn't have anything to do with that crap. Hey, honey—I'm talkin' to *you*, nat bitch."

Moonchild ignored him. "Looks like you think you're too good for us scummy jokers," Spoiler said. "Maybe you oughta show us if that stuff's for real."

She finished her form and stopped. She smoothed back heavy black hair from a face half-obscured by her yin-yang mask. "I do not fight for sport or pleasure."

Spoiler pulled a long face beneath his air-scoop nose and nodded. "Well, how about *self-defense*, then?"

The crowd parted. The young German joker the others called Rhino charged Moonchild. He was heavy, but he wasn't slow, and he had his name for a good reason.

She danced aside, out of his path. A savage hooking blow with the foot-long horn that grew from his face grazed her hip. Instead of lumbering on into the side of Croyd's bunker, the joker dropped his weight, turned, skidded, stopped facing Moonchild with one fist on the muddy ground, propped like a lineman on one massive arm.

Jesus! Cosmic Traveler shrilled. *He's serious!*

The Krauts don't do joker kid gangs the way we do back in New York, J. J. Flash responded. *They got no Killer Geeks or Twisted Sisters. Last German joker to get any sound bite was that twisted little freak who got waxed at the Democratic Convention in Atlanta back in '86. This boy figures he's got to show some real fiendish class to keep up.*

Moonchild was not used to the sort of kibitzing Mark increasingly had to put up with. She tried to put it from her mind and concentrate on summing up her opponent. He looked as if he massed two hundred kilograms, heavy gray folds of hide hanging on a squat frame. He clearly had metahuman strength, to move that bulk so quickly, and he had to be agile to come so close to tagging Moonchild on his charge. On the other hand, the tiny eyes glaring at her from the blunt-muzzled face seemed to be having trouble focusing on her six meters away, and the joker's sides were heaving as if he were winded.

Yes. I can run from him, and I can hide from him. A sidestep, a sprint, and I become one with shadow. It was what her strict code called for, flight over fight if at all possible.

Even as Cosmic Traveler weighed in with enthusiastic approval, she knew she couldn't do it. She had a responsibility to Mark and the others. The new recruits seemed to take her existence as a challenge. Unless she proved herself formidable, they'd just keep trying their luck with her—or with Mark, who in his own persona had no ace powers and was far from robust, even for a nat.

I must best him without hurting him, she thought. *Beat without humiliating him.* No one ever said being an ace would be easy.

"Leave off," she said. "Are we not comrades?"

The pig eyes flicked right and left, assessing the crowd. No mistake: it wanted blood. "You're a nat," he said. "I'm a joker. We fight."

"Is not that the attitude we are supposed to fight *against*?"

This time Rhino looked square at Spoiler, who stood at the front of the crowd with his hands on his hips. Glancing that way herself, Moonchild saw that Brew and Luce had arrived as well and were hanging out at the rear. As was the badly disfigured young joker, Eric the dreamer.

"It's come down evolution time," Spoiler said. "Prove yourself or die, nat."

Brew and Luce held obvious if not formalized rank; they could stop this if they chose. They made no move.

While she was looking toward them, Rhino charged. Moonchild leapt high, somersaulted over his head.

Built low to the ground, he recovered quickly, spun to face her again. With a falling-away sensation she realized she had not made much impression on the onlookers. They had all seen that move in a dozen *kung fu* movies. They didn't realize that in most cases it was a special effect.

"Think you're clever," Rhino rumbled. He brought his blocky three-fingered fists up to either side of his lowered horn in a pose reminiscent of a *muay Thai* stance and began to circle her clockwise. She doubted he could manage the freewheeling kickboxer's shin-kicks, but if she got inside the comfort zone of his horn, he could give her a rib-crushing knee.

The onlookers began to jeer, disappointed by the lack of action, the lack of blood. Predictably Rhino was goaded into an advance, spiraling toward her in that mincing Thai step.

As he got near, he tossed his head and that wicked horn. Her guard came up. He whipped a roundhouse shin-kick up and into her ribs and sent her flying.

She tucked a shoulder, rolled, came up to one knee as he charged. She whipped her right arm up and out in a fore-arm block that connected with his horn with a sound like a pistol shot. As momentum sent him thundering past, she fired a punch into his side.

He staggered, stumbled, went to a knee. Then he stood up, hunched over with an elbow pressed to his side. She wondered if in her anger at being caught unawares she had failed to pull the blow enough, had really done him harm.

"We can quit now, before someone gets hurt." Instantly she realized it was the wrong thing to say; to quit now would make him look as if he feared her. *Why cannot I be better at this? Why is it so hard to talk to people?*

He came at her with two quick punches. She blocked them easily, so easily that when the knee-shot they'd been intended to set up came, she hopped half a step away, out of the way of the short-ranged attack, and spun a back-kick into his broad belly.

All two hundred kilograms of Rhino sailed into the air. Spectators scattered. He landed on his butt with a mighty thud ten feet away.

The crowd made impressed noises. She had flashed her own power and speed. He had weight on her and probably strength. Speed and skill were all hers.

Rhino picked himself up, moving as if it pained him. "We've done enough and more," she said. "Why should we hurt each other, to excite these others?"

He shook his heavy head as if her words were water he wished to shed. Surrender was no option to the proud joker youth. *I hope this boy has the sense to take a dive,* she felt J. J. Flash say in her head.

She was surprised. Her image of J. J. was all combative cockiness, not compassion. Rhino rushed her then, lashing out with a roundhouse swipe of his fist.

She ducked, wheeled, caught the horny wrist. She pulled the arm out straight, helping Rhino along the way he was going, put her palm against his suddenly-locked elbow, and levered his horned snout into the mud.

He struggled briefly, but he could not fight without dislocating his shoulder—or breaking his elbow. His nostrils dilated, a vast sigh blew furrows in the mud, and he went dormant.

"Waste him!" the crowd was yelling. "Rip his arm off!" She released him and stepped back.

"So brave, all of you!" she flared at the crowd. "*He* had the courage to fight. If you have the courage to do more than jeer, step forward and prove it!"

The crowd seemed to be held back by an invisible cordon. Spoiler had mysteriously vanished from the front rank. That spinning back-kick would have stove in the chest of just about any man in camp.

She reached a hand to Rhino. He took her hand, pulled himself upright. Then he stared at her.

"I could have stuck my horn right through you, just now," he said, thick-tongued.

"I know."

Soundlessly he began to cry. Then Brew and Luce were shoving their way through. "Hey," Brew said, in that quiet, laidback way of his, "do all of you *really* have nothing better to do than hang here and gawk? And is there anything here you really *need* to see?"

Luce glared the jokers back. "If you *don't* have anything better to do," he snarled, "maybe we should schedule extra *kiem thao* for everybody, huh?"

The crowd became one with the night almost as readily as Moonchild might have. "All right, suckers," Croyd announced in his best carny-barker voice, lighting up one of his death-wick cigars, "step right up and take your best shot at the Queen of the Night!"

Moonchild gave him a dirty look. Brew and Luce had Rhino under the arms now and were helping the sobbing youth to his feet. Moonchild fired a final contemptuous glance at the rapidly dwindling crowd.

She found her eyes locked with Eric's. In them she read a compassion and understanding so profound, they staggered her.

She felt the end of her hour approaching and hurried into the bunker. Some moments were too private to share, even with comrades.

Chapter Twenty-five

J. Bob Belew was sleeping in when they came knocking on his door with a Soviet RGD-5 hand grenade.

Before the plywood splinters settled, Belew was awake and rolling, off the bed. He came up with his Para Ordnance. Explosive entry was not just something you passed around among friends like chlamydia.

He double-tapped the first man through the blown-in door, easily controlling the big handgun's kick. The intruder uttered a choking squawk, dropped his Kalashnikov, and reeled back into the man behind him.

Belew gave the point man two more in the chest. The 180-grain Hydra-Shok slugs expanded in meat, gouging great channels through him. Skinny as he was, they passed right along through to spoil the day of the man he'd stumbled against.

Compulsive tinkerer that he was, Belew had made a few alterations to his miserable back-alley flat with the dull Asian porno prints of Thai cuties in dowdy fifties bikinis shellacked to the wall. He grabbed his jacket and light pack and dove for the window. The whole assembly blew out into the alley.

It was dark and narrow, defined by shacks with crazily angled corrugated-tin roofs that threatened to slump into the right-of-way at any moment. Belew rolled clear of the debris—a new layer added to the accumulation of years—and came up with his pistol in both hands, drawing down on the window in case his drop-ins were following right behind. Instead another flash and crash and swirl of smoky rubble inside; with at least two punctured they had belatedly decided to play it safe by pitching another grenade.

It was that grimy time of day when enough light has spilled over the horizon to spoil the darkness, but not enough to really illuminate. That time of day beloved of cops and marauders: predawn, as in "predawn raid." Fully dressed, of course, J. Robert Belew got up and raced between the slouching buildings, raising a bow wave in ankle-deep puddles.

A stutter of gunshots behind him. Holes splintered open in a rude plank wall right in front of his face. He hit a T-junction in the shanty labyrinth and cranked hard right. He was built low to the ground, not much for sprint speed, but still one hell of a broken-field runner. For one thing, though he aged normally in cosmetic terms, his ability to regenerate meant he had seventeen-year-old cartilage in his knees.

Another slow, heavy AK burst chewed the wall, long behind him. Somebody began screaming, whether in terror, pain, or sudden grief he had no way of knowing.

J. Robert Belew was a man who believed in always traveling first-class. It was just that his definition of *first class* was skewed from the rest of the world's, like so much about him. He loved fine wine, Vivaldi, satin sheets, and beautiful, long-legged women to slip between them as much as the next man. When those things fit the mission profile. On a gig like the present one—free-lance; high-risk factor; no assets; a quick, clean death one of the more favorable outcomes he could hope for and a warm sense of accomplishment about the optimum—he had different criteria. Here he liked a low profile, incurious neighbors, a lot of traffic in the area to cover his moves, and ready escape routes.

You didn't find those things in the middle-class neighborhoods that still managed to cling to existence despite the wealth-devouring propensities of socialism. You didn't even find them in the precincts of the respectable poor, where everybody knew everybody for generations back, and the good people of the Earth stood ready to show their civic spirit by cooperating with the authorities at every chance.

You found them in *slums*. He found them on the Ben Nghe waterfront of District Four, dingy, dirty, dangerous,

ripe with decay, where he wasn't the only *Lien Xo* dog on
the bum, and nobody asked questions—or ever, ever answered them when the Man asked—and the foul Southeast
Asian river that defined the district and gave it its unmistakable *ambiance* lay handy for comings and goings and dispos-
ing of evidence. Such as his own xenovirus Takis-A–positive
corpus.

Voices chased him as he exploded out onto a street, or
at least a broader alley, a short block from the river. He
dodged chicken crates and veggie carts and trussed depres-
sive pigs and bicycles loaded like quarter-ton trucks and the
sort of early-morning people who hadn't waited for the Sixth
Party Congress to tell them it was okay to become entrepre-
neurs. Traffic was at low ebb, and it had nothing to do with
the hour. There had been antigovernment riots the last two
days, and much of Ho-ville was hunkering down in the old
familiar wait-and-see mode.

When he hit block's end, instinctive combat timing
made him turn and kneel just as a skinny dude in generic
black pajamas came flailing out of the alley-tangle with a
stockless AKMS clutched in one hand. *Just like the old days,*
Belew thought with a pleasant rush of nostalgia. He fired
twice.

Only in the movies do people never miss, even if
they're combat-pistol experts, which J. Bob happened to be.
Neither shot hit the boy in black pajamas, but he promptly
fell on his skinny ass anyway. He went scrambling back to
the alley on all fours, clattering his Kalashnikov on sporadic
pavement, as a second triggerman poked his AK around the
bend and started hosing.

The street had suddenly become a wasteland of prime-
time proportions. A fair share of the pedestrians and cycle-
jockeys had been born since ostensible Liberation in '75,
but few of them were hearing full-auto fire for the first time.

Belew went left at the riverfront, jinking around water-
warped crates and sampan drivers in rice-straw hats. Whoever his friendly visitors were—and there were any number
of stinging-ant hills he could've bumped during his several
days of discreet inquiry; that nasty Heisenberg principle
again—they were being cagey. Most of the government's
watchdogs were running in packs down in downtown District One just to the north, and southwest in Cholon, the

two main loci of trouble. They were poorly positioned to intervene in any running gunbattle this far north. Of course that didn't mean the black-pajama killers weren't from the government themselves. The Socialist Republic might think it had splendid reasons to off J. Robert Belew without appearing to have done so.

As he ran, his mind paged through options like flash cards. He had scoped out a number of escape routes in advance. But the riverfront was chaos, always flowing, always changing, always coming-going. It was never predictable, which made it such good cover for his shadow games.

He never relied on set plans anyway; only made them as a form of mental discipline. The opportunity that struck his eye was not on his short-list of preplanned escapes. But his pursuers, half a dozen strong, had younger lungs than he did, if not knees. They were gaining.

A fistful of bullets missed him to the left, crackling with supersonic spite, and shattered a stack of boxes labeled SAIGON EXPORT. The dark reeking fluid that cascaded out sure wasn't the Nam's premium beer, nor even formaldehyde-laced *Giai Phong*. He didn't stop to give it a taste test.

A fortunate toss of the yarrow sticks had caught his eye, a surreal flash between the rickety buildings that crowded down to the water's edge. That was the lovely thing about chaos; it was in essence random, but it was random *within limits*. You had a measure of predictability if you knew the delimiters. This set of circumstances was just the sort of thing to be expected, down by the river.

He dashed between shacks onto a wharf that boomed beneath his feet like a Vachel Lindsay drum. This side of the river was given over to river-people shanties, godown warehouses, and tiny tin-roof houseboats. The far side was choked with motor sampans with barrel-shaped wood or bamboo roofs, all nosing in toward the shore like Sea World dolphins hitting on a tourist with a bucketful of mackerel. The Ben Nghe was a poor cousin of the at least sporadically well-groomed Saigon River. But its left bank—the triangle formed by the Ben Nghe, the Te Canal, and the Saigon—was somewhat upwardly mobile. The boaters on that side were all running rice up from the fertile Delta to ever-hungry Saigon *giai phong*. Bowing to the inevitable, i.e. starvation, the government had recently legalized the trade. The boaters still had rum-runner moves, like all the other recently legitimized *tu san* enterprisers.

A boatman stood bent over in the stern of his covered sampan, fiddling with a balky engine. The boat rocked zanily as Belew jumped in. The boatman looked at him. His lower jaw opened like the rear ramp of a C-130.

"Sorry, Jack," Belew said, "but my need is greater than thine."

The man continued to stare at him. His mouth kept opening wider. If he kept that up, he was going to strain something.

Belew repeated the phrase in Vietnamese. No response. He pointed the 10mm at the man. The boater understood *that* fine: he turned and half dove, half fell into the greasy brown chop.

Shouts from downstream, then shots. Bullets raised quick geysers, not uncomfortably close. Belew holstered his sidearm. He reached out to the wharf for the other object that had caught his eye, which in concatenation with the stalled-out boat had drawn him.

"I hope this boy was bright enough that this thing's not out of gas," he said. He laid his left wrist on the gunwale, raised the U.S. Marine-issue machete that had been lying on the wharf, and brought it down with a *thunk*.

The lead pursuer was still a good fifty meters away. He stopped short, staring in astonishment as the American's hand flew off and a stream of dark red arced into the Ben Nghe. He couldn't handle *that*. He dropped his Kalashnikov and went running in the opposite direction, spewing vomit.

His comrades had stronger stomachs. Several knelt down on a wharf and opened fire. Three kept running after Belew.

He thrust the spurting stump against the sampan's motor. A stinging instant as dirty metal met raw flesh, then a sense of contact and completion as Belew's spirit entered the machine. *A clog in the fuel line*, he knew. *I can handle that.*

He concentrated, frowning slightly. The engine coughed twice and barked into life.

His arm temporarily welded to the engine, J. Bob

steered the craft out into the flow. He headed downstream, as though making for the Delta himself. The Mekong Delta was traditionally fractious and at the moment in a state approaching open rebellion. It was a customary kind of place to blow to when you had to blow Saigon.

Three of his attackers were tripping over each other trying to get down to the wharf he had stolen the boat from. That left three standing by the river downstream. They all stood bolt upright and blazed away at him as the current and the small motor carried him by.

Very few people can hit a damn thing firing an assault rifle on full rock 'n' roll, even a twenty-foot boat not thirty meters away. Near-miss miniwaterspouts showered Belew. A couple of copper-jacket 7.62x39-millimeter rounds did crash through the plank hull, but none close to J. Bob, who lay on his back in the stern. Bracing his right hand on the gunwale, he returned fire, and was gratified to see one gunman drop his rifle in the drink and go down in a heap. He might have been scared, instead of hit, but he didn't seem to move as the sampan pulled slowly out of range. Belew holstered his pistol and rummaged one-hand in his pack.

The two surviving gunmen were joined by their three brethren. Two of them dodged back up to the street to run after Belew in futile pursuit. The rest got into a good old-fashioned shouting match, waving their rifles under each other's noses.

Suddenly one pointed at the receding boat. Belew was aiming a fat black tube at them, something that looked highly reminiscent of a grenade launcher.

One dove off the wharf into the Ben Nghe. The rest scattered.

" 'The wicked flee when no man pursueth,' " J. Bob Belew said, and unscrewed the telephoto lens from his camera. *I can sell those pictures to* Rolling Stone, he thought, *or* Soldier of Fortune, *depending*. He was on the masthead of both publications as contributing editor. The superior man thought of righteousness before gain, but what the hell?

Running the gauntlet of fire had been a final act of calculated ballsiness. That hit squad would be *damned* sure he was heading down to the Delta.

But he wasn't. Out of their sight, he was going to cut left at the Te and then again on the Saigon. North, toward

where that Ozzie soak at Rick's had told him Fort
Venceremos was.

He laughed out loud. He never gambled for money; he
thought that was a waste. But he loved to stake his life and
win.

Chapter Twenty-six

"Village is deserted, Sarge," Mario called back from the point, leading the squad out of the rice fields. He was a slight, intense kid with a Rambo rag tied around his temples. His skin was covered with pebblelike protrusions, which gave rise to the name Mark had briefly known him by back on the Rox, Rocky.

The sergeant stopped. Still strung out single file after coming off a paddy dike, the squad did an inchworm thing behind him.

"Is it, now?" Mario was shifty and smart and had seen some combat during the nightmare siege of Bloat's stronghold. The sergeant thought he had potential to be a good troop, which was why he'd put him in the crucial—and, in an actual wartime situation, highly dangerous—point position.

The sergeant pointed at a pen where a heavy-horned water buffalo with a calf nuzzling her side eyed them with deep suspicion. "Think they'd leave their animals behind?"

He started walking again. Mario stood there slumped, with the consciousness of having fucked up just beating off him like heat off sun-warmed blacktop.

"Mario, my man. Walk with me." The sergeant put a hand on the boy's shoulder and urged him along into the village. He didn't go by "Rocky" anymore; he had fallen under the influence of Lucius Gilbert, otherwise known as Luce, who held that joker names were bogus—slave names.

Moving with egg-walking care, Mark followed along with the others. Mark felt dumb; *he'd* thought the village was deserted too. He hadn't noticed anything but these funky bamboo hootches, like he'd grown up seeing on the six o'clock news. They gave him a sense of *déjà vu*.

"Maybe they're off working the paddies," suggested Slick.

"With a big old pot of rice bubbling on the fire out front of one of their hootches like that?" the sergeant asked, pointing again.

The hair started to rise on the back of Mark's neck. *Where are they? Are they watching us?* He felt like a trespasser.

"There!" Eraserhead screamed, so shrilly it made everybody jump. He flung out a hand to point, so fast his arm stretched to half again its normal length. "I saw somebody there in that hut!"

Mark snapped his head back and forth as if watching a tennis match on speed—him or the players, it didn't make much difference. Yes, he saw them. Faces in the shadows. Some sullen, some openly hostile. Most of them wore a blank resignation he imagined a rape victim got when she knew she couldn't fight back.

"Why are they doing this?" Spoiler demanded in a high-pitched voice. "Why the fuck are they hiding from us?"

"They're afraid of us," the sergeant said. "They think we're monsters—even Meadows, who looks about two feet taller'n any human they ever seen before. Also, we got *these*."

He slapped the receiver of the M-16 he, like the rest of them, had been issued that morning. They were the reason Mark was being so hypercautious. He was afraid the thing would go off by itself.

The sergeant chuckled. "Got no way of knowing we got no bullets."

"But we're here to *help* them!" Mario said.

The sergeant gave him a look. "They heard that one before, son."

Croyd tipped back his bottle of *Giai Phong*. He and Mark, whose squad had been stood down after coming in a little after noon, sat on lawn chairs in front of their bunker. The afternoon sun lit up bubbles the color of Croyd's eyes.

"As far as I know," he said regretfully, "I got no ace powers this time around." He gave a half-lidded glare to a bunch of jokers drifting their way in evident hope of cadging beer. "Not that I've been in any hurry to let these shrabs know that."

"You really dig life as a gecko, man?" asked Mark. He wore a T-shirt tied turban-fashion around his head and nothing on his chest. He wasn't worried about ultraviolet radiation at the moment. He was worried about *hot*.

"Skink, dammit. I'm a skink."

"I thought skinks were skinny, squinty lizards with heads smaller than their necks."

Croyd drew himself up in his chair. At Mark's suggestion he had discovered that he could sit in a lawn chair if he fed his tail through the back.

"See the words you're using?" he asked. "*Sk*inny. *Squ*inty. '*Sk*' words. They *sound* like 'skink.' That's why you associate them with skinks."

Mark looked mulish. "I don't know, man."

"Look, who's the *authority* here? You—all right, you're a biochemist. But I—*I'm* a *skink*. So there."

He had an audience for his outburst. "Naw," said one of the old breed, a three-eyed Joker Brigade vet everybody called Tabasco. "You're a fuck-you lizard."

"Okay," Croyd said. "Fuck *you*." He lunged at the joker, opening his mouth wide. It was shocking red inside and armed with alarming teeth. Tabasco squawked and ran, pelted by the jeers of his buddies.

"You fools wouldn't know a skink if it bit you on the ass," Croyd grumbled. He settled back and resumed his beer.

"Uh-oh," he said at once. "*Now* what?"

For the last ten or fifteen minutes there had been a lot of activity around the wooden headquarters buildings in the center of camp. Now the tall figure of Evan Brewer—Brew—was striding across the parade ground toward Croyd's bunker.

Tabasco was standing on the far side of the group of idlers from Croyd, batting at his buddies' hands as they poked at him. His hand hit something hard and spiky. He stopped and turned to see Brew with the end of his lobster-claw resting on his shoulder.

"You. Down to the quartermaster. Do it now. And you,

and you." He was picking out men from the original Brigade.

He stopped in front of Mark, reached out his claw to touch Mark on the sternum. The spiny tip was strangely cool as it pricked Mark's bare skin.

"You too," Brew said. "The Colonel wants an ace along. Though I don't exactly know how your friends will find you to help you if something comes down."

Even a half day on patrol had left Mark drained. But he struggled to make himself rise. "What's happening, man?" he asked.

Brew's handsome face clouded. "Somebody just took a couple of shots at one of our training patrols."

"The bastards! The nat fuckin' sons of *bitches!*"

The sun had vanished into a cloud *tsunami* rolling in across the South China Sea. Rays of pale light fanned out from the place where it had vanished like the fingers of a cosmic hand. Ambling back from the mess hall—he went along to chow to be comradely and also because there were sometimes big snaggle-tooth bamboo rats to be found— Croyd gestured toward the rec hall with his cigar.

"Spoiler's in good voice tonight."

"Yeah," Mark said. The parade-ground mud sucked at his feet, trying to pull his boots off. He could barely muster the strength to lift them. An hour of flying cover for a rescue mission as J. J. Flash left him feeling completely blasted. They hadn't found any enemies, and no one had been hurt, but the tension had wrung more out of him than even J. J.'s overamped metabolism.

Spoiler tore off his Brooklyn Dodgers hat and threw it down. Then he tore off his T-shirt and threw that too. "It was those Vietnamese Army assholes, you know it was! They think all us jokers are dogshit, do you hear me? *Dog shit.* We ought to go down to that camp and just mop the place with the cocksuckers!"

Croyd stopped to watch. "Oh, yeah," he said, though Spoiler was out of earshot even if he could hear anything over his tantrum. "You don't even know how to fire your M-16s yet. The People's Army has machine guns. *This* should be interesting."

Mark noticed a deputation marching across from the

headquarters buildings. Brew and Luce and a couple of their cronies he recognized from Rick's, Osprey and Purple and his squadmate Slick.

Spoiler was still rampaging around offering to personally kick the ass of the entire People's Army of Vietnam, collectively or one at a time, when Brewer called out, "Hey, why burn up all this energy? Is this display really *accomplishing* anything?"

Spoiler stopped in the process of trying to fight his way through a knot of his pals to get inside the rec hall, presumably to bust up the pool table, which was way the hell off true anyway. He turned to face the older jokers, skinny chest working like a donkey engine.

"It's those fucking nat bastards," he panted. "They were the ones who bushwhacked our boys today."

Luce's cheeks puffed out. "Is that the Vietnamese Army you're talking about?" he demanded. "Is that our *comrades-in-arms...?*"

Brew put a calming hand on his friend's upper biceps. "What happened today was an accident. Things happen. Life's like that."

"Bull-fucking-*shit* it was an accident. Your butthole buddies from down the road were out to bag them some joker meat. What the fuck are we *doing* here? I thought we were supposed to be training to defend the right of jokers everywhere. How the fuck can we do that if we can't even defend *ourselves?*"

Luce was starting to turn colors and ball all his hands into fists. "If the attack today was deliberate," Brew said smoothly, interposing himself a little more firmly, "bourgeois elements had to be responsible. The reactionaries have been kicking over the traces all over the South the last couple of days. And if that's the case . . ."

He shrugged. "Then you may get a chance to fight for joker rights a lot sooner than you think. And for our hosts."

"Why should we fight for them, man?" another young joker asked. "They hate us."

"Well, so what? How important is it for you to have the nats love you? It isn't going to happen.

"The Vietnamese are giving us a shot at being the nucleation point for a whole new phase of joker activism. But more than that, they're giving us a chance to atone for the sins of America. This is Vietnam, man. It's crucial, absolutely crucial. What went down here is the focal point of our national consciousness."

The joker boy looked at him blankly. "Why? Did something happen here?"

Croyd tugged on Mark's olive-drab sleeve. "We better draw a curtain discreetly over this scene. Spoiler's lost his head of steam, and the only thing liable to happen here now is our friend Brewer having apoplexy. Or don't people have apoplexy anymore?"

"They call it having a stroke, now, man."

"Is that so? Damn. It's hard to keep up with slang when you spend two thirds of your life asleep. Of course, I guess you normal people spend a third of your lives asleep, but it's not, like, *all at once*, if you know what I mean."

Mark looked at him with bleary intensity. "Are you sure you're feeling all right, man? You're starting to sound like you need sleep worse than I do."

"Bite your tongue. I never felt better in my life. In my whole damned life. Besides, I told you: lizards don't sleep."

"Huh," Mark said, and allowed himself to be led off to the bunker.

Chapter Twenty-seven

Night, and a *kata* in the rain. This time Moonchild—
and the semisubmerged Mark persona—were feeling guilty
about being so well rested. The rain had returned in mid-
afternoon. Moonchild carried on her martial dance uncaring,
serene and lovely, her heavy black hair hanging around her
shoulders like seaweed.

The sun had been high up in the sky and the bunker
filling with heat like a Cadillac with cement when Mark
opened his eyes. He had slept through reveille, which was
a much-abused record played over the camp P.A. system. It
was a weird note, after even Mark "The Last Hippie" Meadows, Cap'n Trips, had broken down and bought a CD player
for his long-lost head shop, the Cosmic Pumpkin, to wake
up every morning to the firefight sounds of old-fashioned vi-
nyl getting scratched by a needle. Maybe they figured the
cracks in the record would roust out the somnolent better
than the recorded bugle solo.

It hadn't awakened Mark. The miracle was, nobody had
come along to kick him awake when he didn't fall in for P. T.
Nor was he in the deep shit he assumed he was, when he
turned up at H.Q. at ten o'clock in the morning with his
shirt buttoned one hole off to report, heart-in-throat, that
he'd overslept. He had been told not to sweat it and was
given minor make-work jobs to while the day away inside
the perimeter. They hadn't even made him fill sandbags.

Mark was feeling almost human by evening chow. Af-
terward the nightly political meetings were held in several
big tents, lit by kerosene lamps and smelling of wet canvas,
like a militaristic camp revival. Brew taught the one Mark

215

and Croyd wound up at, explaining the history of the Vietnamese war of liberation from a socialist point of view. The young bloods kept getting bored and making noise or dozing off. They were pounced on by Revolutionary Vigilance monitors—other young recruits whose interest in the proceedings had been engaged by giving them red armbands and Authority—written up and told to attend the dreaded daily self-criticism sessions that followed the regular political meetings.

Every once in a while an original Joker Brigader would lose his cool at some quietly dry remark Brew made concerning the American involvement in Vietnam and start yelling. Brew never flinched. He just got this sardonic half smile on his heavy, handsome face, listened to what the retread had to say, and then demolished him without ever raising his voice. His refutations didn't always seem logically watertight to the ever-scientific Mark, but the recipients seldom found an answer to them. Brew fought with words the way his buddy Luce did, toward the same end—total Clausewitzian devastation of the enemy—but his skills were subtler. "Jack the Ripper compared to the Skid Row Slasher," Croyd said, *sotto voce*, when Mark mentioned it to him.

When Brew finished with him, the objecting veteran got handed a yellow slip requiring his presence at the ensuing *kiem thao* session. The veterans accepted them meekly, seeming almost to welcome additional contrition. The young bloods generally had to be threatened with worse, like a good beating by the monitors, or some downtime in the Box. The Box was a recent innovation right out of every direct-to-video prison flick ever made: a tiny tin-roof shed at the foot of the parade ground. Malefactors were locked into it and allowed twenty-four hours or so to enjoy the stunning heat of day and the surprising nighttime chill.

When the indoctrination session ended, the sun was long gone. It was safe for Moonchild to come out and play.

As she moved through her forms, the blocks and punches and startling high kicks, she did not lack an audience. She was an attractive female alone in a camp full of lonely men. The gawkers kept a wet, respectful distance, though, and went easy on the catcalls. They'd all seen how she handled Rhino—or heard, which pumped the act up to more than it was.

Eric Bell stood by himself to the side, near the bunker Mark shared with Croyd, the rain matting his dark-blond hair to his misshapen skull. He was silent, his hands and body at rest.

When she felt the end of her hour nearing, Moonchild finished her practice and turned to enter the bunker. Eric stepped forward. "May I talk to you?" he asked. His voice was low and deep beyond his years.

She tipped her head and regarded him coolly. "You are disappointed that there was no fight tonight, yes?"

The boy shook his head. "Relieved. I don't have much taste for violence."

"Really? Why, then, are you here, in the middle of a military camp?"

To her surprise he laughed. "I might ask you the same question. The answer is, I believe in love. But love isn't all you need, no matter what the Beatles sang. The nats have been grinding our faces in that fact since long before I was born—or you either, I suspect. We must have *strength*, the strength to protect ourselves. *Then* our love can begin its work—not in a spirit of confrontation, but confidently and unafraid."

She dropped her gaze to the mud. "That is very beautiful."

He laughed again. "I was a street poet in Brooklyn before I came here to be a peaceful guerrilla warrior. I picked up a few oratorical tricks back then. It's all sleight-of-tongue."

Her mind filled with an urban street-corner image, young Eric barefoot in torn jeans, addressing an afternoon-rush pedestrian throng. First one man in hardhat and coveralls stopped and turned to listen to him, then a woman in a smart gray executive suit, a delivery boy on a mountain bike, one after another, until the homeward surge stood still to hear the boy poet's words.

He finished his poem, the words of which Moonchild could not quite hear, though they tantalized with the promise of infinite meaning. The crowd barraged him with dead cats and garbage.

She laughed. "That never happened, surely!" she exclaimed, clapping her hands together in amused delight.

His distorted features slipped into a highly charming grin. "Not *exactly*," he said. "You can call that a sleight-of-mind. Another one of my gifts."

She smiled and started to turn away, suddenly shy. "The way you handled Rhino . . ." he said.

She froze, every muscle tensed, as if expecting his next words to strike like a blow.

"It was beautiful," he said. "You could have hurt him badly, yet you did not. You could have shamed him, too. I guess a lot of the guys think you did. But I know better. I saw the way you gave him a chance to strike you when you helped him up, gave him the pride of choosing to do the right thing. That was the most magnificent thing of all.

"You have an ace's powers, but none of an ace's arrogance. You have enormous strengths, but you use them with restraint—yes, and with love. That's what this place"—he gestured around at the dark, rainswept camp.—"what Fort Venceremos is all about. You show us the way that, yes, *we shall overcome.*"

She licked her lips and swallowed. She could find no words.

"I'd like to talk to you more," he said. "I want to know you. May I see you sometime?"

She nodded, almost frantically, agitated by some emotion she could not identify and the coming transformation. "Ask Mark," she said quickly. "He is a good man."

She vanished into the bunker, leaving Eric in the rain.

"Check," Croyd said, moving his bishop. It tipped over his knight en route. "Excuse it. These digits aren't really designed for manipulation."

"Uh-uh," Mark said, shaking his head. "Can't do that, man."

For a being virtually bereft of mimetic muscles, Croyd could muster a hell of an outraged look. "Why the hell not?"

"Revealed check from my queen. Can't put your own king in jeopardy, man."

"Shit." Croyd retracted the move, knocking the white knight down again. "And here I thought I had your back to the wall."

Mark gave him a thin smile. Once upon a time he had been a middling-hot chess player; he'd held a master's rating in high school and college, playing tournaments, memorizing games by the bookload. Time and extensive experimentation with psychoactive chemicals had left certain gaps in his knowledge, and he hadn't had much occasion to keep his skills honed since. He still fancied himself a dangerous player.

Unfortunately Croyd played with the banzai intensity of an amateur. All those classical openings painstakingly committed to memory, all Mark's fianchettos and his Nimzo-Indian Defenses, all his careful strategic analysis, blew right out the door in the face of a player who didn't know enough to know what he wasn't supposed to do. Despite the misfire of Croyd's current attack, Mark saw yet another draw looming a few moves ahead like the face of a glacier.

Somebody rapped on the bunker's doorpost with something hard. "Hello? Anybody in here?"

"Lizards and old hippies, if that counts," Croyd called. "Come right on in."

Brew and Luce entered, Brew folding an umbrella, Luce's face streaming with rain and his T-shirt soaked transparent and clinging to his rather flabby middle. Umbrellas were bogus, apparently.

Gilbert immediately started batting at the air, which was a near-solid blue haze from about the level of Mark's breastbone up, with several of his arms. "You're smoking that damned cigar in here. I don't know why the Colonel permits tobacco onbase. Smoking is a bourgeois habituation, fostered by capitalist consumer fascism."

"That must be why every Viet over the age of three years old smokes," Croyd said affably.

"It can't really be *helping* you," Evan Brewer offered in his sweet-reason voice.

Croyd laughed. "Get real, man. Maybe I'm damaging my tissues and my precious bodily essence. But every two, three months I go night-night and the wild card deals me a whole new set. Where's the damage?"

"Sidestream smoke adversely affects the health of those around you," Luce said primly, folding his lower sets of arms while his upper continued to fan.

"What? Meadows? He's got enough bad habits of his

own. A little cigar smoke won't make him much difference."
He drew on the cigar and released an aromatic jet toward
the log beams of the ceiling.

"So, you gentlemen have something in mind, or is this
a social call? Us old guys need our sleep. But I guess you
know that."

Luce scowled. He liked to think of himself as a youth
in rebellion, although he was old enough to have fathered
most of the second-generation Brigaders. "Colonel wants to
see you. Now."

"Are we in trouble?" Mark asked.

Luce glowered, still feeling the sting of Croyd's "old
guys" crack. Brew shrugged. "He didn't tell us to point guns
at you, for what that's worth," he said easily.

"Can't beat old-fashioned courtesy," Croyd said, standing and sweeping his stubby tail left and right a couple of
times as if to shake the kinks out. He swayed briefly, as if
drunk, then collected himself. "Let's not keep the man waiting."

The Colonel's office was paneled in some dark-stained
hardwood. Mark guessed teak, but he wasn't sure if that
came from Vietnam. It was also small, cozy to the point of
near claustrophobia for three individuals, their chairs, and a
lordly wooden desk.

The room was additionally crowded with two-
dimensional occupants, stuck up on the walls and sharing
frames with Charles Sobel. There was a young Captain
Sobel, painfully earnest, Doug MacArthur chin proudly ajut
as General Westmoreland pinned a medal on his chest.
There were pictures of Major Sobel, a little older, a little
more creased around the eyes, posing with members of the
Joker Brigade company he had commanded in the early seventies. There were a lot of photos of Sobel in civilian
clothes, shaking hands with Jimmy Carter, shaking hands
with Andrew Young, shaking hands with Robert Redford,
shaking hands with the Hero Twins in Guatemala, shaking
hands with Gregg Hartmann, back in uniform to shake
hands with Joker Brigade survivors in front of the Vietnam
Wall, whitewater rafting with Soviet veterans of Afghanistan.
He probably shook their hands, too, but for some reason had
neglected to memorialize it.

"Care for a drink, gentlemen?" Colonel Sobel asked, leaning back in his padded leather chair. Soft New Age music played from a small generator-run CD system. "I have a modest but, if I may say so, fairly high-quality collection of hard liquor."

Croyd asked for Wild Turkey and settled for Jack Daniel's. Mark accepted a cognac without specifying a brand name. Alcohol was not his drug of choice.

Sobel poured some brandy for himself and passed the snifter back and forth beneath his nose, savoring the bouquet.

"*La lucha continua.*" He almost sighed. "The struggle goes on."

He looked at them. "You may wonder at finding me in such decadent surroundings."

"Farthest thing from our minds, Colonel," Croyd said.

"The truth is, life in our materialist consumer-oriented society accustoms one to certain perquisites, certain comforts. It is difficult to do entirely without them. And in truth, why put oneself to the stress of going cold-turkey from decadence, as it were, when there is so much urgent work to be done?"

"No point at all," Croyd said. "We're behind you all the way, Colonel."

He sort of hung his head to one side and gave Mark a big wink. Mark fought an urge to slap him. What the hell was wrong with him?

Sobel nodded. "You gentlemen are aces. Powerful aces. You have a great deal to offer our revolution. And I hope you won't take it amiss if I mention that you're getting up in years. Not that you're *old*, of course, but, simply put, you aren't as young as you once were. Neither am I, of course; why, I'm probably older than either of you."

Croyd raised a three-fingered hand, palm-down, wagged it side-to-side. He was pushing sixty; he had been fourteen when Dr. Tod and Jetboy held the very first Wild Card Day, more or less over his head. His long periods of sleep and the ancillary effects of the wild card virus had kept him in stasis in a sort of indeterminate maturity. His story was not exactly common knowledge. He had told it to Mark in a crystal-meth rush. Over and over.

Not seeming to notice the gesture, Sobel folded his

hands on the desk before him. "What I'm saying is, we're all equal here, but of course I'm willing to take cognizance of both your age and the unique contributions you can make."

"We want to pull our weight, sir," Mark said.

Have you gone completely insane, you drug-addled freak? Cosmic Traveler wanted to know. *Don't you know better than to contradict a man who holds life-and-death power over us? And listen to him—do you* like *filling sandbags?*

"You will do that, and more. 'From each according to his ability; to each according to his need.' You have special needs and special abilities both. You, Dr. Meadows, can call upon your 'friends'—you'll have to tell me how you do that, comrade-to-comrade, one of these days."

"Um," Mark said.

"I'm also aware of your fine scientific background. We have a crying lack of qualified medical personnel. The Republic's medical assets are so thinly stretched—another crime to be laid at America's door, denying this country the aid it needs to expand its medical services."

They got plenty of gelt to blow on guns and tanks and warplanes, buppie, J. J. Flash thought. Mark had a flash of relief—he was feeling centered enough at the moment that he knew he hadn't actually spoken the words aloud. Then he glanced frantically at Croyd, afraid *he'd* say them, or something to their effect. Croyd didn't, but he gave Mark another bulb-eyed stage wink, which was almost as bad.

"I was therefore wondering," the Colonel said, "if you'd mind assuming the role of camp pharmacist. It's far from a full-time occupation; I just want somebody competent to oversee our precious inventory. You're clearly qualified—overqualified, if anything."

"Um," Mark said again, "sure, sir. I'd be happy—"

"And you, Mr. Crenson, your powers—"

"Are unique." Croyd tossed off the rest of his Evil Jack as if swallowing a particularly juicy bug. "Over the years I've learned to be *very discreet* about my ace powers, Colonel. The nat world isn't always very understanding, if you catch my drift. You can rest assured that my powers are at your disposal, whenever you may call on them."

Sobel nodded emphatically. "Of course, of course, I understand. The years of oppression. . . ."

He gazed off at his photo collection. "The Socialist Republic is doing a great thing for all aces and jokers here. A great thing. We owe the Republic a heavy debt. And we may be on the verge of being able to begin to pay it back."

He stood up and turned to face his Wall o' Photos, placing his back to Mark and Croyd. "The Republic is beset by traitors, gentlemen. While all over the world the faint of heart are turning their backs on revolutionary socialism, Vietnam has the strength to keep fighting the good fight. But even she has traitors gnawing her vitals from within."

Croyd raised his head suddenly, as if taken by surprise. "Traitors," he said crisply. "Absolutely."

Traitors? Mark thought. He had immense respect for the Colonel and the scope of his Lennonesque vision, but he was beginning to feel like the Alan Arkin character in *The In-Laws.*

"There has been a news blackout throughout Fort Venceremos," the Colonel said, "but we all know how the rumor mill grinds. You may have heard the stories by now: civil unrest in Ho Chi Minh City, rebellion in the countryside, how the People's Army has been struck with an epidemic of desertions. And while I frown upon rumormongering, I must admit there's a good deal of truth to the stories."

He turned. "We may be called upon to demonstrate that we, at least, are loyal to our hosts."

"Certainly, Colonel," Croyd said, and Mark had a horrible flash that he was doing as good a Peter Falk impression as his lipless lizard mouth would allow. "We're with you all the way." Mark just nodded.

"I knew I could rely on you, gentlemen."

"So we may have to, like, go to war," Mark said. Actually he yelled it to Croyd, as the two stumbled across the flooded compound in hammering rain. Croyd was padding along on his hind legs, though his favored mode was all-fours. That would drown him tonight, or at least require him to swim more than walk. Mark didn't know how geckos fared in water—okay, skinks. Croyd was making heavier weather than usual of locomotion, even allowing for the ankle-deep water.

"Could be," Croyd said. "Some fun, huh?"

"So a bunch of our guys fought *against* the Vietnamese

years ago. You think they're really going to like being on the same side with the government if the shooting starts for real?"

"Who knows? It's in their contract, and these are your pinker shade of Nam vets. I haven't got it all worked out, to tell you the truth. Half the time the vets come on like they're way to the left of Lucius Gilbert. Then they suck down a couple *Giai Phongs* and it's 'we were winning when *I* left.' "

He lowered a horny lid to half-mast and laid a finger alongside his broad snout. It was an alarming sight.

"By the way," he said, "I'm not so sure our Colonel has all his hatches battened down tight. Can't you just see him with a little face painted on his hand? 'Señor Pepe *likes* zee lizards. Don't you want a keess . . .?' "

"Stop that. Colonel Sobel is a great man. He's a visionary."

"He's a dude who had you beaten with rubber hoses in a room with drains in the floor, Mark."

"Never mind that. He was doing what he thought was best; he thought I was a CIA spy or something. Besides, the Vietnamese dudes did the actual beating. Sobel was just watching."

"If making excuses for people becomes an Olympic event anytime soon, be ready to pack your bags for Barcelona next year because you just qualified."

"You don't understand, man. It's good to have visions. Us wild cards *need* visions. Especially since some of us can't see beyond where the next rhinoceros beetle is coming from."

They reached Croyd's bunker, ducked inside. "I'm sorry, man," Mark said, as soon as the rain was off their backs.

"No, *touché*, fair's fair. When you're right, you're right."

Mark shot him a warning look. "All right. I'll stop with *The In-Laws*." He lay down on the pallet he'd made out of blankets.

"So what *are* your powers this time, man?" Mark asked, sitting on a crate that was there for the purpose.

Croyd laughed. "Well, I can climb walls like a son of a bitch. And I can catch bugs with my tongue."

Mark was staring at him. "Hey, *you* try catching bugs

with *your* tongue. It's not as easy as it sounds. If you or any of these jokers tried it, all you'd do is just mash 'em into the ground. Don't want to do that; gets 'em all muddy and gritty."

"Gak," Mark said. "You mean, you don't have any powers?"

"Other than those . . . none I've noticed yet. No levitation, no bolts of lightning from my fingertips, nothing like that. And for once I'm actually weaker than a nat. I thought one time my scales were turning color, but it was just a trick of the light. We get your green-flash sunsets from time to time here in scenic Vietnam."

"What if Sobel finds out you don't have any of these 'special abilities' he was talking about? Unless he's planning on launching a big bug-eradication campaign, he's gonna be pissed."

"Who's gonna tell him?"

Without waiting for an answer, Croyd placed one hand atop the other and rested his head on them. He knew Mark was no informer.

"Hey!" Mark said. "They way you were acting in there, like you were drunk or something—"

"So I was a little giddy," Croyd said without raising his head.

"You're not getting sleepy, are you?"

"Nonsense," Croyd said firmly. "I already told you. Lizards don't sleep."

Chapter Twenty-eight

At the next break in the rain a bunch of the new recruits got sent to a rifle range beside the Vietnamese People's Army camp next door for a little training. The kid with the flesh-bars in front of his mouth eyed his M-16 with disdain.

"Why we gotta fuck with these?" he asked. "I heard they jam all the time. Don't they use AK-47s around here? Now, those guns are *bad*."

The instructor was a tall, narrow Joker Brigade original with a squint and bright-green skin. "You've been watching *60 Minutes* too much, Dillman. The media have distorted the story, as they do anything connected with the Vietnam experience—anything to do with firearms, for that matter.

"After the M16's introduction to combat in the middle 1960s, a number of the rifles experienced failure-to-feed malfunctions, what the layperson will call your jam. Frequently these had fatal results to the shooter. The Army and Colt did a study, announced that nothing was wrong, and proceeded to fix it."

He smiled without humor. "Since that time the M16 has undergone a number of improvements and refinements—what you computer types might call debugging. You now have the privilege to be equipped with the very latest rendition, the M16A2. Consider yourselves fortunate. The Black Rifle *is* the finest assault rifle in the world. You will treat it with respect."

"But what about the AK-47?" another kid wanted to know.

"Heft your rifle, soldier. Is it heavy?"

"Uh, not particularly."

The instructor reached into the duffel bag at his feet, produced a wooden-stock AK. "The Kalashnikov series of assault rifles consists of the AK-47—which is old and out-moded, people, though the People's Army still has a lot of them—the AKM, the folding-stock AKMS paratrooper model and the new AKS-74 family, which are in 5.45-millimeter instead of 7.62 like the older ones. They have several things in common. They are no more mechan-ically reliable than the M16A2, even under extreme field conditions. They have a safety/single-shot/full-auto selector that is loud enough to wake the dead, which is inconvenient on ambush. And, people, they are *heavy.*"

He tossed the rifle to Dillman. The kid caught it, then staggered, almost dropping the weapon.

"A fully loaded AK-47 weighs upward of ten and a half pounds. An M16 weighs less than seven. Those three-pounds-plus seem very, very significant when you have to hump the rifle through elephant grass and up and down hills under our beautiful Southeast Asian sun all day long.

"Do you now understand why you will carry and learn to shoot the Black Rifle?"

The assent was on the muted side. The instructor let it go without comment and proceeded to the instructing part.

Mark took his turn shooting. To his astonishment he wasn't instantly seized with a desire to run off and start gun-ning down Vietnamese schoolchildren the instant the piece was loaded, despite the ready availability of Vietnamese schoolchildren. The rifle had very little felt recoil, and wasn't horribly loud.

It was actually kind of fun.

"As originally issued," the instructor said, "the M16A2 had a regulator restricting full-auto fire to three-round bursts. It was observed that the first thing troops did on be-ing issued the weapon was to disable the three-round regu-lator. Accordingly, the weapons you have been issued can be fired in the unrestricted full-auto mode. You would be well advised not to do so."

Right. The recruits sprayed bullets downrange on full automatic, a magazine at a time. Mark noticed that even at close range few rounds from a full thirty-round mag hit any-where near the X-ring when fired flat out. A couple of the

young guns managed to miss not only the somewhat maca-
bre black man-outline target proper but the paper border as
well with entire magazines.

Mark, obedient to the instructor's orders primarily because he had no idea what the hell else to do, fired his shots
one at a time, aiming each as best he could. Though the others jeered and hooted for him to hurry, he got better than
half his shots into the black at twenty-five meters.

"Well, congratulations," the sergeant-instructor said.
"You killed him, instead of just scaring him shitless the way
most of these homeboys did. Guess which lasts longer in
combat?"

Mark felt both satisfaction and guilt. Though some of
his "friends" had taken human life, it was creepy to feel
good about *shooting* anything. He suspected that if it actually came to action, he would flip the selector to Anything
Goes and empty his mag with the best of them. And he was
unsure he could actually fire at another human with any
hope of hitting him. He knew the hot-and-cold rush of combat and knew that the real thing differed from practice as
death differs from dance.

It's nice to have friends, he thought as they packed it in.
The rain began to fall again.

"I don' know but I been told—"
The Ural-375 lurched up the cracked blacktop road,
southwest into the Tay Nguyen. The sky was clear. The sun
beat on the canvas shell so hard, it seemed damned near as
loud as the rain.

"Nat-born woman got no soul."
It was Mark's platoon's turn to be shipped out for what
Croyd—just transferred into the same squad as Mark—
called sleepaway camp: overnight or longer patrols in the
mountainous Central Highlands of Gia Lai-Kon Tum Prov-
ince. Some regarded the rotation as a welcome break from
Venceremos; it was reputedly cooler in the mountains than
down by the coast. On the other hand, the inhabitants
tended to be Montagnards or ethnic Viets forcibly trans-
planted from Ho-ville, and not at all welcoming.

"Find me one before I die—"
Sobel and his monitors had been stepping hard the last
week or so on rumors that the Highlands were in a state of

virtual revolt. There were a few traitors at work, undoubt-edly in the pay of the CIA. The populace—the ocean in which guerrilla warriors swam like fish—rejected them roundly.

"Take her down, give it a try."

Though he said nothing even to Croyd, Mark felt ap-prehension. He had noticed that often as not, the heavily laden craft taking off from Da Nang rolled out heading in-land and came back with their hardpoints empty. *Maybe there's a test range in the Highlands,* he told himself.

"Sound off!"

"One, two!"

Two squads, about twenty men, were jammed into the Ural. Its wood floor and metal sides rubbed Mark raw at the tailbone and lower back. Gilbert—in command of the pla-toon with the apparent rank of first lieutenant—bragged on it as the most powerful and capable utility truck in the world. That might be true, but it didn't seem to be designed for hauling humans. Maybe the Network had secretly sold the Sovs a design meant for rhomboidal life-forms.

"Sound off!"

"Three, four!"

"Sound off!"

"One, two three, four, one, two—three, four!"

"Y'know," said Croyd, stirring beside Mark, where he had been slumped the past half hour seemingly asleep or dead, "that's kind of catchy."

Mark grimaced. The marching song had a nasty edge to it, in the tone in which it was sung and in lyrics that smacked to him of rape. It made him uncomfortable.

Seated across the truckbed, Dillman gave Mark his death's-head grin. "You're not singing, Meadows. What's the matter? Don't like our little song?"

"Hey," another kid said, "you know how *clannish* nats are. They always stick together in the face of nasty, dirty jok-ers." He and Dillman made a big show of working the bolts of their M16s. It didn't really matter—they didn't have any ammunition—but to Mark it was the thought that counted. He spent the rest of the ride with one hand in his pants pocket, wrapped around a vial of powder. It was orange, and he just hoped the rain held off until the trip was over.

*   *   *

Their new forward base camp was at a gutted church, on a hill surrounded by mountains and overlooking a vast expanse of tea bushes. Croyd paused a moment to light a stogie and gaze out at the vista. Like the rest of rural Vietnam that Mark had seen, the mountains and the plantation were green, more shades of green than he had ever known existed, and all so lush they hurt the eye.

Dirt roads crossed the green tea fields, red and raw as the marks of a whip. The straw hats of black-clad workers bobbed among the waist-high plants.

"Lordy, look at all them slaves just a-workin' away on de old plantation," Croyd intoned in a terrible Amos 'n' Andy accent.

"It's not a plantation," Mark said. "It's a collective farm."

Up until that moment Mark hadn't known Croyd could move his rather forbidding-looking eyebrow ridges. He raised one now. The effect was as if the *pon farr* had hit Mr. Spock while he was visiting the Gorn homeworld, and the resultant offspring was trying to mimic Daddy's trademark "highly illogical, you dumb Earthling fucks" look.

A rain squall swept the plantation—no, *commune*—workers from view as though washing them away. Luce Gilbert emerged from the lead Ural of their two-truck platoon convoy. He wore a cammie baseball cap and a camouflaged uniform whose creases you could shave with. It was obviously tailored; it had sleeves for his upper two sets of arms, the functional ones, and little tuck-and-roll pouches for the lower, semivestigial sets. He began to yell orders for his troops to unass the Urals from Hell and get his H.Q. tent set up among the bullet-pocked stone walls and fallen blackened timbers of the church.

Mark turned around to help unload the gear. A touch on his biceps stopped him. He whirled to find Osprey standing beside him. His talons were lustrous black, with white feathers between. They gripped Mark lightly by the arm.

Mark's eyes rolled. His hand hunted wildly through his pants pocket. Those claws could take a man's throat out like *that*. A spatter of rain hit his cheek. *No, orange won't do, the rain'd be like an acid bath to J. J. Flash. And the sun's still shining, so Moonchild's out. . . . Jesus, does this mean my only chance is to turn into Aquarius?*

"Don't be afraid," Osprey said. His huge, hooked beak was anything but reassuring. "I won't hurt you."

He steered a still-quivering Mark to one side. "Look, what happened back at Rick's . . . we didn't know you, man. Didn't know who you were. We know now. We remember what Cap'n Trips did for Doughboy when the nats were ready to toast him, man. We don't forget our friends."

"Uh—thanks, man."

"Now, the way some of these young bloods talk—" He shook his magnificent eagle head—"Be aware you don't have to worry about *us*, man. But keep an eye on your back, just the same. Some of these kids look at you, they see nothing but nat meat. Know what I mean?"

Mark nodded nervously, glanced around through the downpour. Nobody was paying any overt attention to him. "Yeah. Thanks, man."

"The Rox lives, man." Osprey gave him a feathered thumb up and drifted away. Mark stood watching him, with his boonie hat collapsing around his ears from the weight of the water falling from the sky, fingering the vials in his pocket.

Okay. If somebody tries anything, I turn into Aquarius and hope for the best.

Why did trying to do good have to be so complicated?

Chapter Twenty-nine

They were crashing and tripping their way down through the dense underbrush of a jungle slope, alternately cursing the hill, the jungle, each other, and the clouds of tiny stinging bugs that swarmed around them. Even Croyd, humping along on all-fours behind Mark in the middle of the line, bitched about them. They were too small to catch with his tongue, and they got in his eyes and up his nose like everybody else's.

Eye Ball, Second Squad's point man, loomed up on the deer trail they were following. Walking first after him, bulky Haskell left off griping about being compelled to tote the squad's big black M-60 machine gun to point the weapon at him.

As soon as the column stopped, Mark collapsed by the side of the trail. His lungs pumped air that cut like glass. The muscles of his thighs felt like lye Jell-O. His pack straps were like a cheese slicer cutting him in thirds.

"Easy. Easy, dammit." Sarge pushed forward from the third spot to shore the M-60's barrel skyward. His M-16 had a thick M-203 grenade launcher slung under its barrel; along with Haskell he was the squad's heavy-weapons support. He alone carried ammo, for both components of the compound weapon. "Mario, what does he say?"

The point man had no mouth; his head was a mass of eyeballs, of various sizes and colors, with a boonie hat perched uncomfortably on top to keep the sun off. Mark had the impression the eyes tended to flow together and redivide over time, but he wasn't sure. Eye Ball was one of the few jokers he had met whom he honestly could not stand to look at for any length of time.

Eye Ball was agitated, waving his hands frantically, and not just at the insects that must have been torturing him to the point of madness. He communicated solely by signing. Mario was his official interpreter. A significant percentage of jokers lacked the capacity for speech, so sign was the unofficial second language of jokers everywhere. Mario was the squad's most fluent signer.

"He says he's found something," the slender young joker reported. "He can't say exactly what it is."

"Is it dangerous?" Sarge asked.

Eye Ball held up his right hand and made a motion like a chicken closing its beak with his thumb and index and middle finger. "No," Mark panted under his breath as Mario translated aloud.

"What? You understand signing?" Croyd had sat up when the column stopped, and was craning around Mark to see what was going on. He wore a boonie hat, too, and because his skull wasn't real ideal for holding hats, it was taped under his chin. The effect was of some sort of wharf dowager got up for hard weather. "I never knew that."

"I have a cousin who's hearing-impaired. I picked up some signs growing up. Stuff like 'I love you' and, uh, 'bullshit.' "

Commotion erupted behind, up the hill. Mark heard the voice of Spoiler, currently in the tail position, raised in an unusually shrill squeal of anger.

"Point man for First Squad must've bumped into the boy and scared poor little him," Croyd said unsympathetically.

"Sir," called Studebaker Hawk from just in front of Mark. "Sir, it's, uh, Lieutenant Gilbert. He wants to know why the delay."

"Candy-ass political mother*fucker*," Sarge said, walking back to accept the radio handset from the former Killer Geek warlord, who had become subdued almost to the point of meekness around him. Nobody could quite figure out why; the Joker Brigade vet was gruff and exacting, but even Mark, a highly sensitive kind of guy, thought he stopped well shy of abusive. "And that's 'Sergeant,' not 'sir.' I work for a living. Yeah, Charlie Two Two Six, over."

"He's pissed," Croyd said behind his hand. Mark nodded. The Sarge was a bug on radio discipline; for him an extra "yeah" was equivalent to a screaming fit.

The radio unit looked modern—newer than Mark would have expected, much more compact. The Brigade had cast-off uniforms and an infirmary-dispensary that was a gesture at best, but they had the latest in weapons and commo gear. He didn't know what to make of it.

The sergeant listened for a moment, then said, "We're looking into it." He handed the handset back to the Hawk. "Come on, everybody. We don't want the *lieutenant* having himself a stroke."

He didn't much care for Luce's officially sanctioned assumption of military rank either. Luce had no more training or experience than ... well, than most of the rest of the New Joker Brigade.

Mark and Croyd and several of the others followed the sergeant as Eye Ball excitedly led them to his find. He stopped and pointed at what looked like a particularly overgrown patch of undergrowth.

Sarge frowned, and then his hound-dog features softened. "I'll be damned," he said softly.

He reached up and began to tug at a strand of liana. It gave away, revealing a broken stub of blade.

Suddenly it all made visual sense to Mark—the patches of flat faded-olive surface glimpsed through foliage, fitting together to suggest a rounded form.

"It's a slick," the sergeant said. "An old Huey."

Eye Ball stood by looking multiply expectant. Mario licked his pebbled lips, then spelled out H-E-L-I-C-O-P-T-E-R with his right hand.

They all gathered around, pulling at the brush and the vines enough to reveal the unmistakable sperm shape of a utility chopper, long deceased. Several of the youngsters crowded in to peer through the windscreen, which was totally devoid of glass.

"Shit," Eraserhead said in disappointment. "No dead dudes inside."

"Didn't burn," Sarge observed. He pointed at the streamlined housing humped above the crew compartment. "Looks like they caught a couple rounds from a twelve-seven heavy machine gun in the engine and autorotated in."

"You look thoughtful," Croyd said to Mark, settling himself down drowsily as First Squad came tromping down the trail to see. "What's on your mind."

"I—" He shook his head. "It just seems, like, real sad to me somehow."

"What's this? The Last Hippie wasting sympathy on a machine? All this indoctrination in dialectic materialism must be getting to you." He put his head down on his forefeet and lay still.

Luce Gilbert came downhill in his natty cammies and posed for a picture with his foot propped on the dead Huey's duckbill snout. Mark just stood there with tears coursing down his cheeks. He had no idea why.

Mark flattened himself behind the moss-grown log his rifle was propped on and willed himself to become one with the spongy mulch of rotting vegetation below him. Its smell, rich with decay and edged with fermentation, made his head swim. He had a bunch of branches stuck to his hat, which made him feel like a walking salad. The afternoon sun ricocheted among the leaves of the trees like a lightspeed pinball.

"Damn!" Croyd exclaimed beside him.

Mark jumped. "Wow," Croyd said. "For a moment there I thought you'd just found out *you* could levitate."

"You scared me," Mark hissed.

"What are you whispering for?"

"We're supposed to be on *ambush practice*."

"Yeah, but it's broad daylight. Hard to take it all seriously. Aren't ambushes supposed to happen at night? Isn't that in the rules?"

"You can have ambushes in the daytime."

Actually Sarge had grumbled mightily about having to run ambush drill during the day. But the platoon was only doing maneuvers in daylight, since they'd tried a nocturnal patrol night before last and Luce fell into a stream. For some reason it had taken the members of his First Squad almost fifteen minutes to haul him out, dripping and sputtering.

"Mark Meadows," Croyd said, "jungle warfare expert."

Mark grunted. At least Croyd seemed all the way awake today. Lately he seemed always on the verge of dropping off; yesterday Mark could have sworn he saw his outline began to shift, as if he were beginning to metamorphose right before Mark's eyes. Croyd told him the sun was boiling his brain, which may have been so, but Mark was glad he'd roused him anyway.

He was settling his mind back on blending into the landscape when a scream raised him up off the humus all over again.

Croyd jerked as if startled awake. "*Now* what?"

Thirty meters away through the undergrowth Haskell was hopping around clawing at his stocky body. "*Army ants! Army ants!*" he shrieked. "I'm being eaten alive! *Aieee!*"

Mark jumped up, martial make-believe forgotten. They had encountered nasty stinging white ants before. If the machine-gunner had gone to ground in the midst of a swarm of those, he was running a serious risk of anaphylactic shock. That meant Mark would be needed in a hurry. The sergeant had received medic cross-training, but he wasn't real current.

Haskell was dancing around his M-60 as if paying it bizarre ritual homage. The pink cilia around his mouth waved like a stadium crowd at a play-off game. The ground around the heavy weapon, and indeed the machine gun itself, was alive with a white swarm.

"Whoa, look at the size of those suckers," remarked Croyd, who was following Mark. "And check out the size of their *jaws.*"

The sergeant had one hand on Haskell's shoulder, trying to get him to stand still, while the other brushed at the half-inch insects that covered him. "Here, here, settle down," he said in a low, level voice. "You're okay. Those aren't ants."

"*They're all over me, they're all over me!*" Haskell shrieked. "*They're eating me, Goddammit!*"

"No, they're not."

All of a sudden Haskell stopped hopping and squalling. "They're not?" he asked in a normal voice.

"Feel any bites?"

"Uh ... no. Just them mosquito bites I been itching since last night."

The sergeant picked one of the insects off Haskell with his fingertips, held it up before his face. The creature opened and shut sweeping mandibles that looked a third as long as it was.

"Soldier termites," Sarge said. "They don't eat people."

He stuck the tip of his forefinger between the jaws. They pinched it, indented the skin deeply, then released. Mark thought the bug looked outraged at being had.

"The 'Yards—that's short for *Montagnards*—use 'em to close wounds, instead of stitches. They pinch the wound shut, get a termite to close its jaws on it, then bust the body off and leave the head holding on. Works fine."

"Wow," Mark said.

"Bugs won't eat you, but they *will* eat everything else that isn't metal. Including the furniture on your pig, there." He nudged the M-60 with the toe of his cloth-topped jungle boot. The weapon was crawling with termites, all gnawing away to see what was edible.

"All right, everybody. Time to shift. We put our ambush right in the path of a swarm."

Haskell grabbed up the machine gun and began to dust insects from it. The sergeant looked at Croyd. "What are you waiting for, brother? Chow down."

Croyd reached out and tweaked the mandibles of the insect the sergeant held. "Too spicy for my tastes," he explained.

Chapter Thirty

Standing out in the black and the rain, Mark felt he really understood erosion for the first time. If he just stood there till, oh, about noon, he figured all of him would have washed away.

A joker shaped like an oil drum with a low dome of a head passed down the line of shivering troops, handing out Ripstop magazine pouches.

"Y'all guard these with your lives," said Sergeant Slumprock, the platoon sergeant. He was another original, a good ol' boy from Oklahoma, stubby and powerful, with a general melted look to him. Nobody knew if Slumprock was a joker name or his by-God surname. "Have 'em ready to hand at all times. God help you if you load one of them suckers into the magazine well of your M-16 without Lieutenant Gilbert, Sergeant Hamilton, or myself orderin' you to do so. Got that?"

"Yes, Master Sergeant!"

He glared around at them with tiny blue Poland China–hog eyes beneath brows so pale they were only visible because the early-morning rain darkened them up some. He looked as if he wanted to run the old "I can't *hear* you" gag on them. But like Hamilton, Second Squad's leader, Slumprock didn't really go in for hardass movie-drill-instructor games. You didn't want to give the man any static, but he didn't walk out of his way to step on your face either.

"All right. Everybody keep your heads out there. Now git your asses in them trucks."

* * *

"Villagers say no deserter here," Pham the translator said. He was a skinny little guy with not much in the way of a chin, dressed out in PAVN khakis and a rain-glossed pith helmet. He held his nostrils pinched, which made him talk funny, and he looked as if he wasn't sure which disgusted him more, jokers or the Montagnard villagers huddled miserably under their freshly loaded guns.

Mark stood by Croyd with his M-16 held so muzzle-low, the flash suppressor was practically in the mud. Like those of the rest of the platoon, his hands and face streamed blood from dozens of tiny cuts. They had humped half a klick through elephant grass for their surprise visit to the suspect village. The stuff was higher than Mark's head and edged like razors.

Lucius Gilbert stood with top two pairs of arms akimbo and a steady stream of rain sluicing off the bill of his camo baseball cap, staring from the Vietnamese interpreter to the young Montagnard to the old Montagnard with a face like a relief map of the *Chaîne Annamitique*. "When I talk to you, why do you have to talk to him, and then he talks to the old guy?" Luce demanded. "Won't the old fuck deign to talk to us directly?"

"He no can," Pham said haughtily. "He no speak Vietnamese. Him *moi*."

"That means 'savage,'" Croyd said brightly. He was propped on his tail with his rifle cradled in his arms. He claimed it was uncomfortable to hold in a ready-to-fire position. "The Viets don't think the 'Yards are human. Of course, the 'Yards return the favor."

To Mark the twenty or so villagers, squatting in the rain in ponchos made from what would probably be colorful blankets if there were enough light to bring out colors, looked more like Andean Indians without derbies than Southeast Asian hill tribesfolk. Then again he wasn't really sure what he thought they *would* look like. Mostly they looked pathetic.

Mark glanced at Sarge, standing beside a hootch with his M-203 held ready. The brown canine eyes would not meet Mark's.

I'm trembling, Mark realized.

"Tell them," Luce said to Pham, "that we have a good

tip that they're harboring deserters. Mention to them that that's a pretty serious offense."

Pham spoke rapidly to the younger, who spoke to the elder, who grunted. The grunt came back down the chain.

"Him say no deserter here." From the way Pham was glaring at the elder, Mark suspected he had said more than that.

Suddenly Luce's upper right hand lashed out, seized the old man by the wrist, and dragged his hand out from under the blanket. "Just like I thought," Luce crowed, holding the captive arm up for display while the old man glared holes in his face. "A Timex watch. Takes a licking, keeps on ticking. *Some* tribal people."

He let go the old man's arm. "Have it your way, you soul-bought old puke. All right, everybody, search the village. Really shake it down."

"I don't like this," Mark muttered to Croyd from the corner of his mouth.

"Just remember, you volunteered."

"*There!*" Gilbert's strident yell cut across the whitenoise rain. "That man! What's your *problem*, soldier? Why aren't you following orders?"

It was Eraserhead, the squad fuck-up, still standing there in the middle of the village with the little toy Cub Scout–size pack that was all he could carry pulling his shoulders back like modeling clay and the butt of his M-16 planted in the mud.

"I ain't going," he said.

"What the *fuck* did you say?"

Eraserhead raised his round little chin. Water beaded on his rubbery dark skin. "I ain't going in no huts! I saw *Platoon* and *Apocalypse Now*. They probably got all these crossbows and punji sticks and booby traps and shit just *waiting*."

In three strides Luce was beside him, grabbing him by the biceps. He pointed. "Get your *ass* in that hootch. Right fucking now."

Eraserhead pulled away from him. Luce held on. Eraserhead squealed in pain as his upper arm stretched.

"Lemme *go*! I won't do it!"

"You bogus little fuck!" Luce went wild, pummeling the boy with four fists in a frothing fury. Eraserhead's malleable flesh dented and flowed beneath the storm of blows.

Sergeant Hamilton was between them, thrusting Luce back with a strong left arm. Luce staggered, almost went on his ass in the mud, caught his balance. Eraserhead sat down in a puddle and began to cry.

"What the fuck do you think you're doing?" Luce yelled.

"You got no call to go beating on my men, sir," Sarge said in a low voice.

"That man disobeyed a *direct order*."

"Then there's disciplinary procedures to follow. You can't lay hands on him."

"Look, just spare me the *petit-bourgeois* horseshit, will you?" Gilbert started forward as if looking to try the sergeant on for size.

Then he stopped. He had belatedly realized that both barrels of Hamilton's weapon were trained on the center of his little hill of belly.

"You're going on report for this, Hamilton!" Luce shrieked, screwing his face up so tight it almost pushed his Lennon glasses off his nose. "You'll bake in the Box for fucking *weeks!*"

"That's fine, sir. Charge me if you want. But remember this: lay hands on one of my men again, I'll kill you."

He turned away, put a gentle arm around Eraserhead's shoulder and helped him up. "You okay, son? Nothing permanent out of place? Good. Why don't you come along, cover me while I search that old hootch there?"

They were out of the jungle but not out of the rain. The hills their patrol route ran up and down were steep-sided hogsbacks, lightly forested. It probably would have been very pleasant, if Mark didn't have a heavy rucksack on his back, infected leech bites on his right hip, and a rifle in his hands that felt fully as alien as any Kondikki artifact. And if he wasn't expected to tote it all up and down slopes that ran with slick-mud water like a polluted water slide.

He had just helped Studebaker Hawk down a meter-high drop-off when both feet squirted out from under him. He sat down hard. He began to slide. He shot past the Hawk, who was so startled that he lost his balance, too, and fell sideways. Fortunately there was a bush he could grab and prevent himself and the radio from following Mark.

In his own personal rivulet, bouncing over moguls, flailing his long arms and legs and going, "Whoa! Whoa! Whoa!" as if that would do any good, Mark shot clear to the bottom of the hill. He landed in a narrow hollow between hills, sitting in the midst of what at the moment was a full-blown stream. Fortunately this had some rocks in it to stabilize the slippery mud, otherwise he might not have stopped till he hit the South China Sea.

Croyd came slithering down next to him. "You're such a show-off, Meadows. Can't you just walk downhill like everybody else?"

Not trusting himself to reply, Mark let Croyd help him to his feet and out of the torrent. Croyd's skin felt clammy, and for all Croyd's banter he seemed sluggish and strange.

"You doing okay, man?" Mark was taking inventory and finding to his amazement that he hadn't lost anything: hat, ruck, rifle, wits.

"Fine. I'm fine."

The rest of the squad reached the bottom of the hill. They were on their own today. For some reason Luce had stuck close to First Squad since the village raid, and sent the two squads out separately.

Sarge had memorized their route so that he wouldn't have to take his map out of its sealed pouch and have it melt in the rain. He sent Mario, today's point, down the hollow along a trail following the temporary stream. The rest of the squad trudged after.

"You don't sound fine, man."

Croyd half shrugged and half shivered. "I don't think I'm entirely warm-blooded. I react to changes in temperature a lot more severely than I usually do. It's all a matter of heat economy, I guess. I don't really know what that *means*, but I read about it somewhere, and it seems to me it applies."

He looked at Mark. His gold eyes lacked their customary shine. "You know all this stuff; you're a scientist. I wish I'd gone to college. Hell, I wish I'd finished high school. I'm always making these plans to continue my education, but I never follow through." He shook his head. "I guess it's tough to go to school when you sleep for months at a time."

"Have you ever thought about video courses, man? I

mean, you can, like, order VCR cassettes, watch 'em whenever and then take the tests when you're ready."

"Say, that's a really good idea. Didn't think of that one. That's another trouble with this stop-and-go lifestyle, you tend to lose the ramifications of all this new technology."

Mark was about to remind him that VCR technology was not exactly new when someone behind them began to scream.

Chapter Thirty-one

The latter half of the squad was clumped on the trail like a gall on a treelimb. On the ground in their midst someone was flopping like a fish and screaming as if he didn't ever have to breathe. Mark shed his ruck and went racing toward them. Sarge arrived the same instant, ordering the squaddies to stand back and let him through.

Eraserhead writhed in the mud. His right leg bent like a bow—not a bad sign in itself; though his body and limbs would bend and stretch, they wouldn't break. But the leg disappeared into a hole in the mud beside the trail.

Haskell and the Hawk had him by the shoulders. They pulled on him. His right leg stretched until his bloused pant leg pulled out of his boot and his leg, thinned like a rubber band under tension, was bared. His lips skinned back from his teeth and his head thrashed from side to side. Only the whites of his eyes showed.

"Lay off that!" Sarge barked. "You're doing more harm than good. Dig him out, dammit!"

"With what?" Only Mark and Croyd still had their entrenching tools. The others had covertly thrown theirs away.

"Meadows, Croyd, use your E-tools. The rest of you, use your belt knives or use your bare hands. Just *get him out.*"

They attacked the sodden earth. Eraserhead began to thump in a circle around his trapped foot, shrieking hysterically. Haskell and Mario had to pin his shoulders.

"A pot," gasped the Hawk, clawing up mud though his hands bled from nicks by shovels and knives. "He's got his foot in a fucking *pot.*"

"Careful, careful," Sarge urged. "Get it out of there slow. Somebody—no, fuck it. Spoiler, gimme your Ka-bar."

As pale as the rest of them, Spoiler handed over his heavy knife without argument. "Sheath too." The former gang member unfastened his sheath from his harness and gave it to him.

The sergeant sheathed the knife, reversed it to grip it by the sheath. "Hold that sucker steady," he murmured. Mark and Eye Ball reached in to hold the pot firm. Sarge rapped it carefully with the knife pommel. Eraserhead screamed.

On the third hit the crude pot cracked. Sarge tapped it a few more times to extend the crack. Blood spilled out. The fired clay was thick, and bore the marks of the fingers that had shaped it.

They opened the pot. It was a vicious kind of egg. The inside of the shell was lined with sharp bamboo splinters, smeared with chocolate-brown shit.

They had to hump Eraserhead back to the old church on a stretcher fashioned out of rainslicks and long black M-16s. It took seven hours. Eraserhead sobbed the whole time, though Spoiler raved and threatened to kill him if he didn't shut up. Mark thought he was crying more from fear and a certain outrage than pain, but by the time they got him to their base camp, his foot had swollen to twice its normal size, and streamed clear serum from a score of red-rimmed holes.

The rain broke not long after they arrived. Just before sunset a polliwog-shaped Mi-8 Hip utility chopper motored in from Da Nang. It touched down beside the church, and a crew of khaki-clad medics bundled the now-quiescent Eraserhead aboard. They seemed to be trying to hold the stretcher at arm's length, to avoid all contact with the patient. *Most dinks—uh, Vietnamese—don't think black people are human, any more than they think jokers are*, Sarge had told him once. Eraserhead was both.

Mark had wanted to ask Sergeant Hamilton why, if the Vietnamese were so prejudiced against jokers and blacks—and Sarge was both those things too—he had volunteered to come back and fight for them. He hadn't had the nerve.

"Stay hard, man," Mario called after Eraserhead. "The

Rox lives!" Some of the old-timers sneered, but none said anything.

As the Hip lifted off, Croyd came out of the apparent trance he'd been in since they finally stumbled back up the hill. He rose from the base of the church's pocked wall and wandered over to stand next to Mark.

"All right, everybody," Sarge told the quiet crowd after the chopper's rotor thunder had dwindled enough to permit speech. "We all got better things to do than stand around with our mouths open collecting flies. Or if not, I can sure as hell *think* of a few."

"But, Sarge," Slick said, "that thing the kid's foot got stuck in—"

"Punji trap. Old piece of shit, left over from the last war. Like that old crashed Huey we found, remember? It don't mean nothin'."

He walked off. The crowd began to break up. Mark watched with single-minded intensity as the helicopter lost itself against a distant slab of slate-colored cloud that seemed to be balancing just above the horizon with the half-set sun for a blinding fulcrum. He felt a sense of isolation and dread. There were monsters thronged around them, in all that evening green. One of their youngest and most vulnerable was being taken away into the land of monsters, and there was nobody to look after him.

A star came out, visible just above the band of cloud. Mark shivered.

Croyd yawned, stretched, and took a cigar from the camo fanny-pack he wore in front of his smooth-scaled belly. "Penny for your thoughts."

Mark shuddered. "I wonder what'll happen to him."

Croyd scratched a match alight on his pectoral scales and fired up his smoke. "If we're lucky," he said between puffs, "we'll never find out."

He whipped the match out and dropped it into the red clay at their feet. Glaring at him with ecological fervor, Mark bent over to pick it up.

"What's your sweat, man?" Croyd asked. "It's organic. It's just *wood*. Soldier termites think it's a tasty *hors d'oeuvre*. Something exotic, a break from the same-old same-old."

"Oh." Mark straightened, feeling sheepish. He also felt

surprise. He thought the trendy activist side of him had died with Starshine, in orbit around a far, cold world.

Croyd yawned again. "Uh, y'know, man," he said, looking down at his splayed skink feet, "I was wondering if you could do me a favor when we get back to Venceremos tomorrow."

"What do you need?"

"Well, you're the Brigade pharmacist now and all. I was wondering if you could maybe slip me a little something to help keep me, y'know, *sharp*."

Mark looked at him and sighed. Maybe nothing did change.

"I guess," he said in a carefully neutral tone.

"Now, don't get me wrong, guy. I just need to keep my"—*yawn*—"my *edge*, if you know what I mean. Lizards don't sleep."

"Of course not," Mark said.

"What does it mean," she asked, accepting a tin plate of steaming rice and vegetables, "when the jokers say, 'The Rox lives'?"

"It means they come from a TV generation that never learned to tell the difference between reality and spun-sugar Steven Spielberg Technicolor bullshit," said Eric the Dreamer. To the light of his bunker's single lantern his eyes showed the depth and shimmer of the layered glazes of a seventeenth-century Japanese cup. It was hard to say what color they were—harder, perhaps, to say which they *weren't*. From somewhere in the depths of her, Moonchild summoned the knowledge that such varicolored eyes were called "hazel."

He nodded his heavy jut-encrusted head at the plate, which his guest had yet to touch. "There's no meat in there, if that's bothering you," he said. "I don't eat it myself."

"Koreans are not necessarily vegetarians," she said. "We are a harsh people in some ways, I suppose." She dropped her eyes. Her black *yin-yang* half mask and a heavy fall of black hair hid most of her face in shadow. "But I eat no meat either. It is against my . . . my principles to take life."

He took a bite, chewed slowly, watching her the while.

She found she couldn't look at him for any length of time without her cheeks growing uncomfortably warm.

"Strange to find you in the camp of Mars, then," he said. "We are an army, Ms. Moonchild."

"Isis," she said quickly. "Isis Moon. 'Moonchild' is an ace name. I don't know where I got it, to be honest. There are so many things I don't know. . . . To use an ace name seems so ego-bound, yet that's how Mark and his other friends refer to me."

"Isis, then. If I may."

"Oh, yes—Eric."

"So why are you here? This seems like a funny place to find a pacifist."

"Perhaps *pacifist* is not the right word to use—oh. Forgive me if I seem to contradict you."

He shook his head, mouth full.

"This food is excellent. The vegetables are crisp and flavorful."

"Thank you. The Sterno-can cooking method adapts well to stir-frying. Sorry I'm not able to offer you *kimchi*. This probably tastes a little on the anemic side to you."

"Oh, no, not at all. It's wonderful."

"You still haven't answered my question."

She lowered her eyes again. "I lack the skill with words that I have with my body. I have no gift of verbal evasion."

She took a few bites in silence. He let her. He watched her closely.

"I do not forswear—is this the word? I have not renounced the use of force. There are times when it is necessary to defend the weak or needy, or to defend oneself. But I do renounce the doing of *harm*. Therefore I use force to subdue an attacker without hurting him, so that I can leave his presence. And so, with luck, he can cool down, let go his anger and perhaps through meditation realize that there is no need for violence."

"But there *is* need for violence sometimes. However gently applied, the means you use to subdue your attacker still are *violence*."

She sighed. "As I say, I have no skill for debate. The—violence—I use is restrained, defensive. None suffer it who do not intend harm, and even they suffer as little as possible."

He smiled, shaking his head. "That's a sweet sentiment. I really applaud you for it, Ms. Moon—Isis. But what happens when your attacker isn't just coming after you in the heat of passion? What happens when he really comes to kill you, and he *won't* cool down? When he keeps picking himself up and dusting himself off and coming after you?"

"You saw how I dealt with Rhino. His anger and his fear of seeming weak before his peers caused him to come at me after it was obvious he could not best me, nor harm me unless I let him. I met his attacks, and finally he desisted."

"That's fine," Eric said, gesturing with his fork. "But you're an *ace*, Isis. How about the rest of us, who don't have your metahuman strength and speed and skills, and God knows what else?"

She looked at him. She moistened her lips with a neat pink tongue. She could find nothing to say.

"That's why we're needed. The New Joker Brigade. The nats aren't going to be satisfied with their laws and their hate rallies much longer. Their thirst is only going to be quenched in a flood of joker blood—and ace blood, too, don't jive yourself. They got a taste of it at the Rox. Do you think the lynch mobs will calm down and start loving us humble jokers after you've roughed them up some and given them time to think about it?"

Her mind filled with images of a nat mob coming for her with torches and knives and rope, their white-dough faces twisted into hate pastries. There were dozens of them, hundreds, thousands—too many for her to deal with for all her skill and metahuman traits, surrounding her so that she could not run. Coming to kill her.

"But if you hurt them, do you not lower yourself to their level?" Desperation tinged her voice.

"If that's so, why isn't it lowering yourself to the level of your attacker to use violence at all?"

"Perhaps . . ." She looked all around now, everywhere but at him. "Perhaps we can agree to disagree, yes? I live as I do and act as I do because I have sworn to. If I cause lasting harm, if I take life, I lose what powers I have."

"Nonsense. Your powers come from the wild card virus, not some mystic vow."

"*Please*. I know what I speak of. Could—could Peregrine fly without her wings?"

Eric looked thoughtful. "I read somewhere her wings aren't near big enough to lift her weight, and that in reality she flies by a kind of telekinesis. Sort of like the Turtle."

"But she cannot. She cannot fly if her wings are bound, or if they are damaged. If she lacked her wings, she would not *believe* she could fly, and so she could not. It is the same with me."

"But the world isn't about what you *believe*. It's about what *is*."

She raised her head and looked him in the eye. "Do you truly believe that? You, who call yourself the Dreamer?"

He looked at her a moment. Then he laughed. "Got me with that one. But let's see. I dream of a better world and ask, 'Why not?' I don't imagine the better world *really exists*, here and now, just because I dream it. That's what I'm doing here in Fort Venceremos. Laying my life on the line alongside Colonel Sobel and the rest of the comrades to make the world that better one I dream about. Okay?"

"Perhaps I am naïve. That is why I am here, as well, to work—yes, to *fight*—for your better world, Eric-*sonsaang*. But mine is the gentle way. It must be so."

"Let's hope you enjoy the luxury of keeping your feet on that gentle path."

For several minutes they ate in silence. The bunker was smaller than the one Mark shared with Croyd, lower-ceilinged. It was also neater.

"You're fascinating," Eric told her. "Where do you come from?"

"I was born in Korea," she said. "My father fought with *Inmun Gun*—the army of the Democratic People's Republic of Korea. He was captured during the invasion of the South. At the end of the war he refused repatriation to the North, as so many did.

"My mother was a nurse who tended him in hospital when he was stricken by appendicitis. They fell in love. When he was finally released from the internment camp, they married."

She laid her spoon across her plate. Her appetite had faded. She chided herself: *how long since you actually took*

*food with these lips, this tongue? And he'll think you don't
appreciate his cooking.*

"I was born. My father worked in a factory. I don't remember much about my father. When I was very small, he
returned to the North. He was never happy with life in the
South."

Eric nodded. "The feverish drive to feed the insatiable
appetites of Western consumer-junkie culture. The materialism and greed."

"So I believe. My mother seldom spoke of him . . . we
moved to the country. She ran a village clinic. I remember
she was quiet, not saying much, interested only in helping
people.

"My great-grandfather took care of me. He told me stories of the ancient *hwarang* knights and their traditions of
duty and honor and skill in the martial arts—they were
much like the Japanese *samurai*, you see. He himself was
descended from the *sulsa*, the Knights of the Night. They
were a special sect of the *hwarang*, an elite, trained in
stealth and hidden ways. They were much like the *ninja*, of
course, but unlike the *ninja* they were never outlaws. He
taught me much about their ways; he did not want the skills
to die."

She gazed into the flame of the wick suspended in a
bowl of fish oil that was the only light. The fire danced *kata*
in her black eyes.

"When I was seventeen, I came to America to attend
the University of California at Berkeley. My recollections
become confused after that."

"That's fascinating, Isis," Eric said, holding her with
those beautiful eyes, "and I want to know as much about
you as I can—I want to know all about you, if you'll let me.
But it wasn't what I *asked*."

He laughed gently at her crestfallen expression. "No,
you didn't do anything wrong. I just didn't ask it clear
enough. I wonder where you *come from*—here, now. How
did you get into the middle of a well-guarded military base
without anyone spotting you? Where do you go after you go
into Meadows' bunker? And what's your relationship with
Meadows, anyway?"

"I am Mark's friend," she said deliberately. "Friend"
was what he termed his alter egos, after all. And she truly

felt herself to be his friend, so it wasn't a lie. "Mark's ace ability is to . . . call upon us."

Eric raised an eyebrow. " 'Us?' "

"He has other such friends."

"Yeah. Okay. I remember seeing Jumpin' Jack Flash on Peregrine's Perch once—one of the few times I watched TV since I left my parents' house. He's one of Meadows' 'friends,' isn't he? And Starshine, isn't he another?"

Pain rippled across Moonchild's face. She stared at the planking floor on which she sat cross-legged. "Yes," she said, all but inaudibly. She longed to pour out her loss, *their* loss, to this deformed and beautiful young man, to share the pain. But she sensed resistance from Mark and the others. She would not go against their wishes. Not yet.

"Did I say something wrong?" Eric asked.

"No. It was a memory . . . a memory only."

"So how does Meadows call you? How does such a beautiful woman come into the midst of us, and where do you go when you're gone?"

He was leaning forward, face almost touching hers. Her breath was coming rapidly, as if she had been sparring for minutes on end. *Can I tell him? Can I trust him? How can I not?*

Thunder detonated. Moonchild cried out and clapped her hands over her ears to keep the drums from imploding. The earth rocked. Fine red dust filtered down between the planks in the low ceiling.

She leapt up and began to dart outside, convinced the bunker was about to collapse on them both. She grabbed Eric in passing, to rush him to safety. He went limp, becoming deadweight.

She stopped. She was strong enough to have hauled him bodily out, but she didn't want to risk dislocating his shoulder.

"Come *on!*" she cried. "We must get outside."

She saw he was laughing at her. "That's exactly the wrong response to artillery," he said.

"Artillery?"

"Have no fear. It's outgoing, from the 152-mm guns in the People's Army camp next door."

She frowned. She let him go, went up the steps made of crates to look out.

The whole southern sky lit up in a yellowish flash. A heartbeat, and the noise hit her like a tidal wave. She set her jaw, made herself endure the awful sound.

"Pretty bad, isn't it?" He was standing beside her. She could scarcely hear him for the ringing in her ears.

"Whom do they shoot at?" She thought she could see faint trails of light arcing away across the night. West, into the mountains.

"Nothing in particular. It's just practice firing, that's all."

Just practice firing, that's all. And Sarge Hamilton had said that the punji trap that injured poor Eraserhead was a relic of the War of Liberation, that the young joker's stumbling into it had been a bad accident, happenstance of a country still recovering from a horrid military upheaval a decade-and-a-half ended.

Mark Meadows was no jungle-warfare expert. But even he could recognize green bamboo when he saw it. That punji trap was new.

. . . At first she thought the spasm that passed through her was a product of recalling the truth of that trap, and all that it implied. A second shock passed through her, tangible as the blast from the distant guns.

Grandfather! My hour's up! I'm about to change. . . .

She tore away from Eric, not knowing till then that he had laid a comforting hand on her arm, running across the compound with her long black hair flying.

"Isis!" he shouted. "Isis, come back! It's all right, the guns can't hurt you."

She felt tears squeeze from her eyes and whip across her temples. Her transition back to Mark was intensely personal, private. For others to witness it would be a violation.

She felt guilt at shutting Eric out. He was open with her. How could she hold a part of herself back from him—especially a part as fundamental as where she came from and where she went?

Another spasm wracked her. She almost stumbled. Her molecules were stirring, getting ready to realign themselves. The change was almost on her.

She reached the bunker, hurled herself inside, dove behind the cheap painted rice-paper screen Croyd had scrounged somewhere as a privacy shield.

It was Mark Meadows who hit the palette floor. A crack like the gun-thunder echoed in his ears as air rushed in to replace the atmospheric gases that had been sucked into the transition-vortex, to make good the mass difference between compact Moonchild and gangly Mark. The screen lay across him like the wings of a big origami bird.

He picked himself up. Croyd was lying on his back on his bunk, drumming his sucker-tipped fingers on his belly. He looked at Mark with big golden eyes.

"So how was your date?" he asked.

Chapter Thirty-two

"The Man says burn the village," Sarge said, "we burn the village." It was a sort of *post facto* mantra for him; behind them the bamboo hootches were already ablaze, sending clouds of dense smoke to join the overhang of gray.

Sarge's German shepherd face was grim. Behind him the squad was chatting excitedly, elevated by what had happened.

"Did you see the looks on their dumb nat faces when we torched their shacks?" Haskell asked. His mouth tendrils waved like cheerleader arms.

"Yeah," the Spoiler said, marching along turning his rifle around in his hands, pointing it this way and that. His eyes shone in his backswept skull. "We really dissed 'em, man. We laid some hurt on them. Too bad we couldn't burn some of *them*."

"Payback for the Rox begins now!" Studebaker Hawk cried, pumping his fist in the air.

"The Rox lives!" the squad shouted. Sergeant Hamilton frowned.

Beside the trail the elephant grass stirred, and Croyd emerged next to Sarge, popping up on his hind legs. He was the only one who could move easily through the taller-than-head-high, razor-edged grass. Sarge whipped his M-203 up to cover him, then lowered it again.

"Whaddaya say, guy?" Croyd asked. His golden eyes were wet, gleaming bulbs in the heavy, humid air. "Just like the old days, huh?"

"Shut the fuck up and get back in line," the sergeant

growled. Croyd giggled and vanished back into the tall grass.

They had found deserters in the Highland village, a pair of them, teenagers with buzz cuts and skinny limbs. One of them glared angrily at the foreigners and tried to shake their hands off whenever they touched him. The other soiled himself as he was being dragged out of a hootch and curled into a fetal ball as soon as he was thrown on the ground by a pair of boys from Slumprock's squad. He had to be prodded to his feet with the muzzle brake of an M-16 when the search was done and First Squad was ready to march them to the trucks that would carry them back to the Old Church base camp.

Hamilton's squad was to continue the patrol. But there was something they had to accomplish first.

"The order has come down," Lucius Gilbert announced, strutting around in his baseball cap. "We need to start teaching these traitors to socialism some *lessons*."

Given the daily rains, Mark was surprised how readily the hootches burned. A few white-phosphorus grenades did the trick. They burned with a prodigious quantity of smoke, while the occupants stood by watching with faces so blank that not only all emotion but all thought might have been erased from them.

Mark marched along, bowed by the weight of his PAVN-issue ruck on its American frame and a rifle he had no intention of using. They were nothing compared to the weight on his soul.

I'm turning into one of the people I protested *against,* he thought. *What's happening to me?*

If he ever hoped to recapture the golden Radical of that famed confrontation in People's Park, he feared those hopes were dead now. His hands were blackened. His soul stained.

But all I'm trying to do is what's right!

"Not always too damned easy to figure what's right," said Croyd, popping out of the grass at his side. He jumped, as much because he realized he was thinking aloud again as from being startled.

"Especially when politics come into it." Croyd had recently developed the habit of talking very rapidly. It was no surprise to Mark, who had seen it before. "People always think politics are about right and wrong. That's crap. Politics are about *power*."

"But we're trying to reform the world, make it a better place, man," Mark protested. "That isn't about power."

Croyd patted the receiver of his M-16. "What is it that comes out of the barrel of this baby, huh? Hey, how are you going to make the world a better place without you have power?"

"There's, like, good power and bad power, man."

Croyd laughed and slapped him on the arm. "Hey, hey, Mark my man. You're coming right along. Pretty soon you'll be saying there's good murder and bad murder, huh?"

Mark licked sweat off his upper lip and blinked very rapidly. His eyes filled with tears at the injustice of Croyd's words. *Gotta make allowances,* he told himself. The war between fatigue poisons and amphetamines for possession of Croyd's metabolism was escalating.

By the time he thought of a comeback, Croyd had slipped off in the weeds again.

It rained for an hour and stopped, leaving everything dripping and steaming. Their patrol route took them down into jungled ridges, not canopy rain forest—you could find that, too, in the *Giai Truong Son*—but tall trees spaced far enough apart to let the sunlight in to produce thick, foot-tangling undergrowth, green and wet and just swollen with the scents of decay. There were as many nuances to the smell of decay in the jungle as there were shades of green. There was the lush, sweet, overbearing stink of rotting grass and leaves, fermentation, full and round and fruity, the sinus-invading cat-in-the-crawlspace staleness of animal death—just a hint, but even a hint was noticeable, impossible to ignore, like even the most discreet of tigers at the *bal masque*.

Eye Ball had point this afternoon. They had reached a level spot, where the trail widened in a little clearing. The squad began to look at Sarge, who was marching more quietly than usual, hoping he'd allow them to fall out and take five.

They had mostly filed into the clearing when Eye Ball stopped dead on its far side, near the great trunk of a tree that had fallen at an angle, creating a lean-to of roots and

limbs and draped lianas. He seemed to be listening, which
meant he was watching with especial intentness, the eyes of
his head stirring, rolling.

Suddenly he turned and ran back across the clearing as
fast as he could, clutching his rifle with one hand and signing frantically with the other.

Sarge didn't have to wait for Mark or Mario to translate.
"*Ambush!*" he screamed, as flashbulb-flares began to flicker
from the tented debris beneath the fallen tree.

"*Get down!*" the sergeant screamed. Instead the patrol
broke like a dropped plate, shattering away from the muzzle
flashes into the brush on the near side of the clearing.

Mark heard the *thunk* of Sarge's grenade launcher,
slung beneath the barrel of his M-16, and the crash of the
40mm round exploding off in the woods. His long nose had
plowed up a little mound of black mulch just this side of a
fallen moss-grown log of much more modest dimensions
than the one that blocked their path through the clearing.
He had no idea how he'd gotten there.

"Man! Look at these *bugs*."

Mark's gut spasmed. He half-rolled onto his side, bringing his rifle up awkwardly. Croyd Crenson had dropped
down beside him on his belly and was staring raptly at the
assortment of insect life just pullulating in the rotted wood
a few inches from their noses.

The ambushers' guns were rattling in crowded staccato
bursts, like giant woodpeckers on speed. "Christ!" Mark exclaimed. "What are you doing here? You'll draw their fire!"

"What? Cap'n Trips actually showing a sign of *self-
interest*?" Incredibly, Croyd produced a stogie and lit it with
a lighter from his camo fanny-pack.

"What the hell are you *doing*?" Mark hissed. "They'll
smell your smoke!"

"Naw. They won't smell anything but gunsmoke and
their own sweat—and shit, probably." The adrenal fear-rush
of deadly danger seemed to be having a calming effect on
the amphetamine-soaked Croyd. Mark was not in a mood to
appreciate the biochemical subtleties of the fact. "They're
just as scared as we are."

"What are you talking about?" He started to push the
slim, vented snout of his M-16 over the low log. A burst of

gunfire chewed up the log, spraying his face with friable punky wood and writhing white grubs.

"They haven't hit anybody. Or haven't you noticed?"

As if taking a cue, Sarge called, "Anybody hit? Sound off." The squad members called out negative replies.

"Eye Ball's okay, too, Sarge," Mario yelled from somewhere behind and to the left of Mark.

"Hey!" Mark said. "They stopped shooting!" He started to peek over the log.

Croyd grabbed him by the arm. His grip was clammy and not strong, but emphatic just the same. "Hold on to your horses, boy."

"Open fire!" Sarge yelled. "Start busting caps! *Right now!*"

Mark glanced at Croyd, then held his M-16 up over the top of the log and fired off the whole magazine in a shuddering spasm.

Croyd nodded. "Flashback time again. That's just the way they used to do it, in Nam Round One."

Return fire was cracking past overhead, more desultory than before. "Why'd they stop shooting?" Mark asked, dropping his spent magazine and trying to cram in another. He dropped the fresh mag three times.

"Same reason you did. They all went dry at once. Sarge Hamilton ordered everybody to shoot so we'd grab *fire superiority*." Croyd took a hit from his cigar. "Basically that means making them keep their heads down."

Mark's fingers were scrabbling in the dark soil for the fallen magazine like the legs of some giant jungle insect. Suddenly he stopped, took a deep breath. Then he carefully picked up the full magazine and pushed it into the well with a click.

"How come you know all this stuff?" he asked Croyd.

Croyd popped a huge pale beetle into his mouth with his tongue and rolled over onto his back, as if bullets weren't passing with miniature sonic booms inches above his nose. "I read books. I never did finish my education, but I can read." He looked at Mark. "All the fear went out of you just then, didn't it? What happened?"

Mark stared at him. He had studied the workings of the mind enough to have no sentimental notions about the insights of the crazy. Crazy people thought crazy things. But amphetamine intoxication or no, Croyd was being very perceptive, out here on death's green edge.

"Yeah. I let go my fear. Now I feel calm."

Croyd eyed him with glittering gold interest. "How'd you accomplish that?"

"I died. On Takis—off Takis, I mean. In orbit. I—part of me died. *I* died."

"No white light?"

"No. Just dead."

"So what happened just now?"

Mark shrugged. "I panicked when Eye Ball came running back and those people opened up. But talking with you, I suddenly thought, 'What the heck? What's it matter?' They can't do anything to me that hasn't been done before."

The attempt to make the enemy keep his head down had failed, unless they were hip to that blind-firing trick too; a brisk little firefight was in progress. To Mark it all seemed to be happening to someone else, far, far away. As if he were watching it all on TV in his parents' den in smug southern California safety.

Croyd was studying him with speed-freak intensity. "Uh-oh," he said.

"Why 'uh-oh'?"

"Holy shit!" It was the normally calm Slick, his voice sliding on a glass sheet of panic. "Sarge, they're getting around behind us!"

"Excuse me, man," Mark said, unbuttoning a pocket of his camouflaged blouse. "I'm gonna roll behind this bush. . . ."

"Hey, it's cool. I've seen you change before."

Mark stared. Only K. C. Strange and Tachyon had actually seen him turn into one of his "friends." Well, yes, about half of New York had seen it on the evening news, at that apartment fire the last night with Sprout and Kimberly Anne, but that was an accident. The only reason the jumper girl—Blaise's main squeeze of that moment—who had befriended him on the Rox had gotten to witness the change was that Mark was half-convinced it wouldn't work.

"Remember that night we both did up some windowpane? You tried this new batch of powder you'd been working on and turned into this giant raccoon. I thought I'd flipped out totally."

Mark stared at him. A friend he didn't even *know* about? He shook his head. *No, he was tripping. . . .*

Fresh gunfire from the left—the heavy, slow clatter of an AK. Mark slammed the contents of the tiny vial in his vest.

Croyd yelped and rolled away from the flames that enveloped Mark. "Jesus! What's *in* that stuff?"

"Me," said Jumpin' Jack Flash, Esquire, flexing his fingers. Orange flames capered from tip to tip.

He looked at Croyd, who was flat on his belly several meters away. "So what was that 'uh-oh,' anyway?"

"You ever read Joseph Campbell? *Hero with a Thousand Faces?*"

"Yeah. I thought it was pretentious jive."

He swooped up ten feet in the air and hovered, arms akimbo. "All right, you jerks, you haven't hit anything yet. Try your luck with me."

For a moment all was silence except for the dripping of rain from a billion leaves. Then gunfire reached for him from behind the huge fallen tree.

"Your aim still sucks," he said. He rolled his left palm open. A line of fire stabbed into the heart of the great trunk.

The tree exploded as the water trapped in it flashed into steam.

J. J. Flash laughed as half a dozen black-pajama-clad ambushers went rolling backward from the blast. They picked themselves up and ran off into the bush, elbows pumping.

Shots from the left. J. J. felt the shock waves of their passing slap his face. He pivoted, jetted flame from his palm. Another tree, this one standing, blew up, fragments black against an expanding ball of plasma. As the top half of the tree crashed down, another set of ambushers fled.

Laughing, Jumpin' Jack Flash cast his fire-lances far and wide. Miniature suns flared. Trees fell. Ambushers ran for their lives.

Then all was still. A few birds began tentatively to sing.

Wreathed in smoke, J. J. Flash looked down on his fellow squadmates. They stared up at him, faces blank.

He conjured a guitar, a Fender o' Flame, alive in his hands. He struck a chord, reverberating off through the jungle. The smoke whipped away. He floated against a low, cement-colored sky.

"It's a gas-gas-gas," he said.

A raindrop struck his shoulder. He yelped in sudden pain. "This is what I get for being overconfident," he said, and darted for the cover of an intact stand of trees.

When the squad, still pale and unsteady on its feet—whether from the ambush or J. J.'s demonstration—reached the point where Flash had vanished, they found Mark sitting in the rain, humming "Give Peace a Chance."

Chapter Thirty-three

"Hey, bay-*bee*!"

Moonchild ignored the wolf calls from around the bon-
fire that leaped higher than Giraffe's mottled mauve head.
Normally she would have stopped to upbraid the young
men for their sexist behavior. Not tonight. She would have
to fight one or many of them, and they would come at her
with such ferocity that she was afraid she might hurt one inadvertently. These war dances, which had begun after the
gloves came off and the New Brigade was put on combat
status, put the boys in a badger-savage mood.

As she walked on, a fight broke out behind her. The
nonparticipants gathered around to urge the fighters on with
howls and jeers and the throb of Public Enemy for
soundtrack. Beer had been banned from the camp, but she
doubted that the youths had tea or the heavily chemical-
flavored water in their cups and canteens. Even pariah Mark
had heard rumors of secret stills inside the wire. And the
raggedy army of vendors that had gathered outside the
gates, despite Sobel's fulminations and the best efforts of
the Vietnamese authorities, were willing to provide anything
at all for a wad of Vietnamese *dong* or, better, a few dollars
carried across the water in a back jeans pocket.

She owed her very presence to that enterprise, in sad
fact. The store of potions Mark had mixed in Athens was
running low. And there were limits to the kind of drugs he
could get his hands on as camp pharmacist. He was severely
worried about the purity of what he was able to scrounge;
given the powerful effect of his potions, he didn't even want

to *imagine* the possible effect of a bad trip caused by tainted components. But so far his luck had held.

She veered in the other direction then, to carry herself wide of the Boxes and their reek of human filth marinade. Sobel had five of them now. They still had a waiting list.

Behind her someone started screaming. Her reflex was to turn and run back, to help. But to interfere would be anticommunitarian—acting against the popular will. She kept walking.

She was learning a lot here in the struggle-capital of Fort Venceremos. All Mark's personae were.

She reached the entry to Eric's solo bunker, paused. From inside came sounds of conversation, male laughter, hard as brass. For a moment she concentrated on centering herself. Then she rapped on the peeled-pole lintel.

"Come," Eric's voice called.

She advanced into gloom that seemed more intensified than diminished by the low-turned kerosene lantern. Eric the Dreamer sat with three young jokers, new arrivals. The one sitting cross-legged with his back to Moonchild when she entered still wore Killer Geek colors—a violation of New Joker Brigade policy. It surprised Moonchild; Eric was a vocal upholder of Sobel's discipline, one of the few among the young bloods who was.

Her resolve faltered. "Am I interrupting something?"

The young blood with the colors squeezed out a low wolf whistle. "Stop that," Eric said softly.

"Hey," said another through a mouthful of teeth like curved yellow knitting needles. "I thought we was like all pals here. Share and share alike. No property."

Eric looked at him. The boy with the teeth suddenly paled. He shot to his feet, staggered against the doorframe next to Moonchild, then managed somehow to eel out without touching her. His two buddies followed, stumbling all over each other in their eagerness to get outside without coming in contact with the slim young woman.

"What did you do to them?" she asked Eric, who still sat cross-legged and serene, like a slender youthful Buddha.

"Showed them the error of their ways," he said with a smile. "We don't tolerate sexism here."

"So you have the power to give nightmares as well as beautiful dreams."

He held his hands palm up and open on his thighs. "To every *yin* there must be *yang*. You're Asian; surely that's no surprise."

She shook her head as if trying to drive away the omnipresent bugs, swarming in that especially frenetic way they did just before the rains hit again. "It doesn't matter," she said.

"They brought disturbing news," he said. "Word on the street back home is the government massacred the jokers they took prisoner on the Rox."

"No!"

He nodded. "It's the rumor. But I believe it. Don't you—really, deep inside?"

"I can't. The government—it's America! They'd never do anything like that! They wouldn't permit it."

"Then why," he said calmly, "are you here and not there?"

She was in his arms, clinging to him like a baby monkey, weeping. He sat statue-solid, statue centered, holding her and whispering endearments into her hair until she cried herself out.

She rose. He looked up at her, calm and unsurprised as she stood over him. Her hair fell heavy across his forehead, his face. She put her hands on the tortured badlands of his cheeks.

She bent and kissed his knobbed and scablike lips.

His eyes widened in surprise. Her tongue slid over his lips, insinuated itself between. He accepted her, caressed her tongue with his, then thrust it into her mouth.

She broke away, straightened. She reached up and removed the half mask, pulling it off over her hair. The right side of her face was stained with a port-wine birthmark like a splash of paint.

"Tsk, tsk." Sitting back propped on the heels of his hands, Eric shook his head. "In a camp full of jokers you hide such a small deformity. I'm not ashamed to show my face."

If he was trying to bait her, she refused to rise. "My mask is symbolic. And it is fitting that I wear it. Understand, I am a creature of the night."

She stepped back into the shadows and was gone. Eric uttered a soft cry of surprise, started to stand.

"Wait," her voice said. She seemed very near, but squint as he might, he could see nothing.

A bare foot emerged into the wan light-pool of the lantern, a leg, and then she was standing again before him. She was nude. Her breasts were small, pink-tipped and conical. Her pubic bush was a dainty vertical band, very sparse.

"I am a creature of light and darkness," she said in a husky voice, "mostly darkness."

Standing astride him, she drew off the denim vest he wore, pulled his white T-shirt up over his head. The skin of his chest was ridged and folded. She ran her lips over it.

He caressed her head with his rough hands. Her fingers worked inexpertly at his belt and the buttons of his jeans. After a moment he grinned at her and guided her hands away.

"I guess there are some things even an ace can't do," he said. She stood up, an uncertain look on her face. He unfastened the pants himself, slid them off.

He grasped her by the hips, kissed her in the midst of her bush. She gasped and grabbed his head with both hands. Her breathing went stop-and-go as he ran his tongue down the centerline of her pubic thatch.

The tip of his tongue slid down between her smooth-muscled thighs, parted the tangled hair, found the lips of her pussy and teased them apart. Her fingers drilled into the sides of his head.

A strangled sound escaped him. He pulled his head back. She looked down at him in confusion and disappointment.

"Careful, love," he said. "You damn near squashed my head there. Don't forget, you've got an ace's strength."

"Oh, dear. I am most terribly sorry." She started to pull away, blushing, almost weeping in embarrassment.

He grabbed her by the buttocks and buried his face in her. She put her head back and moaned, practically collapsing onto him.

In less than a minute she cried out, sharply, sounding almost frightened. She rocked her hips forward into the sweet, insistent pressure of his tongue. She dug her fingers into his shoulders, froze, relaxed her hands to keep from harming him.

She pushed him away. "That was quick," he said, looking up at her with her juices shining on his misshapen face. "You're easy to please."

"It was so . . . so intense," she said breathlessly. "I was not expecting it."

"Don't tell me nobody ever did that to you before."

"Not . . . that I recall."

Eric shook his head. "Then I can confidently say your taste in men has improved, Isis."

He straightened his legs. He put his hands on her waist and drew her down. She allowed herself to be drawn to her knees, down.

She went rigid as the head of his cock touched her pussy. Then she sat down upon him, moaning as he entered her.

"Ahh—" He took her face in his hands. "Haven't you ever done this before either?"

"I—I don't know." She threw herself forward, breasts flattening against his chest, arms looping around his neck. She put her chin on his shoulder and rested her cheek against the roughness of his neck.

He drew up his knees, put his hands up behind her back, and began rocking his hips. The friction of his corrugated chest on her nipples was both painful and delicious. The sliding within her made it hard to concentrate, hard to breathe.

She heard the voices yammering within her. She firmly pressed them down. She did not ask much for herself—she did not know how. But this was what she wanted to do. This moment was hers.

She came again, three times, before they finished together, he lying on his back, body arching into her, braced at shoulders and heels as his head thumped heedless on the planks, she upright and astride, head tossing, hair waving like anarchy's flag. Their hands were locked at the ends of outstretched arms. They cried, and strove together.

Drops of sweat fell into the midst of the desolation of Eric's chest. Then she collapsed onto him. He held her, murmuring and caressing her hair.

When she was in control again—too soon, too soon; her control was so iron and constant that liberation had been as sweet as the physical pleasure—she raised her head and smiled at him.

"No dreams?" she asked, teasing, tentative lest he take offense.

He laughed, out of breath. "Whoa! I'm enjoying the dream we have here together. *You're* generating this one, babe, and you're doing just fine."

She slid partway off him, slippery with sweat, resting an elbow on the harshness of a plank. "It is a dream, isn't it?" she said, holding down the babble of voices within, but marking their presence. "All this—it's not real, is it? It's the hatred and injustice and war outside that are real."

Her mind filled once more with the pastoral symphony of visions Mark had experienced at that first rally, when he and she and the rest first laid eyes on beautiful Eric. A land of peace and nature and harmony, where no smokestacks broke the sky and the words and stares of bigots no longer assailed jokers like thrown stones.

"That's real, Isis. *That's* the reality. It's the rest that's the dream—the nightmare. What we're doing here, we're dispelling the nightmare. Breaking the spell of the dark magic of Western values, Western materialism, Western linear thought."

The ANC burned twenty jokers in a township last week with gasoline, J. J. Flash's outraged thought broke through. *In Calcutta a mob killed a hundred and fifty the week before that. I don't mind you taking the high hard one from Elephant Boy here, hon, but tell me what the fuck those atrocities have to do with Western goddam values.*

"Is something wrong?" Eric asked.

She shook her head. "Voices. . . ."

"All the voices of the past," he agreed. "Telling you that what *is* is right. Jokers and aces are different. They must be bad. All that matters is getting ahead, the bottom line. Nature exists to be subjugated by Man."

That's Lenin you're quoting there, you little commie creep! Flash thought.

"Hush!" Moonchild said aloud. Eric blinked. It came to her that it had been a long time since anyone told him to shut up.

Hurriedly she kissed him. "Not you, never you. The voices in my head."

The tension of hurt anger flowed out of him. He kissed

her back. "We all have those voices, babe," he said, only a little dubiously.

She touched him at the forehead, the line of his curly dark-blond hair. She ran the fingertip gently down the face, tracing every fold and protrusion, as though burning them into her central nervous system. She kissed his lips.

"You are the most beautiful man I've ever seen," she said, forcing her voice through her throat with difficulty. "I love you."

He grinned, buried his face in the base of her throat, began to lick the hollow and nip gently at her clavicle. She gasped. His hands began to move about her body, doing amazing things.

An alarm tolled in the back of her head. *The change is coming.*

"Oh!" She jumped up with metahuman ease, to her feet in a quick pulse. He stared up at her, completely lost.

"Did I do something wrong?"

"No, I—" She snatched frantically at her clothing, lying in a pile by the shadowed bunker wall. Her ancestors alone knew what would happen if she didn't have everything she came into the world with when she translated out again. "I have to go."

Clutching the clothing to her breasts, she leaned in to quickly kiss his lips. "It's nothing to do with you," she said. "I love you."

"You're going out there naked?" he asked in amazement. She was already gone.

It was Mark Meadows who collapsed on the crating floor inside the door of Croyd's bunker in his own brief private whirlwind. He was gasping, from nervous tension and humiliation as much as exertion.

Nobody seemed to be looking her way when Moonchild darted out of Eric's bunker in a flash of moonwhite skin. Then she found the shadows and was lost to view. There were advantages to being a nocturnal ace.

Croyd was sitting on the edge of his bunk, wearing dark sunglasses and rocking back and forth. He wasn't holding his usual beer—the ban and all. He didn't mind; he was beyond depressants now.

"What's happening?"

Mark sat with his knees up and his head hung between them. He felt weird. He had just been, well, fucked. His cock felt distended and sore.

He had never doubted his own sexuality, at least when it came to orientation. He wasn't attracted to his own sex, had never had even any particular impulse to experiment with it. And here he'd just had sex with a *guy*.

Okay, so he wasn't himself at the time. The worst thing was he was actually still feeling turned on, residue from Moonchild—he hoped. *Why can't I have a normal sex life?* He was glad he came back to himself fully dressed. What Croyd would make of him stumbling back naked with a hard-on from a Moonchild date with Eric the Dreamer, God only knew.

Croyd just kept rocking, off in a world of his own. He was dangling off the edge right now like one of those Aztec pole-dancers, soaring at the end of what Mark knew to be an increasingly frayed rope.

Croyd twitched, stared at Mark as if seeing him for the first time. "How's it going, man?" he asked. He scratched himself with sudden intensity. "Say, dude, feel free to speak up next time you see me with fucking *bugs* all over me."

Mark bit his lip. There were no bugs on Croyd.

Things fall apart; the center cannot hold.

He didn't even know if the quote came from J. J. Flash or from himself. But it was true enough.

It was going to be a race to see which fell apart first: himself or his surroundings.

Chapter Thirty-four

"The gloves have come off." Colonel Charles Sobel's voice rolled out over his assembled troops like a wave of righteousness. "The forces of reaction are on the march across the Socialist Republic of Vietnam. The eyes of the world are upon us; make no mistake about that.

"And make no mistake about this: we are locked now in the fight for the rights of jokers everywhere. This is not just politics. It is *survival*, for everyone touched by the wild card."

Comfortably far back in the crowd, Croyd Crenson circled thumb and forefinger and jacked off the air.

"Stop that," Mark hissed. "Somebody'll see."

"No way. They only have eyes for Magic Man and his line of miracle bullshit up there."

Left and right and to the front of them, the Joker Brigaders seemed absorbed by the spectacle of Colonel Sobel in his glory. And spectacle it was: torches flaming to either side of his podium, their light writhing on his face and the painted faces and bare chests of the honor guard of joker youths that surrounded the dais.

"It's not bullshit," Mark insisted. The uncertainty in his eyes made his words weak.

Croyd studied him. "You're a military brat, aren't you? Your dad just retired as head of the Space Command, didn't he? Old Charles is mashing all your daddy buttons at once."

Mark flushed. "That doesn't have anything to do with it."

"We have learned from the mistakes of the American imperialists whose crimes we have come to atone for. We

271

haven't got any off-limits here, no rules of engagement to keep us from doing the right thing. We know what's right, and by God, we *will* do it."

The crowd erupted in applause and hoarse cheers and cries of, "Rox lives! *Payback time!*" The young recruits who made up the majority of the New Joker Brigade were skeptical and wary of the original Brigaders, if not downright hostile—and the hostility was becoming daily more pronounced, especially since the Originals uniformly sneered at that optimistic slogan of the young, *The Rox lives.*

None of that hostility seemed directed toward Sobel. He told the boys what they wanted to hear.

Off to the side, quiet and slim in the dancing shadows, stood Eric, awaiting his cue. Mark couldn't make himself look at him.

"We are *righteous*," the Colonel thundered. "We are armored in righteousness, and we have the irresistible impetus of history behind us.

"The nats have oppressed you. And now they are trying to do it again, here in the haven provided us by the Socialist Republic of Vietnam. The gloves are off; you've all seen your brother jokers carried in on stretchers—or carried out in body bags!

"But the tide shall turn. The tide *is* turning, and it turns here, at Fort Venceremos! Our fight is the fight for jokers everywhere, and as the name of this base declares to the world, we *shall* overcome!"

As the applause erupted with redoubled violence, Mark's mind filled with a panorama of Final Battle: nats and jokers locked in combat on a field where the mud was soaked with blood and the sky was filled with fire. The New Joker Brigade sent up a roaring crescendo of approval as the dream reached a climax of slashing and smashing and burning and crushing.

And then it was done, and a band of weary, wounded jokers, their uniforms tattered and scorched, slumped upon the weapons to survey their victory. The battlefield was drowned in blood. *Nat* blood.

The crowd went insane. Mark had his eyes squeezed shut and his palms pressed over his ears in a futile effort to shut the horrific visions from his brain.

"That good a show, huh?" he heard Croyd comment, through his hands and the mob's fierce ecstasy.

He dropped his hands and opened his eyes. Tears poured forth. "I don't understand," he sobbed. "We're supposed to be struggling for, for brotherhood and tolerance. But here the colonel's deliberately trying to whip up race hatred for the nats!"

He shook his head. "What's going on, man? What's going on?"

Croyd took his cigar from his mouth and surveyed the scene with fine amphetamine detachment. "Looks like Armageddon to me," he said.

"You sound like you approve of all this!" Mark said, pitching his reproof to carry above the blood-lust cries of the mob.

Croyd produced a lizard shrug. "Hey, I don't have any problem with kicking nat ass. Nats never did much for me; shit, they hunted me like a dog, back when I was being Typhoid Croyd. Croak 'em all; no scales off my ass."

He paused, looked confused. "Except my family. But they, *they're* far away. Yeah, that's it. They're out of it. So fuck a bunch of nats. *Fuck* 'em!"

He was shivering and babbling now. The hellbrew of amphetamines he was pumping through his system to fend off sleep was starting to kick him over into delirium.

Mark provided his friend with stimulants because Croyd asked him to; what Croyd did with them was Croyd's responsibility and Croyd's concern. Croyd the Sleeper never articulated it, but he had a deep fear of sleep, almost pathological in its intensity, and Mark knew why: there was no knowing when Croyd would wake up to find the wild card had dealt him the Black Queen. If there was one thing worse than being an enormous pink bat or a great big skink, it was being dead.

But Mark had purely selfish reasons for wanting Croyd awake. Croyd was his sole friend, his sole ally, a raft of comradeship in a strange and murderous sea. If he nodded off, for days or weeks or even months, Mark would be all alone.

There was Eric, of course. But he was Moonchild's connection; he had no interest in Mark. Mark suspected that if Eric knew the truth about where Moonchild came from, he would not be so interested in her either.

He'd care, he felt her think. *He'd still care. He's very caring.*

Mark looked at Eric, discreet and powerful. He shuddered.

"Colonel? Colonel Sobel, sir?"

One of the Colonel's flying wedge of escorts laid hard hands on Mark as he tried to intercept Sobel on his march back to his quarters. Sobel recognized Mark, nodded them off. They fell back, glaring hate.

Sobel put a hand on Mark's shoulder, brought him along. "Walk with me, son. What's on your mind?"

"Sir, I'm, uh—I'm not, like, trying to criticize or anything, but didn't it seem like you were trying to stir up antinat sentiments with your speech tonight?"

"Hell, yes. I *was.*" He laughed at Mark's confused expression. "I was trying to instill fighting spirit in a unit that's still pretty much civilian, a unit that's trying to cope with taking real-life casualties for the first time. You don't do that by beating around any bushes."

"But isn't that racist? I thought the Brigade was about tolerance."

"The New Joker Brigade is about two things. One: atonement. Two: survival. It's us against the nats, son. Here in Vietnam we have a chance to carve out a sanctuary for the wild cards. A place to build a better life, based on sharing and caring, socialist discipline and solidarity. A beachhead from which to take on the whole corrupt, capitalist, white bread nat world. I don't see much room for sentiment in that agenda. Do you?

"Besides, toleration is a dead white-male concept. It has no relevance to the oppressed. To what we're doing here and now."

Mark felt like crying. This wasn't the way he'd expected it to go. And now—damn Croyd!—he felt as if he were betraying his father, in the doubts that surged unchecked through him now.

Distraught, he blurted another question that was eating at him: "Why aren't there any Vietnamese jokers in camp?"

"There are no jokers in the Socialist Republic of Vietnam."

"That's craz—I mean, that can't be true. The wild card virus was dispersed widely enough—"

Sobel faced him, laid hands on his shoulders. "Son," he said, "you ask a lot of questions. I appreciate how concerned you are, and I admire your ethics. Truly I do. But remember, you left the normal nat concept of civil liberties back home when you left the white-bread USA. And also remember, a lot of communities these days are taking steps to protect themselves against people asking the wrong kind of questions."

"The wrong kind of questions?"

"*Destructive* questions. Insensitive questions. Questions that stir up bad feeling or dissent. A lot of our American colleges are taking the lead in that these days.

"Asking too many questions will weaken us here, what we're doing here. That hurts jokers everywhere."

Mark tried to speak. Words would not come.

"Don't bother yourself with questions, son." The Colonel smiled and patted Mark on the shoulder. "The time for questions is past."

He walked away and left Mark standing.

Fueled by repression, desertion, ethnic and sectional tensions, and the Socialist Republic's lack of economic progress compared to its noncommunist neighbors, full-scale guerrilla war flamed up. Determined not to be among the last few communist dominoes to topple, the Republic reacted with fury. The New Joker Brigade was thrust into the fire.

Squads began coming back to Venceremos with hairy tales of firefights and nighttime ambushes. And more. Several youngbloods began strutting around with necklaces of human ears. Swaggering talk of torture, mutilation, and village massacre made the mess-hall rounds.

Not everyone approved of the atrocity talk, among either the Originals or the new kids. There were angry words in the mess, shoving incidents, out-and-out brawls.

Then, the night after Mark and his squad had returned from a grueling two-week patrol in the Highlands, the Joker Brigade original named Tabasco was stabbed and left to die on the parade ground.

*   *   *

"How could that happen?" Moonchild asked. She was lying naked on her side next to Eric, beneath a blanket to fend off the surprising night chill, listening to rain drum dully on the sandbag-reinforced roof.

Eric lay on his back with his hands behind his head, staring at the play of shadows thrown on the ceiling by the single fish-oil candle. "How could what happen, babe?"

"The murder of that man. Tabasco. Who would do such a thing?"

Eric shrugged. "Tabasco pressured a lot of people. He made enemies."

Moonchild pulled herself up on one elbow. "Pressured people? How? About what?"

"Some of the things going down out in the bush. He was hung up on old times, how the New Brigade had to make up for all the bad things he and his buddies did way back when." He shook his head. "He didn't seem to realize that that war's over and done with. It's history. It has no *bearing*."

She frowned. "You sound almost as if you approve of his murder."

"When people start getting shot at, it changes them. Changes their outlook. You go ragging on them at your own risk."

"I can hardly believe you are so callous. He was criticizing people who bragged of murder, of rape. Terrible crimes."

He looked at her with half a smile. "Are there really such things as crimes in a war? Look, the people who are suffering are deserters and traitors. They're a threat to the Socialist Republic."

He put his fingers beneath her chin, raised her face. Tear-trails shone on her cheeks. "Besides, they don't think we're human. They think anyone touched by the wild card is a devil. They'd do worse to us."

"Do the Vietnamese in the government think any better of us?"

He shrugged. "Probably not. But it doesn't matter. They're behind us, whether they love us or not. They're giving us what we need."

"And what might that be?"

"A place to *stand*, darlin'. It's coming down Holocaust

time—you should know that as well as anybody, after what
your friend Meadows has been through. The nats fear us.
They know what we are: *homo superior*. We're the future,
babe."

"You don't believe that!"

He raised his head to look at her. His eyes were like
amber beacons, burning through her. "I do. It's true. Look at
you—aren't you superior to any nat?"

She bit her lip, trying to order her thoughts, form a denial that would not sound foolish. "I am stronger than most
nats, faster," she said. "I can conceal myself in shadow. I recover from injury with unnatural quickness. But these things
do not make me *superior*. Not in a moral sense."

He laughed and laid his splendid head back down. "A
moral sense? How moral is genocide? That's what the nats
have in mind—for me, for you, for all the little ace and
deuce and joker babies in the world. Lights out."

She shivered. She could feel much truth in what he
said. But it did not make all that he was saying *right*.

"The Vietnamese are giving us a place to make a stand.
A place to settle, once the fight is done. A place to build the
dream."

"Is that the coin they use to purchase our souls, then?
Land?"

"Call it space, if that makes you happy. Call it tolerance;
call it a fighting chance. That's more than anyone else is
even willing to offer us. So we owe them."

"Is that all there is to it? That we 'owe' it to them to kill
for them?"

"It's the dream, babe. The *dream*. It's greater than
anything—you, me, the whole Brigade."

Her mind filled with those seductive pastoral images
again—the happy, liberated jokers about their appropriate-
technology pursuits. Moonchild shook her head.

"No, no, please. No more pretty pictures. We are talking about pain here, pain and killing."

"Is that really wrong? If a toe becomes gangrenous,
don't you have to amputate it or lose the foot? If the foot
gets gangrene, don't you have to amputate it so as not to lose
the leg? If the leg is gangrenous, don't you have to cut it off
or die? You don't cut off your toe because you don't love it.

But there comes a point at which a part is beyond saving, and endangers the greater whole."

"But a man is not a toe. He's a *life*."

"Aren't you forgetting the Way? Aren't you falling prey to the Western illusion that the individual is greater than the group?"

She hung her head. "We are becoming what we fight against."

"No." He kissed her forehead. "Can't happen, hon. Because we're *righteous*."

Chapter Thirty-five

The villagers stood outside the bamboo fence that encircled their collection of hootches, a sad huddle beneath the guns of Second Squad. The morning mist of the valley wound about them like living gauze, shifting and twining, and detached the surrounding mountain peaks from the planet, so that they seemed to float on cloud. Mark felt a sense of strangeness as great as any he had known on Takis; it was as if the valley and village and the mountains were on another planet, remote from Earth.

The evidence lay on the damp earth before them: an ancient American M-2 carbine with a skeleton stock that may have folded before it turned to rust. Decrepit as it was, sniff tests revealed the tang of burned powder and lubricant that betrayed it as the weapon—or one of them—that had been fired at the patrol on its approach. The villagers claimed not to know whose hand had held it.

Why were there no young men in the village? They had all been drafted into the People's Army, of course. The villagers responded sullenly to the questions shrieked at them by Pham, strutting to and fro before them like a cock keeping an eye on his hens, but they answered.

It was just that no one believed their answers.

Crouching beside the weathered stone gate, Haskell looked up from the radio that Croyd had humped up here and shed. His pink mouth-tendrils quivered.

"Word is to waste 'em," he said. "Comes right from the Man Himself."

"All *right!*" Spoiler yelled, and pumped his fist in the air. *"Payback!"*

Mark felt an iceball the size of Takis form in his stomach. *No!* his mind yammered in several voices.

"Bullshit," Sarge said.

Haskell looked mulish. "That's what they say. I'm just passing the word along." His expression said that word didn't make him any too unhappy.

Black lips drawn back to show businesslike white canines, Sarge strode forward and grabbed the headset away from the younger joker. He turned his back on his squad to speak.

Mark glanced at Croyd. Croyd was propped on his tail, whistling "Mack the Knife," which Mark thought was in pretty damned poor taste. He alternated whistling with talking to himself. At least he was being quiet about it. Mark had managed to impress upon him the importance of not raving out loud. Given Croyd's state, it was quite a diplomatic feat.

A white T-shirt was still plastered to Croyd's dorsal scales from the predawn rains. He had one four-fingered hand up inside it, scratching at those invisible bugs. Across the shirt's front was written SLEEP IS FOR THE WEAK in jagged ink-slash letters. It was a tribute to that legendary outlaw, the Sleeper. Croyd had seen a fresh recruit walking around in it during that last downtime in Venceremos, the time Tabasco died. He had demanded it. After a quick consultation with his comrades the kid had peeled it off his back and handed it over, in deference to the witchy reputation that had earned Croyd the right to a bunker of his own, and to his increasingly savage unpredictability. Also, Croyd *was* the Sleeper.

Croyd caught Mark's eye and gave him a weird lizard smile. Mark didn't know how to read it.

Sarge threw down the headset and turned. "No," he said. "No way."

"What the fuck do you mean?" shrieked Spoiler. He racked the bolt of his M-16. The clack was shockingly loud in the echo chamber of mist and mountains. "We got our goddam *orders!*"

Sarge faced him squarely, hands down by his sides. "So did the Nazis at Nuremberg."

"What does fucking cheese have to do with anything?

You're talking history again, old man. This ain't fucking history. This is *now*."

He turned to face the others. "Who's with me? Who's for jokers, who's for payback for the Rox—and who's with this nat-lover?"

The squad passed looks around like a red-hot iron bar. Haskell was grinning through his tendrils and caressing the humpbacked receiver of his M-60. The two newbies, Stewart and Ram, sidled over to stand near him, fingering the long black rifles they halfway knew how to use. Stewart's thin face was flushed behind the constantly running sores that covered it. Ram let his head with the heavy horns curling from the sides tip forward. His wide nostrils flared.

Pham made a pistol of thumb and forefinger and pointed it at the villagers. "Bang," he said. "You dead."

Croyd pumped the charging handle of his own M-16. Mark turned to him, feeling his facial muscles go slack with shock. "Croyd! You're not going along with this, man?"

"Rock and *roll*," Croyd said. He held the rifle by its pistol grip while his left hand wandered back up his shirt in its endless quest for nonexistent vermin. "Rock 'n' fucking *roll*. Nats are out to get us, and they're everywhere. Hiding in the mist all around—can't you *feel* 'em, Mark?"

He stared searchingly into Mark's face. "Mark, man, you're *changing*. Your face is flowing, all funny . . . are you turning into a joker too?"

"I'm still in command of this outfit," Sarge said. "We're not wasting anybody. Spoiler, put your piece on safety and hand it over to me until you settle down."

"*Hand* it to you?" The young joker was so furious, he wheezed the words. "Hand it to you? You old fuck! You're just a fucking nat-lover. A *fucking nat-lover!*"

"Hand me the piece."

"You want it?" The words were doubling Spoiler like blows to the gut. "You *want* it? Well, fucking *here!*"

He swung up his M-16 and fired a burst into Sarge's belly and chest. Blood and bits of tissue sprayed his face and soggy cammies. Sarge fell heavily, the front of his own blouse smoldering from the muzzle flash.

Spoiler held the weapon on the supine sergeant for a moment, muscles standing out on his forearms, until it became apparent Hamilton wasn't getting up again under his own power. Then he spun around and held the weapon two-handed over his head in a parody of a boxer's victory salute.

"Yeah! I laid some *power* on the fuck!"

Before he knew what he was doing, Mark had crossed the damp meters of intervening earth and plowed into Spoiler in a windmill of fists. He got in two good cracks on the face, rocking Spoiler's streamlined skull left and right. Pain flashed through his knuckles; it was the first time in his life he had actually hit anyone.

It felt good. He tried to do it again.

Spoiler had fallen back under the initial fury of Mark's assault, not to mention its unexpectedness. He had dropped his M-16. Now he stiffened the fingers of his right hand and drove them hard into Mark's solar plexus.

Mark doubled. It felt as if he were out in space again, with the endless vacuum sucking all the air from him in a whoosh and still pulling, trying to pull his guts out his mouth.

Spoiler snap-kicked him in the face. His head whipped back. His long, lanky body started to straighten as bright lights ricocheted around his brain like pinballs. *See what happens when you lose control, you moron!* Cosmic Traveler screamed.

Spoiler turned, rammed a side-thrust kick into the middle of Mark. Mark jackknifed again. He was beginning to feel like some sort of flexing toy. Spoiler planted his kicking foot, pivoted around it to slam a fairly creditable spinning back kick into Mark's temple.

As a general rule, you don't go out when you're hit in the head unless something is seriously *broken*. Mark didn't go out now. It was just that the planet blindsided him, and none of his limbs wanted to work, and his stomach had decided his body was too dangerous to be in and was trying to get out, and his brain seemed to have come loose from its moorings and be rolling around in his skull. He wasn't *focusing* well, so to speak.

As if from the next valley over, Spoiler's voice came to him, bragging how he'd showed *him*. "You want we should make 'em dig like a big grave?" Haskell asked.

"Naw. Why fuck with that? Hey, I know—let's play a little game. Pham, why don't you tell that granny there to haul ass for the hills. I could use some moving-target practice."

Mark stirred, groaned. For a time his being had diffused to the tops of the mountains. Now it was coalescing again. All the pain in his body gave it something to collect around, the way an oyster protects itself from an irritant by sheathing it in pearl.

"What about him?" he heard Haskell say. "What about the old nat?"

"Fuck him," Spoiler said. "We'll wax the nat cocksucker in our own sweet time. Right now it's showtime—Pham."

Mark heard the translator bark something in Vietnamese. Wails went up from the villagers like a flock of frightened gulls. He tried to move his hand. It felt like a lead spider. A raindrop struck the back of it. Mark knew he was about to trade the pain that was pounding him now for something infinitely worse. He kept willing that hand to move.

"Pham, tell her to move, or I'll just start spraying the whole slant-eyed lot of 'em!"

"Hey—holy shit, Spoiler, the old nat's *on fire!*"

Spoiler turned to see Mark's body wreathed in orange flame. "Hey, so he torched himself somehow. Saves us the trouble—"

The burning man stood.

Somebody screamed. The blazing figure was smaller than Mark by a head. As the squad and villagers watched, the flames seemed to be sucked *into* it.

Spoiler saw a flash of orange sweats and knew he'd been had. He made the worst mistake of his life.

He brought up his M-16.

The bolt of plasma struck his skinny chest dead center. The shriek that exploded from his mouth was the loudest sound anyone there had ever heard a human being make. Spoiler didn't will it; all the water in his lungs flashed instantly into superheated steam and blew out the pipe of his throat, forcing his head back and blasting from his mouth in a visible steam-whistle cloud that melted his lips from his teeth.

For a moment he stood, head back, a neat round hole burned right through the middle of his chest. With a boom like a sheet hung on a windy laundry line his whole body burst into flame as air rushed back to replace that ionized in the plasma jet.

Spoiler collapsed, his burning body flopping to random impulses as his neurons took their final shots. He never felt the fire. The plasma jet had flash-boiled the fluid in his spine. The sudden, savage overpressure had imploded his brain.

Haskell screamed like a wounded horse and hauled up his M-60, firing the huge weapon Rambo-style from the waist. Flash pirouetted, rolling his hand to show the burly joker his palm. Metaflame slagged the barrel as a round detonated in the chamber. Back pressure blew out the receiver. Haskell shrieked as jets of high-velocity gas burst through the weapon's sides and gashed his arms and ribs like razors. He dropped the weapon to roll on the ground, a kicking knot of agony.

The rain was falling heavily now. Each drop raised a red welt on Flash's fine Jewish features. He held up his hands; they were beginning to blister.

"Anybody else?" he screamed. "You're hot to do some killing—c'mon and let me show you what *hot* means!"

Pham's hand dove inside his shirt for the ancient Tokarev he kept tucked into his pants, out of rain's way. Flash grinned through blistered lips and gestured. The front of Pham's shirt vanished in a puff of flame. Pham screamed, dropped the pistol to bat at his scorched chest as if to put out flames.

"Take off, you little commie scumsuck, or I'll fucking melt you." Pham lit out in a stumbling run across the beanfields, falling every half dozen or so steps, picking himself up again to stagger on. He seemed very motivated.

"You villagers, clear out!" Flash shouted. "Go!" They stood and stared at him like so many sheep. They had no idea what was going on.

He blazed a line of fire at their feet. As one they turned and bolted for the hills, streaming around both sides of the village like a cattle stampede.

"Fire," J. J. Flash said, grinning through cracked and swollen lips. "The universal language."

Lying unattended on the ground, the radio was spitting out Lucius Gilbert's voice from the next valley over, demanding to know what the fuck was going on. He wasn't re-membering much about proper radio discipline.

"Somebody grab that thing," Flash said, no longer able to keep his pain from his words, "and tell that puke we are walking. Going over the hill."

He looked around at the joker faces. "Or am I the only one?"

He looked at Croyd. "What about you, Crenson? Are you with me, or are we going to go 'round and 'round?"

Croyd threw up his rifle, grabbed Flash by the fore-arms, and waltzed him around in a frenzied circle. "It's a gas-gas-gas!" Croyd shouted. "Rock 'n' roll! Rock and fucking *roll*!"

"Yeah," Flash said, disengaging himself. "Easy, there, bud, or the meat's gonna start coming off in your hands. Who else?"

"I'm with you," Slick said.

"Me too," Studebaker Hawk said. "These assholes are too crazy for me. Anyway, I used to run with the Princes. Trips was always on their good-guy list for what you did for Doughboy. Seems to me you've done a lot more good for jokers than that loony dickwad Sobel is ever gonna do."

"Yeah, hey, thanks for the testimonial." He was swaying now, hugging his hands under his armpits to save them from further damage. "Anybody else?"

The new boots Stewart and Ram had run at the sight of Spoiler going up in a blaze of glory. Haskell was rolling from side to side, and the hatred glaring from his tiny eyes was answer enough. One by one, the others stepped forward to join Flash's impromptu mutiny.

"Great," he nodded. "It's, it's a gas-gas-gas. Uh, Slick, can you take over for a little while? Make like you're Louie-Louie—I gotta go now."

Not comprehending, Slick nodded.

Suddenly Flash stood at the center of a small hurricane. Dirt and debris and even rain were drawn to him in a swirling cloud. When the miniature tornado cleared, Mark Meadows stood there, swaying. His face and hands were still shockingly blistered, as J. J. Flash's had been.

"Long live the revolution," he croaked, and pitched for-ward, unconscious, at Croyd Crenson's splayed feet.

Part Three

The Feel-Like-I'm-Fixin'-to-Die Rag

Chapter Thirty-six

"Mark."

Seated cross-legged on the mat-covered floor, Mark looked up. Lou Inmon's great feathered head was stuck in the door.

"We got company," Osprey said. "Could be bad."

Mark's veins got cold. Not for the first time he wished that Croyd were up and around, rather than out cold and being lugged around as baggage by the mutineers. Exactly what a giant lizard could do to help if they'd been discovered was a bit problematical. But at least Mark wouldn't feel so isolated, so *alone*.

"Government troops?" he asked. It had been a constant high-wire dance, in the weeks since the breakaway, trying to keep his little band accessible to the steady stream of deserters from Venceremos without exposing them to the People's Army or the wrath of Sobel's die-hard loyalists.

Osprey shook his head. " 'Yards. They just *appeared*. Put the villagers seriously uptight."

A thin, middle-aged Vietnamese slid into the hootch, keeping as far away from Osprey as possible—after initial wariness the villagers were beginning to see their joker guests as benevolent monsters, but monsters nonetheless.

"Mock," the villager said. "Will Dark Lady appear? Will Dark Lady help us? All *moi* number ten, steal our women, eat our dogs."

Mark sighed. *Moi* meant *savages*. Ethnic Vietnamese treated the Montagnards as animals—pests. *I thought racism and intolerance were white-European-male kind of things,* Mark thought wearily. He had been learning differently.

"You shouldn't call them that, Thich. They're people too."

Thich looked skeptical. "Them steal. Dark Lady come?"

Mark stood up. "If she's needed, she'll come." Thich bobbed his head and pulled back. Mark went to the door.

There were half a dozen of them, squatting in the middle of the village with carbines and shotguns across their thighs, smoking in the heavy evening sun angling in between mountain peaks and slate sky. Like most Vietnamese Mark had seen, they were small and seemed to have been wound out of wire on human-shaped armatures. Two wore turbans, and all had on wire bracelets and blankets with holes in them for their heads like serapes.

He spared them only a glance. The man with the bandaged left hand who stood in the middle of them was tall only by comparison with the Vietnamese, but he attracted Mark's attention like a giant electromagnet.

Mark's hand jumped toward a pocket of his cammie blouse. Then he sighed, and his hand dropped away.

"Mr. Bullock," he said, "you're one persistent guy."

"Last time I saw you, you were helping those DEA agents track me down," Mark said, dipping up hot rice with his fingers. "Why should I treat you like a friend, Mr. Bullock? Er, Belew."

J. Robert Belew looked up. The glow from the fish-oil lamp underlit his eyebrows and gave his features a Satanic cast. "What if I said I didn't walk in here without taking, shall we say, measures to ensure my safety?"

"I'd say you were full of shit, man. We're in the middle of a whole lot of my friends, and I don't just mean aces. If you're planning to make any moves, you better have brought the People's Army to back you up. And even if you did, they'd never get here in time to keep you from being slagged."

"Threats, Doctor? That doesn't sound like the gentle Captain Trips of old."

Mark hunched a one-shoulder shrug. "I don't put up with as much abuse as I used to."

Belew laughed. "I came in here with six underfed Montagnards with about twelve rounds of ammunition among them. If I don't walk out alive, not one blessed thing will happen, except my aged mother will be very sad in a dignified and well-bred way. If not exactly surprised."

He set his own bowl aside. "Satisfied? Or do we need to go through more macho posturing?"

"I'm not posturing, man. I'm making my position clear."

"Very well, Dr. Meadows. Let me make my own a little clearer: if I'm not your friend, why did the DEA agents never actually *catch* you?"

"I had a little bit to do with that. And my friends, yeah. But to tell you the truth—I know they're like the big heroes and everything back in the States, but I never thought narcs were all that bright."

Belew laughed. "You should've seen these two. Heckle and Jeckle."

"So where are they now?"

"Playing drop the soap for the Turkish national ace in some awful slam in Istanbul."

"You're putting me on."

Belew solemnly shook his head. "I set them up. They never suspected a blessed thing until the Turks found the coke in their luggage. And all the while they thought they were putting one over on *me*." He paused to chuckle. "Naturally the United States and the Governor will get them out of it. *Eventually.*"

Mark laughed long and loud. When he was finished, he shook his head. "I know I should feel sorry for them. But they tried to kill me, they hurt a lot of innocent people, and they endangered a whole lot more. The heck with them."

"Indeed."

"Why'd you do it? Why were you trying to help me?"

"May I speak frankly with you, Doctor?"

Mark gave him the Big Doubt eye, one eyelid at halfmast, the opposite brow arched Mr. Spock style. "Why do I have the feeling you're going to do anything but? But go for it, man."

It was Belew's turn to laugh. "I like your style, Dr. Meadows. I thought you were just another naïve hippie burnout. But you've got something to you. Some steel in your spine."

"I'd rather you think of me as a hippie, if it's all the same."

Belew showed him a raised eyebrow back. "A hippie, in

command of a hundred armed men and getting set to take on the whole Republic of Vietnam?"

"So call me a combat hippie. This isn't exactly the role I ever had in mind. But you were about to be frank, Mr. Belew—"

"Never give me a straight line like that, Doctor. But yes. With all due respect, my helping didn't actually have much to do with you personally. It was more to put a spike in the wheels of the people who were after you."

"You got something against the DEA? Uh, you want a beer?" He held up a couple of bottles of *Giai Phong* with the necks between his fingers.

"No thanks. I'm trying to cut down on formaldehyde. No, I don't have anything against Drug Enforcement; I've done contract work for them. That's a career option I have a sneaking suspicion is going to be closed from here on in.

"I have something against the people they were fronting for."

Mark stopped with his beer halfway to his lips. "You going to give me a line about some kind of big conspiracy behind the U.S. government?"

"No. I'm going to give you a line about a *worldwide* conspiracy. It's not exactly behind the government of the United States, but it has its claws in governments all around the world."

Mark set his beer down. "That's very interesting, Mr. Belew. But I've been having kind of a busy life lately, so I hope you'll don't mind if I just cut this short—"

"I thought hippies were naturally drawn to conspiracy theories."

"So I'm an unorthodox hippie. All the conspirators I ever knew, they, like, had a hard time figuring out what to eat for lunch by six o'clock at night."

Belew laughed again. "Look, Doctor, I've taken substantial risks in order to come here and talk to you—as you yourself were at pains to point out. Why not listen to what I have to say before you dismiss me as a random lunatic?"

"I never thought you were a *random* lunatic. You seem like a pretty single-minded lunatic to me. But, okay. I'll listen." The only thing this was keeping him from, after all, was Moonchild's evening exercise, and Mark was none too eager to let her out to agonize over Eric. Besides, the sky was clear, and that meant stars. Mark was still not sorry to miss them.

"Very well. You're certainly aware that anti–wild card sentiment is very prevalent today. It takes the form of anything from verbal abuse to legal strictures to mob violence and assassination. But doesn't it sometimes strike you that the hate campaign is fairly well orchestrated?"

"You mean, like Leo Barnett and the fundamentalists?"

Belew smiled and shook his head. "Barnett's a well-meaning fool—all right, you don't have to agree with his goals, and obviously you don't, but he sincerely believes he's doing the right thing. Of course, as that malignant but astute dwarf Alexander Pope informed us, the road to Hell is paved with good intentions. But Barnett is an outsider, a hillbilly barbarian at the gates. I'm talking about entrenched men, powerful men. Insiders."

"How'd you find out about this conspiracy?"

"I don't suppose it would surprise you if I told you I used to work for the CIA?"

"No," Mark said. "Are they in on it?"

Belew gestured with his good hand. "Yes and no. The CIA is not monolithic, any more than most governments or even governmental agencies throughout the world are. Group dynamics are more complicated than that; that's where most conspiracy buffs make their mistake.

"But yes. There is a sizable faction within the CIA that is connected with the conspiracy. As there is such a faction within the Drug Enforcement Administration."

Mark gave him a narrow eye. "How did you find out about all this?"

"Do you remember the attempt to rescue the hostages in Iran in 1980 with an all-ace strike team?" Mark nodded. "I commanded it. That's when I first became aware of an anti–wild cards conspiracy."

"I thought you military types blamed Carter for that."

"No. Carter was spineless and a fool, though he showed a certain grace when he accepted responsibility for the mission's failure. Of course that was wrong, too; I was the commander on the ground, I lost almost half my people, so the fault was legitimately mine."

"I can't tell you how confident this makes me feel."

"I'm being straight with you, Doctor. I need you to believe the unbelievable. What better way to establish my *bona fides* than being honest about my own failures?"

Mark waved a noncommittal gesture.

"I'll spare you the details. I will say that I found reason to believe that the mission was intended to fail from the inception, in order to embarrass not just aces in general but Carter, who was felt by certain parties to be soft on wild cards."

"Why didn't you, like, report it?"

"To whom?" A small smile. "One of the men I suspected—suspect—was a National Security adviser, who's very well connected. I'm a cowboy, a shadow operative—contract man. Who'd believe me?"

"You expect me to."

Belew laughed. "You have firsthand experience of the conspiracy."

Mark rubbed his chin. Bristles scraped his palm. He had stayed mostly clean-shaven since going on the run after the trial. He was going back and forth now about whether to grow a beard or not.

"So that's why they were after me so hard."

"On the operational level, yes. The reason these particular boys pushed so hard is that one of them conceived himself as having a personal grudge against you. His partner was killed in that shoot-out in your upstairs lab, back in New York."

Mark slammed his open hand down on the floor so hard, the beer bottles and earthenware bowls danced. "I wasn't even *there*."

"Western linear thought was not this boy's strong suit. You're a bad guy; in his mind you were responsible."

"*I'm* a bad guy? How many crowds of bystanders did *I* hose down with machine guns in Amsterdam and Athens? Jesus!"

"DEA has a simplistic worldview, even by cop standards. To get back to the point, Agent Saxon was set on your trail because the conspirators within DEA were morally sure he'd have no qualms about killing you."

"Why?"

"You are one of the most potent aces in the world. Killing you would be a triple *coup*: it would bring you back onto

CNN Headline News as a major ace crimelord—no, save the indignant denials; *I* know it's not true—which would boost public perception of aces as a serious threat. It would neutralize a potentially dangerous opponent. And it would be a welcome victory in a War on Drugs whose poll ratings are beginning to grow just a trifle threadbare."

Mark sat staring down the neck of his mostly empty bottle as if he'd find an oracle in there. It made sense to him. He never had figured out why the DEA had pursued him across the entire Eurasian landmass with such vindictiveness. Even if they really believed he was a major drug supplier—which he never had been, except occasionally to Croyd—it seemed entirely out of proportion.

Belew's seeds were beginning to germinate in his mind. As a matter of fact, he secretly *was* inclined toward conspiracy theory. Even if his rational mind knew better.

And Belew read him like a road sign. "The real conspirators are smart men, shrewd men, used to playing power games for blood. These aren't a bunch of your standard fanatics huddled in some cellar making bombs from *The Anarchist's Cookbook* by candlelight, like the Symbionese Liberation Army nut cases your wife used to run with."

Mark looked up at him, eyes big and round as a frightened cat's. "How'd you know about that, man?" He would have sworn not another soul in the world knew of it.

"I've been studying you for a long time, Doctor," Belew said, his mellifluous voice almost a whisper. "I'm very good at what I do. 'Military intelligence' isn't always an oxymoron. That's why I was able to keep credibility with the DEA while steering them into a series of near-misses with you. I had a clear, accurate mental image of you and could make a fair guess what moves you'd make. They were working from their profile, which was *ab initio* all wet."

In the stretching silence a rhinoceros beetle crawled across the woven mats. Mark stared at it, wishing Croyd were here instead of doing his personal version of the Big Sleep; he'd be happy for the snack. But then, that was probably all behind him now, unless he still hadn't exhausted his bug-eating karma.

He raised his eyes to Belew. "All right. Say I buy this conspiracy for a minute. What's your role in it? Why were they letting you come along for the ride?"

"Since I finished my twenty in 1979, I've never been an actual employee of the U.S. government. I'm a contract man, as I mentioned. A mercenary, if you like."

Mark grunted.

"My usual employer has been the CIA. As I said, I have also done piecework for Drug Enforcement."

"So how—?"

Belew grinned. It took forty years off him. "I allowed the DEA to think I was working for the CIA, and Central Intelligence to believe I was—"

"—working for Drug Enforcement." Mark shook his head. It wasn't a denial; he could see how spook agencies could outsmart themselves in their cloak-and-dagger games.

"So, what's your big interest in *me*?" he asked.

"The same reason the conspirators are interested in you: you're a powerful ace. Plus, the very fact of their interest in you. If they want you dead, I want you alive. What your enemy wants, you deny him. 'When the enemy is at ease, be able to weary him; when well fed, to starve him; when at rest, to make him move,' Sun Tzu says."

"Why, man? Why should you give a damn what they do to wild cards?"

"Because I am one, Mark."

Mark's eyes narrowed in disbelief. Belew laughed softly. He held up his left hand and began to unwrap the bandages.

"They caught up with me in Saigon," he said, "and I had to use my ace to make a quick exit, stage right. Not elegant, I admit, but everyone has to improvise sometime."

The bandage came off, showing a puckered stump. Four fingers and a thumb protruded from it like a cluster of pale tubers. "Regeneration's just one of my gifts."

Mark nodded. "Okay, man. You're an ace. What do you want with me?"

"I want to help you."

"Do what?"

"Just what you're doing."

"What *am* I doing?" Unfortunately it was not a rhetorical question. Mark had no clue what he was up to. He regretted spilling the fact right out there on the mat.

"Preparing to bring down the Socialist Republic of Vietnam," Belew said.

Chapter Thirty-seven

"Or at least liberate the 'liberated' South," Belew added.

Mark's hands made random motions in the air before him. He had no real idea what to say to that; his hands were just on autopilot. "You're crazy, man," he managed to say at last.

"You're not the first to make that observation. Crazy I may be, but you have to admit, I'm pretty darned functional."

"Why would I want to overthrow the government?"

"Because if you don't, they'll kill you. You and the jokers who deserted the New Joker Brigade to join you. And all the villagers who've befriended you. It's not a game any more, Doctor. Last week the People's Army did a whole village of Montagnards with flamethrowers down in Kon Tum, for resisting forced relocation. It's just like the bad old days."

Mark looked at his hands a final time and dropped them on his thighs, where they lay like dead birds.

"You've done a wonderful job of burning your bridges, son. You can't go back to the World. You can't go anywhere that has extradition with the U.S., or anyplace the conspiracy's agents can easily reach out and touch you. You can't stay here, because sooner or later the army will find you, or your wacky pals from Fort Venceremos. You can't go back and you can't stand still."

"What can I do?" The words peeled off his suddenly parched lips like flakes of paint.

"Sun Tzu said something else: 'In death ground, fight.'

You're caught in the killzone, Mark. You have to fight, and fight to win."

Mark shook his head again—and again it wasn't really denial. It was more that he refused to process that statement just yet. "I still don't see what you want in all this."

Belew raised his left hand. "One," he said, tapping the sprouting forefinger, "I'm what you call a dedicated anticommunist. I've spent my life fighting the commies. Now I find myself just about out of business, with a very few exceptions. Vietnam happens to be one of them.

"Two"—he touched the middle finger—"we have the chance to knock one of the conspiracy's pet projects into a cocked hat. You've made a good start already. I want to build on it."

"What are you talking about?"

"The New Joker brigade," Belew said. "A wholly-owned subsidiary of the anti–wild cards gang."

Mark stood up. "No. Bullshit, man. I met Colonel Sobel. He's the reason I *joined* the Joker Brigade. He'd never be part of something like that. He's *devoted* to wild cards, man. Totally devoted."

" 'They say he's a decent man,' " Belew quoted. " 'so maybe his advisers are confused.' "

"Is that Sun Tzu again, man?"

"*Raising Arizona*, actually. Think about it, Doctor. Why on Earth would the Socialist Republic of Vietnam offer sanctuary to aces and jokers?"

"They're *concerned*, man. They're trying to fight injustice."

Belew smiled a slow smile. "How do the Vietnamese feel about wild cards?"

Mark bit his lip. "Most of them hate us. They think we're, like, devils."

"Some wild cards resemble devils closely, Doctor. Did you know the parade ground in Fort Venceremos is now ringed by posts, and that on each of those posts is a human skull? Did you know that some New Brigade squads have taken to ritually eating their kills on patrol?"

Mark looked away. He wanted to call bullshit on the compact man, but he'd heard stories from the many deserters who had walked in since his flight. That was why they were splitting to an uncertain fate in a distinctly unfriendly land: they were sickened and scared by what the New Joker Brigade was turning into.

Belew left that flank alone for a moment. "Do you think the Vietnamese who happen to be in the government like wild cards one whit better than their cousins in the villes?"

"They're socialists. It's their beliefs—"

Belew snorted. "Right. Their beliefs. We all know how well wild cards fare in these revolutionary socialist paradises. It's been known for years, if not widely discussed, that Stalin was about to set in motion a plan to exterminate all wild cards in the Soviet Union when he died. And *glasnost'* has turned up plenty of evidence that jokers were being plowed under wholesale before the old monster packed it in as well as after. To bring it closer to home, does the Socialist Republic admit to having any wild cards of its own?"

"No" It was scarcely audible.

"You've seen the spore-distribution maps. They're right up your professional alley. Statistically, is it likely—is it *possible*—that nobody in Vietnam's expressed the virus?"

"No. There must be . . . hundreds at least."

"Thousands. Are they dead, Doctor? Or are they in camps? Those aren't very *caring* alternatives, Dr. Meadows."

Mark could only shake his head.

"I knew Sobel, back in the old days," Belew said, more softly now. "He was a good man. He was also something of a fool. I don't think either has changed."

"Then—"

"He's a tool. The contact men for the conspiracy—the hands behind the screen that pulled the strings to make the Brigade happen—are O. K. Casaday, CIA station chief for Thailand. By a remarkable coincidence, I think he's one of the men who blew us up in Iran. The other is a Vietnamese colonel in the PPSF named Vo." Belew smiled. "I believe you've made the latter gentleman's acquaintance."

Mark nodded. "His . . . men had me worked over."

"And who else was in attendance?" Belew asked, in a tone that said he knew.

"All right. Sobel was there too. But don't you see? It was self-defense for him. For Vo, too, I guess. Here I was, new in-country and claiming to be an ace—"

"Oh. So you practically *forced* them to beat you up." Mark shut up. "You have a quick hand with excuses for people who do you dirt. Undoubtedly I'll take advantage of that trait at some future date."

Mark sucked in a long breath. "What makes you think there's going to be a future date, as far as you and me are concerned?"

"What choice do you have?"

Mark fluttered his hands. "Okay, man. What choices have I? Go ahead and tell me, dammit. You got me; I'm fresh out of ideas."

He felt the easing of confessional. It had twisted him for days. The men of Second Squad—and most of First, who bolted when Second radioed that they were going over the hill—the dozens of desperate men who had found their way to the little deserter band over the weeks. Even the villagers who a month ago had been their enemies. They all seemed to be looking at him for answers.

And he *didn't have any*.

"Very well," Belew said. "You can fight. You can give up. If you fight, you'll probably die. I won't try to dance around that. But if you give up—?"

His voice rose into questioning silence. Mark nodded ponderously and supplied the answer: "The way things are in the Republic now, they'd probably just wipe us out to be done with us. Or—or hand us back over to the Brigade."

"And how would they treat you?"

Mark shuddered. Inside him a voice cried, *no! It's wrong! Eric would never let something so terrible happen.*

"So we have to fight?" Mark shook his head. His pale-blue eyes blurred with tears. "But *how*, man? I'm a lover, not a fighter."

"You've got a warrior within you. Literally, as it happens, and more than one, on the evidence."

Mark looked at him, wondering again. "No legerdemain to my knowing that; I can watch television news with the best of them. That street-corner transformation to Jumpin' Jack Flash raised quite a fuss."

And got Sprout stuck in Hell, Mark thought with a pang of guilt. Not to mention setting his feet on the long, strange path that had—for the moment—culminated in a mountain-village hootch in the *Giai Truong Son.*

Belew held up his fully grown forefinger. "First, trust yourself. Since you went underground, you've pulled off a number of escapades that would do credit to a trained and seasoned operative—and just staying alive is a major accomplishment, my friend, when you have such heavy hounds on your trail. You busted your kid out of Reeves D&DC. You led the DEA on a ten-thousand-mile chase. You survived combat missions with a bunch of untrained kids and a handful of superannuated noncoms. You shot your way clear of Chuck Sobel's personal heart of darkness, and you've weathered the best efforts of the NJB and the whole Socialist Republic to put you down for good.

"In between there somewhere you dropped stone out of sight for a solid spell—coincidentally, about the same time one Blaise Andrieux, Dr. Tachyon's jumped body, and the body Tachyon had been jumped into all vanished as well. Dr. Tachyon's pet spaceship disappeared around about then, too, and there were some unusual sightings in the skies of the southwestern deserts shortly thereafter. I'd say you've had some most unusual adventures, Doctor. Don't sell yourself short."

"What's your next point?" Mark said after a moment. He didn't look up.

"I won't say, 'Trust me'; that would be an insult to your intelligence. But *use* me, Doctor. I'm in the business, and I'm very good at what I do."

"Yeah, your side did so well last time."

Belew laughed. "I did my part. Nixon puppied and pulled us out. I wasn't consulted. The point is, I know the land, I know the people, I know the tricks."

"So what's in it for us wild cards?" Mark challenged.

"You mean, aside from the chance to keep breathing?"

"I mean beyond just us, man, just me and my people. You say this, this conspiracy and the Socialist Republic have set us up for a fall. Fine. So what's to keep us here? I mean, if survival is all that's at stake, we can, like, make our way to Thailand or somewhere, blow off to the four corners of the Earth."

"Aren't you tired of running?"

"I'm tired of fighting too. Give me a *reason*, man. Something beyond just saving my ass."

Belew drew in a deep breath, let it blow out beneath his splendid mustache. "Very well. Why did you agree to join Sobel's fight in the first place?"

Though Moonchild's memories of Eric turned the word to ash in his mouth, Mark said, "The dream. A—a sanctuary for wild cards. Somewhere we'd just be free to *be*, man." He shook his head bitterly. "I guess that doesn't sound like any major military goal or anything, man."

"It sounds like an eminently straightforward goal, Doctor," Belew said, "and well worth fighting for. Why not keep fighting for it? Only—*really* fight for it, not for a sham. Not for the bullet in the back of your head, which is what's waiting for you when Vo and the conspiracy are done with you?"

The image bloomed in Mark's head like one of Eric's dream-visions: a place where wild cards need not live in fear of the nats. It *was* one of Eric's dreams, it was *the dream*. But—for real, as Belew said.

Belew leaned forward, gray eyes intent. "It's yours to make happen. You hold it right"—he held forth his good hand, palms upward, fingers open; then he clenched the fingers into a fist—"*here*."

Mark was tempted. He couldn't deny the appeal of Belew's words. *You weren't able to deny the appeal in Sobel's words, either,* a cynical inner voice said. But this really *was* different; this was Mark taking command of his own destiny, his own path to the Dream, not following another man's.

But his experiences of the last couple of years, on Earth and Takis, had not run off his back like water from a duck's back. He understood that there was Dream, and there was Reality. And the Reality was he and his merry men were in deep, and he didn't know this man from the pope.

Mark's lips came off his teeth in a skeptical grimace. "I don't know, man—"

"I've already helped you, Dr. Meadows. Rather significantly, if I do say so myself."

Mark raised a brow at him.

"Consider the ease with which the villagers you encountered accepted you."

"We were working a new area, place we hadn't patrolled before. The locals used to snipe us 'cause we were government, but they didn't have much against us personally. Yet."

"Does that really explain how ready they were to take in jokers? Physical deformation is a serious matter in Asia. It doesn't just turn people off, it indicates supernatural evil.

But here"—he waved his good hand around the hootch—"they seem to've given you the keys to the city. How does that happen, I wonder?".

"I suppose you think you know."

Belew grinned beneath his splendid mustache. "Of course. The only bets I ever make are sucker bets, my friend. Who was in charge of your band of merry pranksters when you reached that first village?"

"I—no, Moonchild was." When he'd returned to consciousness—fortuitously, right after the sun set—the first thing he had done was slam a silver-and-black vial. He feared the burns J. J. had sustained from the rain would become infected if they weren't healed, and that had meant calling Moonchild.

It had been a tough call. She was practically coming off the wall at the thought of what their defection would do to her relationship with Eric—even though they had not parted on the happiest of terms. She had been trying to talk the others into going back to plead their case before Sobel when they hit the ville.

"Didn't they seem unusually receptive?" Belew asked.

"She's Oriental too. That probably opened them up to her."

"But she's Korean, if I'm not mistaken. People hereabouts don't have fond memories of the Koreans. The ROK army fought here during the War, and they didn't make many distinctions between friendly Vietnamese and unfriendly ones. They were a bit more abrupt than we dared to be."

"Okay, man," Mark said, "you tell me."

"Hai Ba Trung."

"Excuse me?"

"The legend of the Trung sisters. One was married to a Vietnamese lord who was executed by the Han Chinese, back in A.D. 39. The two of them led a revolt against greatly superior occupation forces. The Han finally defeated them two years later, and they drowned themselves in a lake in what's now Hanoi. Female war leaders are a respected tradition around here, despite the fact that the Viets can be every bit as chauvinistic as the rest of Asia."

"They were reacting to Moonchild as a war leader?"

"A resistance leader, more to the point."

"Wasn't that, like, taking a lot on faith?"

Belew's grin cut way back into cheeks. "They did have help."

" 'Help?' "

"I split from Saigon a good six weeks before you parted company with the NJB. You don't think I spent all that time sitting on my hands?"

"You're shitting me now, man. You couldn't have known."

"Oh?" Belew tipped his head to the side. "Does the name 'Dark Lady' ring any bells?"

Mark swallowed.

"All right. You win. You're so damned slippery, I'll never be able to prove you're giving me a line."

Belew's grin widened improbably. "See? We're getting to know each other already."

"What do you want?"

Belew leaned forward across his lotus-crossed legs. "You say you want a revolution? You joined the New Joker Brigade to change the world for the better. Okay, Doctor." He held his right hand out, palm up. "Here's your chance. *Grab it.* You have nothing to lose, and you know it."

"Grab it *how?*"

"Take it to the max. Vietnam's primed to explode. Light the fuse."

"I can't decide for the others, man."

"Then don't. You lead; they'll follow."

"Why don't you lead this revolution, if you're so hot for it?"

Belew shook his head. "Not my style. I'm a shadowboxer. A gray-eminence type. I don't want a throne."

"But you're looking to be the power behind one? I won't be your puppet, man."

"I won't do anything to you that you don't let me."

"You're a sneaky son of a gun."

"And you're a charismatic *naïf*, who is also an incredibly powerful ace." Belew's face split again in a grin. "And admit it: together we make one hell of a team, don't we?"

Chapter Thirty-eight

"Weak sisters." Colonel Nguyen said, sitting back in the chair to Moonchild's left with his head arrogantly tipped, smoking an American cigarette in a black holder. He was tall for a Vietnamese, five-ten or eleven and lean, with a USAF mustache and khaki PAVN walking-out dress with all Vietnamese insignia carefully removed. He wore what Mark—buried currently beneath the expressed persona—recognized as American full-colonel eagles pinned to his lapels. His English was excellent, if occasionally archaic. He was almost as handsome as he obviously thought he was.

He rolled his head to give a highly overt eye to Moonchild. She disliked him. She felt guilty for it.

"Weak sisters are the greatest threat to our success."

The meeting was taking place in the lantern-lit ballroom of a brick French colonial villa outside a remote Highland hamlet. The hardwood floor was black-mottled with mildew, and lizards ran the walls between patches where the whitewash had peeled away in sheets. They made Moonchild nostalgic for the sleeping Croyd.

The eleven resistance leaders and Moonchild were seated around a long table of imported oak. J. Robert Belew presided at its head. Though the shape and seating arrangements of tables had a history of being bones of contention at Vietnamese negotiations, Belew had handled the matter simply by pointing at the long oblong table and telling people where to sit. The attendees complied without demur, primarily perhaps because their hosts had the most powerful factions present, roughly a hundred New Joker Brigaders and a recently arrived company of one hundred seasoned irregulars from Cambodia, who had been—and as far as Mark knew might still be—members in good standing of the notorious Khmer Rouge.

"So all that stuff about Khmer Rouge massacres was just imperialist propaganda, huh, man?" Mark had asked the previous afternoon when the Cambodian contingent rolled in.

"Oh, no," Belew said. "The stories are understated, if anything. They were exterminating angels in a way the Manson family could only dream about. Their main man, Pol Pot, is, demographically speaking, the top genocide in history. Stalin? A wimp. Hitler? A weenie. The KRs rubbed out a third of Cambo's population."

Mark gaped at him. It felt as if all his blood was draining into a seething pool in the pit of his belly. "These people were *involved* in that?" His words ended in a strangled squeak.

Belew shrugged. "I'm not sure. Probably. Lot of them are early-to-mid thirties now, which would've made them early-to-mid teens back in 1975. Golden age of the Khmer Rouge, those middle teens."

"What are they *doing* here?"

"We fought the Vietnamese together, after they invaded and ran the KRs out in '79."

"But—mass murderers—they're your *friends*?"

A shrug. "War, like its pallid reflection politics, makes strange bedfellows."

"And why are they here *now*?"

"They're combat vets. And we have *history* together. Blood is thicker than water; I can rely on them."

Mark ached to ask about the thickness of the blood they'd shed, and he also did not fail to notice Belew's use of the singular first-person pronoun. But somehow he had lacked the stomach for further questions.

Or, more accurately, further *answers*.

Now Moonchild glanced uncertainly at the Khmer Rouge leader, a round-faced, innocuous little man in glasses named Suon San, who sat on the table's far side next to Belew's Montagnard buddies, who answered to the names Bert and Ernie, and across from Colonel Nguyen. He smiled at her and nodded politely, shyly almost.

Colonel Nguyen slammed his hand on the table. "Anyone who collaborates with the enemy must pay the price!"

The man on Moonchild's left laughed softly. "A fine way to speak, for a man who stills wears the uniform of the People's Army—complete with rank badges he was never entitled to, in any man's army."

The colonel purpled. The speaker was even taller and more dapper than he, in his white linen suit and Panama hat. His name was Dong. He was an out-and-out crimelord from Ho Chi Minh City, whose grandfather had been a chieftain in the *Binh Xuyen* criminal sect, wiped out by Ngo Dinh Diem.

"We've all collaborated, in one way or another," said the man to his left. Nguyen Cao Tri was quite young, his accent likewise Saigon. He represented his father, who was a power in Saigon *giai phong*'s more respectable resistance wing. Though his father's followers were primarily *thuong gia*—"trading persons" ("yuppie wanna-bes," was how Belew put it)—the younger Nguyen held himself like a soldier. He had made NCO during his compulsory military service, no easy task in the People's Army.

"*I* haven't," said the man who sat at J. Bob's left hand, next to Colonel Nguyen. He was short but muscled almost like a Westerner, bulkily powerful, and his iron-gray hair was cropped close to his head. He was Nguyen Van Phu, the third Nguyen in the room, none of whom was related. He was an authentic by-God VC, who had spent his whole life as a resistance fighter. In his day he had fought the French, the Americans, the ARVN, and the victorious North Vietnamese—who had been more assiduous about wiping out their former VC allies than any other group in the country's history. He had spent eight years in a communist "re-education" camp. He had entered the ballroom limping; he carried an American bullet in his left hip, a PAVN one in the thigh.

"Perhaps you would care to cast the first stone," said Ngo An Dong from across the table. The fiery young warlord of the southern *Cao Dai* sect, he wore oddments of military uniform and a red headband around his bushy dark hair. Belew described the *Cao Dai*s as "zany but well motivated." Ngo was another former PAVN noncom.

"I won't shrink from taking strong action," the ex-VC replied, ignorant of or just ignoring the biblical reference.

"You're talking terrorism," young Nguyen Cao Tri said. "The purpose of terror is to terrorize."

Colonel Nguyen laughed. "I'm glad there's at least one other *man* here. Fools will be tempted to betray us to the government if they are not given adequate—" Pause for word. "—*disincentives*. Our first priority is to make sure the penalties of crossing us outweigh any benefits."

"I disagree," Moonchild made herself say.

He narrowed his eyes at her. "The *woman* speaks," he said deliberately. "It is because you are nurturing that you speak that way, no? Your woman's heart bleeds for the unfortunates whom we would discipline."

That was true, but she sensed that that line of argument would not get far with the exclusively male assemblage. She felt Belew's gray eyes on her. He sat up at his end of the table serene and centered as an Occidental Buddha. He was testing her. She hated him for it.

If only they had listened to me, gone back to Fort Venceremos to explain to the Colonel why J. J. killed Spoiler. The Brigade is still fighting for justice, no matter how far off the path some of its members have strayed.

Yet how can I back out now?

"I feel compassion, yes," she said slowly. For some reason she could not bear to fail in front of Belew, and she hated him still more for that. "How can we help the people by doing them harm? But more crucial, from your male perspective, is that by resorting to terror against noncombatants, we defeat ourselves."

Nguyen puffed up as if to spit an interjection. Wondering at her lack of civility, she plunged on. "If we brutalize civilians, they will come to hate and fear us more than they do the government; they will come to see the government forces as the lesser of two evils. Just as villagers were driven to join the Viet Cong after they saw their homes and loved ones burned in napalm attacks."

She glanced then at Belew; the remark was a barb. If it found its target, he showed no sign. "Also," she went on, missing the single beat, "we play into the hands of the government: we allow them to portray us as bandits."

"The world media are accustomed to making excuses

for communist regimes," Belew said. "They've been doing it for seventy-three years. They're going to have a powerful inclination to treat us as bad guys. We might be wise not to make it any easier for them."

Though his body language still bespoke tense anger, Colonel Nguyen made an airy wave. "What do we care for world opinion?"

"We wish to be recognized," said Duong Linh. The assembly's elder statesman, except for Belew himself, he sat at the far end of the table. He was a wispy man with a wispy gray beard and round eyeglasses, who closely resembled Ho Chi Minh. A leader of Vietnam's sizable community of covert Catholics, he had been born in Hanoi. As a youth in the early 1960s he fled south to Hue. He attended seminary school for a time, then dropped out, married, and began to raise a family. His wife, three children, and mother were killed in the communist massacres during Tet, 1968. He himself escaped only by chance. He had spent five years in the dreaded *trai cai tao*—"camp/transform/re-create," reeducation camps. Since 1987 he had been living underground.

It was perhaps not surprising that he appeared elderly, though he was only in his late forties or early fifties.

"That gives us an immediate interest in what the world thinks of us," Duong said in his barely audible voice. His accent had more soft Hue drawl than Hanoi harshness.

Colonel Nguyen grunted. "Very well," he said without grace. "Then certainly we must all agree our first priority is to engage the government's forces in battle, secure a victory as quickly as possible to establish our credibility—"

Before she could stop herself, Moonchild blurted, "No."

"Your impertinence disgraces this council," Nguyen said, turning to her. His posture was still sprawled and casual, but the words squeezed from him like toothpaste from a tube, betraying his anger. His left hand suddenly swept around in a backhand slap to Moonchild's face.

Her own right hand snapped up and caught Nguyen's hand an inch from her face.

He jumped to his feet, his wooden chair slamming over backward with a clatter that sent the lizards scrambling up the wall to the shadow-hidden rafters. Fury leached the color from his face. His American .45 appeared in his hand.

Moonchild was already up. As the tendons stood out on the back of the colonel's hand, drawing his forefinger tight on the trigger, she whipped around in a spinning back-scythe kick, blinding fast.

Her foot struck the pistol. The weapon shattered like a rubber ball dunked in liquid nitrogen and hit with a hammer.

Colonel Nguyen stood there, the skin practically slumping off his face in surprise, holding the grip that was all that remained of his pistol, pumping the now-flaccid trigger. He threw the ruined weapon down and stamped out of the ballroom.

After an interval of very silent silence, Chou, the Hoa leader, spoke: "He'll be back." An ethnic Chinese, Chou compensated for having been a law professor at *Minh Mang*, the university in Ho Chi Minh City, by affecting warlord drag: thinning hair drawn back in a queue, Fu Manchu mustache, and two revolvers with what Moonchild very much feared were real ivory grips belted below his capacious belly.

The farmer who represented the Annamese secessionists from central Vietnam laughed. "Small loss if he doesn't."

The conferees sat very quietly to hear Moonchild's objections to engaging the People's Army in direct battle. These amounted to the fact that, desertion-riddled and dispersed though it was, PAVN was still mighty big and mean and would smash them flat in open conflict unless weakened substantially. It was a cogent argument, even the self-effacing Isis had to admit. Of course, her articulate advocacy might not be the only reason for her listeners' respectful attention.

The discussion moved to the particulars of indirect strategy. Moonchild gratefully let the cup of conversation pass from her. She was uncomfortable standing out. Besides, her hour was drawing to a close. She would have to leave shortly.

A couple of Suon San's bandy-legged little gunslingers walked in escorting a man in a yellow American-style polo shirt and white slacks. He was taller than most of the attendees, more squarely built. Belew rose to greet him with a smile.

"This is Kim Giau Minh," Belew said, shaking the new

arrival's hand. "He's an expert in the very kind of warfare we've been discussing. He fought as a counterinsurgency commando in Cambodia. His father was a North Korean engineer, and during his hitch in the People's Army, Kim here was sent to North Korea's famed schools for aspiring terrorists, where he studied death and destruction alongside the best and the brightest of Provo, ETA-*Militar*, and Nur al-Allah henchmen."

Shaking hands around the table, Kim smiled and bobbed his close-cropped head shyly, as if embarrassed by vast praise. He came to Moonchild and his eyes lit.

"I have heard much about you," he said in English, vigorously shaking the hand she offered him, then, *"Choum boepgetsumnida. Kim Giau Minh rago hamnida."*

She stood there staring at him with horror seeping down over her face and body like blood from a scalp cut. She did not understand a word.

He said something else. The words struck no sparks of meaning in her mind.

He took her hand in both of his. *"Asimnikka?"* he asked, frowning with concern.

"I'm sorry," she said. She pulled her hand back, turned, and ran.

Blindly she stumbled out of the derelict villa, off the grand veranda, several steps across granite flagstones laid to keep expensive European shoes from contact with the red mud. She dropped to her knees, hands on thighs, weeping soundlessly.

The Khmer Rouge standing to the left of the doorway with his Kalashnikov slung started forward. From the other side of the door Lou Inmon cleared his throat, held out a warning claw, and shook his head. The Cambodian stopped.

Grandfather, that had to be Korean *he was speaking to me. And I did not understand a word.*

What am *I?*

She breathed deep, from the diaphragm, trying to find her center. She wasn't sure she ever could again.

Isis.

She stopped breathing. She had thought her name without willing it.

Isis. Do you hear me?

It was as if a voice was speaking in her mind. A . . . familiar . . . voice.

"*Eric?*" she whispered.

"*Yes, Isis. It's me. Surprised?*"

"*Yes.*"

"*Limited telepathy is one of my gifts, hon. Very limited, I'm afraid. I think our—closeness—gives me better range with you. By the way, you don't have to talk out loud. Just think at me and I'll hear.*"

Where are you?

"*Not far, I think, though I can't say for sure. Where are you?*"

—Why?—

"*We've been looking for you. We want you to come back. We want you to come* home, *Isis.*"

Is—is that all?

"*I won't play games with you. Rumor has it that you—you in person—are having a confab with some of the Republic's heaviest criminals and traitors. The Colonel would very much like to find out where this is all going down.*"

You want me to inform?

"*I want you to remember whose side you're on: ours. The wild cards'. These people are dangerous to our hosts. That makes them dangerous to us—all of us, hon. You included.*"

She forced her breathing to a regular rhythm. She glanced back at the porch. Inmon stood with his great raptor head averted. The Khmer watched her with undisguised interest.

I—that is, one of us, one of Mark's friends killed Spoiler.

"*Don't sweat that. Spoiler was a hothead. Haskell told us he drew down on Jumpin' Jack Flash. It wasn't Flash's fault . . . Haskell's fine, by the way. We got the infection in his arms under control.*"

I am pleased for him. J. J. intended him no harm.

"*We assumed that, or he'd be toast like Spoiler. Look, all is forgiven. Please come home.*"

Mark led a mutiny—

"*No hay importa, babe. His hand was forced. The Colonel says it's a nonissue. Come back. We want you. We need you.*"

And you?

A pause, then: *"Sure, babe, I need you too. That goes without saying—"*

"Isis?"

She jumped, came up on one knee, turning. Belew stood behind her.

"Are you all right? You left the meeting pretty precipitously."

"Isis. Just tell us where you are. You don't have to do anything; we'll come find you."

She stood unsteadily, hung her head. "I am sorry if I have caused shame."

"You'll be a hero—"

Belew was shaking his head. "No. Indeed, I'd say you knocked their socks off in there when you busted Nguyen's popgun for him. I couldn't have dreamed up a better demonstration of what you're all about if I had a year and infinite beer."

"Isis—"

Eric, I love you. But she felt the contact stretch, and snap, and fall away into a void within her. She reeled. Belew caught her arm, helped her keep her feet.

She would not show him her pain. "What—what of what I said?" she asked him, stepping away and holding up a hand to forestall further help. "Did I pass that test too?"

He grinned. "With flying colors."

"And you agreed with me?" For some reason it was very important for her to know these things. She could not imagine why.

"Well, I think you're a little bit of a bleeding heart, it's true. On the other hand, if the colonel and that commie hard-case Nguyen Number Two had their way, we'd have half the country after our hides. Just as you pointed out."

"But that which I said about the bombers—you were not offended? I—aimed it at you."

He shrugged. "Sorry. But it missed me clean. Special Forces were the hearts-and-minds boys; we *saw* how the populace reacted when granny and little sister got turned into crispy critters."

She made herself stand erect, head up, shoulders back. She wanted him to know she was back in control.

"What of strategy?"

"You were spot-on. We need to soften PAVN up big-time. Otherwise they steamroll us."

"Oh." She had been prepared for assault, carping criticism at the least. Agreement caught her off guard.

"By the way," Belew said, "Kim is half-blind from worry over what he did to upset you."

"I am sorry. I—"

"It's okay. I calmed him down. I understand; it's just the time—"

"That is a sexist remark!"

"Not time of *month*, kid. Time of day. Your hour's almost up."

She looked at him. "How can you know so much?"

"I do my homework. Now, *git*."

Ten minutes later Mark staggered back into the ballroom. Belew had requested that he return after he came back to himself. The conferees looked up at him, then bowed their heads.

"Hello?" he said tentatively.

Bert the Montagnard stood up and shook his hand. "Please permit me to be the first to congratulate you," he said in flawless Oxonian English. He had a gold incisor.

Mark blinked at him. He hadn't even though the 'Yard spoke *Vietnamese*.

"What's going on?" he asked Belew.

"Big news. The Command Council here has just voted your friend Moonchild in as head of the resistance. You're her deputy and official representative to the Council when she's unavailable."

He stood up and slapped Mark on the back. Mark thought his eyes would fall out and roll away across the floor and under the table.

"But I'm not—"

"Yes, you are," J. Bob said. "Congratulations. You always said you wanted a revolution. Now you've got one."

Chapter Thirty-nine

The Su-25 strike aircraft—what NATO called a Frogfoot—began to rock in the ground effect as *Podpolkovnik* Sharagin lowered his flaps for landing. The stubby little Sukhoi, with its two jet engines set on the wings just outboard the fuselage, was not exactly a pulsing mass of power like its sexy cousin the Su-27 Flanker, but it felt light and inclined to skate compared to how it had handled on takeoff, with its hardpoints crammed with napalm canisters and rocket pods for delivery against supposed rebel positions in the rugged *Giai Truong Son*.

And supposed *is just the word for it*, Sharagin thought. The People's Army had a worse Vietnam War complex than the Americans did. Vietnamese officers remembered how much *they'd* dreaded American airstrikes, and so every time their patrols got fired up, they shrieked for air support. Which meant the lieutenant colonel and the ground-attack air company he commanded were running up a lot of time on their engines.

The problem was the rebels were probably smart enough not to hang around for the airstrikes to come in on their heads. Sharagin would have been that smart. The Viet Cong *were* that smart, like the black-asses in Afghanistan, where Sharagin won a chestful of medals to wear on the breast of his walking-out dress when he went drinking—like every pathetic soak in Moscow—and the dubious honor of this command.

Of course the People's Army had *not* been; they gathered in vast Warsaw Pact–emulating clumps where the Yank bombers could *find* them, pursuant to the vision of that nitwit Vo Nguyen Giap, who based his entire strategy on building for a one-two punch: a massive popular uprising in support of the heroic Liberation Forces—which never materialized—and a single great stand-up knock-out battle with the enemy, which worked exactly once, at Dien Bien Phu, and consistently got the Viets' yellow asses kicked every last time they ran it on the Americans.

Of course the Americans finally beat themselves, and everybody called that turtle-headed old quack Giap a genius. Then the Vietnamese went into Cambodia and spent the last twelve years proving the Americans weren't the only ones who hadn't learned a fucking thing from the Vietnam War. And today's People's Army savants thought their current crop of opponents would be just as idiotic as they had been and wait obligingly for their nice napalm showers. *Nyekulturnyy* assholes.

The runway had been scraped in the red clay of a Central Highlands plateau and surfaced with perforated steel plating. Western analysts always went into raptures about the ability of Soviet aircraft to land and take off under highly vile conditions. Sharagin was proud of his ship's ruggedness, too, but it didn't mean it was fun to land on an airfield this wretched. The way you bounced around when you set down, you just *knew* a wheel strut was going to come jamming through the bottom of the plane and straight up your bunghole. . . .

"Be advised runway damaged is not yet repaired, *Kulikovo* Leader," the tower informed him. Only his passion for radio as well as other species of discipline kept him from cursing the Vietnamese controller out loud. The rebels had dumped a half-dozen mortar rounds on the runway's end before dawn. *Of course* the holes hadn't yet been repaired. Sharagin was used to the standards of Soviet Army Frontal Aviation—which was to say he hadn't exactly learned to regard efficiency as his birthright—but these slant-eyes were simply ridiculous.

He wasn't even sure what he and his boys were doing flying their planes into harm's way in support of a regime that even lowly strike jocks like him knew his own government was not going to stand behind if the rebellion truly caught. *Rodina Mat'* had let Eastern Europe go without a peep. The Baltic republics looked as if they might make their

self-proclaimed secession stick. What beyond a weird macho Evil Empire nostalgia made STAVKA think it was worth
screwing around in this humid hellhole? It wasn't as if the
slopeheads were ever going to come close to paying the
USSR what they owed her for their War of Liberation, let
alone—

Frenzied Vietnamese blasted through his headphones
like static. "Speak English, you yellow monkeys," he snarled
at the tower, discipline momentarily forgotten.

Then he heard the voice of his wingman, who trailed
him by half a kilometer, yelling something about the colonel's left wing.

A glance at the board. No red lights. No precorded
feminine voice. If something was wrong, the bloody *plane*
didn't know it. Were his circuits so screwed up that his port
engine was on fire without any telltales lighting? He turned
his helmeted head to look.

A man dressed in orange flew formation with Sharagin.
He was just drawing even with the cockpit, barely beyond
the wingtip. He smiled and waved.

The problem was he'd neglected to bring a plane.

"Yob tvoyu mat'!" the colonel yelled.

The flying man held out an open palm. Sharagin saw an
orange flash.

An explosion rocked the airplane.

Jumpin' Jack Flash, Esquire, glanced back over his
right shoulder. The Froggie must've had a short run to its
target; it blew up into a wonderfully gratifying yellow fireball before it splashed down on the runway and went hurt-
ling down it like a flame *tsunami*. Above his head a green
canopy with one red panel blossomed as the airplane's zero-
altitude ejection seat reached the top of its arc and popped
its chute.

He clucked and shook his head. Clearly communists
weren't big on color sense.

Great big glowing green balls went whipping by to the
right of him. That Frogfoot behind him was obviously trying
out its 25mm Gatling. *Ooo, I'm sooo scared,* he thought. The
stars on these boys' tails were blood red, not Socialist Republic yellow. Soviet marksmanship didn't impress him any
more than the Vietnamese version did.

He dropped till the runway was whipping right below him and he could feel the morning sun heat off the metal warming his belly. He was pleased to see the cannon shells going off among the hangars. He wasn't so jealous of his job that he hated to see the bad guys do it for him.

I'm so glad we wound up on the other side from these buttholes, Mark. I didn't like the War either, but it never meant I loved the commies.

Following Soviet doctrine, the airfield's planes were well reveted, with U-shaped earth berms shoved up around each aircraft in its parking place to protect it from blast damage. The open sides all faced the runway. It had never occurred to anybody that this would be a *problem*: aircraft weapons fire straight ahead, as a general thing. . . .

Flash just flew, slowly, right down the line, squirting sizzling jolts of flame right into those puppies in passing. He could not tarry long enough to make sure of slagging any individual target—guys in khaki shorts and pith helmets were starting to run around and shoot at him with Kalashnikovs. But he heard explosions behind him and felt their quick, hot pressure. And exposure to superhot plasma was not going to do sensitive avionics any good, even when the plane didn't go up. . . .

With a rushing roar the trailing Frogfoot passed overhead, tucking its landing gear up as it accelerated.

To one side of the runway's far end a pair of attack craft sat with their canopies up, waiting the word to take off. J. J. gave each of them a blast through the tails. He circled left for another pass.

Some fairly heavy ordnance was going off around him; the air shuddered from automatic antiaircraft fire. Like all Vietnamese airbases, this one was surrounded by AAA and SAM pits—God knew who they thought was going to be coming after them in airplanes; maybe they were nervous about the Chinese, who hated the Vietnamese as much as the Vietnamese hated them. The problem was even the finest antiaircraft defenses are not designed to take on man-sized targets flying deck-level, at highway speeds, directly over the base itself. The gunners were shooting pretty much every direction except at him.

Don't let it go to your head, he cautioned himself. He was not bulletproof, and if, say, an exploding 57mm shell hit him, not even Moonchild's regenerative capabilities would put Jumpin' Jack back together again.

As he began his triumphant return engagement, he noticed the pilots had hopped out of their waiting Sukhois and were racing away across the plateau in their flight suits, trailing assorted hoses behind. "Smart boys," he said, and gave their abandoned planes the for-true torch.

He was halfway back down the runway, spreading hot mischief, when he noticed the Frogfoot that had waved off its landing approach banking around as if to come back.

"Oh ho," he said aloud. He'd always wanted to play chicken with a fighter jet.

No! You irresponsible buffoon! You can't be serious—

J. J. Flash grinned. Cosmic Traveler seldom managed to get his oar in when Flash was expressed; different personality types, to say the least. *He must think I'm about to get up to something majestically ignorant.*

And of course I am.

He broke off his strafing run, banking toward the aircraft. Making sure he didn't stray out over the flak pits, he flew above the buildings lined up along the runway, out past the revetments. As he did so, he cut in some serious *flame*. He surrounded himself with a roaring, brilliant nimbus of fire till he was blazing along like a meteor on terminal guidance. People on the ground stopped screaming and shooting to *point*.

The Frogfoot had its nose aimed at him and was blitzing back. Time to move. Risking the ground guns, he streaked straight toward the inbound strike plane, flaming like a dozen Buddhist priests.

White smoke blossomed from under the Frogfoot's starboard wing. *Missile launch,* Flash knew. The only kind of missile that would lock onto him and permit itself to be fired was a heat-seeker. And he was giving the IR-sensing head a *mother* of a picture to look at.

He whipped a one-eighty and flew right back at the tower.

He didn't have too big a clue as to the flight time of the missile. He knew the damned things were fast, faster than a fighter could go full-throttle—and *he'd* been straining to keep up with a porky Frogfoot, slowed way down for landing approach. He flew in a straight line toward the tower for two full seconds, feeling his scrotum retracting into his belly, expecting the missile to nail him. The Traveler was yowling in his head like a cat in heat.

He saw startled faces through the polarized glass of the tower. He saw open mouths, then assholes and elbows as the crew realized they'd been had and rushed for the exits. He cut the flame F/X *slam*, pulled up vertical, shot a hundred feet in the air, and hovered.

The heat-seeker, suddenly deprived of prey, went ballistic. Inertia kept it rushing down the path its target had been taking when it suddenly went out.

It hit the tower in a shower of glass and flame.

J. J. Flash pumped his fist. *"Yeah! It's a gas-gas-gas!"*

The strike pilot banked his plane and accelerated away from the airfield, east toward the coast, as if embarrassed to hang around the scene of his missile *faux pas*.

It was likewise time for Jumpin' Jack to make like a hockey team and get the puck out of here. The Viets were pitching sufficient lead-particulate pollution into the air that somebody might get lucky, after all. Somebody might also get *smart*, and send out for attack choppers, and he knew he couldn't handle them.

He went low, seriously low, so far down he could reach his hand and scrape all the skin off his palms on red clay if he wanted. Between the buildings he flew, accelerating to his maximum thrust, which, while not much by the standards of jet aircraft, looked awesome to the man on the ground. It also reduced Cosmic Traveler to a mewling wreck inside him as the walls of the hangars flashed past.

There were armed dudes in front of him. He kicked his flame-aura back in. They threw away their guns and ran like bunnies.

He whipped between two flak pits, extending his arms to give each a flying finger in passing, as they stared open-mouthed at a target they couldn't depress their guns to track.

He had cost the Socialist Republic and their Soviet butt-brothers some heavy change, but nothing on the scale of even a pissant little war like this one. A blip on the scope. PAVN had other strike planes, other airfields, other air-traffic towers.

But nobody was going to feel quite as *safe* in any of

them from here on in. That was the win that had him laughing out loud as he hit the plateau's rim and let every bit of the wild, exhilarant energy blasting through him go in a blinding supernova flash, so that as he dove over the edge out of sight, he seemed simply to *vanish*

If there was one thing Jumpin' Jack Flash, Esquire, knew, it was how to make an *exit*.

Chapter Forty

Propelled by an arm the size of an elephant's trunk, a fist slammed against the side of Ngo An Dong's head and snapped it around. Sheet lightning went off in his brain. His red Rambo headrag got loose and slipped into his eyes.

The spectating trio of PASF officers looked at one another in amazed approval as Rhino stepped back, rubbing his horny fist. "These monsters really are good for something," said one.

"Yes," agreed a second. "But we should tell him to go easy. We don't want him killing the dog."

"Yet," added the third.

Through red-and-black haze that filled young Ngo's skull limped the realization that you could, too, be too brave; it wasn't like *rich* or *thin*. Getting caught in a piddling little raid on a supply depot near the coast proved that. Now the dashing young warlord could only hope that he could find some way to die before he broke. Even the spirit of Woodrow Wilson—venerated by his sect—could not help him now. The fog crowded awareness from his brain.

"How many aces are working with you traitors?" the first officer asked. Ngo tried to spit defiance, but all that came out was blood and part of a tooth, and they slopped down his hanging lower lip.

"*Khong?*" the interrogator said: *No?* Then he turned to the squat American joker and said, in that English every People's Armed Security Force officer assiduously studied against that happy day when the Americans woke up to their responsibility and started shipping major loot to the Socialist Republic so that its hardworking cops could fight crime like

Miami Vice, he said, "Hit him again. Only this time not so hard."

The door opened. Colonel Vo Van Song of the PPSF stalked in, smoking a cigarette and gazing around with slit-eyed disapproval.

The interrogating officers went rigid. Though none had had the pleasure of meeting him before, they recognized him at once. Colonel Vo had a Reputation. He was one of those delightful chaps who feel it is better to be feared than loved, by your own side as well as by the enemy.

"What have we here?" he hissed in English, for the evident benefit of the guest torturer. His words were slurred and slouched and misshapen, like jokers. "Is this what passes for modern police techniques with People's Armed Security?"

The third officer stepped to a rickety wooden table and held up a pair of big alligator clips, dangling from thick red-and-black cables. "We were simply softening him up before we put these on, sir," he said brightly.

"Oh, so? And perhaps even as we speak you are having an iron maiden brought up from the basement? A rack, maybe?"

He plucked the cables from the PASF man's limp fingers. "The first important rebel leader to fall into our hands, and you interrogate him with *this*?"

The trio wilted into the collars of their summerweight tan uniforms. They knew what was coming. In the complicated food chain of the Vietnamese internal-security apparatus, the People's Public Security Force occupied a much higher niche than PASF. And PPSF was a noted credit-jumper.

The colonel signaled. A pair of basic legbreakers in PPSF khaki lumbered in. They undid the heavy leather straps that bound the now-unconscious *Cao Dai* leader to the chair, put hard hands under his armpits, hoisted him up, and hauled him out with his bare toes scraping on the cement floor.

"The Socialist Republic is grateful for your efforts on her behalf," Vo said in his horrible voice, taking another drag on his cigarette. "She is also grateful your clumsiness did not deprive her of such a valuable prize. Good day."

He threw the cigarette down beside the green-patinaed drain grating in the middle of the floor and walked out.

"Have a nice day," the squat joker said to his back. The door slammed shut.

"Tight-assed Northern cocksucker," the second officer hissed. The PASF men were all Annamese, local boys.

"Did you hear his voice?" the third one asked. "He spoke as if he had a cleft palate. Chilling."

The first nodded sagely. "It's true, what they say of him."

"Arrogant Tonkinese piece of shit," the second said.

"One of those men he had with him didn't even look Vietnamese," the third officer said indignantly. "He looked . . . *Korean*." He practically spat the last word.

"Indeed." The first officer stood staring at the door. "A wise man might wonder why loyal officers of the state such as ourselves should run like dogs to the summons of a Northerner with a broomstick up his rectum," he said at length.

"That's true!"

"Injustice, that's all it is."

"Has it ever been different, since the Tonkinese won their Short Victorious War?" the first officer went on quietly.

"Not for one day!" agreed the second quickly. He wasn't a weatherman, but he knew which way the wind blew.

"That's right!" said the third, who *didn't*, yet, but was determined to let it carry him along withal.

"War of Liberation, they called it," the first officer said, his spine uncurling from the beaten slump Vo had put into it. "War of conquest is more like it, wouldn't you say?"

The third jumped as if the alligator clips had leapt off the table and bit him. "But that's—"

"Loyalty," the first officer said, clearly and firmly. "Loyalty to our homeland—Annam. It is time to recognize invasion for what it is, violation for what it is."

"We must be men," the second officer said. "We must refuse to be victimized." He'd been reading American self-help texts as part of his study plan.

"Absolutely!" the third man almost yelled. He'd finally gotten the drift and hoped the others wouldn't interpret plain slow-wittedness as dissent. "Men! Not, uh, not dogs."

"There is," the first officer said, "but one thing to do."

And they all three turned as one to the horrid *Lien Xo* joker, who had stood there throughout it all not understanding a word that was said, and smiled. He smiled back with his grotesque leathery lips.

"Thank you," the first officer said, in English again. "You have been of great help. Return to your unit now and tell your colonel to await our report."

"In Hell," the second officer said in Vietnamese, as the being shambled out.

Because the three shared a single thought with total clarity: that night they were going to slip away across the paddies and join the rebels. The answer was blowing in the wind.

Ngo An Dong was unfortunate enough to come partially back to himself as the Soviet-made GAZ jeep pulled away from the police station and its bad suspension began to jolt his tailbone. He had osmotically absorbed the fact that he had fallen from the rice pot into the cook-fire.

The two who had hauled him from the interrogation room were sitting up front. There was something vaguely familiar about the back of the driver's head; it seemed kind of *square* for a Vietnamese head, somehow. Ngo had gone to Saigon University after he got out of the Army, and was fairly sophisticated; he assumed the blow to his head had broken something and he was hallucinating. He hoped a subdural hematoma would finish him before the legendary Colonel Vo got him to wherever he was taking him.

The colonel sat beside him, which struck him odd somehow. He made himself turn to look his future tormentor squarely in the eye.

And screamed.

There was no Vo. Instead a man sat beside him wrapped in a black cape, grinning at him from the depths of a cowl. His face was hairless. It was also *blue*.

"Those assholes swallowed my act hook, line, and sinker. Did you see that, Kim?" He reached forward to grab the driver's shoulder.

Kim Giau Minh, playing the driver, nodded his head. The cowled man settled back in the rear seat. Ngo caught a glimpse of what seemed millions of tiny lights in his cape. Lights like . . . stars.

"I'm slick," he said, rubbing blue hands together, "so slick. I don't see why Mark doesn't choose me more. I'm really a lot more useful than the others. Much more *versatile*. Don't you agree?"

Ngo nodded, though it made his head ring like a temple bell. The apparent fact of his escape from torture, degradation, betrayal, and death was beginning to penetrate the fog. If the blue man had asked him to confirm that he was Queen Victoria—another celestial personage for the *Cao Dai*—he would have nodded too.

The blue man looked at him closely. "Say, you wouldn't have a sister, would you? I don't get out too often."

Dawn was graying-out the clouds over distant jungle. The patrol boat prowled between banks covered in grass grown thick and high from the summer monsoon. The crew kept their thumbs on the firing-switches despite the fatigue of a night's patrol. The half hour before the sun actually popped the horizon was prime time for ambushers.

The boat was a Soviet copy of an old American RAG— River Assault Group—design, made especially for the Border Guards Directorate of the KGB. With the Soviet withdrawal from Afghanistan it had been retired from service on Central Asia's Amu Dar'ya, where it and others of its class had been engaged in trying to prevent arms from being smuggled south cross river to the 'Stan, and dope from coming north. The boats had not been a conspicuous success in either endeavor. But the Vietnamese armed forces were intent on resembling the Americans they had outlasted a decade and a half before as closely as possible, so they just *had* to have the craft when they hit the market.

The rating drowsing upright in the forward twin 12.7 mount jerked fully awake. "Did you feel that? Did you?" he demanded in a shrill voice, tracking the gun barrels left and right at the mist rising off the river.

The warrant officer in command stuck his head out of the armored cabin. "What's going on?" he yelled over the engine throb.

"I felt something hit us! Didn't you feel it?"

"*Vang!*" yelled the man from the after-machine-gun mount. "Yes! I felt it too."

"It was just a snag, Linh," the warrant officer said. "A sunken branch caught on a bar. All kinds of things get in the river in the monsoon. Go back to sleep."

Thump. The fifty-foot craft rocked perceptibly. The warrant officer lurched, had to grab at the hatchway for support. "What in the name of all hells is going on?"

The impact seemed to have come on the starboard bow. A rating ran from the armor-plated cabin to peer down into the heavy water.

"Look!" he shouted, pointing. "I see something down there. Something gray, going away fast."

Linh pointed his guns that way. "Shall I shoot? Shall I shoot?"

"If you do, you'll blow To into tiny pieces, you cretin!" the warrant shouted. "Helm, cut the throttle. We need to find out what's happening—"

"*It's coming back!*" To screamed.

The engine sounds died. The boat slowed perceptibly as it coasted into the current, wallowing from side to side. And suddenly it rocked sharply.

To went headfirst over the rail.

At once he began thrashing, splashing, and screaming. If he could swim, he was keeping the fact well hidden.

"Nguyen, throw him a line. Linh, keep a lookout. If you see anything, shoot it."

To's shrieks rose an octave, and he actually came halfway out of the water. "Oh, Buddha, oh, Jesus, it's got me, help, help, help!"

The warrant officer ran to the side—not as near as To had been. The rating was bobbing hysterically up and down, waving his arms. "Shoot!" the warrant officer yelled, dancing back. Then: "No! Don't shoot!"

Linh, who was tightening his thumbs on the butterfly trigger, cranked up the barrels of his heavy machine guns in time to chew up the tall weeds on the bank instead of To.

And then To was staggering in the shallows, pushed to relative safety by some unseen force. "AHH! Ahh. Ah?" he said. He scrabbled up the bank on all fours, then sat down and covered his face with his hands.

"Now, shoot!" the warrant officer commanded. Linh dutifully began to rake the murky river just shy of the bank, throwing great brown sheets of water over To. To screamed and ran off into the weeds.

Linh stopped shooting. There was a terrific bang, so loud that the warrant officer thought for a moment a round might have cooked off in the chamber. The little boat rocked back.

When it fell forward again, it just kept *going*. Slowly but unmistakably.

A rating ran from belowdecks. "The hull's all caved in!" he screamed. "We're sinking!"

"Ridiculous!" the warrant said. A big air bubble rolled to the surface, right in front of the bow.

A metal ammo box came sliding forward down the deck. The boat was settling heavily by the bows now. The warrant officer slammed his pith helmet on the deck.

"Why couldn't the filthy Americans-without-money have sold us a boat with a metal hull?"

A shape burst from the water, big and sleek and streamlined and silver-gray. It hung in the air a heartbeat, grinning all over its rostrum at them. Then it fell back into the river with a splash that swamped the deck clear to the gun mount.

Linh turned and fled, screaming, "Sea monster! Sea monster!" The warrant officer grabbed him and started punching him.

"It's just a dolphin, you coward!"

"Dolphins don't sink ships," Linh sobbed.

The beast broke the surface again fifty meters away, streaking off in a racing jump. Cursing, the warrant officer released Linh and jumped to the twin machine guns. The dolphin was moving away incredibly fast, shooting up out of the water at regular intervals.

The warrant officer fired the ammo cans dry. He never came close to hitting the dolphin. It vanished around a bend in the river.

He had to wade through ankle-deep water to abandon ship.

"What's bothering that damned dog?" the sentry demanded.

His partner had his heels dug in and was holding the

leash with both hands in an effort to keep the straining, snarling German shepherd from pulling him off his feet and dragging him out of the white high-noon glare of the floodlights that illuminated the ammo dump's perimeter.

"I don't know," he said between panting breaths. "He's never acted like this before."

"Stupid animal. I should put a bullet between his ears. That would calm him down."

"No! He must sense something. He's a good dog." The handler sounded wounded. He'd been through training with the dog; his fellow sentry was just somebody he'd been assigned to walk the wire with tonight. The dog was his *buddy*.

"I don't believe it."

"Here. I'll let him go. He'll show you." He released the animal.

The dog sprinted forward in a black-and-tan blur. They saw him race into the black of the compound, saw his shadowy form leap as if at a victim's throat. But there was nothing there.

Except the dog suddenly flipped over in the air and came down on its back so hard the two sentries heard the air burst out of its lungs. The shepherd rolled over and ran away with its tail between its legs, casting fearful looks over its shoulder.

The sentries looked at each other and began to unsling their assault rifles.

A woman appeared out of the darkness. Literally; it seemed she came into existence at the edge of the light—neither sentry saw a flicker of motion before she was abruptly *there*, running right at them. She wore tight-fitting black. Half her face was obscured by a black mask.

The dog handler's hands were numb from holding the leash. He almost dropped his Kalashnikov. His partner got his weapon free first, started to raise it.

The woman ran up to them, jumped, sent both rifles flying away with a double kick. She burst between them, sprinting right for the three-meter fence.

She leapt into the air. Incredibly she soared up and over the high fence, tucking into a ball to spin over the razor-wire coils that topped it. As the sentries watched, jaws dropping, she hit the ground running.

When she reached the far edge of the lightspill, it was as if she simply winked out of existence.

Behind the two sentries the ammo dump erupted in a cataclysm of light and noise.

The village security officer made his way home along the nighttime trail with the wobble-legged swagger of a man returning from a whorehouse. Which was just what he was doing.

To the last man who saw him alive he looked distinctly green. That was because he was being watched through an AN/PVS-2—a so-called starlight scope.

J. Robert Belew tightened his index finger on the trigger. The American-made M-21 sniper's rifle roared and slammed his shoulder. The security officer dropped into the short grass with the pratfall abruptness of a man who isn't rising again this side of Judgment Day.

Leaving the rifle resting on its bipod, Belew rose and stole forward. He had two Khmer Rouge with him for security. They were small, watchful men, men from whom the youthful fire that had led them to drive the sick and old and crippled from hospital wards before their guns into the streets of Phnom Penh—and to shoot, laughing, those who had not the strength to stagger—had long since died away, leaving them cynical, alert, attuned to survival for its own sake. Perhaps because it was all that was left them.

Though the Red Khmers as a movement were still as fanatically committed to their zany Maoist brand of revolutionary socialism as ever, few of the men who had taken part in the gang rape and murder of a nation still believed. They had seen too much. Now they were *warriors*, pure and simple, with no values and no past to fall back upon. Their ethics were those of the primal warrior through all human history: loyalty to buddies, qualified loyalty to a leader, if he had luck. Beyond that it was them against all humankind.

In their eyes Belew was both a comrade and an extremely lucky leader. To him they were *useful*, which made their moral failings irrelevant. He felt safe with them watching his back.

Belew dew his Para Ordnance sidearm in case he had misjudged and his quarry had friends following along behind. He paused, knelt beside the body. He felt the throat, held the back of his hand before the man's nose and mouth. No pulse, no breath. No sounds came out of the wall of elephant grass from which the late security officer had emerged.

Voices were calling from the other direction, inside the bamboo fence of the village a couple of hundred meters away. Belew took a piece of paper from his pocket, thrust it into a pocket of the man's blood-blackened tunic, and ran lithely back to where his rifle lay.

He picked up the weapon, folded the bipod, and slung it. Slinging a piece was usually the mark of a slovenly troop, something no self-respecting Special Forces soldier would dream of doing in the field. Except if Belew ran into real trouble there was no way he was going to *fight* with the cumbrous, slow-firing M-21. His sidearm would serve better.

There were torches bobbing his way from the village now. " 'Paranoia strikes deep,' " he murmured softly. Not *all* his aphorisms were classical.

The villagers would find a list of government informers on their late security officer. This would, with luck, have Ramifications.

For instance, the villagers would probably assume the security officer was trying to defect to the rebels and that the *government* had burned him. The official's family would blame the government. The government would grill everyone in the area to find out who else might be disloyal, while going nuts trying to figure out who actually popped the poor son of a gun, since they knew *they* didn't do it.

Meanwhile officials in nearby villages would be thinking furiously. The fact that one of their own had bitten it would remind them of their own mortality. Even if the rebels weren't responsible for this killing, it might give them unhealthy ideas. And say the government really had rubbed this guy out: what if the government suddenly took the notion *they* were disloyal?

Finally, life was not going to be too comfortable for the people whose names were on the list, either.

The assassination, then, was not merely a random act of midnight murder; it was a *cunningly planned* act of midnight murder. An engine for generating maximum paranoia and ill will, it would put a lot of people seriously uptight and cause them to do much soul-searching about where their loyalties lay. He didn't think many would come down foursquare for the Socialist Republic after this one. And even though most people wouldn't do anything, he was planting seeds, planting seeds.

Best of all, he thought, as he slipped back to his quondam Young Genocides, to give them a thumb's-up and be answered with flashes of teeth and eyes, *Mark will never connect the act to Major J. Robert Belew, USSF, retired.* Belew genuinely liked and respected the boy, but he was in ways too good for this world.

What he didn't know couldn't hurt him.

Chapter Forty-one

Moonchild flinched as the TV spots hit her. She felt the exposed skin of her face redden under their assault. She could not endure them long, she knew. She would make herself stand them long enough.

"We, the Revolutionary Oversight Council for Free Vietnam, have agreed upon a platform of goals. We seek to secure freedom for the people of Vietnam, freedom in its many forms. These include first and foremost the freedom of conscience, the freedom of expression, the freedom to enjoy the fruits of one's own labors. . . ."

She could feel the skepticism of the small but dedicated band of reporters on the other sides of the lights and glass camera eyes. Crews from CNN, CBS, RTL, and the French national news agency had all made their way to this former mining camp in the jagged spine of the *Chaîne Annamitique*, plus some print media. J. Bob had set it up, of course; he had contacts everywhere.

Belew sets so much up, she thought as her mouth transferred words from paper to sound. *Maybe it is too much.*

The statement was brief, indicating nothing of the hours of violent wrangling that had gone into its composition. It was tough enough to keep the ethnic-Vietnamese factions, such as the *Cao Dai* and the Annamese separatists, the Hoa, and the Montagnards, from trying to cut one another's throats, let alone *agree* on anything. The minorities were no more tractable than the haughty Vietnamese. Even though FULRO, the Unified Fighting Front of the Oppressed Races—represented by Belew's friends Bert and Ernie—had existed since the sixties, when it fought both the

333

VC and the South Vietnamese government, its Cambodian and Montagnard members feuded incessantly with each other. They only gave it a rest when they combined to beat up on the Muslim Cham of the coastal region.

The coalition's continuance required Moonchild's all-but-constant presence as peacekeeper. In the early days she repeatedly found it necessary to wade in physically to break up fights or keep an overly aggressive debater under control—as she had done with Colonel Nguyen, now one of her most vehement supporters. There was less of the physical stuff now—the ability to take on an opponent who had the drop on you with a gun and win deeply impressed the Vietnamese, who had enough intimate acquaintance with deadly force to know that sort of thing belonged normally in the movies. But she was still an all-but-indispensable control rod, whose presence was necessary to keep all those hot rebel heads from achieving critical mass.

It meant that Revolutionary Council meetings had to take place at night for the highly UV-sensitive Moonchild to be able to attend. Fortunately night is the natural medium of conspirators and rebels; no one thought twice about it. Her playing the part of *sulsa*, a *ninja*-esque Knight of the Night, only enhanced her status among the rebels. It only built the legend, the mystique—with, inevitably, more than a little help from J. Bob Belew.

But it also meant that Mark often had to take his Moonchild powder more than once a night. Playing the sporadic presence, who appeared mainly when and as she was needed and was otherwise not seen, added fabric to Moonchild's cloak of mystery. Sometimes, though, she had to come and stay for more than an hour, to maintain her credibility and prevent internecine bloodshed.

Mark had long ago learned that doing one of his personae even twice in a twenty-four-hour period had savage aftershocks, mentally and physically. His island-hopping passage of the Aegean as Aquarius had left him weak and sick and talking in voices other than his own for several days. The time Isis Moon was spending expressed was taking a toll on Mark and all his friends. Not even Moonchild's healing powers could make up the costs.

And he was far, far away from reliable sources of the drugs that made up his powders. He had Belew funneling stuff to him from old connections in the Golden Triangle drug trade. J. Bob would not vouch for their purity. That made Mark happy, yes indeed.

Moonchild finished, looked up for questions. As Belew had warned her, they weren't friendly.

"What about the environment?" a reporter asked. "How can a supposedly free regime protect the environment from pollution and exploitation?"

She smiled slightly. She feared Belew was a devil, but he was a cunning devil, she had to admit. Remoteness, and the consequent difficulty to government forces seeking to decapitate the rebellion, was only one of the reasons for selecting this site for the press conference.

"Did you look around yourselves on your way in, please?" she asked. "You must have seen the great scar gouged out of the side of the mountain. This was a strip-mining camp. There are many such across Vietnam, just as there are horribly polluted factory sites and clear-cut forests. To the Socialist Republic, Nature is something to be subjugated and exploited with a ruthlessness unknown to even the most rapacious capitalists of the West. Everyone has seen the terrible environmental costs this philosophy exacted in the former East Germany. The same heedless forces are at work here."

"What about the homeless?" another reporter asked quickly, eager to drop *that* subject.

"The government of the Socialist Republic has *created* homelessness, not combated it. Its housing policies have fallen greatly short of meeting the needs of its urban populations. Its solution has been to try to herd unhoused masses into *khu nha moi*, New Economic Zones, which are no more than the old New Life Hamlets that were such a shame of the former South Vietnamese regime. You would call them concentration camps. And to create these New Economic Zones, the Socialist Republic has forcibly displaced minority populations such as the Hmong, the Nung, the Muong, and the Khmer. Such displacement, by the way, has been defined as genocide by the United Nations.

"Understand, also, that as in the USSR, in the Socialist Republic indigence is a *crime*. People you would see living on the streets in the West are here arrested and shipped to *trai cai tao*, reeducation camps. As with the environment,

Free Vietnam cannot offer magical solutions. We *can* promise to be less brutal and ineffectual than the current regime."

The journalists shifted and rumbled. Moonchild felt stirrings of contempt for them, and put the feelings down with shocked surprise and self-reproach. But while the facts she had recounted were news to her and Mark, these people had to have seen their truth before, have known them. But they chose to act as if they were untrue, and to present that pretense to the public as fact.

She was beginning to understand Belew's virulent contempt for the media. It made her uncomfortable, as agreeing with the ultraconservative spook always did.

She moistened her lips, which felt not just dry but strange, as if they were developing cold sores. She hated the lights.

"Are there any more questions?"

"Why do they want me for their spokesperson?" Moonchild asked, picking her way down the steep slope. She saw better at night, by moon or starlight, than she did in artificial illumination. But the mountainside was brushy, the footing unreliable.

"Let me count the ways," Belew said. He was actually moving with more confidence than she. It did not occur to her that for all her intrinsically superior physical abilities, *he* was the one with experience of the land. She just took the fact as a reproach. "You're an ace. You're beautiful. You're charismatic. You're photogenic. *And* you're not Vietnamese. The Viets are adept at not taking the rap for their mistakes—look at what they did to us Americans. If the rebellion pulls a rock, they can point their finger at a foreigner and say, 'It's all her fault.'"

"Oh." She misstepped, slipped, caught herself on her hands as gravel slid rattling away from beneath her feet. "I am sorry. I am so clumsy."

"A gentleman never disagrees with a lady," Belew said, extending a helping hand, which she declined. "Fortunately I know when *not* to be a gentleman. Nonsense, dear child. You are far more coordinated than any nat or most aces. You're simply upset and fighting yourself."

She stood upright again, came close to him. "If you know so much, tell me what I am!" she whispered fiercely.

"You're what would be called, in the current vernacular, a babe."

She clenched her fists. "No! You know what I mean. Why could I not speak Korean when Kim addressed me?"

"Maybe because you're not Korean."

She felt her knees lose all cohesion, as if the collagens binding her sinews had dissolved. Even the stars, stabbing down hard as needles through clear thin mountain air, could not heal her with their ancient light. She felt a stab of Mark's remnant dread of them.

"What am I?" she whispered. The escort of jokers and *Khmers Rouges* slipped and slid past them down the trail, eager to put as much mountain up-and-down between themselves and the press-conference site as they quickly could.

"What *am* I?" she asked, tears running down her cheeks.

"I don't *know*, darlin'. What do you think you are? How do you account for being trapped inside the six-four male body of the world's Last Hippie?"

She shook her head. "I don't know. Something must have happened. To me and the others. We were . . . *lost*. Somehow we found—shelter—in Mark's psyche."

"Did you lose your grasp of Korean along with your separate existence?"

"What are you trying to do to me?" she sobbed.

"Trying to lead you to the truth," he said with quiet intensity. "I don't know what it is. But if you just wander, and wonder, and don't try to confront the facts of who and what you are—whatever they are—you're never going to hold up. You'll lose your center. And with it the resistance will lose its own."

She covered her face with her hands. "You think Mark has—what do you say?—a split personality."

" 'Multiple-personality disorder' is the current catchphrase, unless they changed it again while I wasn't looking."

She grabbed his biceps. "I'm a fantasy, then? I don't *exist*?"

"*Mu*," he said evenly. "Zen negation. That question was never asked, the way the *rōshi* Jōshū unasked the question

of whether a dog has Buddha nature. Was it a fantasy that
shattered Colonel Nguyen's .45-caliber manhood into a zil-
lion pieces? Is it a fantasy that's about to pinch my arms in
half?"

"Oh," she said. She let go and stepped back. "I'm
sorry."

"Maybe it's time you quit hiding behind apologies.
Where's Mark, right this instant?"

She placed a hand between her breasts. "Inside."

"All right. When you're not here, where are you?"

"Inside . . . Mark."

"That's right. So, is Mark unreal?"

"No."

"Are you?"

"But, Mark is the real one. He becomes us—"

"Bullshit."

She shut her mouth.

"Mark is the baseline personality, as he calls himself.
What's the difference? You don't lose your consciousness
when you're inside him, now, do you? I know he hears the
voices of all of you. Once in a while he even speaks in
them."

She hung her head, felt the tears drip from her eyes.
"That's true."

"So you never *don't exist*. It's just that sometimes you
have no physical reality. Visible, anyway—I sure as heck am
not pretending to understand the mechanics of your coming
and going.

"Look, child. You are real, you are here. How can it
matter where you really came from, or what you're doing
here? You're a fact. And if you let brooding about an unan-
swerable question like who you *really* are—and who on
Earth can ever wholly answer that question, anyway?—if
you let that dissolve you, you are going to leave a whole lot
of people who depend on you sinking without a life pre-
server."

She began to tremble. He put his arm around her. She
stiffened, then stopped fighting the contact and melted
against him.

"Isis. Isis, do you feel me?"

She went rigid. Belew held her, firm but not constrict-
ing. His left hand was a bandaged stump again; he'd been

up to tricks, which was why the government-owned mine site was available for the rebels to hold a press conference in.

"Isis, where are you?"

Eric?

"Accept no substitutes."

Eric, what's happening to me?

"An attack of conscience, maybe?"

I'm doing the right thing.

"Really? Then where's all that grief coming from? All that guilt? I can feel it there, down inside you, surging like a black, stormy sea."

You really are a poet, Eric.

"I'm the voice of your conscience, hon. Do you feel good about what you're doing?"

—Yes—

"Then why do you weep so, my love? You're helping the exploiters, the bigots. The ones who want to see us burn, to see our joker flesh blacken and shrivel from our bones—"

She felt an image begin to form in her mind, an image bright with flame. She pushed it down.

"What? You're fighting me? Can't you bear to see the truth?"

I won't be manipulated anymore. Not even by you. No matter how good your reasons are, I won't have it.

The glow came back, persisted, grew. She shook her head, fighting. Her body began to tremble uncontrollably. Flashes of light were stabbing in her head, themselves threatening to white out the dream Eric was trying to force into her mind.

"You can't run forever, baby. You can't hide. Just as your ragtag reactionary lynch mob can't play keep-away with us and the People's Army forever. We will win. We are righteous.

"Why won't you come back where you belong?"

She turned her head aside, vomited all over Belew's arm. *"Isis, what's happening to you?"*

"What's happening to me?" she screamed.

Belew wrapped both arms around her and threw himself sideways, dragging her off the trail. The two went rolling and bouncing down the mountainside.

Chapter Forty-two

Moonchild got a soft-slippered foot into Belew's gut as she rolled onto her back, pulled him over her and launched him into the night. Then she caught herself, stopped rolling.

She got to all fours. Her arms and legs were shaking so hard, it felt as if she would fly apart. She vomited again.

She heard brush stir. Belew was coming back. She had no idea why he was assaulting her. Perhaps his conservative *machismo* was driving him to rape. She tried to get up, to fight or flee, but her body would not respond.

Then his arms were around her again. *Go away!* she wanted to shriek. But she could not produce words.

A whistling of wind, a stinging inrush of debris, and it was Mark huddling in Belew's arms, shivering violently.

"Now you see what I was up to?" the spy asked softly. "I thought you might still consider that transition a private matter."

Mark spat to clear his mouth. "What *happened*, man? The change never hit me that hard before!"

"Moonchild's having an existential crisis, in a way the Existentialists never *dreamed* of. Her emotional state made the transition bad. Also—" he shook his head—"it was as if something else was eating her, as if she was listening to something from far away, that was riling her up more."

Mark tensed, forced himself to relax. *He knows too much. He sees too much. Can I trust him?*

Do I have any choice?

You always got a choice, bunky, J. J. Flash finished for him. Mark made himself shake his head. "I don't remember anything about that, man," he said, "just that she was upset."

340

As always the lie tasted like copper in his mouth. He'd always hated the taste of lies.

Belew stood up, helped him to his feet. "How are you handling it?"

"I . . . I don't know." That tasted of truth. "I'm gonna have to sort this out—"

To the north the sky lit, silhouetting the hunchbacked peak they had just skirted in white. A moment later a rumble reached them, through the ground and cold air. The sound and lights went on and on, pulsing irregularly.

"Airstrike!" Mark cried. He tensed to run.

Belew touched him lightly on the arm. "No. It's okay. Sov-bloc planes don't fly at night. It's artillery."

He stood for a moment to watch the display. "Our unbiased, impartial media friends ratted us off to the People's Army. What did I tell you?" He preened his mustache with a thumb.

"I know it's bad of me . . ." he said. His teeth were white beneath his well-tended brush. "But is it too much to hope a few of them got caught in the barrage?"

Torches sent strange, misshapen shadows chasing each other between tents and bunkers like imps in a Bosch painting. Jokers swarmed around the two men making their way into the belly of Fort Venceremos, half-naked, sweat-slimed, painted or scarred when they weren't feathered or scaled or otherwise disfigured by the wild card.

"Aces, *a*ces, let's get in their *faces*," chanted a joker. He brandished a torch in a fist covered all over with short bristles.

"I hear you, man," another jeered. "Aces are just nats with some *spice*."

"Just *meat*, man."

"Gimme *six*."

"You wave that fucking torch in my face anymore," said the man in white, "and you'll fucking eat *it*."

He was about medium height, beefy in shoulder and chest. His tight-fitting white suit had the black hood thrown back at the nape. His dark hair was short. His eyes were green, dangerous, and not on the same level. His face seemed to have been assembled from whatever parts were to hand in a bin. He walked with a hitched and swaggering gait.

They came to the parade ground, passing between poles. He tossed a thumb at the white-bleached human skulls that topped them. "I kind of get behind your *decor*, though."

His partner just lumbered silently at his side. He was taller by a head. From the mask that hid his face to his pointy-toe cowboy boots he was dressed entirely in black. Except for the white straw cowboy hat with the peacock feather in the band, of course.

A teenaged joker planted himself solidly in their path. He had torches in his outstretched hands and a face whorled like a thumbprint. The skin on his bare chest and arms was normal human skin. As if to counteract that, he had cut vertical gouges in his torso from collarbone to the waist of his jungle-cammie trousers.

"So you're the mighty aces from back in the World," he said. "Hear me: we don't *like* aces. And we aren't part of your fucking world anymore. We got our own New World Order, here. It looks like you just don't *belong*."

"Oh, no?" the man in white said. "We'll see about that, asshole."

The tall man took off his cowboy hat and handed it to him. Then he grabbed his mask by the crown and pulled it off.

The joker screamed.

The crowd surged back. Someone turned and vomited. The whorl-faced joker dropped his torches and ran.

The man in black had half a face. From the onlookers' point of view it was unfortunate he had any. What remained looked like hamburger that had been left on the counter for three-four days and then set afire with charcoal starter.

"Now that we got that out of the way," the white-clad man said, handing back the hat, "we got an appointment with your boss. Now, do you let us get to it, or do we start kicking your ugly asses?"

He laced his fingers and cracked his knuckles. "I'd really hate that," he said. "It's not *professional* to put pleasure before business."

*   *   *

"Gentlemen." Colonel Charles Sobel rose from behind his broad, empty desk. The exacting order of the photo-crowded office made it seem an island of sanity in the chaotic sea of Fort Venceremos. "I can't tell you how glad I am that you're here."

Then he tipped his head to the side, and his noble Doug MacArthur profile took on some wrinkles. "What's that smell?"

The man in white jerked a thumb at the one in black. "Him. He's *dead*. Or didn't you know that?"

Sobel rubbed his chin, nodded slowly. "I've read your dossiers, of course, Mr. Ray."

"Call me Carnifex. Sir."

Sobel paused, nodded again. "Very well, And you are Bobby Joe Puckett."

The man in black nodded.

"Also known as Crypt Kicker," Billy Ray said. "He's a ball of laughs."

"Please be seated," the Colonel said.

"I'm fine," Carnifex said.

"The dead don't need to sit," Crypt Kicker said.

Sobel raised a brow at him, as if surprised he could speak. "Initial reports indicated you were lost in the last assault on the Rox, Mr., ah, Kicker."

"He was fried by a dragon, he got left below the bottom of the Hudson River when the Rox disappeared, he went boiling up to the surface in the giant air bubble that got left behind, and *then* he got hit by the Turtle's tidal wave," Carnifex said. "They found his dead ass wrapped around a light pole on Staten Island."

"It sounds as if you had a trying day."

"He told Battle he didn't need to shower before we hit the Rox," Carnifex said, "because he knew he'd wash up on shore."

"Mr. Battle, yes," the Colonel said. "I'm very grateful to your superior for providing us with your services. You are badly needed."

"Yeah, I'm so happy I could puke that he sent me out here among all these damned monsters of yours, Colonel. And stuck me with the biggest monster of all for a partner."

He leaned forward and put his black-gauntleted knuckles on the desk. "I still don't get it, Colonel. You're out here playing butt-boy for about the last pack of commies left on Earth. Just what the hell is the CIA doing, looking out for that particular endangered species?"

The smooth, tanned skin of Sobel's face writhed briefly, as if it had live mice beneath it. Then it firmed. "Believe it or not, Mr. Battle does possess a social conscience. If you knew him as I do, you'd understand."

He folded his hands. "I realize you are confused and resentful at the unexpected turns of events that brought you here. I hope you're not going to have any problems working with us."

Carnifex straightened. "I do my goddam job. I'm the very best." He dipped his head right, raised it again. "Nobody said I had to like it."

"What Mr. Battle says, I do," Crypt Kicker said. "He said obey you."

"If I get to kick some butt, I'll do fine, Colonel," Carnifex said.

Sobel smiled. He picked some invisible lint from his immaculate uniform sleeve. "I think I can promise you that, Mr. Ray."

He leaned forward. "Our situation is grave here, gentlemen. The rebels have been having everything their own way. They still don't have any military strength to speak of— some support among urban capitalists greedy for a chance to exploit their fellow men, some sympathy from primitive minorities who resent the modernizing influences of social reform. A number of soldiers of the People's Army have deserted to them, it's true, but they're all cowards and weaklings, of course.

"But *psychologically*"—he shook his magnificent head—"they're picking us apart. Not just the standard assassinations, sabotage, and other acts of terrorism. You would not *believe* the reports we're getting: beautiful, bulletproof women who walk through shadows. Burning men who fly through the air and shoot down jet aircraft with fireballs from their hands. Sea monsters attacking river-patrol craft. The site of that press conference the traitors gave last week, the mining camp—it was abandoned after the workers and security detachment reported one of the big ore shovels came to life and began attacking them. Even the administrators and technicians claimed it was true, and they were Russians."

He shook his head. "Someone—or some *thing*—impersonated a high official of the Socialist Republic's security apparatus, a dedicated, loyal officer well known to me personally, and helped a major leader of the rebels to escape government custody." He leaned back. "Our people are strong, gentlemen; they are *righteous*, as we in the New Joker Brigade are righteous. But they're starting to lose heart. They're afraid. They feel they're up against some supernatural enemy."

Billy Ray looked at Crypt Kicker and cracked his knuckles. "Naw," he said with a nasty, lopsided grin. "You're just suffering what we call your severe ace infestation."

The grin went wide and feral. "Fortunately, Colonel, you just called on Ace Exterminators."

Chapter Forty-three

"Thanks, guys," Mark said wearily, forcing a smile. He sat cross-legged on the floor with his elbows on his thighs, rubbing sunken eyes and wondering if he'd ever sit in a chair again.

The men of his original runaway squad stood in the doorway of the hootch or crowded together close outside—Slick, Studebaker Hawk, Mario, and Lou Inmon, Osprey from First Squad, their eyes shining. Eye Ball was missing; he had continued to insist on walking point and had gotten cut down in a chance meeting with a government patrol on the way to an ammo-dump raid.

They had brought news; great news, Mark supposed. The sugar plantation near his current village command post had a satellite dish. The news had come down it.

The Soviets had pulled an East Germany on the Socialist Republic. They had not quite told the regime that they were willing to guarantee its fall if it looked as if the rebels were running into difficulty. But they had announced that, effective immediately, all fraternal assistance to Vietnam was suspended indefinitely. The freighters in Haiphong Harbor weighed anchor and steamed into Tonkin Gulf. The administrators and skilled technicians were pulling out of the huge, environment-wrecking logging and mining and construction camps. Starshine would be proud.

Soviet personnel in military installations the length of Vietnam blandly shook their heads when their Vietnamese counterparts begged them to fly airstrikes against the waves of resistance passing like peristalsis throughout the country—even in the militant North, ancient Tonkin, the actual *winner* of the Vietnam War. The Soviet commander of the giant Da Nang airbase, near Fort Venceremos, ordered all Vietnamese brusquely off the premises. The Soviets were evacuating their huge civilian and military complements from the Socialist Republic and could not afford to have outsiders getting underfoot. The Soviets, he said, would be more than happy to hand the facilities over to the government of Vietnam when they left—whoever that government happened to be.

Mark felt his head drop forward on his neck, as if the people it contained were too heavy for his muscles to support. Tears dripped to the back of his hands. Misreading his body language, the others drew back to leave him to his triumph.

All he felt was numb. Dead from the neck both ways. *Maybe that's a blessing,* he thought. The voices in his head were still for the moment.

In the shadows stood J. Bob Belew, sipping tea from a cracked old French porcelain cup. "We're winning," he said.

Mark shook his head. It was as if he had not five—four now—personae, but dozens of them, hundreds, and each was filled to bursting with a different emotion. He raised his hands, moved them ineffectually in the air. The only possible release he could see for all those volcanic emotions was to throw his head back and open his mouth wide and just vent them in one long scream.

Except, once started, that scream would go on forever, as near as he could calculate.

". . . How? . . ." he managed to ask in a strangled voice. "How—is it—*possible*? There's so many of them. There's—so few—of us."

" 'In war, numbers alone confer no advantage,' " Belew quoted. " 'Do not advance relying on sheer military power.' Sun Tzu."

Mark shook his head. "Just words, man. I need . . . *answers.*"

Belew laughed. "All right. First of all, don't give yourself—or Moonchild—*too much* credit. What's happening here is as close to inevitable as anything ever is—it's like the 'historic process' the Marxists are so fond of, only they're the ones it's grinding into cotto salami. Soon or late—this year, next year, 1999—what is happening now would happen anyway. What you, your friends, all of us, are is merely a catalyst."

Mark stared at his hands. They had come to seem great and ungainly to him, as he himself did, in contrast to the tiny and graceful Vietnamese. Even Moonchild felt bloated around them.

He didn't know whether he felt resentment or relief at what Belew said. Part of him wanted to trumpet, *I am too important!*

Another part was happy to avoid the blame.

"Next," Belew said, ticking off right-hand fingers with his bandaged stump, "don't discount the numbers of 'us.' Our name is legion. If you take passive sympathy into account, I'd say upward of half the population is with us—and I'd say an overwhelming majority from the old DMZ south, in Annam and Cochin China. But even in the North we have support, if the demonstrations in Hanoi are any indication. There's a twenty-four-hour vigil going on at the lake where the Trung sisters drowned themselves, you know, and the authorities are afraid to break it up."

"Hey, I was at People's Park in '70, man. We had the people then too. *They* had the guns."

"That didn't stop you then, I notice, Mark. Or were you not really the Radical?"

All Mark could do was thrust his face into his palms and sob. When he could see and speak again, Belew was squatting Vietnamese-style on the mat nearby, not close enough to threaten, but close enough that Mark could feel his presence.

"I don't know, man," Mark said brokenly. "I've never known. All I've done since, the experimentation, turning into my friends, all that—it was all so I could *know*. Know that just once, in this fucked-up, useless life of mine, to know that I was a *hero*."

He dabbed his eyes clear, raised his head, matched Belew gaze for gaze. "Whether I was or not, man, it didn't matter. Radical won that fight, yeah. The other side won the war."

"You're beginning to grasp the essence of strategy, son, which is the difference between winning a battle and winning a *war*. But just the same, I have to disagree with you. *You* won. Trust me; I was on the other side. I know. We cut and ran and left South Vietnam in the lurch, because in the crunch Nixon didn't have any balls in his pants. You—Radical, whoever—you helped cut his nuts off. You might as well feel proud."

Mark laughed. It wasn't much of a laugh. But it was a laugh.

"Well, anyway, we didn't win it all. There was no revolution. We had the numbers, but they had the guns."

"No," Belew said, "you didn't win it all. But you did exercise leverage on the government—mainly, of course, because our government was sadly lacking in will. At home or abroad.

"That's why People Power fizzled out so badly, with the Tiananmen massacre. People thought that what ran the Shah out of Iran and Marcos from the Philippines was the popular will, peacefully expressed. But it wasn't that at all. The army and the secret police—the enforcers—lost faith in their main man to hold the center. And if he went, the army and the secret police wouldn't be the biggest, baddest, most untouchable gangs around anymore. They'd be a mass of individuals, each liable to be hunted down and killed by the friends and family of anybody they wasted trying to defend their boss. People in the West underestimate the socializing effect of the blood feud in these ceiling-fan countries.

"That's what happened in Guatemala. The Hero Twins got to exploit Soviet aid to an extant underground movement, plus the intense racial hatred the Indians harbored for *mestizos* and the Spanish. They dealt themselves guns *and* numbers. That's what we've been trying to do here. That's why we're winning."

"But all we're doing—we're picking at them. It's like the bugs around here." A pang for Croyd, still asleep, still being bundled along as baggage. "They bite you and bite you, and you go, like, half crazy. But you don't stop what you're doing."

"That's right. Because unlike your swarming bugs, *we* don't bite at random. Each bite is calculated to make the enemy feel the most insecure, to make us seem most supernaturally powerful to them—and to the population we're trying to attract to the cause. People want to go with a winner. We seem to have a hundred aces on our side, and we strike where we please. What does it matter that the strikes don't amount to anything much, singly or taken all together? We live in the world of *Maya*, Mark, the world of illusion. Perception is reality. The perception we are creating is that we are invincible.

"Add that to the marvelous job the Northerners, the Tonkinese, have done of instilling the resentment of the conquered in their 'liberated' southern brothers, and the standard hash that communist rule has made of the economy and of everyday life, and you have a highly receptive audience. The Viet in the village and the Ho-ville street looks at Rumania and East Germany and even the USSR and asks, 'Why not?' And that's why we're winning."

"And what are we winning? A chance for brother to exploit brother?"

"Come on, Mark. That's not your brain talking, it's sixties nostalgia. You've lived on the fringes of Jokertown, and you've lived here. Who has it better, the despised minority members in their New York ghetto—even with Barnett and his crazies on the loose—or the dead-average ethnic Vietnamese in the villes?"

Mark hung his head. "Back home."

Belew nodded. "I'm not saying it's *perfect*, Mark. It's lousy in a lot of ways—I'm a wild card too. That's why I'm here."

"Bullshit."

Belew's head snapped back. Mark cursed as seldom as he did.

"You're taking another shot at the title, man," Mark said accusingly. "You didn't win it all back in the sixties and seventies. You're trying again to do it right this time. You're just like—like . . ."

His voice trailed away. He could not speak the name that had come into his mind.

"Like Colonel Charles Self-Righteousness Personified Sobel?" Belew laughed. "Guilty as charged. We're middle-aged assholes trying to erase the failures of our youth. Did you think you were going to shame me? I know what I am: I'm a man who always does what he believes to be right, and I'm not embarrassed when what's right happens to gratify my less noble instincts—which I don't think are necessarily ignoble, by the way. I legitimately want Vietnam to be free—I fought and spilled my blood to that end in the first round, and I've done it this time too. And I *am* a wild card, Mark, and I do know a hawk from a hernshaw."

"What the heck *is* a hernshaw, anyway, man?"

"Nobody knows. Don't let the junior-college *Hamlet* commentators tell you the word is really 'handsaw,' though. That's hooey."

He reached to touch Mark on the knee. "I also know that's not what's really bothering you, son. I know you feel like one of those two lizards walking on a cloud in one of Vaughan Bodé's old *Deadbone Erotica* strips, the boys who suddenly realized that what they were doing was impossible and plunged to their deaths."

"You read *Deadbone*, man?"

"Did you think conservatives couldn't be cool? Okay, so most of them aren't. But most of them aren't real conservatives, either, they're New Dealers warmed over and allowed to congeal. Or are you practicing age discrimination here? Think about it, if *young* equated to *hip*, Vanilla Ice would be a busboy."

Mark laughed. He had spent his life fighting against everything J. Robert Belew was and stood for. But he sure *liked* the dude.

"But if, in the long run, you let the mere fact of something's being impossible slow you down, you wouldn't be here, would you? You would never have turned up all those wonderful friends who can walk the shadows and fly through the sky and hide behind the face of anyone in the world, would you? You'd never have flown to an alien planet and back, and done God knows what along the way. The cloud-dancing isn't what's eating you either."

Mark sighed. "Okay. I don't know what I *am*. Anymore. Am I a man? Am I four—uh, *three*—men and a woman? Am I nuts?"

"Isis Moon's little episode has still got you down, eh? I suspected as much."

"Well, she had a *point*, man. I always bought what she told you, that she had been born and raised and lived her life and all, and that something happened and next thing anybody knew, she was trapped inside me."

"Doesn't that seem a little farfetched?"

Mark looked at him. After a moment Belew laughed.

"All right. *Touché*. You're getting pretty Zen as we go along here, Mark. *Still.*" He turned a hand palm-up, questioning.

"All right. I wondered, too; I'd have to be brain dead not to. I did some research.

"There are three people named Isis Moon in the whole United States, at least that I could track down; heck, one of 'em lived at the commune I hung out at after I sprung Sprout, outside Taos."

At the mention of his daughter's name he swallowed hard and paused. It was as if he had picked away a scab to find a wound the size of the Grand Canyon gaping in his flesh. He had to look away, hurry himself past, lest he pitch in headfirst and fall forever.

"They're all ex-hippies, New Agers, or both. None of them's Korean.

"J. J. Flash—his real name's John Jacob Flash, you may know that, he mentioned it on *Peregrine's Perch* once or twice. There is a John Jacob Flash in Manhattan. He's a Wall Street broker. J. J.—Jumpin' Jack—met him once, on Peri's show. They're the *same man*. I mean, the broker is a bit paunchier, though he looks like he works out. But they're the *same*—same looks, same gestures, same smart mouths.

"But Jumpin' Jack is a *lawyer*, not a stockbroker. Flash-the-broker isn't an ace—he's tested negative for the wild card. And Jumpin' Jack doesn't think of himself as an ace either; that's jargon he picked up. Where he comes from—where he thinks he comes from—he's called a 'superhero,' just like in the old comic books."

"Which you loved."

"Is there *anything* you don't know about me?"

"What you're telling me now, Mark."

Mark sighed again. "No one knows it. Not even—not even Tach. But it's got to come out, now, man, or my head will explode."

"We don't want that. Don't let me interrupt."

"I checked Damon Strange—cool name, you gotta admit. Too bad he's such a weenie, Cosmic Traveler is. I mean, I even got his name wrong, his ace name—the real song title is 'Mystic Traveler,' it's an old Dave Mason song. Now, there's a Damon Strange in Albuquerque, New Mexico, who's a lawyer, No connection there. There is also an insurance adjustor of that name in Fort Lauderdale, Florida. I've got his picture, and he looks a lot like the Traveler, though he isn't blue. He had a car accident in 1983 and has been a veg since—Florida courts won't let 'em turn off life support. Sorry for being insensitive, man."

"You're a biochemist. You know what brain death means. Why tiptoe around?"

Mark took a breath. "Yeah. The thing is, this Strange in Florida had his accident two days before Cosmic Traveler first appeared. As near as I can pin down, his EEG went flatline *ten minutes* before I took the potion for the first time.

"Traveler won't let me have anything about his real past—Aquarius won't either, though I think he's French-Canadian. But that spooked me, man. And then, to find out Moonchild doesn't speak any Korean—"

He shook his head. "What am I, man?"

"What do you think?"

"I don't know. Sometimes I think I somehow managed to draw in these souls that had gotten loose from their bodies and were wandering through the cosmos—from alternate dimensions, like?"

Belew nodded.

"But this thing with Moonchild—maybe I just have the world's most vivid multiple-personality disorder, man. Though I always thought, like, with an MPD, the identities had no memories of one another, weren't even aware the others existed. My alter egos hardly shut up, these days."

He looked at Belew. "You know everything about me now, man. Tell me what I am."

"Okay."

Mark rocked back, stunned. He expected another "*mū*" out of him.

Belew stood, put hands behind hips, stretched. He looked toward the open door of the hootch.

Outside was turning mauve and gray-blue as the night prepared to descend like a lead weight in a Monty Python skit. The insects were out in the day's most profuse profusion, and the night birds were, too, scything through their clouds with happy savagery. Somewhere a box played Public Enemy.

That was a band Belew could respect, Public Enemy.

He wasn't fond of their message or their sound. But they weren't *wimps*.

"I don't know where your friends come from, Mark. I don't know if they're unmoored psyches who happened to roost behind your baby blues or whether you're just nuts. Or all of the above.

"But, Mark, I know what you are.

"You're a hero."

He came over and slapped the stunned Mark on the shoulder. "It's what you've wanted all your life. Wise men—men who think they're wise, anyway—always tell us to beware what we ask for, because we might actually get it. Well, you did.

"Now you just have to deal with it." And he walked out the door into evening air that hummed as with ozone after thunder.

Chapter Forty-four

The rope-handled wooden box was longer than tall or wide and God knew how old. The stencils on its side were weathered to near-invisibility: U.S. ARMY MORTAR ROUND 81MM M301A3 ILLUMINATING. It sat in the middle of a clearing in the woods in the Kon Tum foothills east of Pleiku. The grass had been cropped close by grazing water buffalo. An array of other junk was scattered around the fringes of the clearing, including a clapped-out Ural truck.

A tall man with blue-black hair and a notable jut of jaw stood at the clearing's edge, gazing intently at the box. A curl of blue smoke rose from it.

The box burst into flame.

Standing at the muscular man's side, Mark jumped despite himself. "Hoo!" he half whistled, half exclaimed. "Uh ... yeah. Yeah. So you can, uh, do that too."

"Mark," Croyd Crenson said, in a baritone Diskau would have killed for, "the problem right now really seems to be finding something I *can't* do."

He chuckled from the depths of his heroic chest. He laced his fingers together and flexed. Muscles heaved the skin of his bare arms and the olive-drab cloth of his T-shirt like the Loma Prieta quake.

"I feel great. Really great. I've never felt this way before. Except maybe when I'm just starting to hit the amphetamines, and they give me a rush instead of just keeping me going."

Mark moistened lips that, despite the humidity, were dry as the thousand-foot cliffs of the Khyber Pass. "Great, man," he said, though it cost him effort. Croyd was his friend. To feel this way—

"Dr. Meadows."

Mark sighed and turned. At least he had convinced the coalition's Vietnamese rank-and-file to quit calling him "your Excellency."

It was one of Bui Bam Dinh's Annamese peasant guerrillas, a tiny brown man in black pajamas, a conical straw hat that overwhelmed the rest of him, Ho Chi Minh slippers, and an AK-47 with black electrician's tape wrapped around a cracked foregrip slung over one shoulder. He was the classic *Time* magazine portrait of a VC, circa 1966.

"Yes, Bui?" The man was also one of the leader's cousins, or in any event part of his extended family. As far as Mark could tell, there were about twenty family names in common use in Vietnam. Telling everybody apart was not simplified by the Western media's habit of calling Vietnamese by their last names, which happened to be personal names, not family names, as in most Asian cultures. Thus "Uncle Ho" for the late northern leader, used with jocular familiarity by people who thought "Ho" was a first name, like Frank or Ed; and thus Ho's foremost general, Vo, was universally known as "Giap."

This Bui was actually a blood relation of the rebel leader, in any event. He bobbed his head and smiled. He modestly kept a hand before his mouth, but Mark could see it was full of steel Soviet teeth.

"There is someone," he said. "Perhaps you would wish to come and see."

"*Xin vui long,*" Mark replied. As always he was surprised at how rapidly he was picking up Vietnamese. Moonchild handled the rising, fallen, and "broken" tones far more gracefully than any of the other personalities—another mystery, since Korean was not a tonal language. "Thanks. I'm coming."

He glanced back at his friend. Croyd was staring at the derelict Ural. He had his right arm stretched out straight, palm down, fingers extended. He waggled his fingers slightly.

Obediently the truck was hovering about four inches off the ground.

Mark swallowed. "Later," he said.

* * *

The newcomer sat on the hootch's mat floor in a sprawl of complete collapse. He was gaunt. His clothes were shreds, scorched, torn, rotting from his frame, revealing fading yellow bruises and oozing sores. The tip of the gigantic lobster claw that was his right hand had been broken off. His eyes, sunken deep below what had been a domineering brow and was now a jut, stared through the bamboo wall of the hootch, outward toward infinity.

Evan Brewer wasn't looking so dapper and self-assured today.

"They fragged us," he said in a voice that made it sound as if each word tore away the lining of his throat in sheets. "I wasn't in the bunker, but I think they were going for both of us. They didn't want to hear about *socialism* anymore; all they wanted to talk about was how good nat blood tasted when you drank it, how it felt when you rubbed it on your skin."

Mark glanced at Belew, who shrugged. Mark had ordered the best medical care to be made available—several *Medicins sans Frontières* doctors had joined the rebels' permanent floating headquarters. In fact medical care per se wasn't much of an issue, though supplies were low: the professional classes were deserting the regime en masse North and South, and physicians were leading the way.

If only Mark's special pharmaceutical needs were as well tended to. The doubt about purity of his powders was one more constant strain. There was nothing to do about it but roll the bones, roll the bones.

Brewer had waved away medical attention. He needed to try to force the memories out of his mind in the form of words before his body was dealt with.

At one time Mark would have been kneeling at his former tormentor's side in a frenzy of codependency. Now he sat, watching, listening, withholding evaluation. *Maybe my conscience died with Starshine*, he thought. *Maybe that's why I'm so heartless*. Except, of course, gentle warrior Moonchild had always been his voice of compassion; Starshine was righteous indignation.

"I was in the latrine. It was just luck. Lucius was sacked out on his cot. They rolled a white phosphorus grenade right under him."

He broke off in a shuddering fit. Mark felt an urge to put his arms around him and try to comfort him. The impulse died without moving him to action.

"The blast blew off two of his arms. I got the fire put out by beating it with a blanket, rolling him in it. Mostly."

He shook his head and shifted his unseeing gaze from horizon to Earth's core. "It took an hour and a half for the chopper to get there. The base is ten minutes' flight time from Venceremos. It took ninety minutes.

"We'd given him the last of the morphine—people've pretty much looted out the pharmacy, but the Colonel still had a private stash in a safe in his office. Nobody messes with the Colonel—yet. The way some of the young bloods are talking—"

He shook that off. That was information, incidental, not the poison he needed to purge. "So he wasn't screaming when the Hip came in, just thrashing around, moaning some, starting to come out of it. When they carried him aboard the chopper, you could still see those little flecks of white phosphorus where they'd eaten into him, glowing like little stars. Like little radioactive cancers, just eating away at him." Mark shuddered.

"So after the Viets dusted him off for medical attention, what did you—" Belew began.

Brewer turned his eyes to Belew, and for the first time they focused on something close at hand. They were practically black, and it was the kind of black something would turn if it could be heated so hot it emitted light in the ultraviolet, light too hot to see.

"He *never got* medical attention. Colonel Sobel went out himself to check on him the next day. He never arrived. Don't you see, man? They got him up one, two thousand feet, and they *rolled him out of the helicopter.*"

There was a time when that would have sent Mark out the door with puke spilling from his mouth. It shook him badly, but the fish heads and rice he'd had for lunch stayed where they were. In fact he couldn't help thinking how long ago they'd gotten there.

"The Colonel called them on it. Said they had to've murdered him; he was on the chopper when it left Venceremos, and he was fucking nowhere when it landed. *And do you know what they told him? Do you know what?*"

"What?" Belew asked gently.

"They said there's a war on. They said there's an emergency shortage of medical supplies. They said, *'If your pet monsters want to murder each other, that's not our concern'!*"

... Mark found himself standing in the door of the hootch, taking in air in giant gulps. The monsoon had pretty well petered out, but the rebels had come low enough down that the air was thick and sticky. Eventually he came back to his place.

Brewer was looking off to nowhere again. He sat as if he was never going to move. "What happened then?" Mark asked.

Brewer's chest and shoulders heaved in something that was half sigh, half sob. "Things were crazy. Too crazy. The young bloods were telling me, telling me to my *face*, that they were sorry they'd missed me, that they were going to do the job right real soon." He shook his head. "All the Colonel is doing is talking about how these new aces he's bringing in are going to turn the tide. It's as if he's in his own private world."

Belew shot a significant look at Mark. *I know you think the Colonel's crazy, man,* Mark thought, *but he's under stress, he's watching his dream unravel—*

And we are pulling at the threads, Moonchild concluded with infinite sadness. *I worst of all. Oh, Eric....*

"What aces?" Belew asked softly.

Brewer shook his head. "They hadn't actually showed. They were all a big secret. Somehow I wasn't interested in hanging around to see who they were. I went over the wire that night."

The words Brewer released into the room overrode the ones tumbling around in Mark's head. Thankfully.

"There was nothing else for me to do. Maybe I'm a coward, man. But there wasn't anything left to *fight* for there. Nothing I could understand. I could stay there and die, and it would all be for nothing. I thought I was ready to die for *la causa,* you know, for *la lucha.* But not ... for nothing.

"They chased me. One of the boys, joker-ace, used to run with the Geeks, he could smell the way a bloodhound could. Maybe you remember him. Little guy, and his face was all sad eyes and these humongous nostrils."

Mark nodded. "Madison."

"Yeah. After he hit camp, he started calling himself that instead of his joker name, Sniffer. I talked him out of that; I was real concerned about his *dignity*.

"They set him after me. He found me in an abandoned village next to a derelict sugar plantation. You maybe know the one? We went through it on patrols a lot, before moving up into the Highlands. It wasn't abandoned then. The rebels, they—you—are right up against the wire at Venceremos every night now. They ran off the overseers, and the villagers fled. They wanted to get away from *us*. Made me sick when I heard about it. But that was before *I* had to run away.

"I killed him. I shed joker blood." He held up the claw. "He was all over me, trying to strangle me, yelling that he'd found me. I jabbed this into his eyes and pushed as hard as I could. I pushed for all I was fucking worth. He screamed and struggled and flopped around, and then suddenly he was still. I had to break the end off my claw to get out of there."

He put his face into his flesh palm. "I went into the sugar cane. It's all dry and overgrown. I heard them thrashing around, coming after me. Then somebody started letting loose with flamethrowers. I don't know if it was the Brigade or the People's Army. Some of the boys got caught; I heard them screaming, worse than anything I've ever heard. Worse than Luce—he was too screwed up to scream very loud, even when he was conscious."

He held up both his hands. "I got away. I hid in the woods. Eventually some of your bandits—your rebels— found me. I thought they were going to kill me. But they put me on a truck and brought me here."

"We still get deserters out of Fort Venceremos," Mark said. "The locals know to be on the lookout for them."

Brewer sat with his head tilted, looking as if he had something more to say. Tears dripped from his face. Belew looked at Mark. Mark shook his head.

They rose and went out into the open-hearth heat of afternoon. "Sounds like your hero Colonel Sobel's just about departed controlled flight," Belew said, with unaccustomed nastiness.

Mark felt too hollow to flare back at him. "He's a good man," he said dully.

"Yes, he is," Belew said. "And so what? A lot of good men have done a lot of harm, over the years."

"I suppose you'd rather be a bad man," Mark snapped, finally rising to it.

"Well, you recall what Mark Twain said about Hell: it's where all the interesting people will go. I'd hate to miss out on good conversation in the afterlife."

"Hey! Hello!"

Belew and Mark looked in different directions and at each other. Then, as one, they looked up. Mark felt as if he was part of a bad television skit.

Croyd was hovering thirty feet in the air. He waved.

"I just found out I can do this," he said airily. "Whoops!"

He tipped forward in slow motion, hitting about a sixty-degree angle before he stabilized.

"Sorry," he called. "Still having a little trouble with my vertical hold. Or would you call it trim?"

Chapter Forty-five

"No way," Belew told the Revolutionary Oversight Council.

It was an L-shaped cinderblock building, blocky and overgrown, off in the woods not far from the clearing in which Croyd had been experimenting to see what powers he had awakened with. Nothing remained by way of furnishings—the long collapsible table and the auditorium chairs were formerly the property of the nearby village's executive committee, its governing apparatus, whose members had sensibly made themselves scarce or jumped to the rebellion. Still, Mark was convinced it was an American-built school. It just had that familiar *feel* to it.

And while the French and the communists both had their more than somewhat slightly conspicuous failings, who but Americans would have thought to build a flat-roofed building in rain-soaked Vietnam?

Young Nguyen of the *trai cai tao* faction gave Belew the fish eye. Dong, the dapper gangster, showed no emotion, but telltale sweat domes popped out along his hairline.

"I don't mean any disrespect to our representatives from Saigon," Belew went on. "I simply do not believe it is in the interests of the rebellion to commit the bulk of its forces to a defense of Saigon at this time. We have the advantage of dispersal of forces, the will-o'-the-wisp's upper hand. The government has many targets and cannot possibly strike them all. If we concentrate in Saigon, they'll have just one."

In the place of honor at the other end of the table—directly opposite Belew—Mark swallowed. *He's got a point.* He made himself stand straight.

"You could be passing up a very fine opportunity, my friend," Dong said, in that head-back, hissing way of his. His mannerisms made Mark think of a Vietnamese William Buckley. "Our nation's rightful capital has taken up arms in support of the rebellion. The mayor, Vo Van Kiet, is ready to declare for us."

"The soldiers in Saigon are expelling their officers," Nguyen Cao Tri said breathlessly. "They've called on Moonchild to come and lead them. This is what we've all been waiting for."

"A massive popular rising was what Vo Nguyen Giap was always waiting for too," Belew said. "He never did get it. And the times he judged the time was ripe and gambled on getting it, like Tet '68, he lost his shirt. Even if the world media did turn it into a victory for him, after the fact."

"But we already *have* a revolt," Mark pointed out.

Belew shrugged. "The Saigon mob is fickle. Mobs are, everywhere. But the Saigon mob is worse. You can relax, by the way, Dong," he added with a cool grin. "I mean 'mob' in the sense of the rabble in the streets, not your people."

That did not much seem to mollify the crime boss, though he was too cool to show his agitation in any very overt way. Several of the other Saigon representatives were shouting and jumping up and down. Ernie had to wedge himself between Nguyen Cao Tri and the equally tough, equally young, and equally hotheaded Ngo An Dong to head off an incipient fistfight. A Southerner himself, the *Cao Dai* leader obviously had little love for the big-city boys.

"Gentlemen!" Mark rapped, hardly even remembering to be abashed at raising his voice. "Are we here to fight the government, or are we here to pound on each other while our enemies recover their strength and laugh at us?"

Silence bit like a guillotine blade. Shamefaced, Ngo and Nguyen stepped away from each other, avoiding one another's eyes and those of Mark, who stood at the table's head, stern and looming as a teacher confronting unruly third-graders. They forgot to take umbrage at the fact a dirty *moi* had laid hands upon them. Or maybe they understood by now that a display of racism would get the inhumanly tall American *really* pissed off.

Mark stood there, blinking, briefly at sea. The council-table commotion had bumped him off balance, as it always did. Mark always thought of Asians as reserved, polite. Generally they were, in his experience. But if something got them going, they carried on like a cageful of jays. Not the kind he used to smoke either.

All right, a voice in his head said—and it was his own—*you've got center stage. What do you do now?*

The old Mark, with a score or two of large dark eyes turned on him like spotlights, would have stammered, turned red, and sat down. This Mark took his balls in his hand, metaphorically speaking, and plunged on.

"I think this is too good an opportunity to pass up," he forced himself to say as quickly and smoothly as he could. "Saigon has great, uh, symbolic importance, both for the world and for Vietnam as a whole."

There you go again, you scramble-brained addict, Traveler sneered from his box seat in the back of Mark's skull. *Recklessly putting us all smack in the middle of the bull's-eye again. You stumbled there for a moment, didn't you? Wasn't that incipient common sense tugging at your sleeve, trying to get you to think again before you senselessly put us all at risk?*

That did it. Mark drew a deep breath, inflating himself to his full six-four.

"I also think it's time to put up or shut up," he said firmly. "If we say we want a revolution, we can't very well hang around scuffing our feet when we *get* one."

He looked around the room. "You, Ngo; you, Nguyen. What do you think you're doing? You, Bui—you say let the big-city Southerners fend for themselves; you ask what have they done for Annam? But the question isn't what they've done for you. It's what the Northerners and the communists have done *to* you. Are your petty jealousies more important to you than getting the Tonkinese boot off your neck? Are your chains so comfortable that you're willing to stay in them so long as you can make sure your neighbor doesn't break his?"

He slammed his fist on the table. It startled him into brief speechlessness. *Oww!* Cosmic Traveler whined. *That* hurt.

His audience had jumped as one and hadn't seem to notice the break in his rhythm. Maybe they thought it was a pause for effect.

"I tell you what I'm going to do," he said, and his words seemed to rattle off the thickly painted cinderblock walls like bullets. "I'm going down to Saigon and do what I can to help."

He glared around the table. "The rest of you can stay up here and make faces at each other until you all have long gray beards, if that's what you want to do. I'm outta here."

The Council jumped to all its feet at once, yelling. At first Mark—who had actually gotten himself so worked up he was in the process of stomping out of the school— thought they were hooting him from their midst. Then he realized they were *cheering*.

All but Colonel Nguyen, who sat back in his chair with arms tightly folded. *Great*, Mark thought. It was about the way life worked—his life, anyway. Colonel Nguyen thought Isis Moon walked on the water now. But he had no use for *Mark*, and when Mark appeared before the Council rather than Moonchild, he got these tremendous testosterone attacks.

A glint in the PAVN deserter's eye touched off realization in Mark's mind like a magician's flash paper: *He thinks I'm sleeping with her. Well, for Christ's sake.*

"What does Moonchild say upon this?" the colonel asked in his best bone-piercing voice-of-command. The conferees stopped in the midst of their acclamations and turned and looked at him, bewildered. "She is the Field Marshal of the Revolution."

Field Marshal of the Revolution? Mark thought.

Gotta admit it has a ring to it, said J. J. Flash.

At the foot of the table J. Bob Belew rose. He cleared his throat.

Mark looked at him glumly. *Here it comes. He can put the kibosh on everything I've said and done. And I thought I was doing so well.*

And just what is a kibosh, anyway?

"May I remind the Revolutionary Council," Belew began in his best orator's voice—which was pretty damned good, and Mark felt a spur of *Isn't-there-anything-he can't-do?* jealousy rake him—"that Dr. Meadows is Moonchild's fully accredited voice on this Council?" He hit the word *doctor* hard. The Vietnamese had an almost German regard for titles, especially academic ones.

"With her own lips Isis Moon said, 'He speaks with my voice.' Is that not true, Colonel?"

The colonel found something highly fascinating to look at on the tabletop. "It is."

Belew nodded. "Then his words are hers; she has spoken. And now I'll speak.

"Earlier I raised the voice of caution. Caution has its place. There's also a time to cast caution to the winds. Dr. Meadows has shown us that that time has come. Let me remind you of the Duke of Montrose's famous toast."

He raised the cracked white-enameled metal cup he'd been sipping tea from and declaimed, " 'He either fears his fate too much, or his desserts are small, who dares not put it to the touch, to win or lose it all.'

"Gentlemen—to Saigon!"

Mark walked along with his head down. The moon was high, shaming the stars and the broken clouds, who seemed to be scurrying to get out of her way. He hoped the clouds didn't get too far. He had mostly stopped worrying the place Starshine had been the way a child does the gap of a missing tooth, but he still took the stars best in small doses.

The water buffalo had worn a trail in the head-high, razor-edged buffalo grass. It felt strange to walk these trails freely, without fear of ambush or booby traps, after the paranoid weeks of patrol with the New Joker Brigade. But the people who laid the traps were his devoted followers now.

Moonchild's, rather. And that was fine. He didn't have much ambition to be a great captain. From the former DMZ to the Mekong Delta, the rebels ruled the night. It was appropriate that they should follow Moonchild.

A footstep behind him. He stopped, spun, clutching the familiar silver-and-black vial hung on a rawhide thong around his neck. If he turned into Moonchild again right now, he was certain he'd flip out—that was why he had appeared at the Council *in propria persona*—but the thought of getting wasted on his moonlight cruise by a government infiltration team, or maybe the NJB's new heavyweight aces, was too much to take. He wasn't acting in fear of his life; he was *disgusted*.

"Just me, Mark," the quiet voice of J. Bob said.

Mark stood watching his backtrail as Belew materialized out of the dark. He did not initially remove his hand.

Belew grinned and preened his mustache with a thumb. "You still don't trust me, do you?"

Mark moistened his lips and dropped his hand as if the vial had grown hot. Then defiance surged up within him.

"No."

"Good. 'The Master said, A gentleman in his dealings with the world has neither enmities nor affections; but where he sees Right he ranges himself beside it.' I do like you, Mark, but that'll never stop me doing what I see as right. It never has yet."

"Me neither." Which had maybe not always been true, but was now.

"Good." He came alongside Mark and patted him on the shoulder, inviting him to continue his walk. Mark did.

"A couple of days ago I told you not to give yourself too much credit," Belew said.

"I remember," Mark said.

"I'll bet. I'll bet you remember every negative thing—or thing you could take as negative—that was ever said to you. And I bet you'd be hard pressed to remember a single compliment. But remember this: don't sell yourself too short either."

Mark made a helpless side cut in the air with his hand. "Moonchild is the one who's doing it. I'm only along for the ride."

Belew stopped and turned. The magnet of his personality made Mark stop and turn to face him.

"Hogwash," Belew said. "It wasn't Moonchild facing up to the Council—and facing bad old me down—back there."

Mark shrugged. "I'm just her mouthpiece, you said so yourself—"

"I was touching up the stragglers, Mark. Every man on horseback needs a few outriders, though history usually manages to overlook the fact. Yes, Moonchild is the figurehead of the revolt. And our best evidence is she's merely a part of you."

Mark's mouth drew tight. He moved his head from side to side, not shaking it, quite.

"That's moot. The fact is, *you* did it in there. All by

yourself. You know what you are, son?" He clapped Mark on the biceps. "You're a leader."

"Oh, no, man, you got it all wrong—"

"I never get things *all* wrong, though I've pulled some sockdolagers in my day."

"Some what?"

"Nineteenth-century slang. Don't mind me. The important thing is, I know what I'm talking about."

A strong forefinger stabbed Mark in the sternum. "*You* are the real leader of the revolt. Don't ever forget it."

Denial bubbled up in Mark so furiously, he couldn't find words to vent it. He just shook his head.

"You'll see," Belew said. He took Mark's arm and steered him into motion again.

"Now, something else. Don't take anything for granted. Walking out here alone like this—" He shook his head. "The bad guys have gotten lucky before. And not all the bad guys wear PAVN khaki; you and your foxy alter ego in the yin-yang mask have roused some pretty fierce jealousies. Not everybody thinks it's too swell that *farang* types are leading this revolution. And remember what Confucius said about the gentleman, affections, and the Right. We won't always walk the same path, maybe, and I won't necessarily warn you when I head another way."

"Me neither," Mark said, from sheer bravado.

"Excellent." Belew put fingers in his mouth and whistled.

To both sides of the trail the elephant grass parted. On the right were Montagnards in their ponchos and bracelets. On the left stood Khmer Rouge in red headbands.

"You were safe," Belew said, "*tonight.* Your guardian angel J. Robert was looking out for you. But there's one thing you should bear in mind, son."

"What's that?"

"What happened to the Duke of Montrose." The guerrillas faded back into the high grass. Belew turned and walked back down the trail, whistling. He would have called the tune "*Marlbrouck S'en Va-t-en Guerre.*" To Mark it was "The Bear Went Over the Mountain."

Chapter Forty-six

Belew's warning to the Council about presenting the government with too convenient a target so that a single blow could decapitate the rebellion was perfectly correct. Moonchild had not needed to be told in fact. To his surprise, neither did Mark.

It seemed strangely natural for him to spend the next few days divvying up the rebel forces: who should stay behind in the bush to keep raising trouble and who should go to Saigon; how the rebel forces should split up to infiltrate down to the southern capital so that even in a worst-case calamity the government could not catch them all on the march at once. Mark had always heard the military cliché "never divide your forces." Maybe there were times when that was right. But in the core of him, he knew it wasn't right *now*. He acted out that insight with a confidence that frankly amazed him.

When he faltered, he had Moonchild there in his mind to offer suggestions and soft, soothing words of encouragement. J. J. Flash of course took to antigovernment guerrilla warfare like flame to tinder, and what he had to offer was the basic insight that *a hundred small fires are a lot harder to put out than one big one—and when they all get bigger and combine, they turn into a firestorm.*

Even Cosmic Traveler calmed down enough to offer suggestions, and some of them were actually useful. Who knew better how to keep out of harm's way than a confirmed coward with an infinity of faces? For all their popular support—which seemed to be causing total consternation to the world's media—they were still fighting a war of weakness against strength. Trav was weaker than *anybody*.

Mark suspected his main goal was to get back to Saigon. Now that he'd had time to consider, the Traveler realized he felt much safer in a city than in the paddies or mountains or rain forests. There were four million faces in Saigon, and he could imitate any of them. He couldn't turn himself into a stand of bamboo.

Only Aquarius, immovably hostile to land-dwellers and all their doings, remained aloof. That was all right. Of all Mark's personalities Aquarius was the only one who was almost always content to let Mark go along in his own way. Better silence now than another voice in the peanut gallery.

Belew watched everything Mark did, his scrutiny unobtrusive but minute as a circling sparrow hawk's. He himself said nothing. Either Mark was making all the right moves or the American soldier of fortune figured he was setting himself up for an error he, Belew, could capitalize upon for his own agenda. Mark found he didn't care. Somewhere he had gotten out of the habit of second-guessing himself.

The tribes came together and flowed apart again, like cloud masses. The storm moved down upon Saigon by divers ways.

The enemy was not totally paralyzed. Despite the Soviets' defection, the People's Armed Forces were able to keep both strike craft and helicopters aloft. The rebels generally kept good dispersal, which made them tough to find from the air, and exposed only a few at a time when they got caught. They moved by night, knowing that Soviet-bloc ground-attack aircraft, choppers as well as jets, flew only during daylight.

But sometimes the government pilots got lucky. And PAVN patrols were still thick on the ground, and while some of them were looking mainly to desert, others were still loyal, motivated, and mean. The government still had its spies and informers. It took its toll.

But the guerrilla forces continued to trickle toward Saigon, in a thousand rivulets, like water down a cliff face. The government seemed powerless to stop them.

After a brief respite Mark found himself resorting to the black-and-silver powder even more than before. Maybe Belew was right; maybe he was capable of being a leader himself, maybe he had commanded respect in his own person when he made the decision to go down to Saigon. But Moonchild was still the figurehead of the revolt, the mysterious ace whose quiet word could soothe all tempers and settle all disputes.

Sometimes when she was out, Moonchild felt Eric, probing for her mind. She sealed herself against him. She had chosen her Way. It was too late to change direction.

And then, coming down out of the *Cao Nguyen Di Linh* into the Cochin lowlands northeast of Ho-ville, Mark's contingent met white-flag emissaries.

"We're here to talk to Moonchild," said the leader of the three jokers. They were scarified, painted, and feathered. In the mottled forest shadow it was hard to tell what was the wild card and what was self-inflicted.

J. Bob Belew turned his head aside, spoke in steadily descending tones. Then he looked back at the three.

"I was telling my boys," he said conversationally, "to waste you if you looked like causing trouble. They're Khmer Rouge. Ever hear of them, or hasn't the Cambodian Civil War come out for Gameboy yet?"

"Save your breath, nat-lover," said a second joker. "You'll need it for screaming."

The leader held up a three-fingered hand. "Easy. We're here under a flag of truce."

Mark pushed forward. "Let's keep everything cool," he agreed. He realized Belew was casting him as Good Cop in a standard Mutt and Jeff routine. He didn't see anything to do about it.

The lead emissary frowned him up and down. "We're here—"

"I'm Moonchild's personal representative. Ask anybody here."

The young joker looked mulish. "We have our orders—"

"Let's just plow these fools under," Belew said harshly. At the tone of his voice the Khmer Rouge brought up their Kalashnikovs with a multiple clack of safeties. "We have places to go and promises to keep."

"—but, hey, we're not slaves," the joker leader finished. "I guess we can give the message to you."

Fighting to stifle a grin, Mark said, "Okay. Let's hear it."

"The Colonel wants a meet." He said *Colonel* without notable affection. "He wants to kiss and make up."

"He thinks Moonchild will betray her cause."

"Moonchild's a wild card." The joker studied Belew, who as always looked creased and cool despite exertion in the midday heat. "So're you, I'm guessing—you're the one they call the Mechanic, aren't you?"

Belew performed a mock bow. "I have that honor."

"If you say so. We got briefed on you." He looked to Mark. "We're all wild cards. Like it or not, that's our cause. Colonel thinks we should be together."

"We're on our way to pull down the government of the Socialist Republic," Belew said. "I can't see your Colonel wanting to get together with us on that."

The joker boy shrugged. "Fuckin' Viets think *Cambodians* are black," he said. "How much are they ever gonna love us jokers?"

Mark felt his heart jump. The young joker grinned. "Things aren't like we thought they were when we signed up. Colonel might be closer to your way of thinking than you imagine."

"I'm willing to concede you were right last time, son," Belew said. "Don't press your luck."

Mark stood looking into the darkness. This was hilly country, forested, not yet flattening out into paddies. The insects were raising their avant-garde orchestration on the soundtrack.

"Wild cards shouldn't fight each other," he said.

"It's a trap," Belew said.

"I'm going as Moonchild. She can take care of herself."

"She's not Golden Boy. She's not bulletproof. And even if she *were* the Golden Weenie—no amount of metahuman power can save you forever if enough people want you bad enough."

Mark shrugged. "If there's even a *chance*. Don't you see? I came out here for a dream—the dream behind the New Joker Brigade. The dream's still valid, man."

"Didn't you hear what your pal Brewer said? Didn't

you *see* those yahoos today? The dream's become a nightmare."

"Maybe it can come back. I—I have to believe that."

"You have to believe in the Tooth Fairy too." He turned, walked a few paces away. "It's Sobel, isn't it? Your search for an all-knowing Father God figure who can tell you everything's okay."

Mark felt his cheeks go hot. "What, are you jealous because you don't get the role?"

Belew laughed. "Okay. You got me again. Although maybe, just *maybe*, this is a little too serious for us to be scoring points off each other. . . ."

"Since it's so serious," Mark said, "I suppose it's too serious for me to point out that you started it."

Belew walked away three steps, walked back. He raised his hands in the air. It wasn't like him to waste so much motion; Mark had never seen him this agitated.

Unless, of course, he was playing a role.

Belew let his hands drop to his side. "I can't stop you, can I?"

Mark held up a vial. Inside, it was silver and black. "Not unless your KRs can see in the infrared."

Belew drew a deep breath through the flared nostrils of his sometime-broken but still-aristocratic nose. "Nobody's indispensable," he said, "but some of us are less dispensable than others. I wish you'd reconsider."

"It's something I have to do."

J. Bob arched a brow and looked at him closely. "Is there something here you're not telling me—"

With a faint pop Croyd appeared beside them. "And of course there's always me, if things go wrong."

They looked at him. "I beg your pardon?" Belew said.

"I overheard your little discussion. Mark wants to go and meet Colonel Sobel. I just thought I'd pop in and set your minds at ease: I can keep an eye on him. An ear, anyway."

"How'd you know what we were talking about?" Mark demanded.

"Oh. A new talent I just discovered I had. Clairaudience. And, uh—"

"Teleportation," Mark said.

"Teleportation. Yeah." He held his hands out. "So don't worry. Nothing can go wrong."

It was a temple in the forest, small, with plaster walls and sweeping wood-beam pagoda roof. By decree it had been neglected for years. The wood was weathered, swollen with water and faded by the sun.

Moonchild stood poised before the entryway, hands by her sides, every sense stretched as far as it would go. As agreed, she had come alone.

Nothing. Her night vision was excellent, catlike, but otherwise her senses were no more acute than a nat's. Her powers of concentration augmented their range. They picked nothing unusual out of the synesthetic forest background noise, the smells and sounds, the movements windblown and movements furtive.

It didn't mean there was nothing there. She would have to have faith. Either in Colonel Sobel and his dream . . . or in herself. She went inside.

By the light of a pair of candles she could see that the iconoclastic communists had stripped the temple. All that was left was the meter-high statue of the Buddha himself, sitting potbellied and serene with the candles by his knees, and before him a scatter of offerings: bits of candy, flowers, Vietnamese *dong* notes with petitions and prayers scribbled on them in the modified Roman characters Vietnam had adopted in the seventeenth century, dropped by the faithful and hopeful, undeterred by official disapproval.

"Good of you to join us, Ms. Moon," said the tall man standing on the Buddha's right hand.

"Thank you, Colonel," she said. "I'm willing to do anything I can if it will help us work together instead of against each other."

A second man stepped from the darkness at Buddha's left. The light did fascinating things in the folds of his face. "I'm glad to hear you say that, hon."

She looked at him. Her hands knotted to fists, slowly unfolded. It was what she had hoped for. It was also what she feared.

"Eric," she said.

He stepped forward, embraced her, kissed her. She gave him her cheek.

"What's this? Too good to kiss an ugly joker now?"

"Eric, don't. I—"

He stepped back. He was grinning at her. "Or are you just ashamed?"

"I have done nothing to be ashamed of."

He looked at her. She dropped her eyes.

"I have tried to do the right thing," she said. "It is not always so easy to know what is right."

"Yes it is." The Colonel's voice was low and compelling and rich with overtone. "In this case it is. Come back to us, Isis."

The tip of her tongue protruded briefly between her lips. "Are you willing to forsake the government's side, then?"

A low laugh, smooth and rich as melted chocolate. "Not on your life. World revolution's the only hope any of us wild cards has. *Real* revolution, the socialist, Marxist, Leninist, Maoist revolution, not this phony fascist reaction your little friends are trying to push off as revolution."

She backed up an unconscious step, shaking her head in confusion. "I don't understand. Your emissaries said—"

"That the Colonel might be closer to your way of thinking than you imagine," Eric said. "Right? Because that's what they were told to say."

"Is—" She could barely make herself say it. "Was that a trick?"

Eric shook his head. "No, my love," he said, catching hold of her gloved hands, "because I know you. Down inside, the way you think is the way we think. You know our way is right. There's no reconciliation with the nats, with their world or with their ways. You *know* that."

"My people—"

"Fear you and hate you as much as they fear and hate their government. Maybe more. Don't you see they're using you? As soon as their rebellion succeeds, they'll tear you to pieces. They won't need aces then."

"*No!* They need me. They love me."

"So do I," Eric said with a rueful grin. "Doesn't that count for anything?"

She hugged him fiercely then, and her tears ran hot down his neck. "Oh, Eric, I've missed you so! But I could not stand what was happening at the camp, what we were turning into—"

Gently he pushed her away. "I told you before," he said softly. "We're in a war for survival. There's no room for sentiment."

She tossed her head to clear her eyes of tears. "There is always room for compassion."

"You talk easily enough of compassion, Ms. Moon," Sobel said. "How much compassion will the nats show us when you've broken the back of our solidarity?"

Us? she thought. She wanted to scream at him, *You're a nat! What would you know about it?* But she still felt toward him as if he were a parent. She could not show anger to a parent; she could only hope to change his mind, to make him *see. . . .*

"The lynch mobs are out there in the night, Isis," Eric said in a low, intense voice. "The hounds are baying for our blood. Don't bring them down on our necks, my love. Don't be a party to—"

Her mind filled with horrific images, burning babies and shredded women. "No!" she screamed, holding futile hands over her ears. "Eric, *stop! I won't let you in my mind anymore!* That's *rape.*"

Eric stepped back, ruined face stark, hands held out from his sides. He looked to Sobel.

"I'm sorry you see things that way," the Colonel said. The room filled with jokers and guns.

Chapter Forty-seven

Moonchild's first thought was, *I must keep them from hurting each other.*

Beyond that her main concern was to keep from getting shot up too badly for her healing to handle. She was careful not to underestimate people who lacked ace powers: Bruce Lee said that in the martial arts all skills are *learned skills.* A nat or joker might be her master. Besides, some of the New Joker Brigade were aces as well as jokers.

But there were just too many of them, a dozen or more in close confines, bumping elbows and getting in each other's way. She moved swiftly, decisively, twisting weapons away, aiming nerve-center strikes to numb arms and legs—which has a real mystic-Asian-fighting-arts ring to it, though nerve centers shouldn't seem too damned esoteric to anyone who's ever banged a funnybone.

Her brain filled with terrible pictures again, momentarily overwhelming her vision. A wooden rifle butt cracked against the side of her head. She dropped to her knees.

The mind-tearing pictures were gone, replaced by heartbeat pulses of white light. She thrust a leg out, swept it around. The man who'd clubbed her went down in the act of raising his weapon for another crack, tangling with half a dozen others, kicking and cursing and flailing.

She head Sobel's voice bellowing like an angry *carabao* above the noise. A weight landed on her back. She jackknifed forward in a throw made more of expediency than art, sending her attacker flying into a phalanx of his fellows.

An image came into her mind: herself held down on the wood floor of the ravaged temple, her uniform in shreds about her, while jokers pinned her wrists and ankles, and others knelt between her legs and by her head to ravage her. *"No!"* she screamed, shaking her head, her black hair whipping paint and sweat-streaked faces.

As she was distracted, a youth stepped forward and jammed the muzzle of his Kalashnikov into her belly. Even the ugliest dream Eric could generate couldn't slow her reflexes; her left hand whipped up under the muzzle brake, snapped the barrel toward the ceiling before finger could clench trigger.

The boy had his weapon set to full automatic. The noise was enough to implode your head. Everybody froze comically in place, fixed by the gut realization of what a burst of 7.62mm bullets could do in a room jammed full of bodies. Coughing and blinking in the rain of red dust dislodged from the rafters by the gunfire, the ambushers momentarily lost interest in Moonchild as they frantically checked themselves over for perforations.

It was time to leave. Time to leave the Colonel, her would-be father, and his betrayed trust, time to leave Eric and his poisoned dreams, time to leave the New Joker Brigade cursing and fighting in its madness. She made for a window, delivering hammerfists and backhands to temples, hard enough to temporarily blind the recipient with the sparks behind his eyes, not hard enough to shake anything permanently loose. She reached the wall.

It fell in on her in a cascade of masonry and plaster dust.

A masked and black-clad figure stepped stiffly through the hole. It towered above her like a redwood, gazing down on her with a single eye.

A horrible smell of decay enfolded her. Behind her she heard a snarling: "Get out of my *way*, you morons! If you hadn't fucking jumped the gun, the bitch would be *toast!*" She glanced back to see a savage threshing-machine fury of motion, and jokers flying in all directions.

The essence of command, as J. Robert liked to point out, lay in the ability to take snap decisions. Moonchild took a couple here. She decided that the hole in the wall was her handiest exit, especially since its lone guardian seemed none too agile. She also decided he must be one of Colonel Sobel's vaunted new aces and that she therefore ran small risk of the eternal shame of taking a life by delivering a strike to his midsection with every gram of strength and every milliwatt of *ki* she could focus.

She stepped right into him and *punched*. He took a step back, turned the blank, dark eye of the filter that covered his eyehole upon her. Then his right arm lashed around backhand with the awful, inevitable majesty of an avalanche.

Nobody and nothing had ever take a full-force blow from her unscathed. Not Durg at-Morakh, the toughest and deadliest opponent she had ever known. Not second-stage Swarmlings tall as young houses. *Nothing*. She was so completely shocked that she stood there dumbly to receive the counterstroke.

It swept her right past the giant figure and out into the hot-black night. She landed on clay tamped to tennis-court consistency by the sandals of the furtive faithful. Too stunned to make a good landing of it, she hit on her cheek and shoulder and rolled over like a log.

Stench. She gagged and opened her eyes. A shadow blotted the stars. A monstrous hand reached down to her.

She kicked at his legs, trying to sweep him. It was like the *muay Thai* toughening exercise of kicking palm trees: the most fanatically savage kickboxer never brought the tree *down*. Neither did she.

He grunted, bent low, grabbed her by the shoulder. Pain blazed through her shoulder like a flashfire. She rolled right, breaking his grip, came up to her knees.

The cloth of her uniform had melted away where he touched her. Smoke rose in thin wisps. The skin exposed was reddened and beginning to blister.

"Ah can hurt you if Ah want," the being said in a voice like sand in the gears.

He was working his way around her, trying to pin her against the temple wall. The pain that flamed in Moonchild's shoulder was lighting up an emotion highly unfamiliar to her—an emotion Mark Meadows himself always repressed when he could: *anger*. She had been betrayed, manhandled, and psychically raped. Now this weird monster in the mask had burned her and spoiled her costume. She was getting royally *pissed off*.

"I'm glad you leave me no other way," she said, rising to her feet in a spasm of motion, "than straight *over you*."

She sprinted toward him, driving herself with all the fury in her quick-firing ace muscles. She didn't get much runway, but she didn't need it. As he stood there with arms outstretched to capture, she jumped high in the air and delivered a jumping sidekick with both feet to the notch of the creature's clavicle. She felt a dull snap, and he toppled over with the grandeur of a felled tree.

She fell back to the ground, sprang up, hurled herself through the air in a forward snap-roll right over his supine body. She sprinted toward the enfolding safety of the woods and their shadows.

She had almost reached them when something seized her long hair from behind and brought her up short like a dog on a leash, with such violence that her neck almost snapped.

Light-needles stabbed through her brain. She reacted without thought, without intention, flowing with the momentum her own inertia and the sudden grasp on her hair provided. She flung herself up in a backflip, using the gripping hand as a pivot, snapped around to stand momentarily upon the broad not-quite-even shoulders of the man behind her. A second backflip set her on the ground facing him.

He spun, tossed away a handful of black hair. "That was a pretty cute trick," he rasped, in a strange, raw voice. "Nobody plays cute with Carnifex twice, babe."

He wore all white. His eyes were a green blaze of anger and hate and savage joy. He seemed at some point in the past to have been disassembled and then put back together by a careless child. Another might have taken him for a joker, but Moonchild's warrior eye recognized him for what he was: a mass of old hurts, imperfectly if completely healed.

He watched her scrutiny with a smile that would probably have been twisted if his mouth were perfect. "Normally I pull up my hood for fighting," he said, gesturing toward the back of his neck. "But I thought a fox like you deserved the sight of my handsome face."

"You're the one the German ace Mackie Messer killed, at the Democratic convention in Atlanta," she said.

His face twisted. "He didn't *kill* me, babe. He just messed me up some. I came back; I always do. And I kicked his twisted faggot ass for him good when we had our re-match on the Rox."

That made no sense to her. The youthful assassin had exploded on live TV moments after gutting Carnifex with his buzzsaw hands. An estimated billion people worldwide had seen it.

Carnifex was grinning at her. "*Reminding* me of him is going to cost you extra in pain," he said.

She slid into *Bom-So-Ki*, cat stance, weight on rear foot, right front forward and cocked, hands bladed and held before left shoulder and face to strike or to defend. "We shall see," she said.

"Yeah," he snarled, "and you'll *feel*."

He lunged for her. Firing blows from what seemed a hundred random directions. With blinding speed she blocked them. In moments her forearms were numb from slamming against his, her right thigh was a mass of bruises from intercepting kicks to belly and groin—a vulnerable target for a woman, too, though not quite as crippling as for a man.

She knew at once that he was stronger than she was. Normally that wouldn't have mattered—*all skills are learned skills!*—since he was not devastatingly more powerful, Starshine or Golden Boy or Harlem Hammer powerful, the way the unwieldy one who reeked of death was. She was quicker, if only slightly, and her skill was vastly greater.

As she curled up like a boxer under his untiring blowstorm, the realization hit her that it *didn't matter*. Carnifex on the attack was like Croyd at chess: complete abandon. But this wasn't the wildness of an amateur who knew no better, who didn't know enough to fear. This man was skilled and seasoned. He just didn't feel he *had* to fear.

As soon as she learned how fast and strong he was, her thought was to defend and let his fury spend itself on her defenses. She had been kicked in the belly once, in the left knee once, a cut was vomiting blood from her forehead near the hairline, her left eye was swelling. His attack was as ferocious as ever.

She had jabbed a few times, launched tentative kicks, more to feed his flames so he'd burn out more quickly than as serious attacks. That was obviously not working. He had

started out pretty heedless of defense, though, and her lack
of response was only making him more careless.

So be it, she thought. She stepped into him, her right
hand lashing up and around in a backfist that caved in his
right cheek.

He didn't flinch, didn't pause. He came back with a
straight right that caught her in the nose and sent her
sprawling on her rump with blood pouring over her mouth.

He lunged for her. She jumped to her feet, turned a
side kick, a perfect stop-thrust to his solar plexus that
blasted the air from his lungs and sat him down on his butt
in turn.

"So you're not invincible," she said, circling.

She glanced around, looking for an opening to quick escape. Jokers had formed a leering ring around the combat-
ants. They drove back the shadows with flashlights and
torches. *Eric betrayed me,* she thought. The realization
made her sag as if all her joints had loosened at once.

"Kill her!" the jokers screamed. "Rip her tits off!"

Carnifex wiped his mouth with his hand, looked at the
blood on it, laughed. *"Tae kwon do,* uh?" he said. "Well, try
a little *ass-kick fu."*

He drove himself at her headlong off the ground, like
a guard trying to cut down a rushing tackle. She brought
double fists down on the crown of his skull. At the same
time she brought a knee up hard in his face.

He uttered a groan and collapsed to his knees before
her. His right hand lashed out, seized the great muscle of
her thigh, *pinched.* It was an attack she had never experienced, never even contemplated. Unexpectedness as much
as pain made her gasp and drop her guard. He drove a left
into her belly.

She fell. He was on top of her, hot breath and hard
muscle, groping for a pin. By sheer synapse-speed and desperation more than skill she threw him off, rolled over and
over. She jumped to her feet, stood swaying to the head-
rush. Waves of pain washed over her.

He took his own sweet time standing.

"Had enough?" he asked.

She flicked glances left and right. Jokers with lights and
guns, backed up by the tall man, who was back on his feet
and standing calm as if she had never snapped his collar-

bone. She lowered herself, as if into fighting stance, and suddenly leapt straight up.

Carnifex grunted, "I *hoped* not," and jumped with her. Twenty feet in the air they soared, face-to-face, arms clashing like sabers.

They hit and rolled. She was quicker to recover. Spread-eagled facedown in a spider position, she whipped three quick kicks into his face. They weren't strong blows; they couldn't be from that posture. They were meant to disorient him, give her space.

She leapt up. He rose with her, but he was swaying now, ever so slightly. He tipped toward her, reaching.

She brought her open palms violently together on the sides of his head, an eardrum-bursting blow. He bellowed. She turned to run.

He seized her right wrist with his right hand, put his left hand on her ribcage, and wrenched the arm from its socket.

Chapter Forty-eight

For the third time in ten minutes Belew checked his pocket watch. For the third time in ten minutes a whole hour had failed to pass. He grimaced and put the watch away.

I've been out of the bush too long, he chided himself. *I'm turning into a Nervous Nellie.*

From the southwest, where three kilometers away lay the temple in which Moonchild was to meet with Colonel Sobel, came the *pop-pop-pop*ping of gunfire, distance-faint. It rose to a crescendo, faded, came back strong, in irregular pulses. The rhythm of a firefight.

"Maybe I'm not so nervous after all," he said. The jokers and Viet rebels who stood clustered before the main house of the derelict plantation turned nervous faces toward him, then looked back to the noise, as if by sheer concentration they could see through ten thousand feet of trees and brush.

Belew picked up the handmike of the radiotelephone resting on the ground by his feet. He spoke into it with the falling inflection of Cambodian.

Nothing. No reply, not even a hum to announce that the Khmer squad he'd sent to shadow Mark to the rendezvous were even on the air. Their radio might have malfunctioned—common enough even in the high-tech nineties, and the radio was more sixties—but his old-soldier's gut told him they had joined their erstwhile victims in whatever lay Beyond.

"Ave atque vale, boys," he murmured. They had been good troop and loyal comrades in their way, but he sus-

pected the world would not much miss them. He put them from his mind, turned and walked toward a corner of the great peeling-whitewash villa.

There was somebody who *could* see across three klicks, or at least hear. Crenson insisted he needed isolation so that he could concentrate, so he had stashed himself away in a toolshed behind the main house. Belew wondered if this incarnation's olfactory senses were diminished to nothing as a minor balance to its unprecedented array of powers: a tribe of rock apes had inhabited the shed until the guerrillas had chased them off this afternoon. The stink was enough to stun a goat.

The gunfire was beginning to die away as Belew reached the door of the shed. It stood slightly ajar. *I'll miss the boy, if that was it for him,* he realized. Remembering to breathe through his mouth, he stuck his head inside.

"Croyd? Crenson?"

A snore answered him.

"Holy shit!" He jumped inside, bringing up the penlight he carried in a pocket of his trousers.

Croyd the magnificent, in all probability the most multitalented and powerful ace the wild card world had known, lay curled in a ball on a pile of faded-out *Playboys* that the monkeys had shredded and shat upon, blissfully asleep.

"Hey, bitch! Do you like the taste of joker cock? It's all-you-can-eat time coming up!"

Desperately Moonchild held her hands before her face, trying to escape the horrible blinding pressure of the flashlight beam. The tiny cage gave her nowhere to run, nowhere to hide. The light seemed to blister her palms.

The sweating jokers pressing in on the cage from all sides hooted and jeered. Their faces were twisted like modeling clay into reifications of hate. Their lusts washed over her unimpeded, like the glare of the flashlight.

Isis Moon was a creature of night, of shadow. To be *exposed* like this, helpless before a mob of jokers screaming for her body and her blood, was an agony as keen as having her arm dislocated.

"That's enough, boys." It was the voice of Colonel

Charles Sobel, smooth and solid as hand-rubbed mahogany.
"Don't use her all up. We have to save something for later."

"Fuck you, nat!" a joker snarled. Moonchild was
shocked to see the hate-filled glares the New Brigaders
turned upon their commander. But he shed the anger as a
duck's back sheds water. Seemingly unaware of it, he stood
beaming by until the jokers fell back.

The cage was bamboo and black iron. Even after her
captor, the green-eyed man with the peculiar uneven appearance, had roughly pulled her arm out and slid it back
into its socket, she lacked the strength to break free. And
the encircling torches kept the shadows well at bay.

She did not find it surprising that the Socialist Republic
kept cages at hand.

She became aware of a low rumble like thunder, which
seemed to come from all around. She had no idea what it
might be. She had more pressing concerns.

Carnifex was pitching a fit just beyond the bars of
the cage. "She's my prisoner," he raged. "*My* prisoner, dammit!"

Colonel Sobel showed him a smile, infuriatingly bland.
"I appreciate your efforts in apprehending this criminal," he
said, "but our claim to her is senior to yours."

"Want I should thunder on 'em?" Crypt Kicker asked.
Moonchild shivered. She remembered his touch with horror. He had held her still while Billy Ray relocated her
shoulder. Even without the searing acid he could apparently
exude at will, there was a quality to his touch, a hard immo-
bility, like something . . . dead.

Billy Ray cast his green eyes around the clearing before
the temple, taking in Moonchild in her cage, Sobel, and his
retinue—Colonel Vo, a couple of PAVN officers in pith helmets, Casaday from the CIA, a big sloppy Aussie journalist
with a crumpled linen suit and a drunkard's nose—and the
torches, and the screaming, sweating jokers with guns. Lots
of jokers with guns.

"No," he said. "Fuck it. Fuck 'em all." He turned and
stalked off. A beat later Crypt Kicker followed.

"A hostile young man," Colonel Vo said. "He bears
watching."

Sobel laughed. He was emcee of his own big show now,

and feeling grand. "Not to worry, Colonel," he said. "His heart's in the right place."

The secret policeman looked dubious. "From the looks of him, it could be anywhere."

Freddie Whitelaw mopped his brow with a handkerchief. It was already so soaked that all it did was redistribute sweat around his shining expanse of forehead.

"Colonel Sobel," he said, "what are your intentions now in regard to your, ah, prisoner?"

"I'm having her tortured to death," he said cheerfully. "Some of my boys are quite ingenious in that line, did you know?"

Freddie's jaw dropped. "You're joking, surely?"

The Colonel shook his head. "It will *encourage the others*, as the old saying goes. The rebels will see the penalty for their treachery firsthand. And of course they'll see irrefutable proof that this Field Marshal of their counter-revolution is only too human, ace or not. We only await the arrival of the television crews to commence our little lesson."

"Sir, you—you can't be serious!" Whitelaw stammered.

Sobel dropped a comradely hand to his shoulder. "Have no fear, my friend. I promised you an exclusive on this story, and you shall have it. The TV news people will just have to wait until you publish to release their footage. Who better to break this story, after all, than a long-standing member of our socialist confraternity?"

He steered the journalist away from the cage. Looking over his shoulder, Whitelaw caught Moonchild's dark eyes with his wildly rolling ones and gave his head a desperate shake.

She nodded back. *No, there is nothing you can do. I understand. This is my karma.* She wondered if he knew her for his old drinking buddy from Rick's. Mark had never come out and blurted his powers to him, but it would not surprise her if he had done his research into the ace called Cap'n Trips.

Sobel and his official hangers-on had drifted over to the front of the temple, where the NJB commander was pointing to things and holding forth in his grand way. The jokers had for the moment grown tired of screaming abuse in her face, since Sobel had decreed death on the spot for anyone who went farther than that, and had mostly fallen away into little clumps to shoot the breeze and gamble and grumble about why the media types were taking so long and keeping the real fun from starting. For the moment she was alone with her misery.

—She felt the pressure of shadow. She looked up.

"Hi, hon," said Eric Bell with a strange, sad grin. "I told you you'd come back to us."

She pinned his eyes with hers. "Will you be first in line when they turn me out to rape me?"

He rocked back slightly, as if she'd slapped him. "We're in storm season here. Desperate measures—"

She turned away. "Save your rationalizations. The Brigade has become a pack of animals. They are everything the bigots paint the wild cards to be. They have given in to blood hunger. How soon before you begin to devour your own kind?"

He had no words. She looked at him sidelong. "What? No pretty pictures? Will you not fill my mind with images of the better world to be purchased by my degradation and death?"

He winced, squatted down beside the cage. His right hand was closed tight. Vein and bone stood out on its back as if to burst the skin.

"Look," he said in a fevered half whisper, "we're in the middle of a People's Army armored division. It's on the move even now. Can't you hear it?"

The grumbling noise made sudden sense. She nodded.

"We have your rebel main force trapped in a pincers. By dawn it will be all over."

She turned her face away. "Why do you tell me this? So you can taste my pain for the fate of those who follow me? Soul rape is much to your taste. Perhaps soul torture is as well."

"Isis, *please*." He grabbed the bamboo bar with his left hand. "Those dreams back in the temple—I had to distract you, don't you see. So we could capture you without hurting you."

"So I would be in good health for the torture."

"That . . . that's not my idea. I *had no* idea."

"You attack me with tainted dreams. Yet you believe

your greater Dream can somehow remain pure." She looked at him. "Eric, I pity you. Truly I do."

"Dammit, Isis, give it up! It's not too late! You can join us. I can make Sobel accept it. He has to listen to me! I'm as much a leader as he is. And I'm a joker. He doesn't seem to be aware of it, but the boys are right on the edge. They have a bellyful of taking orders from a nat. If he won't do what I say, we'll . . . make him listen."

He thrust the ruin of his face right up against the bars. "Isis, please! Won't you join us?"

She looked past him to the jokers of the Brigade, eyeing her like rabid dogs, tongues lolling.

"*Mū*," she said. "That question is unasked."

He half-rose from his crouch, waving his fist in despair. "You *idiot*! They'll do it. You have no idea what they're capable of."

"I have every idea of what they are capable of. That is why I refuse to join them."

"Isis, I beg you, I *love* you—"

She shook her head. "That string is broken. Do not try to pull it anymore."

She raised her hands to touch his face through the cool bamboo bars. "Eric, my beautiful boy. Eric whom I loved. Listen to me. *Hear* me. When I met you, we each had a dream, a beautiful dream. I have remained true to mine. I will die true to it.

"You have sold your dream, my love. Sold it for a feeling of power, sold it to feed your own lust for revenge. Sold it to assuage your terrible anger. You have polluted your dream, spewed filth on it like the factories you showed us in that vision the first time I saw you, after you showed us the death of the Rox."

He frowned. "The first time you—but you weren't there then. There was only that nat, the tall one—"

And a wind rose around the cage, drawing clumps of dirt, bits of grass, every stray piece of debris. Eric held up his hands to keep dust from his eyes.

When he lowered them, Isis Moon was gone. In her place was Mark Meadows, absurdly crouched in the tiny cage with his knees to either side of his head.

He gave Eric a sickly smile. "I guess this takes some of the fun out of gang rape, huh?" he said.

Eric dropped to his knees. "Oh, my *God*," he gasped. "I made love to . . . *you?*"

"I don't feel any better about it than you do, man," Mark said. "But Moonchild is real while she's around, if that makes any difference. It wasn't really me."

Eric turned away and vomited.

Then he was back, hanging one-handed on the bars like a monkey. So far none of the others seemed to have noticed the change that had taken place. "If I talk to you, Moonchild hears me?"

"Yeah, man."

"Very well. Isis, I love you. Please God, believe me. I know I used that as—as a weapon, but it's true. I swear it."

"Sure," Mark said sternly.

"It's true. I—never mind. I, I can't bear to see you hurt, Isis."

"I guess you're lucky I turned back into *me*, man."

"No, please. If Isis is . . . in there, they can't hurt you without hurting her. That was never part of my plan. I won't let that happen."

Mark jerked his chin at the surrounding mob. It was about all the motion he could muster in the cramped space. "Just what were you planning to do about it? Your buddies have other ideas."

"It's too late for you to change what's going to happen," Eric said, "so what I do isn't betrayal."

He stuck his fist through the bars. "*Take it,*" he hissed to Mark.

Dubiously Mark opened a hand. Eric pressed something slender, cold, and hard into his palm.

"I didn't know how Mark—how *you* summoned your 'friends.' I knew your drugs had something to do with it. Agent Ray took a pouch filled with little vials off of Isis when he captured her. I was able to steal one."

Cautiously, hardly daring to breathe, Mark rolled his fingers open slightly. A tiny glass vial lay in his palm filled with orange powder. It had a brownish cast to it; doubtless a trick of the torchlight.

"I thought another of your friends might be better able to come and get Isis out. I hope that's true."

Mark nodded. His lips and throat were far too dry to let words past.

"Get her far away from here. And remember—remember that I love her."

He grabbed Mark's hand, pulled it to the bars, kissed it. Then he rose and began walking away.

He had not gotten twenty meters when a voice cried out, *"Hey! He gave the prisoner something!"*

Chapter Forty-nine

Eric froze. Faces turned toward Mark. "Hey, something happened to the goddam prisoner!" another voice roared.

Jokers crowded around the cage. They kept their distance, as if afraid Mark might be radioactive.

Colonel Sobel came striding up. "What seems to be the trouble here?" he asked, his voice a throb of wise forbearance.

The joker who had accused Eric thrust himself forward. It was Rhino, the German punk who hungered for acceptance from his cooler American comrades.

"He gave something to the prisoner," he said, pointing at Eric.

Sobel glanced at the cage. He saw Mark and frowned. "Arranged for your little lady friend to make her escape, did you?" he said. Sadly he shook his head. "Eric, I thought better of you."

Eric didn't say anything. The Colonel drew his .45 and shot him.

The heavy jacketed slug knocked the light-framed boy sprawling on the tamped-down earth. "Holy shit!" a joker screamed. "He shot Eric! *He murdered the Dream!*"

Instantly the crowd transferred its anger at Eric to its nat commanding officer. To Mark, still huddled and helpless, it was as if something very palpable *snapped*.

Colonel Sobel missed it. Colonel Sobel had his Dream, too, and he couldn't see anything beyond it.

Not until a joker covered all over with extrusions like fleshy leaves stepped up and twitched the .45 from his hand.

Sobel frowned then. "What's your name, soldier?" he demanded.

The joker flung himself forward and buried his teeth in his throat.

The Colonel reeled backward. And then the jokers were all over him, snarling and shrieking, darting in, clawing each other in their frenzy to get a piece of the action. Mark heard screaming, weird, unearthly. He saw blood arc, near-black by torchlight.

He saw the Colonel's fine head raise up. And up, and *up*, until it was held overhead at the full extension of a pair of joker arms.

Mark threw up.

The two aces, the Vietnamese officers, and Casaday had trailed some distance behind Sobel when the Colonel walked over to investigate the disturbance by the cage. They were outside the lethal radius of the first explosion of joker rage.

No sooner had Sobel vanished beneath swarming bodies than a wave of jokers came for the little group. One reached taloned hands for Billy Ray.

His first reaction was to bat them away from his blood-spattered uniform. "Hey! Don't touch the merchandise."

The claws came back in a slash and laid open his cheek. That made everything different.

Carnifex smiled.

He caught the raking hand as it went past. With a mighty torque of his wrist he snapped the forearm. Then he shattered the joker's snouted face with a vertical punch.

His own oddly matched assortment of features contorted in a triumphant Bruce Lee grimace. He let the joker drop.

He turned to the charging pack. An overhand right splintered teeth and snapped a joker head back so hard the neck vertebrae shattered like dropped plates. A sideways *shuto* snapped the arm of a second like a dead tree branch. Pivoting, Billy sank the fingers of his left hand into a joker's belly with such force that the tips popped right through skin. He hoisted the howling joker above his head, the blood spattering his face and uni like red rain, and threw him in the faces of his friends.

"I love a par-*tay*!" he cried.

Half a dozen jokers surrounded Crypt Kicker, standing silent and black to one side. They grabbed him, jostling each other for advantages of grip as they prepared to tear him apart as they had the Colonel.

Then they fell back shrieking, their hands and clothing smoking. The black shirt was melting away from the Kicker's big chest and shoulders, revealing desiccated, discolored flesh beneath.

From inside the mask emerged a laugh that sounded like the tank army on the move around them.

O. K. Casaday had his Beretta M-9 out. He stuck it in the multicolored face of a joker and fired. Eyes popped from sockets, brain and blood flew out in a mist.

He looked around. Vo and the two regulars had their sidearms out and were firing into the mob. The Aussie soak had his face covered with his hands, which was probably as constructive a thing as he could be doing.

"Let's get back to the temple!" Casaday yelled. "We can fort up there."

"It's no good," the junior PAVN officer sobbed. "They are too many!"

"Then fucking die here!"

"He's right," Carnifex said, momentarily out of foes. "Even the Alamo's better than the parking lot."

"Him! He's the one! He got Eric offed!"

"Get the fuckin' ace! *Get him!*"

With Sobel turned into organic confetti and Sobel's entourage proving hard to swallow, the mob turned its attention on the cage. The occupant was supposed to be tonight's feature performer, after all.

Of course the victim was *supposed* to be a beautiful, vulnerable young woman. That it wasn't only pissed them off more.

Mark felt a pang as he twisted the plastic cap off the vial. *It doesn't look quite right, man.*

You fool! the Traveler shrilled. *What if it's tainted?*

With luck, J. J. Flash thought grimly, *it kills us quicker than the mob will.*

Mark slammed the contents.

He knew at once that he was fucked.

*   *   *

The earth began to shake. The jokers nearest the cage fell to the hard-packed ground.

A wind began to blow toward the cage from all directions. It scoured dust from the ground, raised it in a swirling, dense cloud that completely hid the cage from view. The jokers turned and scrabbled away, frantic lest they be sucked into the vortex of wind.

The ground kept shaking. The wind grew to a whistle, to a roar. The cloud mounted higher and higher, till it topped the peaked roof of the pagoda.

Lightning split the cloud. And then the whirling pillar of dust . . . *vanished*.

With one horrified voice the New Joker Brigade screamed.

Everyone has them inside, the little monsters. Creatures composite of all our repressed anger, all our pain, all our envy and jealousy and unspeakable desire. Like the sixties themselves, with their bright promise of peace and love and dope and hope that turned to shit in Altamont and the SLA, even gentle Mark, the Last Hippie, had his dark side.

He had been driving himself to exhaustion's jagged edge, the last weeks—and beyond, to the all-too-brief interval in Holland, a halcyon interval of peace between Takis and flight. He had been slamming his Moonchild potion repeatedly, though it took a ferocious cumulative toll. He had been mixing his potions in the worst possible circumstances—on the run, under stress, under less than laboratory conditions. His component chemicals were of dubious provenance and purity.

When he took the unknown potion, he did not summon one of his friends. He opened the gate upon the Pit.

He rose from a crater his lust for substance had sucked from the side of mother Earth. He swelled until he stood a full seventy feet, a manlike figure, mighty with malice, his skin greenish-black, lustrous from a distance, up close rough and abrasive as the hide of a shark. His fingers were tipped with long black talons. Lightnings wreathed his head, which was huge and horned like a longhorn's. His eyes were rattlesnake eyes, slit-pupiled, and they glowed with the yellow flame of Hell. His breath withered the forest where it blew.

Between his massive-muscled thighs he carried a gigantic hard-on for the world.

He was full of hate and pain. He *was* hate and pain. He tipped his enormous head back and roared with the awful joy of liberation. The flames of his gut lit his gullet like Moloch's.

Mark's alter egos took their names from sixties songs. *Hair* was overrepresented, with two, and the others came from King Crimson and Dave Mason and the Rolling Stones by way of Johnny Winter. Many of Mark's favorite groups were totally neglected. There were no Beatles characters, no Dead, no Destiny, no Quicksilver Messenger Service. He had no potion to turn into the Crown of Creation or Mr. Skin or the Ramblin' Man. But maybe now he had a persona for that other quintessential sixties group, Steppenwolf.

Call this one . . . *Monster*.

"What the fuck," O. K. Casaday demanded, "is *that*?"

Standing on the temple steps, Carnifex rubbed his jaw, feeling the knobbed adhesions of countless healed breaks. "That," he said, "is Cap'n Trips' newest secret identity, unless I miss my goddam guess."

Monster bent forward. A vast hand swooped down, caught up Rhino. The German joker squirmed, too terrified to try to defend himself with his powerful horn. For all the good it might have done him.

Monster held him up, studying him with yellow fire eyes. Then he tossed the joker down his throat. His fanged jaw slammed shut on a scream.

The New Joker Brigaders took off in all directions. Odds of several hundred to one didn't look so attractive anymore.

With a squealing clatter like a steamer trunk thrown down a flight of stairs, a tank crashed into the clearing from the far side, shouldering aside young trees in sprays of splinters. "Thank God," the junior PAVN officer breathed, and crossed himself.

Monster swung his massive horned head to bear on the tank. The puny soft things had gotten under cover mighty quickly; it would be inconvenient to root them out. *Here* was prey that would find it harder to get away.

Casaday's big shoulders heaved in a sigh of relief. "T-72. *They'll* handle the son of a bitch."

"Five bucks," Carnifex growled from the side of his mouth, "says you're wrong."

With a whining of servomotors the long gun rose to aim at the center of that broad chest. The commander, sitting half out of the top turret hatch, decided the target could likely be considered armored. He muttered into his helmet mike, calling for an armor-piercing sabot round to be loaded.

A moment, and the loader called the round loaded. Immediately the gunner called ready; he didn't need a return from his laser rangefinder to lock a target that size less than a hundred meters away.

"Fire," the commander said.

The horrific sound of the 125 practically knocked the little knot of onlookers into the cracked temple façade. Hot wind slapped them and stole their breath away.

The monstrous being rocked slightly as the round took him in the center of the chest. Hellfire blazed yellow through the hole. The Monster roared his pain. His voice dwarfed the cannon's.

Unfortunately his hide wasn't as tough as a NATO main battle tank's. The round just passed through him, imparting little energy. He threw out his arms and flexed his muscles.

The hole closed up.

Carnifex stuck his hand out. "Pay." Absently, transfixed by the awful scene, Casaday dug in his pocket for his billfold.

The Monster started walking toward the T-72. Its commander was shouting into his mike, drumming his fist on the low domed turret top to speed his crew. He wanted high explosive this time.

They had about three strides of clawed feet to reload in the cramped confines of the turret. They had considerable motivation. The gunner cranked his cannon to full elevation. It still only bore on the creature's navel, if he had one. He fired without waiting for command, the millisecond the heavy breech closed. The tank rocked back to the recoil as a flame the size of the vehicle itself bloomed from the cannon.

A globe of yellow flame obscured Monster's stomach.

The underlighting flare would have made his features demonic if they hadn't already been. He stopped.

Then he smiled. And grew a foot.

"Shit," Carnifex said.

"Fuck," said Crypt Kicker, who wasn't impressed by much.

"Shitfuck," Carnifex added.

The impact had at least rocked Monster back on his heels. He took a step back, braced. "Bastard sure is hung, isn't he?" Casaday remarked to no one in particular.

The tank commander stood his ground. He was no candy-ass Annamese or Cochin Chinese. He was a Northerner, proud, tough and hard as socialist steel. He grabbed the handles of the heavy 12.7mm roof gun and sent a stream of green tracers arcing at the giant beast, aiming for the eyes.

The thumb-sized bullets bothered Monster no more than a swarm of gnats. He held out his clawed hands, made fists. Lightning squeezed out between his fingers and struck the tank.

Wreathed in sparks, the tank commander threw his arms in the air as the enormous current fired his neurons for him. Then the remaining thirty-eight rounds of main-gun ammo cooked off at once. The turret flew into the air on a column of blue-white flame. The men on the temple steps cringed as it crashed smoking to the ground beside the building.

The Monster threw back his head and laughed.

J. Robert Belew sat with his arms crossed on the wheel of his blacked-out GAZ jeep and stared. "Well, I'll be dipped," he said softly.

The PAVN infantryman the FULRO patrol had picked up while trying to work its way to the temple had told the truth. A rotary-wing squadron had set up an impromptu base in a beanfield seven klicks from the ambush site. Four sharklike Mi-28 Havoc attack choppers sat in the hard shine of generator-powered spots, their motors turning over, their rotors sweeping lazy circles. Soviet-bloc doctrine notwithstanding, this band was tuning up for a little night music.

There had been no way to reach the temple, especially when the tanks put in their appearance. Mark would have to fend for himself, if he still happened to be alive. The priority now was to try to keep the core of the rebel army intact under attack by at least a division of PAVN armor.

Belew had ordered the men to scatter in the woods. The rebels were probably outnumbered, certainly outgunned. Evasion was their best defense, as it always was. Because the People's Army was well equipped with antitank rockets in various shapes and sizes, the rebels were too— they stole them, bought them, or received them from deserters, the way God intended guerrillas should be armed. If they could just melt into the woods and fields, the rebels could not only survive, they might even lay some hurt on their enemies. The key was having enough time to break into cover.

Belew was looking to help buy them that time.

The eagle-headed joker Osprey and the other NJB deserters had given Belew grief. Mark was one of their own. They were determined to wade through however many of their former comrades and PAVN troopies lay between them and him.

The unmistakable sounds of tanks on the prod had changed their minds for them. To the untrained, tanks are totally terrifying, vast prehistoric beasts, deadly and invulnerable.

As a matter of fact a man afoot, in the dark, in vegetation, had it all over a tank; the beast couldn't *see* him. If he were cunning—or had a rocket-propelled grenade launcher, or even your clichéd pop-bottle-o'-gas, he could take the offensive. Belew just didn't tell them that. Shuffling their feet with the guilt of their self-assumed cowardice, the erstwhile New Joker Brigaders joined the exodus from the derelict plantation.

The engine whine's timbre changed, rising, becoming more insistent. The squad had gotten the word to move.

There are two ways to get someplace where you don't belong. You can sneak. Or you can just cruise on in as if you had all the business in the world there.

Belew let out the clutch and drove, fast enough to come on like a Man in a Hurry, not fast enough to look like a charging foe.

As the armorers checked the weaponry slung beneath the Havocs' stub wings, Belew drove up right alongside the nearest ship. The hustling ground crew barely spared him a glance; they recognized the *Gestalt* of one of their own jeeps, and they had more important things on their mind than brass coming out to kiss the brave People's Flyboys 'bye.

The pilot looked out his still-open side hatch and saw a pale, square face. His thick-gauntleted hand fumbled for his sidearm.

Belew quick-drew his Para Ordnance and shot the pilot twice in the chest. The ground crew fled as he vaulted out of the jeep, ran to the chopper to drag the dying pilot out.

The gunner turned a blank visor toward Belew from his station in the nose. Belew gestured with the handgun. The gunner was brave but not stupid. He climbed on out and ran. Sensing what was about to happen, he ran *hard*.

Holstering his 10mm, Belew slid into the pilot's seat. He tore the bandages off his left hand, pressed it palm down onto the helicopter's console, and slashed off his budding new fingers. Then he pressed the spurting stumps against the cool metal.

"Ahh," he said, as his soul entered the metal. There was nothing better than the feel of fusion with a fine machine. It was better than sex.

Well, almost.

J. Robert Belew was a pronounced polymath. But piloting was not among his many skills. With his hands on the controls he could no more fly the Havoc than he could fly by flapping his arms.

But he wasn't the pilot now. He was the *helicopter*.

He sped the spinning of his rotor and leapt lightly into the air. Changing the pitch of his blades, he tipped his nose forward, began to slide slowly forward.

Suspecting nothing, the ship to his right touched off. He swung his chin gun right and blew him from the sky with a burst of 12.7. Magnanimous in his exaltation, he hovered then, permitting the crews of the two craft still on the ground to bail out and escape. Then he destroyed the choppers.

He rose up in the sky, then, a circle-winged hawk of plastic and steel and incipient fire, hungering for prey.

Chapter Fifty

Monster stood above his opponent's pyre, raising triumphant arms to the sky.

Crypt Kicker stood for a moment, seeming to contemplate the creature. Then he put his head down and charged.

He struck the being's shin and bounced. He didn't have the mass to cut its leg from beneath it. Monster stopped his joyous bellowing and gazed curiously down.

Crypt Kicker braced his legs and *heaved*. With a squall of surprised fury the Monster toppled backward into the trees.

The earth shook. Crypt Kicker turned back to face the temple, dusting his hands together as if to say, "Now, *that* wasn't so hard."

"Don't get carried away, you dumb son of a bitch!" Carnifex shouted. He pointed.

Monster was rising, vengeful, from the woods. His eyes blazed like yellow spotlights.

Crypt Kicker turned. A giant clawed foot was poised above him.

The foot came down. It slammed on the ground with jarring finality.

"Sweet Mother Mary," Whitelaw breathed. "The poor sod."

"What's it matter?" Carnifex said. "He was dead anyway." Whitelaw gaped at him in dismay.

Monster turned his blazing eyes toward the temple. The little group turned and bolted into the building, ricocheting off one another. Except Carnifex, who ran around the side.

Monster shrieked. It was a sound like the sky being split in two. He jumped aside, clutching the foot he'd dropped on Crypt Kicker. The sole was smoking.

Crypt Kicker rose from the redneck-shaped impression he had made in the earth. By the woods the soil was spongy with mulch.

Streaming smoke, he began to walk purposefully toward the giant creature. " 'The Lord *is* my shepherd,' " he intoned in his deep, dry voice. " 'I shall not want.' "

Slowly Monster lowered the foot Crypt Kicker's acid had injured.

" 'Yea, though I walk through the valley of the shadow of death,' " Crypt Kicker said, inexorably advancing, " 'I shall fear no evil: for thou *art* with me.' "

Monster raised a fist.

Crypt Kicker raised his in reply. " *'Thy rod and thy staff they comfort me!'* " he screamed, and charged.

Lightning blasted him back twenty meters.

Monster came forward to gaze down at the sprawled body of his antagonist. Crypt Kicker didn't move. He did smolder some.

Monster roared his victory cry and walked on. The night was alive with small, soft things. He longed to hurt them all.

Billy Ray had never run from a fight in his life. He wasn't about to start for this oversized green pukebag, no matter how horny he was.

Carnifex was reckless, but he wasn't stupid. He just knew when to make a tactical withdrawal.

Monster strode by the temple. Carnifex launched himself from the pagoda roof in an ace-powered leap.

Monster felt a tiny impact on the back of his calf. He paid it no mind. Whatever it was was too small to hurt him. His mighty cock vibrated with the lust for pain.

Everywhere were tanks and soldiers. Monster looked, and it *was* good.

It was time to smash.

For all its troops the People's Army had not been able to concentrate overwhelming numbers against the rebels.

The country was too wracked by rebellion. The government could not pull many troops from any one area without simply writing it off. Hanoi was unwilling to surrender a square centimeter of Vietnamese soil to its foes.

That was a mistake.

PAVN had committed its finest armored troops to this fight. If they could claim a one-sided victory over the rebel main force, it would go a long way toward reestablishing its credibility as being in control, in the eyes of the world and, more importantly, in the eyes of Vietnam. It would not matter if rebel losses were insignificant compared with the rebellion as a whole. This is the world of Maya; appearance is all.

The PAVN soldiers were brave. Some of them ran; most of them didn't. They hung in firing at the monster for all they were worth.

Unfortunately the energy of their shells only strengthened him. Their defiance just amused him. And whetted his appetite for destruction.

He smashed, and slew, and tore asunder. Loops of gut hung from his fangs, and blood ran down his claws.

Grunting, sweating, swearing beneath his breath, Carnifex scaled Monster's back. The creature's sharklike hide offered little by way of footholds. He was making his own, plunging his fingers and kicking his feet bodily into Monster. Monster obviously was not regarding him as a sufficient irritant to do anything about.

He wasn't letting himself think about what that implied.

He had just reached the right shoulder blade when another fusillade of tank shells slammed against Monster's chest. Carnifex hugged the reeking flesh. *"Jesus!"*

It was sheer luck he hadn't been dislodged by the explosive impacts. *Hell, I'm lucky nobody's back-shot this big son of a bitch.* But Monster wasn't leaving anybody in his wake in any shape to fire him up from behind.

The vibrations stopped. Carnifex could feel the creature swell with power.

"I'm not getting *paid* enough for this," he grunted. He resumed climbing.

*   *   *

The AT-6 Spiral missile streaked toward the T-72. Belew kept his eye on the target and willed the missile to it, his desire transmitted through the medium of UHF radio signals that guided the rocket. He could feel the missile slide through the heavy moist air with silky, sliding sexual friction. Could feel the impact, and then release as the tank exploded.

He did not pump his free fist and yell, "Yeah!" This was deeper than that.

Eight missiles in the Havoc's load. Eight tanks shattered. He was batting 1.000.

He could see flashes lighting the sky to the southwest. It looked as if there was a major tank battle going on, with some Brobdignagian arc-welding thrown in. Belew had no idea what was happening; his team didn't have the firepower to hold up one end of such a display.

Somebody was giving the PAVN spearhead a hard time. He had the radio turned off; the chatter distracted him, spoiled the purity of his fusion with the machine. For the moment he didn't much care what was going down over there. He was loose in the enemy rear as an airborne killing machine. He was out of weapons that would bust their tanks, but his ship was still gravid with bombs and 57mm rocket pods, and he had plenty of ammunition for his four-barrel 12.7mm Gatling. A modern armored formation sucked fuel and resupply. And that meant . . . *soft targets*.

There, on a black ribbon of paved road: the shiny steel-dachshund shape of a fuel tank-truck. He banked and stooped like a heavy-metal falcon.

With a grunt of Gargantuan effort Monster raised the forty-two-tonne T-64 off the ground, then military-pressed it over his head.

And Carnifex leaned over the *massif* of his right brow. Stiffened to a blade, his fingers speared for the yellow slit-pupiled eye.

Reflexively Monster shut the eye. Despite the dizzying distance to the ground, Carnifex let himself fall. He grabbed a handful of lower eyelash, caught himself. Then he hauled himself up to try to pry the lid open.

Monster tossed the battle tank away. He took Carnifex's

hood between the clawed tips of thumb and forefinger and plucked him off.

Dangling mere meters before that vast, hideous face, in the full smokestack blast of his polluted breath, Carnifex shook his fists in defiance.

"Go ahead and swallow me, scumbag!" he yelled. "I'll chimney up your throat, punch through the roof of your mouth, and *eat your fucking brain!*"

Monster studied him a moment more. Then he flipped him away.

His impertinent foe already forgotten, Monster surveyed the scene. There were broken and burning tanks everywhere. Nobody was shooting at him anymore. He was out of victims.

He raised his claws to the cloudy heavens and roared in disappointed rage. The lust in his loins had not been slaked. He had a world of hurt yet to inflict before he could find release.

Then something caught his yellow eye, a kilometer or so beyond the trees, in the midst of an expanse of cultivated fields. A tiny hamlet, dark, surrounded by its little bamboo fence.

Innocence. *Helplessness.* They drew him like a magnet. His cock pulsating with excitement and need, he lumbered toward the village.

He had almost reached it when a voice spoke in his head: *"Wait."*

He stopped, growling resentment at the intrusion. The massive horned head swiveled left and right, looking for the source of the irritation. Fury beyond fury piled upon the anger that blazed within him. No one told *him* to wait.

"This isn't you. I know it's not."

He raised clawed hands, roared a shattering wordless affirmation: *IamIII!*

"No. You aren't. You're an illusion, an aberration. I'm speaking to the real you. That which is buried deep inside. That which is . . .good."

Monster shook his head, as if to cast forth the insistent voice. He hated the voice. He wanted to find where it came from, and smash, and kill. It said things that must never be said to him.

"Isis . . . Moonchild. It's me, Eric. Your love."

NO! Negation erupted from the molten core of him.

"Yes." Images flooded his mind: Isis and Eric, holding hands by candlelight, walking out along the paddy dikes beneath the moon's benevolent face. Gentle; *loving.*

Monster pummeled his face with the heels of his hands. He would not see these things. He must not.

"Isis. You're still in there. Come out. Fight the evil. You can defeat it, send it back where it came from."

Monster was out of control, reeling blindly in agony. In fear.

Fear fed the anger. As it always does. It was not right that *he* should fear. He was the mightiest of beings; His will be done, on Earth as it was in Hell.

He looked around, desperate. And there was the village, still dark, still silent, still virginal, nearby.

He would slay. He would *rape.* He would wade in horror to the sac of his gravid balls. And that awful voice would bother him no more.

" 'There are more things in Heaven and Earth, Horatio,' " J. Robert Belew quoted aloud, not without relishing the taste of it, " 'than are dreamt of in your philosophy.' "

Orbiting the looming horror at what he guessed was a safe distance, Belew drew a deep sigh. His ammunition cans were empty, his bombs and rockets spent. The monster had been acting crazy for a moment there, but it had pulled itself together. Now it was going to lay waste to the helpless village.

He couldn't let that happen. At least, not without a fight.

J. Bob Belew considered himself a hard man, and generally lived up to his own expectations. But he had a weakness. He thought of himself as a white knight, *sans peur et sans reproche.* All of the things he had done—even the hard things, the repugnant things—had been done out of an unshakable sense of Right. And a white knight didn't let dragons slaughter defenseless peasants.

Even if it cost him his life.

" 'Lord, what fools these mortals be,' " Belew said sadly, speaking of himself. "And worse, what mortals be these fools."

He soared high, savoring a last moment of ecstasy, of flight and power. Then he nosed over and went at the creature's back in a full-power dive.

Monster strode toward the village. His cock throbbed with need. There were women in the village, and children. He wanted to hear them scream as he plucked them to pieces.

The village showed no signs of life. The occupants were all hunkered down in the illegal bunkers beneath their hootches, waiting for the storm to pass. But this storm would not pass. Not until it had dug them out and devoured them all.

His feet were at the fence. Behind him he heard the scream of a tortured engine. He paid no attention; that wasn't the kind of screaming he yearned to hear. He stretched out a hand.

An image burst like a bomb in his mind: himself, poised to give pain. And then, looming over him, a dozen times greater, a hundred, was Moonchild in her black and silver. And at her side stood Cap'n Trips, resplendent in his purple suit, and J. J. Flash, and Cosmic Traveler, and Aquarius—and, yes, the blond one, the dead one, and a legion of others the Monster did not know.

He raised his fists to defy them. It was a dream, a lie! The others weren't bigger than he. They were weak, they were small. He was big. He was greater than anything.

"*All you need,*" the voice said, "*is* love."

He roared his contempt. And the giant faces gazed down upon him, and *love* flowed out.

It burned him like napalm. Like Crypt Kicker's acid. He screamed.

He tried to force the image from his mind. He failed. His dream self lashed out against all those other selves, the soft, self-righteous selves. They would not raise hands in return. They only . . . *loved*.

J. Robert Belew held the helicopter that was himself in its suicide dive. The green-black mass of corruption filled the flat windscreen. He braced for impact, and grinned at his own futility.

"So long, Ma," he said. "You were right all along: I'm coming to no good end."

And the monster blew up in his face.

The excess mass the Monster had drawn into himself in his moment of borning let go in a flash and mighty blast.

Then there was nothing but a village blown down above the heads of its inhabitants—terrified but safe in their bunkers—and a wounded helicopter autorotating to a hard landing back among the trees, and Mark Meadows lying in a fetal ball among bean plants, weeping and vomiting.

And then a great wave of calm passed over him. He rolled onto his back and gazed up at the skies.

The stars gazed back. *Wouldn't you know it,* he thought. Yet they held no terror for him anymore. They were just . . . stars.

. . . He felt the presence of Starshine, joined with his comrades for the fight of all their lives, going away from him. He felt sorrow well up within him. "Wait!" he cried, "Don't go!"

"Don't mourn," Starshine's voice said, *"organize."* And he was gone, and Mark knew he'd never come again.

He blinked the tears from his eyes. The time would come when he would mourn that other self. And then he would be whole, and he would go on, to wherever it was he was heading.

And another voice in his head: *"Isis. Is he—is it—did we win?"*

"Eric!" It was his lips, but Moonchild's voice.

"He's still alive," he said in his own voice. "We gotta help him!"

He picked himself up and headed back for the clearing at a stumbling run.

Chapter Fifty-one

O. K. Casaday lay on his belly, peering through binoculars at the temple. After the Monster's departure the little party had made it to the relative safety of a ridge several hundred meters to the north. The PAVN officers had turned up a squad of infantry, which was currently dug into a defensive perimeter around them. Nobody felt too much confidence in it.

"What do you see, man?" Colonel Vo urged from his shoulder. "What do you *see*?"

"Don't jostle me, dammit," Casaday snarled. "Looks like the Brigaders have pretty well rallied. They're all crowding back into the clearing again."

"Good," Vo exulted. "Excellent! All is not lost."

Casaday rolled an eye away from the eyepiece of his glasses and looked at him.

Freddie Whitelaw sat on his broad bottom, scanning the southern horizon with the telephoto lens of his Leica. "What happened to that horrid thing?" he kept asking. "What *happened*?"

"How the hell should I know?" Casaday asked, sitting up and brushing soil from his tropical suit. "I saw the same thing you did: son of a bitch just blew up."

"What on Earth could have destroyed it?"

"When you find out," Casaday said, "I'm sure you'll have a hell of a story."

The senior PAVN officer had been speaking over the squad's radio. He came forward now with an air of grim satisfaction.

"We have been holding a weapon in reserve," he announced. "We could not deploy it against that . . . creature, because it was in the midst of our own troops. We could not risk so many tanks."

"Typical socialist priorities," Whitelaw murmured. "Worry about the war toys first, and the men last."

"Now that the monster has been dealt with, however that occurred, we can use our fuel-air explosive shells against another menace to our Socialist Republic."

Casaday looked at him in surprise. "You have FAE?" The officer nodded.

"You will destroy the rebels with it, then?" Vo asked, eyes shining with eagerness.

"No. They are too dispersed. To be effective, FAE devices require concentrated targets. Concentrated, like that mass of smaller monsters down there by the temple."

Vo went white. "What are you saying? They're our men!"

"They are monsters. They attacked us. They are rabid, like dogs. They must be destroyed."

"No!" Vo shouted. "You can't! We can still use them! We can still win! They—"

The PAVN officer's backhand blow knocked him to the ground. When Vo blinked away the big balloons of light from behind his eyes, he saw Casaday standing over him, aiming his Beretta at his face.

"But why?" Vo gasped. "It was your project too."

"My main priority," Casaday said, "is wiping out wild card filth wherever I find it. If the project's a write-off, I can still say, *mission accomplished*."

To punctuate his words, a whistling crossed the breaking sky.

When Mark came in sight of the clearing, he saw that a pole had been set up in front of the pagoda. Colonel Sobel's head was stuck atop it. The New Joker Brigade was dancing around and around it.

He stopped, swallowed. *What am I getting myself into?*

But Eric was hurt. Eric needed him—needed Moonchild. Hell, needed all of them. Eric had saved him twice tonight, once from the mob and once from himself.

Mark shut his eyes, willed his conscious self to recede, let himself slip as far into Moonchild mode as he could.

Eric, she thought. *Eric, where are you? I've come to help you.*

"Isis?"

Mark's eyes opened. *Yes*, Moonchild said within his mind. *I'm here.*

Panic filled her mind. "No, you've got to get away from here. It's too late for me—too late for any of us."

Eric, tell me where you are. I'll come to you.

"Isis, you can't. They'll kill you."

Who? The jokers?

"Or the nats. It's a race now, don't you see? Do we destroy ourselves first, or do the nats finish us off?"

She saw him now, staggering from the midst of the exuberant mob. Weak, moving painfully, his T-shirt dyed red with his own blood: Eric.

I see you. Just walk a little farther, into the trees. I'll come for you—

He stopped, cocked his disfigured head to the side. "No, don't! Get away—run! It's too late, I told you. Run!"

Eric— A scream filled the sky.

"Wouldn't you know," came the sardonic thought. "*The nats win again.*"

She heard popping then, too small a sound, she thought, for bombs or shells. Most of the jokers didn't even pause in their dance.

Eric, I love you!

"I love you too, hon."

And then temple, clearing, the jokers, and Eric, all vanished in a single brilliant orange flash. Mark was hurled backward, into darkness.

Epilogue

WHAT A LONG, STRANGE TRIP IT'S BEEN

"So love conquers all."

The room was elegantly furnished, in dainty *fin-de-siècle* French style. Mark perched on one of the antique chairs, looking luridly out of place, like a stork in a drawing room. His cheeks were still sunburn pink from the dragon's breath of the fuel-air blast, and his ears rang.

He was paying half attention to the television droning on: "—White House appears to be backing down from a statement made earlier today by President Bush that he was prepared to dispatch the American Pacific Fleet to prevent what he termed an 'ace-powered criminal mastermind' from becoming president *pro tem* of South Vietnam. The reassessment seems to have been prompted by the People's Republic of China's recognition of the breakaway Republic.

"Meanwhile the survival of the communist regime in Hanoi itself remains very much in doubt—"

Mark looked up at his guest. "At least love helps an old hippie conquer himself," he replied.

Belew laughed. The renegade secret agent had a pair of tubular metal crutches propped by his chair and bandages on his face. He had not made a real good landing after Monster blew up in his face.

"The great work," Belew said. "It goes on and on. 'Man is a rope stretched between the animal and the Superman—a rope over an abyss.'"

"I've been there, man."

Among the other tightrope walkers over the Abyss, William "Carnifex" Ray was lying under guard in a Saigon clinic formerly reserved for Party officials and their families. He

415

was in much worse shape from his aerial adventures than Belew was. Without his body's ability to regenerate he would have been dead, crippled at the least. As it was, the *Medecins sans Frontières* doctors expected him to make a full recovery over time.

Crypt Kicker's condition was stable: he was dead. Whether his condition was critical or not was a different matter. His lightning-blasted corpse lay in a cold drawer in the Saigon city morgue. The bemused attendants were under instructions to open up if they heard knocking.

Croyd Crenson lay in a bedroom here in Mark's official Saigon residence. He was still sound asleep.

"How do you feel?" J. Bob asked Mark.

"I feel strange. Soiled, somehow. *Evil.* I didn't know I had all that in me."

"*Every*body has that in 'em, son," Belew said. "You're just the only one who has such an impressive means of letting it out."

He slapped Mark on the arm. "Just think of all the anger you managed to work out of your system. Does wonders for you, they say."

Mark grimaced.

"Some people say no one ever won a fight," Belew said. "They lie. But there's always a cost. Always a butcher's bill. You pay a price in blood, whether you're scratched or not."

He walked over and touched Mark on the shoulder. "Time for a change," he said softly. "Your public's waiting."

"Thanks," Mark said.

Belew gathered up his crutches and left the room. *I hope I don't have to kill him someday,* Mark thought.

Mark looked toward the window. The night had come down outside. It was time for the new president to address her constituents.

He took his hand from his pocket, held the vial it held up to the light. Black crystals swirled among silver. He brought it to his lips, hesitated. He would never take one of the potions again without that moment of fear, that glass-breaking instant of decision.

He took the potion.

A moment later Moonchild bent to turn off the television. "Good-bye, Eric," she said. There was no pain in the space he had occupied in her soul. Just void. "The Dream is in my hands now."

She stepped to the French doors that gave onto the balcony. She could feel the adulation of the crowd coursing through them like benevolent radiation. Like the healing rays of the moon.

The opportunity before her was great: to turn South Vietnam into a safe haven for all those touched by the wild card; to lay the foundation for a better world. To give peace a chance, the way the song said.

It was also terrible. A fleeting glimpse of such opportunity as this had led Sobel and Eric astray. Had led them to mortgage their souls, to become in the end that which they had dedicated themselves to struggling against.

But we know we'll always try to do what's right, Mark said from just below the surface of her mind. *We won't give in to the temptations of power. Won't make all the same mistakes.*

Yeah, J. J. Flash thought. *Right.*

The white jetliner turned its nose wheel into a quicksilver pool of sun-shimmer on the Tan Son Nhut runway and stopped. Mark's motley honor guard of jokers, Montagnards, and ethnic Vietnamese snapped as close to attention as they ever got. Feeling his heart going all light and drifty in his chest, Mark looked left and right at them and thought it was a good thing he didn't take this presidential trip too seriously.

Especially since *he* wasn't actually the president.

The ramp was wheeled up to the door of the plane. It opened. A slim young woman in jeans and a white T-shirt with teddy bears on it came down the steps. Her long blonde hair gleamed in the sun.

Mark craned his head, looking past her. Then he looked more closely at her. She was studying him with a puzzled look.

They broke toward each other, running gangle-legged and careless, hit and hugged, their tears mingling.

"Daddy!"

"Sprout!" He hugged her again, then held her away to look at her. "Honey, you look all grown up now."

She threw her arms around his neck. "Oh, Daddy," she said, "I didn't recognize you. You look so strong."

"I've been getting lots of exercise, honey," he said. "C'mon. Let's get you out of the sun."

"Daddy, I love you."

He felt tears sting his eyes. He smiled. "Honey, I love you too. More than anything in the world."

Okay, folks, we're ready to roll the credits. Cue up your Woodstock CD to Country Joe and the Fish, "The 'Fish' Cheer/Feel Like I'm Fixin' to Die Rag."

Got it? Okay: Roll 'em.

"Gimme an F—"

TURN OF THE CARDS

Written & directed by
Victor Milán
Executive Producer
Betsy Mitchell
Produced by
George R. R. Martin
Associate Producer
Melinda M. Snodgrass
Edited by
George R. R. Martin & Melinda M. Snodgrass

Guest Stars
[*in order of appearance*]

Helene Mistral Carlysle *was created by*............Steve Perrin
Croyd "The Sleeper" Crenson *was created by*......................
Roger Zelazny
Billy "Carnifex" Ray *was created by* ....John J. Miller
Bobby Joe "Crypt Kicker" Puckett *was created by* ....
Royce Wideman, Jr.

Soundtrack

Novel...Renaissance
Part I...The Grateful Dead
Part II..
written by The Jefferson Airplane; *performed by*
Isaac Guillory
Part III..Country Joe & the Fish
Epilogue ....The Grateful Dead

Moral Support Provided by

Raina Robison
Sean Robison
Melinda Snodgrass
Joseph William Reichert
Mike Weaver
Deborah Armbruster
Karen Turner
Joni and Jim Knappenberger
All the folks in the *Wild Cards* TOPic of the Science Fiction
Round Table on GEnie.

This has been a WILD CARDS *novel.*

"What's that spell?"

Fin

THE VIETNAM WAR
A Personal Statement

I did not go to Nam. I was too young (just). I could have arranged to, had I worked at it, but the truth is I didn't want to.

In the sixties and seventies I had two feelings about the War:

First, I thought the American involvement in Vietnam was wrong, from a moral, political, and military point of view. It's no reflection on those who fought there; they didn't make the policy.

Second, I thought communism was a bad thing. I did not support the government of North Vietnam. I simply believed that the U.S. government had no business spending our lives and treasure trying to make other people behave the way it wanted them to.

Nothing has happened since the end of the U.S. involvement in Vietnam to cause me to amend those views.

This book is not an expression of nostalgia for the war I missed; I'm glad I missed it. It is not a working-out of some weird national angst over the War. It isn't a "Vietnam War book." It's a thriller—I hope, anyway—and a WILD CARDS novel. It's set in 1991, not 1967. I hope people will approach it on its own terms.

VICTOR MILÁN
May 11, 1992

ABOUT THE AUTHOR

VICTOR MILÁN is a former cowboy and progressive-rock D.J., a Yale dropout, a sometime cartoonist and performer, but mainly a writer. He has more than fifty novels to his credit, including *Adah: The World's Delight*, *The War Party*, and *Runespear*, coauthored with Melinda Snodgrass. His most recent book is *The Cybernetic Shōgun*, the sequel to his award-winning *The Cybernetic Samurai*. He is a charter member of the writing consortium who created the *Wild Cards* series. He lives in Albuquerque, New Mexico, with two dogs and a buff-colored rat named Rafe.

Space: the Final Frontier.™
These are the voyages of the Starship Enterprise™...

STAR TREK®: THE CLASSIC EPISODES

adapted by James Blis
with J.A. Lawrer

Here are James Blish's classic adaptations of *Star Trek*'s dazzling scripts in three illustrated volumes. Each book also includes a new introduction written especially for this publication by D.C. Fontana, one of *Star Trek*'s creators; David Gerrold, author of "The Trouble With Tribbles;" and Norman Spinrad, author of "The Doomsday Machine."

Explore the final frontier with science fiction's most well known and beloved captain, crew and starship, in these exciting stories of high adventure— including such favorites as "Space Seed," "Shore Leave," "The Naked Time," and "The City on the Edge of Forever."